池上忠弘先生

(1932–2018)

中世英文学の日々に

― 池上忠弘先生追悼論文集 ―

チョーサー研究会／狩野晃一　編

英宝社

はじめに

　あれは 2018 年 11 月の晴れた日、自宅近くの小高い丘の上にある古墳に、子どもを連れて散歩に出たときだった。風はあったが、陽に当たっていれば暖かな日だったと記憶している。古墳の周りを走る子どもを眺めていると、携帯電話が鳴った。着信画面には池上先生のお名前が見えていた。瞬間的に「これは『カンタベリ物語』の翻訳の件か、はたまたチョーサー研究会で何かお話しになるご相談か、あるいは、もっと勉強しなさいという激励か」という考えが頭をめぐったが、とにかく電話に出た。ところが受話器の向こう側は、池上忠弘先生ではなく、奥様の昌先生だった。それは忠弘先生がお亡くなりになったことを告げる電話だった。淡々と、しかし、しっかりとしたお声で伝えてくださった。あまりに突然のことで、ことばに詰まった。実際にこちらからなんと返したのかは覚えていない。電話を切ってからしばらくは呆然としていたに違いない。子どもが心配して大丈夫かと声をかけてきたほどであったから。

　年を越して 1 月、チョーサー研究会で「池上忠弘先生を偲ぶ会」をひらいた。そこには普段の研究会の倍以上もの参加者が集い、皆さんから一言ずついただいて生前の先生を偲んだ。この追悼論文集の計画もその時に発表して、希望者を募ったところ 20 名を上回る方々が手を挙げてくださった。ただ 2020 年 2 月から始まった新型コロナウィルス感染症の混乱のために最終的にご寄稿くださったのは 15 名となった。忠弘先生が中心となって立ち上げられたチョーサー研究会は、どのような人にも広く間口を開けて、チョーサーに限らず、古英語・中英語・近代英語・現代英語の言語と文学、歴史、美術に関する研究発表や講演を行ってきた。普段から先生は、英語やその文学だけやっていてはだめ、ヨーロッパの方も見ておく必要もあるし、歴史や文化も広く知らなければいけないよ、と仰っていた。この追悼論文集に収められた多様な視点を盛り込んだ数々の論考は、まさに忠弘先生の理想とされるチョーサー研究会のあるべき姿を表している。

先生の中世英語英文学研究の数多のご業績やご貢献の大きさは、ここで改めて繰り返す必要はないだろう。詳しくは記念論文集『中世英文学の伝統』（雄松堂、1997）を参照されたい。記念論文集以降も、日本英文学会で「Chaucer とその時代」というタイトルでシンポジウムを開かれたり、「Anglo-Saxon 語の継承と変容」（専修大学）という大きなプロジェクトで、翻訳『サー・ガウェインと緑の騎士』（言語・文化研究センター叢書4）をはじめ多くの刊行物に携わってこられた。研究会でも「15 世紀英文学研究をめぐる雑感」など、幅広い視点からいかに中世英文学に取り組むべきかというお話をたびたびしてくださった。また研究会の最後には新刊紹介をしてくださった。実物を見せようと、たくさんの書物をキャリーケースに詰めてガラガラと引っ張って来場するお姿は、今でもありありと目に浮かぶ。そのカバンを若手や中堅が「お持ちします」と言って受け取ると「重い！」という反応がしばしば返ってきたものだった。ご逝去後、先生の蔵書整理のお手伝いを少しばかりさせていただいた折のことである。腰の高さの書棚の上に最新の研究書が何冊も積み上げられていた。それらに手を伸ばしてページをめくってみると、赤ペンや鉛筆で書き込みや下線が引いてある。これを見たときに、忠弘先生の文学およびその研究への強い関心と大きな熱量を感じるとともに、先生でもいまだ道の途中であったのかと複雑な思いに囚われた。

　先生を失った私たちは、何か大切なものが手の指の間からこぼれ落ちていく感覚が抜けきらない。もっと先生から学びたかった、得るべきものがあったと思うが、それがもう叶わない無力な感覚。しかし、大切なことは先生と私たちの命のひとときがある部分で重なり合うという僥倖を得たことである。そして、各人（インディヴィジュアル）の一回限りの人生が偶然にも交差したことのありがたみをかみしめたい。

　研究会の一人一人分け隔てなく、有益な助言と温かな励ましのことばをかけて下さった故池上忠弘先生にこの論文集を捧げる。

チョーサー研究会事務局

狩野晃一

目　　次

中世英文学の日々に

— 池上忠弘先生追悼論文集 —

Intoxicating Drinks in Old English

Taro Ishiguro

Most developed countries today have laws that regulate the consumption of alcoholic drinks. The UK is no exception. The Licensing Act 2003, which applies to England and Wales, stipulates, "An individual aged under 18 commits an offence if he knowingly consumes alcohol on relevant premises" (pt. 7, sec. 150). One can only drink an alcoholic beverage in public if they are eighteen years of age or older though there seem to be no regulations against people under eighteen consuming alcohol in private settings. The law assumes that there is a division among drinks or liquids intended for human consumption, between those that contain alcohol and those that do not. We call the former by such names as "alcoholic drinks," "alcoholic beverages," "liquors," or "alcohol."[1] The first citation for *alcohol* in the *Oxford English Dictionary* (*OED*) is from the mid-sixteenth century. However, its use remained a scientific term for the essence obtained by distillation for some time.[2] It was only in the nineteenth century that the word started to stand for the intoxicating ingredient of alcoholic beverages. The *OED* cites a passage from Walter Scott's 1818 work as its first instance: "The landlady filled Dick Ostler a bumper of Hollands. He . . . bolted the alcohol, to use the learned phrase." The last phrase in the quotation tells us that the word still sounded technical.

The other terms, *beverage* and *liquor*, first appeared in English much earlier. These French words have been around from the Middle English (ME) period. The earliest citation for the word *beverage* in the *Middle English Dictionary* (*MED*) is from Robert of Gloucester's *Chronicle* dated about 1300: "A luþer beuerege to hare biofþe hii browe" (Wright 45, line 621).[3] But the word is used figuratively in this instance to mean "a bitter experience; sorrow suffering" according to the editors of the *MED*.[4] Its literal sense, "drink or liquor," emerges in English about a century later in *Cleanness*: "Bryng hem now to my borde, of beverage hem fylles" (Andrew and Waldron 169, line 1433).[5] The fact that the metaphoric use of the word came before its literal use suggests that the word had remained foreign for some time before it was naturalized in the vernacular. The earliest example cited for the other word *liquor* in the *MED*, under "licour," is from the *Acrene Wisse*: "þe bere a deore licur, a deorewurðe wet as basme is, in a feble uetles, healewi i bruchel gles, nalde ha gan ut of þrung bute ha fol were?" (Millett and Dobson 1: 63, pt. 3, lines 626–28).[6] The word in this example does not necessarily refer to anything to drink but to any liquid in general. Its first citation in the sense of "a drink" comes from a century later. The *MED* cites *Arthour and Merlin* as the earliest instance of the word used in this sense: "To þe he drinkeþ þis licour / Þe coupe he ʒeueþ to þi tresour!" (Macrae-Gibson 1: 171–72, lines 2281–82).[7] Neither *beverage* nor *liquor* always meant alcoholic drinks in ME when they referred to something to drink. It could have been something non-alcoholic. And the two words did not exist in Old English (OE).

The Japanese word *sake* refers not only to what the word means in English but any alcoholic drink. It is an umbrella term for all alcoholic beverages in Japanese. In contrast, English seems to have lacked such an umbrella term for the greater part of the history of the language. Speakers of English may not have had any need to linguistically differentiate alcoholic and non-alcoholic drinks in the Middle Ages. They nonetheless talked about intoxication caused by drinking, both favorably when the drinking took place in a convivial function and disapprovingly when it appeared in religious texts. In this short essay, I will examine some OE words that referred to drinks that cause inebriation. There are a few dozen words and compounds that meant something to drink in the language. Some of them expressly referred to a specific type of alcoholic beverage. This essay attempts to discover the OE words that people in early medieval England regarded as representing the intoxicating drink they drank. The term may be different in a different context. I will first discuss the OE words for wine, mead, beer, and ale in OE. The difference in their availability will then be addressed by looking at the evidence in the extant literature, to show which beverage early medieval people prized in England. The last part of this essay will deal with the words used when alcoholic drinks are discussed unfavorably in religious contexts.

People in medieval England, both before and after the Norman Conquest, probably did not distinguish alcoholic from non-alcoholic drinks in the way we do today. They certainly did not have a drinking age. It may have been much safer to drink alcoholic beverages than water when they did not always have access to a clean, uncontaminated water source. Ann Hagen observes, "Water does not seem to have been drunk as a matter of preference by many Anglo-Saxons, any more than it is by people today" (195). She writes that people in early medieval England dug wells and often used cisterns to let the water have a chance to clear before they drank it because their water sources may have been polluted (192-95). In Ælfric's *Colloquy*, we have this famous dialogue: "Et quid bibis?" "Ceruisam, si habeo, uel aquam si non habeo ceruisam" (Garmonsway 47). Having been asked what he usually drinks, this novice monk answers that he drinks *ceruisa* (ale) if there is any, or water if he does not have *ceruisa*. Water was the less preferable option. Ælfric's disciple Bata[8] added the following words to the reply: "Ceruisam uel medonem siue ydromellum, quod est, mulsum, seu lac, si [non] habeo ceruisam" (Stevenson 98). Although Bata may only have expanded the list of semantically related words for a pedagogical purpose, water remains to be the last and the least preferred resort. The novice would drink *lac* (milk) instead of water. Alcoholic drinks seem to have been more readily consumed than they are today. But there was still a distinction between those drinks which cause intoxication and those which do not. Felix reports in his *Life of St. Guthlac* that, after he took monastic vows, the saint "never again took any draught of intoxicating drink or any sort of choice liquor except at the time of holy communion" (Colgrave, *Felix* 85). Felix's words for this "intoxicating drink" are *inebrians liquor*.[9] The people of the time had a specific concept for the group of beverages that cause intoxication. What were their names in OE?

We have OE glosses to those Latin words that appeared in the previous paragraph in Ælfric's *Glossary*: "ceruisa l celea ealu. uinum win . . . medo medu. ydromellum l mulsum beor. lac meolc. mustum must. sicera ælces cynnes gewringc buton wine anum" (Zupitza 315).[10] The *Dictionary of Medieval Latin from British Sources* defines *ceruisa* as "ale," *celea* as "ale, beer," *ydromel* as "(non-alcoholic) potion of honey and water; mead," *mulsus* as "drink prepared with honey; oenomel, drink made from wine and honey; mead," and *sicera* as "intoxicating drink" ("cervisia," "caelia," "hydromel," "2 mulsus," "sicera"). David W. Porter has published a bilingual glossary contained in London, British Library, Additional MS 32246, in which we find the following list: "Ceruisa . Celea . eala . / Uinu<u>m</u> . meru<u>m</u> . win / . . . / Medo . medu . / Ydromellu<u>m</u> . beor . ɫ ofetes wos / Inomellu<u>m</u> . must mid hunig gemenged / Mulsu<u>m</u> . beor . / Mustu<u>m</u> . niwe win . / Sicera . ælces kinnes gewring butan wine / Liquor . wæta" (67). We have thus *ealu, win, medu,* and *beor* as major alcoholic drinks common to both the lists. It is interesting to find *wæta* glossing the Latin *liquor* in the latter list. The OE word continues to refer to a drink in general up to the transitional period between OE and ME. The *MED*, s.v. "wet," cites Lambeth Homily 10 as the last example of the word used in the sense of something to drink other than medicine: "þe oferlifa on hete *and* on wete macað þene mon un-halne" (Morris 101).[11] The *OED* cites the *Ormulum*, "⁊ himm birrþ lokenn himm full wel / Fra luffsumm æte ⁊ wæte" (Holt 1: 272, lines 7851–52),[12] and shows that, after centuries of disuse in this sense, the word re-emerges in the language in the eighteenth century as a colloquial expression for "[a] drink or draught of some alcoholic beverage" ("wet" n. 1 and n. 2).[13]

  A Thesaurus of Old English (TOE) lists *drenc, drync/drynca, wǣt,* and *wǣta* in "04.01.03.05 A drink/beverage," and in its subgroup "04.01.03.05.01 Intoxicating liquor" *ealu, līþ,* and *sicera.* English speakers of the time must have regarded *sicera* as a foreign word. Outside glossaries, the Latin word appears only twice. The two instances of the word occur in the same passage in the OE version of the Rule of Chrodegang: "Druncene mæssepreostas ⁊ se apostol genyðrað, ⁊ seo ealde æ forbytt, 'Þa þe to Godes weofode þeowiað, ne drincon hi win to druncennysse ne siceran.' Sicera an Ebreiscere spræce is ælces cinnes drinc genemned þe man of druncnian mæg" (Napier 74).[14] The first instance of the word in this passage has an OE case ending, but the frequency is so low in the OE corpus that it does not deserve to be a symbolic OE word for alcoholic beverages. Nor does *līþ* frequently appear in the corpus. I will discuss *liþ* below. That leaves *ealu*, which shows up very often in OE. The *Dictionary of Old English* (*DOE*) defines the word as "ale or some other intoxicating drink, apparently brewed," noting that it occurs about 225 times in the corpus though most of the occurrences are in medical recipes ("ealu"). It not only appears as a simplex. The *DOE* entry lists eighteen compounds formed with *ealu*, including familiar ones like *ealubenc*, *ealugāl*, and *ealuwǣge*. The word deserves to be one of the representative OE words to denote an alcoholic drink. But what about the other terms that the OE glossaries listed, *win*, *medu*, and *beor*?

Wine may have been a highly prized, precious drink. It was not something readily bought. Having been asked whether he does not drink wine, the young monk in Ælfric's *Colloquy* quoted above continues: "Non sum tam diues ut possim emere mihi uinum; et uinum non est potus puerorum siue stultorum, sed senum et sapientium" which is glossed in OE, "Ic ne eom swa spedig þæt ic mæge bicgean me win; 7 win nys drenc cilda ne dysgra, ac ealdra 7 wisra" (Garmonsway 47). One had to be rich to buy wine, and wine was not a drink for the young and fools. G. N. Garmonsway writes in the footnote to his edited text of this dialogue that all wine was imported in England. However, it is now accepted that there was some production of wine in early medieval England. Bede tells us at the beginning of his *Ecclesiastical History* that vines grew in some parts of the island: "uineas etiam quibusdam in locis germinans" (Colgrave and Mynors 14). Bede was writing in the first half of the eighth century. During the century, England started to go through significant climate changes, and "the climate became more continental (the summers being drier and warmer and the winters colder)" (Hornsey 242). Hagen suggests that the climate in the early medieval period was much warmer than today (218). Christine E. Fell argues that the vine-cultivation in England was established before the Norman Conquest by pointing out that there are thirty-five compounds with the base *win-* that are "functional and descriptive, such as *winrepan*, *wingetred*, *wingeardseax*, and so on" (78–80). J. R. Clark Hall defines the three compounds as "to gather in the vintage," "winepress," and "vine pruning-knife," respectively ("wīnreopan," "wīntredde," "wīngeardseax"). Although it was not a cheap drink, wine must have been available on some occasions, even to ordinary people. The law of the Northumbrian priests, which Dorothy Whitelock dates to 1020–23 (471), requires a priest to provide wine at mass: "Gif preost buton wine mæssige, gilde XII ór" (Liebermann 1: 381).[15] In *Beowulf*, they drink wine when they are at the best kind of party: "Þær wæs symbla cyst, / druncon wīn weras" (Fulk et al. 43, lines 1232–33).

Mead (OE *medu*) is the oldest known alcoholic drink (Melville and Staub 981). Honey wine is among the simplest alcohols to produce, and its alcohol content ranges between eight and eighteen percent (Martin 852). But it was probably not easy to obtain a large quantity of its primary ingredient, honey, which made this drink valuable in England. Exeter Riddle 27, "Mead," starts declaring its value to men: "Ic eom weorð werum, wide funden, / brungen of bearwum ond of burghleoþum, / of denum ond of dunum" (Krapp and Dobbie 194, lines 1–3).[16] The Laws of King Alfred set the same fine for a thief of bees as for a stealer of gold and horses: "Geo wæs goldðeofe 7 stodðeofe 7 beoðeofe, 7 manig witu maran ðonne oþru; nu sint eal gelic buton manðeofe: CXX scill' " (Liebermann 1: 54).[17] Wulfstan supposedly addressed his report on northeastern Europe to King Alfred, which the OE translation of Orosius's *History against the Pagans* contains in its first book. He says that slaves drank mead while the nobility in a Baltic country drank mare milk, which Janet Bately supposes to have been something like kumis (324): "se cyning 7 þa ricostan men drincað myran meolc, 7 þa unspedigan 7 þa þeowan drincað medo" (17). His report must have sounded shocking to the king.

The OE word *beor* calls for special attention. Scott C. Martin writes that the word "might have been a catchall term" (111), but it does not appear so straightforward as far as OE is concerned. The *DOE* defines it as "an alcoholic drink brewed from various fruits often using honey." The *DOE* editors note, "The etymological connection with Mod[ern] E[nglish] beer need not imply identity of OE *bēor* with, or similar to, modern beer in ingredients or mode of manufacture" ("bēor"). So, the OE word does not necessarily refer to modern beer. The Latin-OE glossaries quoted above show that the OE *beor* translates the Latin *hydromel* and *mulsus*, both of which the *Dictionary of Medieval Latin* defines as a drink prepared with honey, or mead. In OE, *medu* and *beor* seem to be interchangeable. *Beowulf* has a passage that may reveal the interchangeability:

> Ful oft ġebēotedon   bēore druncne
> ofer ealowǣġe   ōretmecgas
> þæt hīe in bēorsele   bīdan woldon
> Grendles gūþe   mid gryrum ecga.
> Ðonne wæs þēos medoheal   on morgentīd,
> drihtsele drēorfāh   þonne dæġ līxte
>
> (Fulk et al. 18‒19, lines 480‒85)

Warriors, drunk with *beor*, boasted that they would wait for Grendle's attack in the *beor*-hall, but in the following morning, the *medu*-hall was painted with blood. Hrothgar's hall, Heorot, is called *beorsele* and *medoheal* here, while they drink *beor* from an ale-cup *ealowæg*. It is interesting to find them drinking valuable drinks with a cup for a beverage of less value. They use ale-cups; yet, they do not drink ale but mead, *beor*, or wine. There are fifteen occurrences of *medu* and compounds formed with *medu*, and ten of *beor* and *beor*-compounds, in the poem. *Win* and its compounds appear nine times. It should be pointed out that *ealu* does not appear as a simplex in *Beowulf*. The poem uses *ealu* only as an element of compounds: *ealo-benc* "ale-bench" (lines 1029, 2867), *ealo-drincend* "ale-drinker" (1945), *ealo-wæg* "ale-cup" (481, 495, 2021), *ealu-scerwen* "(dispensing of ale [bitter drink], i.e.) distress, terror" (769).[18] Mead, *beor*, and wine are what the brave get drunk with at feasts: *beore druncne* (480) and *wine druncen* (1467). The name of the beverage they drink changes, probably for the need for alliteration. But they do not drink ale. Ale appears only as a part of the names of utensils for feasts in the poem.

Ale was of lower value than wine, mead, and *beor*. As we have seen above, our young monk in Ælfric's *Colloquy* answers that he usually drinks ale. Ale was a "staple food" for monks throughout the Middle Ages, according to Martin (245).

Ale of the day may have been what we call beer today. Although the first mention of the production of hopped beer only dates from 1391 (Unger 99), there is evidence of hop production in early medieval England, and there may already have been hopped *ealu* (Hagen 204). Whether hopped or not, *ealu* was a typical drink produced within a monastery, not necessarily for sale but for consumption within the community (Bennett 194).

While they brewed and drank alcoholic beverages in monasteries, their religion warned the monks against overdrinking and getting drunk. An OE poem called *Instructions for Christians* tells its reader to abstain from excessive eating and drinking: "þonne is þæt feorðe þæt he fremman sceal, / þæt he gemettige metas and drincas" (Jones 138, lines 19-20).[19] The Scriptures are full of such warnings. For example, the Book of Isaiah portrays a drunken priest and a drunken prophet: "But these also have been ignorant through wine and through drunkenness have erred. The priest and the prophet have been ignorant through drunkenness; they are swallowed up with wine; they have gone astray in drunkenness" (Isa. 28.7; Kinney 109).[20] This attitude against sacerdotal indulgence may have motivated ascetics to keep away from intoxicants throughout their religious lives. St. Guthlac never drank any "intoxicating drink" after he became a monk, as seen above. Bede says that St. Cuthbert "sedulously abstained from all intoxicants" (Colgrave, *Two Lives* 175).[21] Gregory I, touching on a passage in 1 Samuel, explains in his *Pastoral Care* why Abigail kept silent when his husband Nabal was drunk. Abigail spoke to Nabal in the following morning when he had "digested his wine": "digesto vino laudabiliter dixit" (Bramley 222).[22] Gregory may have been thinking of Proverbs 20.1: "Wine is a luxurious thing, and drunkenness riotous; whosoever is delighted therewith shall not be wise" (Edgar and Kinney 635).[23]

Lið translates the *vinum* of Gregory's Latin in the OE translation of the *Pastoral Care*. The OE reads "ða him ðæt lið gesciered wæs," which Henry Sweet translates as "when his drunkenness had passed off" (Sweet 294). *Lið* is one of the three words that the *TOE* lists in the subgroup "04.01.03.05.01 Intoxicating liquor" mentioned above. Clark Hall defines it as "cider, native wine, fermented drink;

Taro Ishiguro

beaker, cup" ("līð"), while Joseph Bosworth and T. Northcote Toller confine their definition in two words, "strong drink" ("líþ"). Whatever drink of today the word corresponds to, the inebriating nature of the alcohol stands out in the example. The term appears once more in the OE *Pastoral Care*, used metaphorically: "Se þe us oferdrencð mid ðæs ecean lifes liðe" which translates Gregory's "æterna nos dulcedine inebrians" (Sweet 260; Bramley 196). Sweet renders it into "He who intoxicates us with the drink of eternal life" (261). However, the word does not show up often in the corpus. Outside the OE *Pastoral Care*, it appears once each in the OE *Boethius*, the OE *Bede*, and *Bald's Leechbook* (Godden and Irvine 1: 346; Miller 1: 492; Cockayne 2: 63). This word of native origin would deserve to be the representative word for a drink that causes inebriation, but the word's low frequency makes it a less promising candidate.

The intoxicating drink is almost always wine in the Bible if monks drank ale every day in early medieval England. I quoted the earliest citation for *beverage* in the *MED* in the second paragraph of this essay. That passage from *Cleanness* is based on chapter 5 of the Book of Daniel, which describes Belshazzar's profane banquet where the king and his women drank from the precious cups that Nebuchadnezzar, his father, had brought away from Jerusalem (Dan. 5.1-4). The Vulgate says that they drank wine: "Bibebant vinum" (Dan. 5.4; Kinney 972). The *Cleanness* poet expounds on how the wine helped Belshazzar lose his sanity. The wine warmed his heart and "breyþed vppe into his brayn and blemyst his mynde," which Andrew and Waldron translate as "[it] rose as a vapour into his brain and impaired his mind" (169). The OE *Daniel* depicts the same scene. The poem also says that they drank wine: "Sæton him æt wine" (Anlezark 294, line 695).[24] However, the poet describes the king to be drunk with mead, "medu-gal" (line 702). We can observe a similar variation in *Judith*, another OE poem based on a book in the Scriptures. Holofernes and his company came to a wine-drinking feast: "Hie ða to ðam symle sittan eodon, / wlance to win-gedrince" (Fulk 298, lines 15-16).[25] The leader then became "conceited and mead-mad": "modig and medu-gal" (Fulk 300-01, line 26). In biblical contexts, people drink wine, and the intoxication caused by the wine is described by a compound with another kind of alcoholic beverage, probably because the resultant inebriation is the same whichever drink they have consumed.

Nevertheless, ale (*ealu*) rarely appears to cause intoxication in religious poems. The only instance of *ealugal* in the OE poems is in *Genesis* 2410, "ealo-galra gylp" (Anlezark 166).[26] This phrase appears in what God speaks about Sodom. The damned people of the city probably do not deserve to drink a better kind of drink. Ancient people who appear in the Bible are supposed to drink wine, a far better sort of beverage than ale which monks were usually allowed to drink in their monastery.

OE lacked an umbrella term that would designate all the alcoholic beverages that cause inebriation, a word that would correspond to the Japanese word *sake*. Wine and mead were highly prized drinks due to the relatively limited availability of their primary ingredients. The OE *beor* was not today's beer but more like mead, so much so that the word appears interchangeable with other words in poetic variations. The relatively wide availability of ale makes its OE word *ealu* an excellent candidate for such an umbrella term. While monasteries produced their ale for consumption within their premises, the word for ale was virtually absent from passages that negatively depict inebriation. That was due to the nature of biblical stories where wine works as a symbolizing drink that causes intoxication. Therefore, as far as the OE literature that has survived to the present day is concerned, *ealu* seems to have been what people of the time would first think of when they talked about alcoholic drinks in everyday situations. At the same time, *win* or *medu* would come up instead of *ealu* in some other specific cases, such as when they talked about biblical stories or extravagant feasts of the nobility.

Notes

*   This work was supported by the 2020 research grant awarded by Asahi Group Foundation.

1   *Roget's International Thesaurus* lists the following words and phrases under category

88, "INTOXICATION, ALCOHOLIC DRINK," par. 13: spirits, liquor, intoxicating liquor, adult beverage, hard liquor, hard stuff <n[on]f[ormal]>, whiskey, firewater, spiritus frumenti, usquebaugh <Scot[tish]> schnapps, ardent spirits, strong waters, intoxicant, toxicant, inebriant, potable, potation, beverage, drink, strong drink, strong liquor, alcoholic drink *or* beverage, alcohol, aqua vitae, water of life, brew, grog, social lubricant, nectar of the gods; booze <n[on]f[ormal]>; . . . (69).

2   The word originally meant any powder made by grinding. Its use for a specific kind of liquid sprang up in the phrase *alcohol of wine* (*OED*, "alcohol").

3   "They brewed an evil beverage on their behalf" (my translation).

4   William Aldis Wright, the editor of the *Chronicle*, glosses the word merely as "Beverage, drink" (892).

5   "Bring them [i.e., the cups that Nebuchadnezzar took away from the Temple in Jerusalem] to my table. Fill them with drinks" (my translation).

6   "If someone is carrying a valuable liquid, an expensive fluid like a resin ointment, in a feeble container, a precious ointment in a fragile glass, would she not want to get away from a crowd unless she were a fool?" (my translation).

7   "He drinks this liquor to you. He has given this drinking-cup to your store of valuables" (my translation).

8   For Ælfric Bata, see Gwara and Porter's introduction to their edition, especially pp. 1-7.

9   "Ab illo enim tempore, quo apostolicae tonsurae indicium suscepit, non ullius inebriantis liquoris aut alicuius delicati libaminis haustum, excepto communicationis tempore, gustavit" (Colgrave, *Felix* 84). The OE for *inebrians liquor* is *wætan . . . þe druncennysse þurh come* "a drink . . . through which he might come to intoxication," a rather awkward descriptive translation (Gonser 111).

10   The diacritics in Zupitza's edition are not reproduced in the quotation.

11   "Overliving in eating and in drinking maketh the man unwhole" (Morris 100).

12   "One ought to abstain very much from pleasant food and drink" (my translation).

13   The two examples of *wet* in the Lambeth Homily and in the *Ormulum* appear in the same binomial, which may have something to do with its verbal counterpart *eat and drink* which has "been current from Old English until the present" (Kopaczyk and Sauer 21).

14   The passage renders the following Latin: "Vinolentos sacerdotes et apostolus dampnat, et uetus lex prohibit, 'Qui altari seruiunt, uinum ad ebrietatem et siceram non bibent.' Sicera Hebreo sermone omnis potio nuncupatur que inebriare potest" (Napier 72; "The apostle damns drunken priests, and the old law forbids, 'Those who serve the altar will not drink wine and *sicera* to intoxication.' Every drink which can cause

intoxication is called *sicera* in the Hebrew language" [my translation]).

15 "If a priest celebrates mass without wine, he is to pay 12 ores" (Whitelock 473).

16 Craig Williamson renders these lines as "I am man's treasure, taken from the woods, /
    Cliff-sides, hill-slopes, valleys, downs" (538).

17 "Formerly, [the fine] for the stealer of gold, the stealer of stud-horses, the stealer for
    bees, and many fines, were greater than others; now all are alike, except for the stealer
    of a man: 120 shillings" (Whitelock 411).

18 The Modern English translations of the words are taken from the glossary of the
    edition by Fulk et al. For *ealo-scerwen*, see Rowland.

19 "Then the fourth thing that he should do is observe moderation in food and drink"
    (Jones 139). The binomial in the quotation is echoed by that in the Lambeth Homily
    and the *Ormulum* quoted above.

20 "Verum hii quoque prae vino nescierunt et prae ebrietate erraverunt. Sacerdos et
    propheta nescierunt prae ebrietate; absorti sunt a vino; erraverunt in ebrietate"
    (Kinney 108).

21 "Sed et iuxta exemplum Samsonis fortissimi quondam Nazarei ab omni quod inebriare
    potest sedulus abstinebat" ("Moreover in accordance with the example of Samson the
    strong, who was once a Nazarite, he sedulously abstained from all intoxicants";
    Colgrave, *Two Lives* 174-75).

22 "she told him when he had awoke [*sic*] from his wine" (Bramley 223). The passage
    refers to 1 Sam. 25.36-37.

23 "Luxuriosa res vinum, et tumultuosa ebrietas; quicumque his delectatur non erit
    sapiens" (Edgar and Kinney 634). That, of course, did not apply to the dedicatee of
    this collection of articles.

24 "They sat at their wine" (Anlezark 295).

25 "They then went to sit down to the feast, proud ones at the wine-service" (Fulk 299).

26 "the boast of those drunk on ale" (Anlezark 167-69).

Works Cited

Andrew, Malcolm, and Ronald Waldron, editors. *The Poems of the Pearl Manuscript: Pearl,
    Cleanness, Patience, Sir Gawain and the Green Knight.* 5th ed., Liverpool UP, 2007.

Anlezark, Daniel, editor and translator. *Old Testament Narratives.* Harvard UP, 2011. Dumbarton
    Oaks Medieval Library 7.

Bately, Janet, editor. *The Old English Orosius.* Early English Text Society / Oxford UP, 1980. EETS
    ss 6.

Bennett, Judith M. *Ale, Beer, and Brewsters in England: Women's Work in a Changing World 1300-*

1600. Oxford UP, 1996.

Bosworth, Joseph, and T. Northcote Toller. *An Anglo-Saxon Dictionary*. Oxford, 1898.

Bramley, H. R., editor and translator. *S. Gregory on the Pastoral Charge: The Benedictine Text, with an English Translation*. Oxford, 1874.

Clark Hall, J. R. *A Concise Anglo-Saxon Dictionary*. 4th ed., with a supplement by Herbert D. Meritt, Cambridge UP, 1960.

Cockayne, T. O, editor and translator. *Leechdoms, Wortcunning, and Starcraft of Early England*. Cambridge, 1864–66. 3 vols.

Colgrave, Bertram, editor and translator. *Felix's Life of Saint Guthlac*. Cambridge UP, 1956.

———, editor and translator. *Two Lives of Saint Cuthbert*. Cambridge UP, 1940.

Colgrave, Bertram, and R. A. B. Mynors, editors and translators. *Bede's Ecclesiastical History of the English People*. 1969. 2nd ed, Oxford UP, 1992. Oxford Medieval Texts.

Dictionary of Medieval Latin from British Sources. Prepared by R. K. Ashdowne, D. R. Howlett, and R. E. Latham. The British Academy / Oxford UP, 2018. 3 vols.

Dictionary of Old English: A to I Online. Edited by Angus Cameron, Ashley Crandell Amos, Antonette diPaolo Healey et al. Dictionary of Old English Project, 2018. Accessed 16 Aug. 2020.

Edgar, Swift, and Angela M. Kinney, editors. *The Vulgate Bible*, vol. 3, *The Poetical Works, Douay-Rheims Translation*. Harvard UP, 2011. Dumbarton Oaks Medieval Library 8.

Fell, Christine E. "Old English *Beor*." *Leeds Studies in English*, new series, vol. 8, 1975, pp. 76–95.

Fulk, R. D., editor and translator. *The* Beowulf *Manuscript*. Harvard UP, 2010. Dumbarton Oaks Medieval Library 3.

Fulk, R. D., et al., editors. *Klaeber's* Beowulf and the Fight at Finnsburg, with a foreword by Helen Damico. 4th ed., U of Toronto P, 2008.

Garmonsway, G. N., editor. *Ælfric's Colloquy*. 2nd ed., Methuen, 1947. Methuen's Old English Library.

Godden, Malcolm, and Susan Irvine, editors. *The Old English Boethius: An Edition of the Old English Versions of Boethius's* De Consolatione Philosophiae. Oxford UP, 2009. 2 vols.

Gonser, Paul, editor. *Das angelsächsische Prosa-Leben des hl. Guthlac*. Carl Winter, 1909. Anglistische Forschungen 27.

Gwara, Scott, editor, and David W. Porter, translator. *Anglo-Saxon Conversations: The Colloquies of Ælfric Bata*. Boydell, 1997.

Hagen, Ann. *Anglo-Saxon Food and Drink*. Anglo-Saxon Books, 2006.

Holt, Robert, editor. *The Ormulum*, with the notes and glossary of R. M. White. Oxford, 1878. 2 vols.

Hornsey, Ian S. *A History of Beer and Brewing*. The Royal Society of Chemistry, 2003.

Jones, Christopher A., editor and translator. *Old English Shorter Poems*, vol. 1, *Religious and*

Didactic. Harvard UP, 2012. Dumbarton Oaks Medieval Library 15.

Kinney, Angela M., editor. *The Vulgate Bible*, vol. 4, *The Major Prophetical Books, Douay-Rheims Translation*, with an introduction by Swift Edgar. Harvard UP, 2012. Dumbarton Oaks Medieval Library 13.

Kopaczyk, Joanna, and Hans Sauer, editors. *Binomials in the History of English*. Cambridge UP, 2017. Studies in English Language.

Krapp, George Philip, and Elliott van Kirk Dobbie, editors. *The Exeter Book*. Columbia UP, 1936. Anglo-Saxon Poetic Records 3.

Licensing Act 2003. The Stationery Office Limited, 2003.

Liebermann, F., editor. *Die Gesetze der Angelsachsen*. 1903‒16. Scientia Aalen, 1960. 3 vols.

Macrae-Gibson, O. D., editor. *Of Arthour and of Merlin*. Early English Text Society / Oxford UP, 1973 and 1979. 2 vols. EETS os 268, 279.

Martin, Scott C., editor. *The Sage Encyclopedia of Alcohol: Social, Cultural, and Historical Perspectives*. Sage, 2015. 3 vols.

Melville, Gert, and Martial Staub, editors. *Brill's Encyclopedia of the Middle Ages*. English ed., supervised by Francis G. Gentry and Tim Barnwell, translated by Michael Chase et al., Brill, 2017. 2 vols.

Middle English Dictionary. Edited by Hans Kurath et al., U of Michigan P, 1952‒2001.

Miller, Thomas, editor and translator. *The Old English Version of Bede's Ecclesiastical History of the English People*. London, 1891 and 1898. 2 pts. in 4 vols. EETS os 95, 96, 110, 111.

Millett, Bella, and E. J. Dobson, editors, with Richard Dance. *Ancrene Wisse: A Corrected Edition of the Text in Cambridge, Corpus Christi College, MS 402, with Variants from Other Manuscripts*. Early English Text Society / Oxford UP, 2005‒06. 2 vols. EETS os 325‒26.

Morris, Richard, editor and translator. *Old English Homilies and Homiletic Treatises of the Twelfth and Thirteenth Centuries*. 1st series. 1867‒68. 2 pts. Reprinted in 1 vol., Early English Text Society / Boydell and Brewer, 1998. EETS os 29, 34.

Napier, Arthur S., editor. *The Old English Version of the Enlarged Rule of Chrodegang Together with the Latin Original, an Old English Version of the Capitula of Theodulf Together with the Latin Original, [and] an Interlinear Old English Rendering of the Epitome of Benedict of Aniane*. Early English Text Society / Oxford UP, 1916. EETS os 150.

OED Online. Oxford UP, 2020. Accessed 16 Aug. 2020.

Porter, David W., editor. *The Antwerp-London Glossary*, vol. 1, Texts and Indexes. Pontifical Institute of Medieval Studies, 2011. Publications of the Dictionary of Old English 8.

Roget's International Thesaurus. 6th ed., edited by Barbara Ann Kipfer, HarperCollins, 2001.

Rowland, Jenny. "OE *Ealuscerwen/Meoduscerwen* and the Concept of 'Praying for Mead.'" *Leeds Studies in English*, new series, vol. 21, 1990, pp. 1‒12.

Stevenson, W. H., editor. *Early Scholastic Colloquies*. Oxford UP, 1929.

Sweet, Henry, editor and translator. *King Alfred's West-Saxon Version of Gregory's Pastoral Care.* London, 1871. 2 pts. EETS os 45, 50.

A Thesaurus of Old English. 2nd impression, by Jane Roberts and Christian Kay with Lynne Grundy, Rodopi, 2000. 2 vols.

Unger, Richard W. *Beer in the Middle Ages and the Renaissance.* U of Pennsylvania P, 2004.

Whitelock, Dorothy, editor. *English Historical Documents*, vol. 1, *c. 500-1042.* 2nd ed., 1979. Routledge, 1996.

Williamson, Craig, translator. *The Complete Old English Poems*, with an introduction by Tom Shippey. U of Pennsylvania P, 2017.

Wright, William Aldis, editor. *The Metrical Chronicle of Robert of Gloucester.* London, 1887. 2 vols.

Zupitza, Julius, editor. *Aelfrics Grammatik und Glossar.* 1880. Reprinted with a preface by Helmut Gneuss, Max Niehans, 1966.

Bells Ringing for Helen and Criseyde

Setsuko Haruta

> Was this the face that launch'd a thousand ships,
> And burnt the topless towers of Ilium?
>
> Marlowe, *Doctor Faustus*, V.i. 107-8

The famous question is based on an illogical assumption that men would join forces in a large-scale military campaign to retrieve another man's beautiful wife. The mythographers themselves felt the inadequacy of such motivation, and devised other explanations, such as the oath taken by Helen's suitors (who included most of the Greek kings) to help her future husband in time of crisis.

Helen is not only a beautiful woman; she is a person of enormous importance. The purpose of the Greek expedition is to bring her back, not to punish her or to wreak vengeance on the Trojans. After the war, Helen is restored as the first lady of Sparta; she is simply too valuable to be damaged or destroyed.

Helen's importance is both political and mythological. Various legends were created and developed about her. She is believed to be a daughter of Zeus, who raped Leda in the form of a swan. Whoever marries Helen obtains the privileged status of Zeus' son-in-law.[1] It is natural, then, that men regard her as a supreme prize: a woman who brings happiness and prosperity to her partner.

Helen's political importance is hidden under a thin cover. Her official father Tyndareus is king of Sparta, which makes her heiress and queen of the city-state by birth.[2] Sparta, then, basically belongs to Helen, and Menelaus can claim his kingship only through his wife. If Helen changes her husband, the privilege passes to her new partner, who wins the right to rule Sparta as its new king.

Helen's marriage with a foreign prince, therefore, potentially brings a radical change in international/intertribal relationship, which is what happens when Paris elopes with her. Paris is a member of Trojan royal family, and his marriage with Helen allows Troy to claim Sparta as its domain.[3] When we regard the Trojan War, as Herodotus does, as the first clash between the Mediterranean West and the Orient, the meaning of the abduction becomes clear: it is an act of aggression, by which the Orient seized the opportunity to control one of the powerful city-states in Europe. This explains why, once Paris is killed, Helen is quickly married to Deiphebus, a case of a younger brother succeeding to the rights of his deceased elder brother by marrying his widow.[4]

The true cause of the war, then, is not Helen herself but the political tension caused by her dislocation. Under these critical circumstances, the Greeks decide to attack Troy, before their enemies have the time to put their claim in action, either by means of a military invasion or by political negotiations. The Greek kings join Agamemnon and Menelaus, because they recognize the situation as a common threat to all Greek city-states.

This also explains, I think, the Greeks' insistence in calling Menelaus king of Sparta (while his title is now questionable), and in attributing to Helen the misleading epithet "of Troy", as if she were dissociated from her native land, and disinherited by her own people.[5] The verbal manipulations may be interpreted as a kind of political propaganda, and show how the Greeks choose to look at the situation.

From the point of view of the Oriental city-states and the bordering areas, the Greek invasion is a Persian War in reverse. The siege of Troy, an important city-state on the front line against the Greek confederacy, is felt as a great threat, not only to Troy itself but also to all the city-states in the Orient. One after another, the Oriental tribes and city-states send military forces to support Troy, some kings leading their armies themselves. For both sides, it is of crucial importance to possess Helen in person and alive, and to mate her with a male member of one of their royal families.

No extant work has given a full literary treatment to Helen as the central character, with the possible exception of Euripides' *Helen*.[6] Nevertheless, if we are to look for a literary model for Chaucer's Criseyde, we find no figure other than Helen who shares some basic characteristics with her. E. Talbot Donaldson, who probably reached the same conclusion, chooses to begin his essay on Criseyde's literary history with a reference to Helen.[7] The medieval authors had no direct access to the Homeric epics. Helen, as they knew her, was already in the process of demythologization, and her debasement in the later compositions runs in parallel to that of Chaucer's heroine. Helen's influence reaches Criseyde also by an indirect route, through the character of Briseis who, by her transference back and forth between two men, repeats Helen's history in a much diminished and humanized scale.

Scholars have difficulty in establishing the intertextual link between Homer's Briseis and Chaucer's Criseyde. Donaldson thinks that their likeness is coincidental, and Barry Windeatt shares his view.[8] Sally Mapstone, however, demonstrates convincingly that Chaucer could link his heroine with Briseis. In Ovid's *Heroides*, Briseis tells her personal history, and Dictys' version includes the quarrel between Achilles and Agamemnon (where Briseis is given a personal name Hippodamia). *Ilias Latina*, a twelfth-century Latin abridgment of *The Iliad*, was "very likely" known to Benoît, whose romance served as the source of Boccaccio's *Filostrato*. And Chaucer knew that Boccaccio's "Criseida" was modelled on Benoît's "Briseida".[9]

In *Troilus and Criseyde*, Chaucer brings Helen and Criseyde together in one scene, as if to invite his audience to contemplate on the similarities of, and the differences between, the two women. In order to bring about the first meeting of the lovers, Pandarus fabricates a story of "false Poliphete" (II, 1467) who presumably intends to persecute his niece, and asks Deiphebus to invite Criseyde's supporters for a consultation. Deiphebus proposes to invite Helen on the ground that "she may leden Paris as hire leste" (II, 1449), revealing the power relationship between the couple.

When Helen visits Deiphebus' palace, she is presented as an honorable and respected member of the Trojan society. Her manner is graceful, kindly and admirably feminine, much resembling that of Criseyde. She comforts Troilus (who pretends illness) "in al goodly softe wyse ... and gan hir arm right over his shulder leye" (II, 1667-71), a gesture of a mature and affectionate kinswoman, but again resembling Criseyde's behavior when she later visits Troilus in bed: she lays her both hands on him "softe" (III, 72) and talks to him "softely" (III, 182). Helen's attitude toward Criseyde is equally warm and sympathetic: holding Criseyde's hand, she is the first to denounce anyone who intends to harm her (II, 1604-10).

At Deiphebus' palace, Helen is repeatedly addressed, and is referred to, as "queene Eleyne" (II, 1556, 1688, 1703 and 1714). The title puzzles us, because Hecuba is queen of Troy and Andromache is expected to succeed to her position. If Helen is a queen at all, she is still regarded as the queen of Sparta. This indicates that Chaucer, too, believed that the land belonged to Tyndareus' daughter. The English poet had a good reason to be sensitive to the legitimacy of a regal title; his patron John of Gaunt assumed the title of "king of Castile and Leon" after his marriage with Constance (see note 3).

As the heiress of a powerful city-state, Helen is also enormously rich. She carries treasures with her to Troy, which she (rightly) claims to be hers.[10] By associating Helen with her treasures in *The Iliad*, the poet seems to suggest that they include something like a regalia of Sparta.

Chaucer depicts Helen as a lady whose status is firmly established in Trojan society, a position which Criseyde aspires to in vain. Criseyde is of much later composition than Helen; she remains of human size, with human weaknesses and vulnerability, and she is painfully conscious of her limitations. She is under no divine protection, and her environment is realistically threatening; the angry Trojans want to burn her because of her father's betrayal, and she is told that she is under a new threat by "false Poliphete".

Although Criseyde takes pains to maintain her honor (that is, good reputation), Chaucer does not refer to her as an aristocrat; the only noble quality ascribed to her is "womanly noblesse" (I, 287). Criseyde is educated and literate; she reads and writes letters, and has access to a manuscript of "the gest of the siege of Thebes" (II, 82-83). She lives in a "palays" (II, 76) and seems to enjoy a comfortable life, but she feels it her duty to pay attention to the material aspects of her household. She congratulates herself for being her "owene womman, wel at ese" (II, 750), but she has to leave her possessions when she is forced to leave the city of Troy (IV, 1333). In spite of her courtly manners and discourse, Criseyde is a plebeian, a respectable bourgeoise.

Criseyde's pragmatism is explained partly by her non-aristocratic status. As a person of modest social status, she is trained to make compromises in order to avoid offending those who are socially superior. She is also aware of the importance of aristocratic patronage. When she feels her life threatened, she goes straight, not to her uncle, but to Hector, and appeals for protection. When she learns of Troilus' love for her, she fears that, should she refuse the king's son, she may have to suffer the consequences (II, 708-14). After accepting him as lover, she enjoys the sense of security, with the Trojan prince as "a wal / Of stiel" to protect her (III, 479-80).

The sense of security, however, proves to be a mere illusion, and Criseyde has to move to a foreign environment with, unlike Helen, no status attached to her person and no rich treasure to carry with her. In the Greek military camp, she is in an even greater predicament. Diomede understands her need of protection, and loses no time in offering himself; he swears to be her "frend", and hopes to serve her (V, 106 ff.). Neither does he forget to assure her that he, too, is a king's son (V, 932-34). Criseyde complies, but her elusive letter to Troilus shows that she is still afraid of offending the Trojan prince.

Noblemen should estimate a woman's eligibility in marriage by her social status and the amount of her wealth. Helen is "the wife of many husbands"; she is desired, not only for her beauty but more for political, social, and material benefits which she would bring to her spouse. In order to claim the ownership, men should be legally united with Helen in marriage. A medieval equivalent which remotely resembles Helen's case would be Eleanor of Aquitaine, heiress of the vast and rich land of southern France.[11] Kings and princes desired to marry her and, after her separation from her first husband (King Louis VII of France), she was kidnapped, like Helen, by young Henry of Anjou, later Henry II of England. Like Eleanor, Helen is not to be left alone without a husband; it is not a good idea to allow a widowed or separated queen to control her kingdom and her people, as the examples of Dido, Zenobia and Boudicca show.[12]

According to John Pollard, "mistresses were sharply distinguished from wives in Homeric society" (p. 53). While marriage with Helen would bring a man tremendous benefits, Criseyde has no fringe benefit attached to her. Her literary ancestors, Briseis and Chryseis, are captives in war, and are distributed among the warriors as slaves for manual labors and as bed companions.[13] Achilles uses the word ἄλοχος in a very loose sense, but he has no intention to marry a slave; he expects his father to find a wife for him (IX, 393-94).[14]

Criseyde is a widow like Briseis, but she is neither a captive nor a slave. She enjoys her independent status ("I am myn owene womman, wel at ese - / I thank it God - as after myn estat" II, 750-51) and runs her own household. We are not told how long she has been a widow, nor if she has had any suitor before the poem opens. Her response to Troilus' offer of love, however, seems to indicate that no other admirer has approached her; a beautiful widow with a good reputation is not good enough to attract suitors. Calchas' betrayal makes it inconceivable for any man to establish a public bond with a traitor's daughter, although it does not deter Troilus from desiring her as lover. Even Troilus, however, with all his passion and naiveté, recoils from the idea, when Pandarus urges him to claim her publicly (IV, 554-67); the best he can offer to Criseyde is to "stelen priveliche awey" with her (IV, 1601).

Criseyde is thus kept away from the possibility of the legal/public bond of marriage and can serve men's desire only as a mistress/lover. Troilus is not married, but will someday marry a woman whom his father will choose for him.[15] He will conceivably keep Criseyde as his mistress after his marriage, as John of Gaunt kept Katherine Swynford. Diomede is already married to "passing wise" Aegialeia (*The Iliad*, V, 412), but the fact does not worry him when he woos Criseyde; "I loved never womman here-biforn / As paramours", he says (V, 157-58). It is difficult to see the difference between the two wooings from Criseyde's point of view.

As a daughter of Zeus, Helen is destined to marry down. Menelaus, who woos her through his great brother Agamemnon and wins her because he offers the richest gift to Tyndareus, is not among the greatest heroes in *The Iliad*, but he is still a better warrior than Helen's second husband Paris, who proves to be a disappointment to all.[16] In Book III, Helen has to watch their single combat from the city wall and see her current partner defeated by her ex-husband. When she seizes the opportunity to rebuke him, Paris invites her to make love with him, presumably hoping to reassert his masculinity.[17] Speechless, Helen obeys. The audience feels that Helen is a "disillusioned" woman; her "passion [for Paris] had long since died".[18]

Troilus is a king's son, and far superior to Criseyde in his social status, but he is often awkward and inefficient. The narrator assures us that he is a good fighter (I. 470-83 and 1072-8; II. 624-44; III. 1772-75; V. 1751ff., etc.), but famously refuses to give any realistic description of battle scenes (V. 1765-71). Like Menelaus, the young prince depends entirely on his agent (Pandarus) in wooing a woman. Troilus' good looks overwhelm Criseyde for a moment, but he later disappoints her in several things. If Criseyde hopes to enjoy refined and witty conversations with her lover (one of the first questions she asks Pandarus about her admirer is, "Kan he wel speke of love?" II, 503), Troilus fails to live up to her expectation; his first address to Criseyde is a mere ejaculation, "Ha, a!" (III, 65). Criseyde shares to some extent Pandarus' view that love is a "game",[19] but Troilus takes love very seriously to the end.

The greatest disappointment for Criseyde is that Troilus fails to function as "a wal of stiel" (III, 479-81, see above, p. 22); he makes no effort to overcome difficulties at critical moments. In one scene, and only once in the poem, Criseyde appeals for help directly to Troilus: "Help, Troilus!" she cries, and faints (IV, 1149-55). Troilus' response to this crisis is to assume that she is dead, and to proceed promptly to commit suicide. This may be an act of devotion (in *Romeo and Juliet* fashion), but does not improve the situation, and Criseyde has to recover quickly to stop him.[20] After this experience, Criseyde understandably feels it difficult to commit her future to her devoted but impractical lover.

Both Paris and Troilus seem to be unaware of their weaknesses, and remain unashamed. Paris lacks the sense of shame which may be attributed to his uncourtly upbringing as a shepherd, and Troilus' lack of awareness to his extreme youth and his privileged position. Their innocence and good humor[21] make it difficult for their female partners to hate them; they appeal to their maternal instinct and make them feel protective.

Unfortunately for Paris and Troilus, Troy has one male character who is a paragon of both a warrior and a husband at the same time, namely Hector. In *The Iliad*, Paris is contrasted directly with his great brother (VI, 312–41 and 503–29), and the most laudatory epithet for Troilus in Chaucer's poem is "Ector the secounde" (II, 158 and III, 1775). Both Helen and Criseyde recognize Hector as the alpha–male of the Trojan society, and both are interested in him. Helen does not conceal her admiration for him in her warm praises, to Hector himself (VI, 342–58) and at his funeral (XXIV, 760–75). When Criseyde is in need of a protector, she approaches, not the old king Priam, but Hector, and kneels before him in an appealing posture. Her efforts take certain effects: according to Deiphebus, Hector speaks highly of her (II, 1452–56), and he tries to dissuade the Trojans from exchanging her for Antenor, although he does not push his point too far.[22]

Helen is a creation of a half mythological epic world, where characters are often portrayed in superhuman stature. Her divine lineage is of the highest order; her proclaimed father is Zeus, and her twin brothers, Castor and Pollux, are worshipped in popular cults. Helen herself is associated with various goddesses, and legends cluster around her figure. Her title as the most beautiful woman owes much to Aphrodite's judgment; nobody would think of challenging or questioning the decree of the goddess of love and beauty herself.

In Greek antiquity, the process of Helen's debasement is averted by contemporary beliefs and practices. Helen was revered in various cults in Athens and Rhodes as well as in her native Sparta.[23] Pollard suggests that Helen was originally the divine ancestress of Tyndarid dynasty (p. 105) and also a tree-goddess (pp. 101-106). Lindsay sees her as an ancient vegetation deity (p. 305). As a nature goddess, Helen was believed to bring prosperity to the community. This also explains her repeated kidnappings as a variation of Persephone myth (Lindsay, pp. 237-38). Later, she was identified with other nature goddesses: Artemis and Aphrodite.[24] Helen is Zeus' daughter, and her mother is either Leda (for example, in Euripides' *Helen*), Ocean (Hesiod, *Catalogues of Women*) or Nemesis (Hesiod and *Cypria*), "protector of wild creatures, by-form of Artemis" (Pollard, pp. 25-26). Legends extend to include Helen's afterlife: she joins Achilles in "White Island" (Leuke) or, like her brothers, the Dioscuri, she is made a star.[25]

The first appearances of Helen in the extant works of literature are in the two Homeric epics (*The Iliad*, III, VI, XXIV, and *The Odyssey*, IV and XV). She plays a subsidiary role in them, but her character has a powerful impact, both on the audience and on the characters within the poems. She not only "stands somehow for the supreme good, the most desirable goal in the heroic world" (Lindsay, p. 16), but also is presented as an individual with strong and unique personality (see below, pp. 30ff., and 33-34).

Helen also appears in Greek lyrics. Sappho refers to her in exquisite and colorful words: "golden Helen" hatched from an egg of "hyacinthine hue". Stesichorus is said to have been punished with blindness because he slandered Helen in one of his poems; he composed a recantation, asserting that Helen did not go to Troy at all but stayed in Egypt all the while, and regained his sight.[26]

The Greek dramatists are invariably interested in Helen. Aeschylus condemns her, with Paris, in *Agamemnon* (403ff.). Sophocles wrote two plays, one on Paris and the other on Helen, both of which are lost (Pollard, p. 21, and Lindsay, pp. 147-51). Euripides demythologizes Helen on the one hand, exposing her to be an egoistic and culpable woman (most notably in *The Trojan Women*) and, on the other, presents her as a faithful but misunderstood heroine in *Helen*, in a manner somewhat similar to Dryden's remaking of Criseyde into an innocent suspect who commits suicide to prove her faithfulness.

Setsuko Haruta

One thing which remains with Helen throughout her literary history is her beauty. Homer convinces his audience of it, not by portraying Helen herself, but by reporting other characters' reactions. Men are fascinated, almost spellbound, before Helen. Both Priam and Hector treat her very courteously, but the most famous is the scene in which the Trojan elders see her walk on the rampart and say, "Small blame that Trojans and well-grieved Achaeans should for such a woman long time suffer woes; wondrously like is she to the immortal goddesses to look upon" (III, 156- 58).

In later works, Helen's beauty is already turning into a legend; on her return journey, the Cretans gather to see her (Dictys, VI.4) and, on her arrival at Sparta, people flock together to look at her (Guido, XXXIII). Many mythographers seek in her beauty the reason for her survival and escape from any punishment. When Menelaus tries to kill his unfaithful wife, Helen shows her bare bosom, at which he drops his sword.[27] In Stesichorus' recantation, the Greeks cannot stone her to death when they see her face.[28]

Helen's exaggerated beauty came to be regarded as sufficient reason for the Greeks to invade Troy; the beautiful "face" launches a thousand ships. In The Iliad, several characters express this view, most notably Achilles.[29] In The Odyssey, the swineherd Eumaeus blames Helen for causing many warriors' death and wishes her dead with all her race (XIV, 68-69). The Homeric characters, however, do not forget that gods are ultimately responsible for the war; Odysseus says that Zeus afflicted the house of Atreus through two sisters, Helen and Clytemnestra.[30] The Trojan women in Euripides' tragedy, on the other hand, blame Helen for their misfortunes, and Cassandra mocks the Greeks, saying that they wasted many lives for one wanton woman (368-69).

Pollard believes that the story of Helen, "however refurbished and romanticized", has some historical basis (p. 145); "there can be no reasonable doubt that someone or something provoked the war" (p. 22). A simple, dramatic tale of the eternal triangle would please and convince people more easily than complicated political or mythological explanations. The fact does not explain, however, why Helen alone should bear the blame for the three characters involved in the triangle situation.[31]

Cypria, a fragmentary epic which tells the prehistory of the Trojan War, begins with Zeus' plan to relieve the burden (of over-population) of the earth by means of a large-scale warfare. Goddess Themis helps him in devising a plan, according to which Eris, goddess of strife, visits the marriage feast of Peleus and Thetis with the golden apple, a prize for the most beautiful among the goddesses. This triggers a chain of events: the competition of the three goddesses (Hera, Athene and Aphrodite), the judgment of Paris, Aphrodite's promise of the most beautiful woman for him (as a bribe), and finally the abduction of Helen. Zeus' original plan is to help the earth goddess, and it is carried out by no less than six female agents, thus creating a strong impression that women are mostly responsible for stirring up the conflict.

According to another, more historical tradition, the Greeks abduct a Trojan princess Hesione in retribution for the rough treatment the Argonauts suffered from her father Laomedon, and the Trojans retaliate by a similar act of kidnapping a Greek queen, Helen. Here again, the cause of the war involves women, this time as tools of revenge and victims of abduction. Herodotus traces the antagonism between the two worlds (Europe and the Orient) farther back to a series of abductions: of Io, Europa, and Medea (*Historia*, 133). When later generations half-remember or forget other myths and legends, Helen stands for all the goddesses and women who appear in the prehistory of the Trojan War.

When Helen is deprived of her mythological status and aura, her downfall is inevitable. The Romans, who identified themselves as descendants of the Trojan war refugees, were ready to ascribe their sufferings to Helen. To the practically-minded Romans, to organize a military campaign for the possession of one woman would appear to be a foolish and irrational act. Their hero is Aeneas, who deserts an attractive woman and her tremendous offers, and carries out his duty to found a new nation which is to be Rome.

In Virgil's epic, Aeneas gives a first-hand report of the fall of Troy to much interested Dido. When he found Helen in her hiding place, he questioned himself:

"So this woman will live to set eyes on Sparta and her native Mycenae again, and walk as queen in the triumph she has won? Will she see her husband, her father's home and her children and be attended by women of Troy and Phrygian slaves, while Priam lies dead by the sword, Troy has been put to the flames and the shores of the land of Dardanus have sweated so much blood?" He tried to kill Helen, only to be prevented by Venus, Helen's protector and his own mother (*The Aeneid*, II, 567–603). In Hades, Deiphebus' shadow confides to Aeneas that Helen, hoping to gain the favor of the Greeks, betrayed him to be killed by Menelaus (VI, 507–29). As Lindsay puts it, "for Virgil she is merely a vile woman, the Erinys of her own land" (p. 168).

Debasement of Helen's character accelerates in the Middle Ages, when loyalty to one's nation and fidelity to one's overlord gradually gained importance. This is when Criseyde makes her first appearance in Benoît's *roman antique*. Guido's Achilles believes that Helen is not worthy of the venture and sacrifice of so many noble lives (XXIV); Criseyde, too, is the unworthy means of destroying the noble prince of Troy. As the "tradition of cheapening Helen as a woman of shameless coquetry ... [and] emblem of infidelity" (Lindsay, p. 168) develops, so is Criseyde treated as a changeable, lecherous, egoistic, and deceitful woman by many authors.

Helen moves from Sparta (where she is Menelaus' wife) to Troy (where she is married to Paris, and then to Deiphebus), and back to Sparta (and to Menelaus).[32] In *The Iliad*, Briseis moves in a much smaller scale: from Lyrnessus (where she is Mynes' wife [XIX, 290 ff.]) to the Greek military camp, where she is handed back and forth between Achilles and Agamemnon. Chaucer's Criseyde lives in the city of Troy (as a widow, and then as Troilus' lover), and is later transported to the Greek camp (where she becomes Diomede's lover). Criseyde is a counterpoint to Helen in that she moves between the two opposing forces in the opposite directions.

Neither woman seems entirely happy about her dislocation, and the poets evoke the audience's sympathy, Homer by referring to Helen's longing for home (III, 139–45) and Chaucer by quoting Criseyde's soliloquy (V, 729 ff.). From their compatriots' point of view, however, both women change sides and join the enemy.

Helen, although she is native of Sparta, is publicized as "Helen of Troy", and Criseyde is associated with her father who is a genuine turncoat. In the view of their male compatriots, they appear to be doubly unfaithful, betraying both their countries and their partners, associating themselves with male members of the enemy group.

Both Helen and Criseyde are presented as clever women. In *The Odyssey*, Helen instantly identifies Telemachus as Odysseus' son (IV, 137-46). She offers a herbal potion to soothe the young man's emotional pains (IV, 219-32), and prophesies the return of Odysseus by the flight of an eagle, while her husband fails to read the omen (XV, 160-78). In Euripides' drama, it is Helen who instructs Menelaus what he should do to outwit Theoclymenus (*Helen*, 1049-106).

Criseyde is in the habit of thinking logically before she makes a decision. George Lyman Kittredge assures us that she is "an uncommonly clever woman" who "keeps her eyes open, and takes no leap in the dark".[33] In Book II, we see her arguing about the proposition set by her uncle: whether or not to accept Troilus as lover. After being swept away momentarily by the sudden sight of Troilus (II, 610-58), she resumes her inner debate, which goes on till bedtime. Her argument takes a philosophical turn when she asks herself, "To what fyn lyve I thus?" (II, 757), and again, "To what fyn is swich love I kan nat see" (II, 794).[34] Her Boethian monologue on false felicity takes only 17 lines to reach its conclusion (III, 820-36), while Troilus' pondering on predestination goes on for 121 lines (IV, 958-1078).

Both Helen and Criseyde know how to behave and speak under given circumstances. Helen's speeches to Priam (III, 171-224) and to Hector (VI, 342-58) are deceptively open in expressing regret for her own misdeed and gratitude for the generosity of the two Trojan noblemen; they are very different from her spirited rebukes directed toward Aphrodite (III, 395-412) and to Paris (III, 428-36). In her only public utterance (at Hector's funeral), she praises the dead hero for his courtesy and protective kindness toward her, and implicitly encourages other Trojans to follow his example (XXIV, 762-75). Charles Muscatine points out that Criseyde, too, can change her discourse to suit her environment; she speaks to Troilus in the courtly mode, but her speech approaches the language of fabliau when she is with

Setsuko Haruta

Pandarus.[35]

Both women are conscious of their transgressions of the ethos that binds their society. Helen often opens her speech with a wish that she were dead or were never born (III, 172-76, VI, 345-48 and XXIV, 762-64). Although her words sound sincere, it is at the same time a clever strategy to prevent her interlocutor from accusing her. In a similar manner, Criseyde acknowledges fully that she has "falsed oon the gentileste / That evere was, and oon the worthieste" (V, 1056-57), laments over her future infamy and, by so doing, succeeds in extracting sympathetic remarks from the narrator: "Ne me list this sely womman chyde ... for she so sory was for hir untrouthe .... Iwis, I woulde excuse hire yet for routhe" (V, 1093-99).

In other words, both women can play their roles admirably to suit the occasions. Helen can play a graceful queen in *The Odyssey*, and Criseyde acts as a perfect courtly lady when she is with her very courtly lover. In different circumstances, Helen is an outspoken, audacious lady, and Criseyde is a practical, playful woman. When they are exposed to criticism, they act as guilt-stricken women in the anti-feminist tradition.

The intelligence and adaptability of the two women do not help to improve their later reputations; their elusiveness suggests slyness, and their cleverness is linked to deceitfulness. In Book IV of *The Odyssey*, Helen tells Telemachus how she helped Odysseus when he went into the city of Troy, disguised as a beggar (235-64), but Menelaus quickly reminds her of another incident in which she helped the Trojans, too, by testing the wooden horse, impersonating the wives of the warriors hiding inside it (265-89). She also helped the Greeks by signalling to them with torches in a Bacchic dance. In Seneca's version of *The Trojan Women*, she tricks Polyxena into being sacrificed. Guido, too, tells us that she laments for Paris' death only to win Hecuba's sympathy (XXVIII). Helen is thus condemned as a deceitful woman by both the Greeks and the Trojans.

Criseyde is not so deeply involved in the politics of the war as Helen is; she simply obeys the decision of the Trojan council and joins the enemies. She is accused more for her personal infidelity to Troilus, and for her attempts to conceal her new love affair from her ex-lover. One critic interprets her letter as an effort to keep both men interested in her, while another condemns it as being "hypocritical", although it is difficult to see what profit she would gain by such an effort. Criseyde is also blamed for being her father's daughter - that she carries a traitor's DNA which makes her a traitor.

Neither Homer's Helen nor Chaucer's Criseyde appears to be an exceptionally passionate woman; Criseyde, indeed, "although a widow, ... seems ... emotionally virginal" before she accepts Troilus.[36] In the worlds of heroic epic and of courtly romance, however, both transgress the boundary of behaviors assigned to women, and conform to the anti-feminist view that women are by nature shallow, changeable and lecherous, and episodes are fabricated to match their roles. Helen, hearing the rumor of a handsome stranger, goes on her own accord to see Paris.[37] Later, she persuades him to elope with her (Guido, XII). Toward the end of the war, she visits Antenor, who is negotiating a peace treaty, secretly at night, and asks him to bring about reconciliation between Menelaus and herself, and Antenor sets out at dawn to act according to her wish.[38] Shakespeare portrays both Helen and Criseyde as apparently lecherous women who deserve contempt. A recent author on Helen calls her whore in the subtitle of her book, and Criseyde is often called by the same word, although neither of them is known to have engaged in the trade.[39]

European myths, legends and pseudo-history abound with women who instigate conflicts among men. Clytemnestra allegedly causes the downfall of Mycenean dynasty. Medb leads the Connacht men to invade Ulster in *Táin Bó Cuailgne*. In *The History of the Franks*, Gregory of Tours explains the struggles between two kingdoms by the rivalry between their queens, Brunhild and Fredegund. Kriemhild's revenge results in the annihilation of the Burgundians by the Huns in *Das Nibelungenlied*. In *The Most Piteous Tale of the Morte Arthur saunz Guerdon*, Malory tells us how the illicit affair of Queen Guinevere triggers a series of conflicts which ultimately destroys the Arthurian kingdom. Helen's name can be easily added to the above examples. As Chantecleer puts it, "Mulier est hominis confusio" ("The Nuns Priest's Tale", 3164).

The obsession for seeking the cause of men's misfortunes in the acts of women goes back to the roots of Indo-European and Judeo-Christian traditions. In the Greek myths, all existing evils are brought to the human world by one woman, Pandora, and, in the Old Testament, Eve is held responsible for the fall of man. *Radix malorum femina*; women destroy worthy men, as Sir Gawain illustrates by the examples of Adam, Solomon, Samson, and David.[40] It is easy to add Troilus' name to this list, as another example of a worthy man who is victimized by an evil woman.

The male hysteria to blame women shocks an outsider for, in some patriarchal societies, men are expected to take responsibilities on their own shoulders, and to protect women from blame. To those who are brought up in so-called culture of shame, to which medieval Europe presumably belongs, this custom of blaming the socially weak would appear cowardly. The fact that the Greek expedition to Troy begins and ends with sacrifices of two women (Iphegeneia and Polyxena) illustrates this point most effectively.

Both Helen and Criseyde are kinetic women; for men, they are trophies to be won, kept for a while, and eventually lost to another man. Those who enjoy them temporarily suffer later from the sense of deprivation, exaggerate the extent of their loss, and fantasize the lost women. Even while they are in their possession, men feel that they are not entirely theirs, that they once belonged to others and will eventually slip away from their hands.[41] Helen, in fact, is half bird in her origin.

Women with a background similar to that of Helen and Criseyde may themselves lack the conviction that they are attached to any man in particular, that it makes no essential difference which partner they are with. Criseyde regrets that she had to leave Troilus, but expresses her hope to remain faithful to her new lover ("To Diomede algate I wol be trewe" V, 1071). Although disillusioned (and probably disgusted as well), Helen concedes silently when Paris desires her (III, 447). After the fall of Troy, she goes back to Sparta with her first husband, resumes the role of his queen and sleeps with him: "The son of Atreus [that is, Menelaus] slept in the inmost chamber of the lofty house, and beside him lay long-robed Helen, peerless among women" (*The Odyssey*, IV, 304-5). Helen's lack of emotional involvement makes a strong contrast with Andromache's entire dependency on her husband, and her constant worries about the future of her family and of herself (*The Iliad*, VI, 407-39).

Helen and Criseyde are conceived as having a different mentality from most of the female characters found in epic and romance. Male partners are not of their primary concern, and can be replaced by another. In this, they resemble men in the epic world. What strikes male readers as "something uncanny" (Pollard, p. 52) and "a strange sort of innocence" (Lindsay, p. 28) in Helen's character, I think, derives from her emotional independence from such value systems (which are defined chiefly by men) as patriotism and fidelity to men on the part of women. Such emotional detachment is achieved by a woman with "simplicity of innocence" (Lindsay, p. 33), dissociated from society. As a traitor's daughter, Criseyde is a scapegoat to be expelled from the Trojan community, and Helen is "the most socially outcast of all social outcasts" (Pollard, p. 52).

Being aware that their fate is largely manipulated by others, the two women look at themselves from the same detached point of view, regretting the misfortunes they caused for others, but failing to see themselves responsible for them. "She [Helen] owns ... a strange sort of innocence", says Lindsay, "in her passive acceptance of her role and in her refusal to make excuses for herself"; she "never expresses moral repentance" (p. 28). Similarly, Criseyde sees her deed from a detached point of view; "Allas", she says, "that swich a cas me sholde falle!" (V, 1064). Helen weaves the scenes of the Trojan War in a tapestry (III, 125-28), as if she were among the audience of the historical event she is involved in. She also predicts that men will sing about her infamy in the future (VI, 357-58). Criseyde, too, sees her own life from the viewpoint of the future recipients of her story:

> "Allas, of me, unto the worldes ende,
> Shal neyther ben ywriten nor ysonge
> No good word, for thise bokes wol me shende.

O, rolled shal I ben on many a tonge!
Thorughout the world my belle shal be ronge!
And wommen moost wol haten me of alle.
Allas, that swich a cas me sholde falle!"[42]

(V, 1058-64)

The acceptance of fate, however, leads neither Helen nor Criseyde to resignation. The last picture we see of Criseyde is not of a powerless woman in despair, but of a person who hopes to do better in the future: "To Diomede algate I wol be trewe" (V, 1071). Both women survive the war, and their future is left open (except in the works of Henryson and of Dryden). Despite the pressures which forced them to follow a regrettable course of life, and despite their prediction of future infamy, they refuse to fall in despair, and try to make most of their severe circumstances.

Neither does their detachment result in lack of emotions. Chaucer's Criseyde remains "soft" and "tendre-herted" (V, 825) toward others' sufferings. She always acts thoughtfully and gently toward people around her, and her attitude toward Troilus is affectionate, forgiving, and almost maternal. Homer, too, depicts Helen as soft-hearted; she is homesick (III, 139-40), is sorry for both the Trojans and the Greeks who suffer from the war, and for those who are related to her and have to share her shame (III, 225-44). In *The Odyssey*, she joins Menelaus, Telemachus and Peisistratus in weeping for Odysseus who still wanders far from home (IV, 183-86).

If all that Helen does and suffers contribute in making what Pollard calls "Helen's great humanity" (p. 67), Criseyde, who is modelled on Helen, too, has some claim to a similar quality. In the unique scene in which Chaucer brings the two women together, the poet depicts them as sober-minded but well-intentioned ladies, acting tenderly but sensibly, as if to suggest that this is their normal behavior in a right environment.

Notes

References about Helen are to *The Iliad* (Loeb Classical Library, A. T. Murray, ed. and tr. Cambridge, Massachusetts: Harvard University Press, 1924), and those about Criseyde to *The Riverside Chaucer* (Larry D. Benson, ed., Boston: Houghton Mifflin, 1989), unless indicated otherwise.

1 In *The Odyssey*, IV, 561-69, Menelaus is assured of safe return journey from Troy, a peaceful life afterwards, and posthumous place in Elysium, thanks to his relationship with Zeus.

2 Jack Lindsay detects a matriarchal society in the background of the legend in *Helen of Troy: Woman and Goddess* (London: Constable, 1974), p. 57, and Bettany Hughes points out Helen's "position as a matrilineal heiress to a great temporal power" (*Helen of Troy: Goddess, Princess, Whore*. London: Jonathan Cape, 2005, p. 24; see also pp. 71 and 78-79).

3 It is said that a similar consideration prompted Elizabeth I to remain a virgin queen. Chaucer's patron John of Gaunt claimed the throne of Castile and Leon through his second wife Constance, daughter of Pedro (the Cruel, whose tale is told by Chaucer's Monk [2375-90]) in 1371.

4 Marriage of Helen and Deiphebus is mentioned in two non-Homeric epics in the Trojan cycle, *Little Iliad* and *Sack of Ilion*. The two Mycenean brothers marrying the two Spartan sisters, and Agamemnon's determined efforts to win and keep Clytemnestra for himself (by killing her first husband and her children!), and Helen for his brother Menelaus, seem to indicate his political intention to unite the two city-states.

5 Helen is "of Troy" only in the sense that Lawrence is "of Arabia".

6 Euripides' Helen (in *Helen*) is more like Dryden's Cressida than Chaucer's: a stereotype, faithful but greatly misunderstood woman.

7 E. Talbot Donaldson, "Briseis, Briseida, Criseyde, Cresseid, Cressid: Progress of a Heroine" in *Chaucerian Problems and Perspectives: Essays Presented to Paul E. Beichner, C.S.C.* (Edward Vasta and Zacharias Thundy, eds. Notre Dame: University of Notre Dame Press, 1979), pp. 1 and 5.

8 Barry Windeatt, *Troilus and Criseyde* (Oxford Guide to Chaucer. Oxford: Clarendon, 1992), p. 78.

9 Sally Mapstone, "The Origins of Criseyde" in *Medieval Women: Texts and Contexts in Late Medieval Britain: Essays for Felicity Riddy* (Jocelyn Wogan-Browne et al., eds., Turnhout: Brepols, 2000), pp. 132-34 and 139-44.

10 About Helen's treasures (*ktemata*), see John Pollard, *Helen of Troy* (London: R. Hale, 1965), pp. 53‒54; Linday, *op.cit.*, pp. 97‒98; and Hughes, *op.cit.*, p. 80.

11 See Hughes, *op.cit.*, pp. 291‒92.

12 In *The Odyssey*, Penelope attracts many suitors by similar political reasons. See Mihoko Suzuki, *Metamorphoses of Helen: Authority, Difference, and the Epic* (Ithaca; Cornell University Press, 1989), p. 74. Chaucer's Monk includes Zenobia's tale in his tragedies (2247‒374).

13 Briseis' lament over Patrocles' death puzzles the audience, for she says that he was to persuade Achilles to take her as wife (XIX. 295‒99). Was Patrocles merely trying to comfort her, or is she fabricating it, giving utterance to her wishful thinking? Mapstone takes the statement at face value (*op.cit.*, p. 133).

14 See Murray's notes on *The Iliad* (I, p. 406, n. 1, and II, p. 358, n. 1).

15 See Achilles' speech to the messengers from Agamemnon in *The Iliad*, IX, 393‒94, and above, n. 14.

16 Both Helen (III, 16‒37) and Hector (VI, 311‒22) rebuke Paris.

17 Chaucer's Troilus acts somewhat similarly after he recovers from his faint: he embraces Criseyde and declares, "Now be ye kaught ... Now yeldeth yow, for other bote is non!" (III. 1207‒8).

18 See Lindsay (*op.cit.*, p. 28) who also feels that Paris is "oddman out" in the Trojan royal family, and suggests that he originally belonged to a different tratdition (pp. 31, 35 and 205). See also Suzuki, *op.cit.*, p. 38.

19 Pandarus uses the word in I, 868, which is echoed by Criseyde in III. 1126. Criseyde hopes to enjoy the process of courtship involved in the "game". See II. 589‒90.

20 Cf. *Il Filostrato*, canto IV, stanza 117ff. I am tempted to think that Chaucer's Criseyde is testing Troilus. When Troilus previously appealed to Pandarus for help ("Help now!"), the latter promptly replied, "Yis, by mi trowthe, I shal" (I. 1054) and put his promise into action.

21 See Lindsay (*op.cit.*, p. 32) on Paris' character.

22 Criseyde is also conscious of the alpha‒male on the Greek side; she says that Pandarus should forbid her to love ‒ even "outher hym [Troilus] or Achilles, / Ector, or any mannes creature" (II. 415‒19).

23 Lindsay, *op. cit.*, pp. 116, 125 and 209; Hughes, *op.cit.* pp. 247 ff.; and Pollard, *op. cit.*, pp. 98‒99. According to Pollard, all of Helen's cults are post‒Homeric (*op. cit.*, p. 22).

24 Lindsay, *op. cit.*, pp. 174 and 211‒18. In her testament, Henryson's Cresseid leaves her "spreit" to Diana "quhair sho dwellis, / To walk with hir in waist woddis and wellis" (*The Testament of Cresseid*, 585‒86).

25 See Hughes, *op.cit.*, Appendix 4 (pp. 332-41).

26 See Hughes, *op.cit.*, p. 60; and Pollard (*op.cit.*, pp. 20-21and pp. 83-86), who suspects a political reason to explain the anecdote. Euripides bases his *Helen* on this legend, and Herodotus affirms it on the basis of his research in Egypt (*Historia*, II, 112-120). Plato refers to the legend in *Republic* (IX. 586 C).

27 The episode is mentioned in *Little Iliad* and in Aristophanes' *Lysistrata* (155-56).

28 See Hughes, *op.cit.*, p. 160.

29 Homer's Achilles likes to blame women for his misfortunes; when Patrocles is killed, he quickly turns his blame from Agamemnon to Briseis (XIX, 40-73). See Mapstone, *op.cit.*, p. 133.

30 *The Odyssey*, XI, 436-39. We find a similar view in Hesiod's *Works and Days* (156-69). Lindsay points out that the bardic tradition ascribes the destruction of Mycenean civilization to the Theban and the Trojan Wars (*op.cit.*, p. 15).

31 As Hughes puts it, "There are usually many contributory causes to international conflict, to the end of civilisations; the ancient Greeks needed only one: the promiscuity of a beautiful woman" (*op.cit.*, p. 170). About this "scapegoating mechanism", see Suzuki, *op.cit.*, pp. 29, etc.

32 To the above wanderings of Helen, we may add her prehistory of being kidnapped by Theseus, mentioned in *Cypria*. See Hughes, *op.cit.*, pp. 49 and 51.

33 George Lyman Kittredge, *Chaucer and His Poetry* (Cambridge, Massachusetts: Harvard University Press, 1915) reprinted as "Troilus" in *Chaucer's Troilus: Essays in Criticism* (Stephen A. Barney, ed. London: Scolar Press, 1980), p. 15.

34 Criseyde likes to think deeply to the "fyn" of the matters; she also says, "To what fyn sholde I lyve and sorwen thus?" (IV. 764).

35 Charles Muscatine, *Chaucer and the French Tradition: A Study in Style and Meaning* (Berkeley: University of California Press, 1957), Chapter V.

36 Pricilla Martin, *Chaucer's Women: Nuns, Wives, and Amazons* (Iowa City: University of Iowa Press, 1990), p. 163.

37 Dares, 10-11. Guido adds that, since women are amorous, emotionally shallow and changeable, they should not be allowed to go out in public but should be kept at home at all times (VII).

38 Dictys, 5.4 and Guido, XIX. The implication is that Helen used her sexual charm to influence Antenor.

39 In Criseyde's case, Henryson's association of her with "court commoun" (77) is the only exception.

40 *Sir Gawain and the Green Knight*, 2416-19. The biblical texts show that the four men in question are partly, if not entirely, to blame for their own downfall.

41 See Angela Jane Weisl, *Conquering the Reign of Femeny: Gender and Genre in Chaucer's Romance* (Cambridge: D.S. Brewer, 1995), pp. 1-2.

42 Chaucer bequeathed to his future audience/readers the privilege of contemplating which parts of Criseyde's prediction has (and has not) been realized. While Cupid does ring a bell in Henryson's *Testament of Cresseid* (144-45), Dryden uses many a "good word" for his Cressida, and the modern readers (especially women) generally share sympathetic view about Chaucer's heroine.

チョーサーの ‘Pardoner’s Tale’ とその周辺
——免償符 and/or 免罪符

多ヶ谷　有　子

I.　はじめに

　2016 年、リーズ大学で開催された International Medieval Congress（IMC 2016）の発表原稿を、2018 年 2 月に印刷論文として発表した。さらに 2018 年 6 月にそれを敷衍し、充実させて口答発表した。[1]本論はそれを踏まえ、「免償符売りの話」の類話について、新資料も視野に入れ、免償符／免罪符とはどのようなものであったのか、その本質的な悪とは何か、チョーサーの巡礼者のなかに免償符売りが登場する意味は何か、について考察し、類話との比較からチョーサーの視点を探りたい。

　本論の元になった拙論は、チョーサーの『カンタベリー物語』（Geoffrey Chaucer, *The Canterbury Tales*）のなかの「免償符売りの話」（‘Pardoner’s Tale’, 以下 PardT）について、日本における類話を紹介し検討することであった。加えて日本の類話の出典である漢籍を検討し、その源流を探り、インドから中国そして日本へと類話が伝播した可能性を考察した。この考察から、PardT の類話が汎世界的に、一方はインドからイングランドに到達してチョーサーの “Pardoner’s Tale” に結実し、他方は日本にいたって仮名草子等に取り入れられた可能性があることを探った。

　PardT の内容は、Skeat によれば直接の典拠はイタリアの話、W. A. Clouston によれば類話は古代インドその他に多くあり、“Buddhist original” であるパーリ語ジャータカ 48 番、Persian version（ペルシアの類話）、First Arabian version、Second Arabian version、Third Arabian version（アラビアの類話 3 篇）、Kashmir version（カシミール地方の類話）、Tibetan version（チベットの類話）、他のインド仏典説話をあげた。

　ジャータカとは釈迦の前世の話で前生譚といわれるものだが、仏典

ジャータカ No. 48 は日本では『南傳大蔵経』で翻訳されている。[2]Clouston
は日本の類話をあげておらず、日本の研究者も日本の類話については研究
していないため、前述論文では日本の類話についてわずかなりとも明らか
にした。

II.　類話の補遺

　Utter（ハンス＝イェルク・ウター）第二版は（2011）の邦訳版の 763 に、
「宝を見つけた者たちが殺し合う」という項目がある。764 には文献紹介
があり、そこに「Japanese 池田 1971」とある。[3]ただ池田 1971 にはそれに
見合う記述はなく、この種の話を講談で聞いたことがある、とある。1956
年池田氏の博士論文では壱岐島の話「ぼら賣り吉五郎」の記述がある。た
だし、これは吉五郎とは関わりない理由で山賊が互いに殺しあう話で、仲
間同士の毒殺を含む欲張りをテーマとする話とは質が異なる。池田が聞い
たという講談は、おそらく『浮世物語』を原作にしている可能性が高い。
しかし池田氏は『浮世物語』については何の言及もない。講談を聞いたと
いう記述に続いては、"Korean Version" として『朝鮮民潭集』171 頁の「山
上の三屍と金」が紹介されている。
　『朝鮮民潭集』の付録 26 頁には中国の話が紹介されている。「宋の張知
甫」の『張氏可書』（函海本）掲載のものである。函海本『張氏可書』は
国立公文書館蔵の『函海』（昌平坂学問所旧蔵）請求番号 371-0042 で見る
ことができる。ここから、PardT 中国版類話は、明治以前にすでに昌平坂
学問所で知られていたことがわかる。
　この種の類話は、ほかにインド笑話「盗った金塊はだれのもの」という、
ヴィノードクマール＝スィンフ氏からの採話や、中国の「高価な人参を見
つけた兄弟が互いに殺し合う」という兄と弟の死を語る話がある。粗筋は
以下の通りである。
　昔、長白山の麓に幼い時に両親を失った兄弟がいた。貧乏だったが仲良
かった。ある日運試しに薬用人参を掘ろうと、深い山谷の奥へ入って行き、
やがて大きな人参のあり場を探し当て喜んだ。兄弟は喜び勇んで家路につ

いたが、道々互いに独り占めにしたいと考えた。しばらく行くと兄弟は空腹になり、兄は酒を買いに弟は食い物を買いに行った。二人は戻ると道端の石に座って食事をした。食べたあと、兄も弟も「ハッ」と気がつき、同時に何か言おうとしたが、言葉が口から出る前に兄も弟もバッタリ道端に倒れて死んだ、という話である。二人型だが、形は PardT とよく似た話である。

III. 類話のまとめ

以上を整理し、類話を時系列にまとめると以下の通りである。

年	内容
1886	Clouston インドの類話としてパーリ語ジャータカ 48 を指摘。
1934	Tompson Motif Index IV 436 頁 AT763 対応の K1685、Treasure-finders Who Murder One Another に 類 話 と し て 1910-11 シャヴァンヌの仏訳（Contes I 386 No.115 漢訳旧雑比喩経 24 からの仏訳）による紹介あり。
1954	干潟龍祥『本生経類照合全表』66 に旧雑比喩経 24 の項に Cf. として PardT への言及。III 167 注 16 参照。
2004	中込重明『落語の種あかし』246-50 に PardT と『清誠談』との類話関係指摘。カンタベリー物語の江戸時代での日本への渡来ないし原話の共通性の可能性の示唆。III 68 注 17。
2013	西村他『壺の中の女』162-3 に旧雑比喩経 24 について PardT へ言及。III 68 注 16 参照。
2014 以前	神山重彦 ネットの「二者同想」『物語要素事典』167 注 12。

上記表中、III とあるのは多ヶ谷有子編『チョーサー・アーサー・中世浪漫 III』中の参照個所を示すものである。

以上から、中国、朝鮮半島、日本には PardT の類話がかなり見られることがわかる。

IV-1.　免償符／免罪符とは？

PardT で Pardoner が売っているのが「免償符 and/or 免罪符」である。これはラテン語で "indulgentia" つまり "indulgence" である。贖宥状、赦免状、免罪符、免償符などと訳される。カトリック大事典を見る。『カトリック大辞(事)典』は新旧二種類ある。両者の違いをざっと言えば、旧版(大事典)は、第二バチカン公会議 (1965) 以前のものである。Indulgence は「贖宥状」とある。新版(大辞典)は、第二バチカン公会議を踏まえ、Indulgence は「免償符、免罪符」両語を取り、新しい視点で解説されているが、項目の歴史的変化も解説されている。

旧版の「贖宥」によると、「贖宥」とは、罪の許しがあって初めて有効になること、贖宥を買うということはあってはならない、という点を強調している。新版は、「免罪符」という用語を採用し、正確には「免償符」と訳されるべきであるとある。別項に「免償」をあげ、「すでに神のゆるしを受けた罪に対してなおあたえられている有限の苦しみ(罰)が免除させること」と説明する。旧版には「贖宥が屡々罪の赦しと称せられていることは、古来転喩方で罪の罰は屡々罪と称せられてゐた。それを度外視しても、罪はその罰の点に於いても赦されるのであるから、之を罪の赦しとも当然呼び得る。」とある（「免償」『大事典』II 贖宥 730 右）。つまり、罪と罰は別ということである。準えれば、日本の刑法 41 条は、14 歳未満を罰しないと規定している。罪がなくなるのではなく、責任能力がないから罰を与えない、と理解されている。新版では、罪が免ぜられることが前提で、その上で赦免がなされるかどうかということを論じている。

IV-2.　免償符／免罪符についての研究者の紹介

免償符について、二、三文献をあたる。まず、Alastair Minnis の "Purchasing Pardon: Material and Spiritual Economies on the Canterbury Pilgrimage"(2006: 63-82)によれば、"purchasing of pardon（赦免の購入）12" というイディオムは中世英語で確立していたとして、*Prick of Conscience*:

3918-20, *Morte Arthure*: 3497, *Piers Plowman* B: VII 1-4 を例示している。論文では、"purchase" の意味は「得る："acquire, obtain"」というより「"money" などで買う、"buy"」と理解すると何が見えてくるかということについて考察している。(Minnis74)。

R. N. Swanson は、*Indulgences in late medieval England: passports to paradise?* によれば、免償について次のように述べている。すなわち、1300 年ボニフェイス VIII は、ローマでの聖年、ジュビリー（Jubilee: 25 年なり 50 年の節目の記念祭）への参加による一定の免償の布告をした（Swanson 2007: 53）。イングランド人は参加への欲求はあるが実行は困難であった。教皇は、ローマと同等のイングランドの教会への巡礼と、ローマへの旅行よりは安い幾何かの金額の喜捨による免償を認めた（Swanson 53）。免償は、十字軍への従軍、巡礼、聖年の記念祭（Jubilee）への参加などによって得られることになっていた。イングランドにおけるカンタベリーへの巡礼の意識には、免償という意識もあった。1455 年、ニコラス V は、1450 年のジュビリーによる赦免を、当初の記念日にこの恩恵を受けられなかったイングランド、ウェールズ、アイルランドの人々に対して復活させた。(Swanson 54)。教皇の権威をもってイギリス教会に輸入された一級品の、印章付きの、最も普通の免罪符 / 免償符）は Portiuncula（アシジに近い場所）と *Scalaseli* に見られた（Swanson 54）。[4]

　以上のことから、実際には、後世ルターの宗教改革における告発状からも理解できるように、告解、罪の赦し、罰による罪の償い（贖宥によってそれを免じる）という手順が簡略化され、免償符を買うことで、罪の償いのみならず罪そのものが赦されるという理解になり、それが一般的傾向となっていったということは簡単に推察される。

　さらにチョーサーの免償符売りについて、Maxfield は当時の社会的状況をあげている。Maxfield によれば、チョーサーの免償符売りは Rouncivale お墨付き（"brand"）の免償符を携えている。Rouncival とはウェストミンスターとロンドンの間にあるチャーリングクロス村の Hospital of St. Mary Rouncivale（聖マリア・ロンシヴァル病院）のことで、一般に、彼はその代理人のようなものであったろうと説明している。Maxfield の論文は、その

免償符が偽物か本物か？チョーサーの時代にロンシヴァルに悪い評判があったかどうか？チョーサーはロンドンで免償符売り支援をする他の重要な病院もよく知っていたはずだが、彼がロンシヴァルを物語の免償符売りのパトロンにしたのは何故か？などを問題にしている（1993: 148）。

　Maxfield によれば、当時の病院の主たる仕事は、メディカルな治療 "heal" というより魂の癒し "cure" とよい死の準備をすることであった。中世を通して、イングランドとウェールズには約 1100 の病院があり、そのうちロンドンには少なくとも 34 はあったようだ。病院はそれぞれの "quaestorii or quaestores" と呼ばれる者を遠く広く派遣していた。"quaestorii or quaestores" とはラテン語で、それに対応する英語 "quaestor" とは下級の役人の一種で、財務的な仕事をしていたと思われる。彼らは通常、"pardon" と呼ばれる免償符許可証 "certificates of indulgence" を携えていた。そのため彼らは通常 "pardoners（免償符売り）" と呼ばれていた。Maxfield によれば、免償符売りは何世紀にもわたって一般的には尊敬されていたようだが、同時に神学的批判もあったようである。その後、様々な背景や事情があり、免償符売りの堕落が始まったと説明している（148-50）。

　中世後期のイングランドの人口は、現代の基準からは驚くほど少なく、多くとも 3-4 百万を超えないという。"priest" と呼ばれる教区司祭は 26,500 人、つまり全人口の約 1-2% と見積もられている。他に、"monks（修道士）" や "friar（托鉢修道士）" がおり、その数はおそらく 6,500 人を数え、さらに各教区司祭聖職者には数人の "clerk（書記）" がいたと考えられている。ここで Maxfield が言いたいのは、聖職者や半ば聖職者の数が多く、かつ、あるいはゆえに、成功して裕福になっているのは少ないということで、つまり、こうしたことが堕落の背景にあったということである（150）。

　チョーサーの時代はまだ印刷機が発明されていなかったが、免償符がグーテンベルク以降急激に普及した背景には印刷機の発明があり、その結果、多量の面償符の印刷が可能になり、ついには宗教改革を招く一端となったのである。

　早稲田大学の館蔵インキュブラ「ヨーロッパ 15 世紀活版印刷本 Part. 3」によれば、1481 年の免償符を見ると当時の様子が推察される。[5] 解説によ

れば、オスマン・トルコによるロドス島攻撃に対しルドルフ・フォン・ヴェルデンベルク伯爵が教皇の代理人となり、アウクスブルクの有力な印刷業者ヨハン・ベームラーが印刷発行し、ヨハンネス・デ・カルドーナによって頒布されたものである。これは 1481 年に 2 回印刷されている。通例、贖宥状の販売の際には購入者の名前と日付が手書きで記されるが、これはその箇所が空欄となっている。印刷が可能となり、大量生産ができるようになり、こうした免償符が大量に売られ、その結果、本来の免償の意味が希薄となり、さらに宗教的意味は空洞化して忘れられ、免償を買いさえすればすべての罪は赦されるという理解に至ったのである。そのうえ免償を購入すればいかなる悪業も可能になるという理解を生むことになり、こうして聖職界の堕落は加速する結果を招くに至ったことは想像に難くない。

IV-3. 15 世紀の魂の救済に[6]

　森田安一「宗教改革前夜の死のイメージ―スイスを中心にして」には、ホルバインの絵をもとにした木版画が掲載されている。森田氏も言っているように、この絵の右側は教会の内部である。そこにはメディチ家の紋章が掲げられており、メディチ家出身の教皇がおり、悔悛の秘跡が行われている。司祭は告解者に罪の許しを与える一方で、金を出せという合図をしている。そのそばでは堂々と免償符が売られている。絵の左側は教会の外である。ここではダヴィデが悔悛の情を示し、神は彼の悔悛を受け入れている。神に直接祈りを捧げて赦しを乞うダヴィデを神は赦している。右と左の絵の対比に教会の腐敗とあるべき姿が見えてくる。

　実際には、後世ルターの宗教改革、ホルバインの絵からも理解できるように、告解、罪の許し、罰による罪の償い（贖宥によってそれを免じる）、というルートであるべき手順が簡略化され、免罪符を買うことで罪の償いのみならず罪そのものが赦されるという手順になり、それが一般的傾向となっていった。教会の正式見解と現実がどうであったかは明らかである。教会の見解としては免償符というべきであろうが、現実は免罪符であった。

V.　免償／免罪と魂の救済のための巡礼

V-1.　PardT と日本の類話の宗教性

　以上を考察するにあたり、巡礼、免償符売り、免償という三つのキーワードに留意したい。日本の類話と PardT を対照させると、日本の類話は宗教性という側面が希薄である印象を与える。日本の類話が伝わった大本の旧雑比喩経の書き方をみれば、旧雑譬喩経 24 は短いが、互いに悪意をもったために殺しあった、という教訓が見て取れる。旧雑譬喩経 22 の「市に禍を買うたとえ」の場合も、平和な暮らしに飽いてわざわざ禍を招くのは愚かである、という教訓も明白である。経典全体を読めば、仏教説話に共通する倫理的指針があることは確実である。悪意をもってはいけない、そうすれば自分もまた滅びる、ということである。この話が中国に入ると、現実的な立場から欲をかいてはいけないという色合いはあるが、信仰的意味合いは大幅に薄れてくる。日本には旧雑譬喩経も入ってきてはいるが、日本の類話は旧雑譬喩経ではなく漢籍、中国の類話を元にしている。そのために信仰的意味が薄れているとも推察できる。日本人の気質とも関わりがあるかもしれない。中国経由であるために現実的な話になったのか、時代が下がってより合理的な考え方に立つようになったのか、という考え方もありうる。

　それに対して、チョーサーの Pardoner の話には多少なりとも宗教的な含みがある。貪欲の罪が扱われ、それを貪欲な Pardoner が語ることの皮肉がこの作品のミソである。基本的にキリスト教世界であった中世という時代

的背景は大きい要素である。しかし、当時の日本も、基本的には神仏混合的宗教的背景がなかったわけではない。この延長線上には国民性などという要素もありうるが、本論ではそこまでは踏み込まず、カンタベリーへの巡礼と日本のお伊勢参りを並行させ、物語の語る巡礼の性格ということを考えてみたい。

V-2. カンタベリー巡礼とお伊勢参り

　この点については、すでに、2014年の「カンタベリー巡礼とお伊勢参り」『チョーサーと中世を眺めて』で、チョーサーのカンタベリーへの巡礼と日本のお伊勢参りの比較的考察を発表しており、一部と重複する点がある。

　西洋の巡礼も日本のお伊勢参りも、本来は信心から出発したものである。確かに、カンタベリー物語にしろ、お伊勢参りを物語る『東海道中膝栗毛』にしろ、信心から巡礼という要素は強いとは思えない。

　パゾリーニの映画『カンタベリー物語』の第7話に「赦罪状売りの話」がある。この映画は、粉屋の話や貿易商人の話など、ほとんどが艶笑譚ファブリオであるが、PardTは、特に筋立ての面白さとか不条理性の面などから選ばれているのであろう。[7]この映画を見れば、どんな意図があるにしろ、監督は意図的に『カンタベリー物語』から信仰的要素を排除し、一つの側面を見せたかったことがわかる。

　物語そのものに戻る。物語はともに、一見、その内容は娯楽であり、信仰の問題を考えなくとも充分楽しく読める。この世を織り成す人々の滑稽さ、愚かさ、恥ずかしさを皮肉や風刺をこめて描き出し、軽妙に笑いとばしている。しかし、これらの作品のなかで、元来巡礼に基本的要素である信心・信仰的な側面は完全に払拭されているとはいえない。

　『カンタベリー物語』の巡礼者は、よく言われることではあるが、中世社会の縮図を象徴している。これらの人々は誰を取ってみても、人間としての欠点や弱さを持ち、'General Prologue' やそれぞれの 'Tale' に、それぞれの職業や身分、地位に伴う小狡さ、誤魔化し、気取りや慾、俗物根性が見え隠れする。チョーサーは彼らのそうした人間的欠陥を鋭く見抜き、批

判の的に曝す。一方、弥次・喜多の場合、貧に窮して旅に出るというわけ
で、動機そのものからして信仰からは離れている。では、二つのこの作品
は、巡礼といいながら信仰的側面との接点はないのであろうか。

VI.　結び：『カンタベリー物語』と『東海道中膝栗毛』におけ る信仰する心

　『東海道中膝栗毛』の場合、主要な登場人物は弥次・喜多の二人で、彼
らが道々出会う人々との掛け合いや事件が、その時代そしてその土地の風
俗や人々の気質を伝える。二人が出会うのは彼らと同じ庶民である。その
同じ庶民が、人間の持つ小狡さ、厚かましさ、誤魔化し、小賢しさを本能
のままに露にし、それが滑稽に描き出されている。弥次・喜多の旅の途上、
起こる事柄は異なるが、いずれも弥次・喜多の浅知恵、ささやかな慾、怠
け心、貧すれば鈍した厚かましさや卑屈さが相俟って、事の決着のつき方
は多様である。根っからの悪人も飛び切りの善人もいない。登場人物はす
べて向う三軒両隣にちらちらする凡人である。弥次・喜多が接する世界の
狭さがそのまま物語に反映されている。そのことによって、狭い階層なが
ら人間社会がいかに多様で重層的かつ複合的であるかを見事に描き出して
いる。
　肝要なのは、庶民の中にあって特に優れているわけでもなく、また特に
劣っているわけでもなく、その心栄えについて云々するにも及ばないごく
並みの並である弥次・喜多が、伊勢神宮にいたれば、それまでの悪ふざけ
すれすれの振る舞いに終始していた二人が、それなりに襟を正し、宮廻り
をし、殊勝にお参りをすることである。弥次・喜多の旅のほとんどが滑稽
で埒もないものであっても、旅の終りがお参りであることが、この物語が
巡礼話であることの意味がある。この世に生きる人々がその日その日の生
業の中で、己の身の丈で己の持つ才覚の範囲で生きていくとき、人はどう
あるかということを、弥次・喜多道中は滑稽の薄幕を通して鮮やかに描き
出している。日常生活は人様々な生き方をするが、いかに手垢がつき、染
みだらけの日常であろうと、寺社を前にしたときには襟を正し、殊勝な心

で神仏の前に手を合わせる、いかなる出鱈目をしていても、ここという場では正道を心の軸に合わせる、これがこの世に生きる人の区別（けじめ）というものである。この区別（けじめ）があるか否かが、人として生きる世の中が成るか成らぬかの分かれ目なのである。巡礼をテーマにする作品ならば、この一点が作品の中になければならない。この一点は『カンタベリー物語』ではどのように描かれているであろうか。

　チョーサーの描く巡礼者はいずれも人間的欠陥を免れていない。一見理想的に見える教区司祭もまた人間的欠陥から免れることのない、チョーサーの作り上げた登場人物の一人である。しかしそのことは、教区司祭の人格を貶めるものではない。中世社会の縮図を描くチョーサーが一人教区司祭だけを理想的な人物に描くことこそ不自然である。チョーサーの描く巡礼者はいずれも、弱さも脆さも、狡さも怠惰も備えた、閑として不善なす不完全な人間たちである。それゆえにこそ、彼の描く巡礼の一行が社会の縮図であることの意味は大きい。この世はそうした有象無象の人々が、日常の手垢に塗れ、不徳の致す所業の積み重ねでなりゆく場所なのである。その中で、人々は、角突き合わせつつ、諍いしつつ、小競り合いしつつ、はたまた、団栗の背比べの無駄な競争をしつつ、押しあい圧し合いして暮らす。しかし、そうした人々の寄せ集めでありながら、巡礼地を目指す一点だけは変わらない。教区司祭の話にじっと耳を傾けるという設定が、そのことを物語っている。弥次・喜多がお伊勢では襟を正して手を合わせたように、チョーサーの巡礼者も教区司祭の話にはじっと耳を傾ける。聖地巡礼への道中は俗世界の塵芥や溝水に塗れたものでありながら、それでも聖地に向かう心根は失われていない。『カンタベリー物語』の巡礼の意味はその辺にある。

　Minnis によれば、Jubilee 聖年は 1370 年、1420 年にあった。1370 年はカンタベリーで高い成功を得た年で、カンタベリーでは 1291 年、1328 年、1395 年でも成功であったという。これらカンタベリーの成功例のことは、チョーサーの念頭にあった可能性があろう（Minnis73 参照）。

　ウィクリフ派なりロラード派の極端な主張は、カンタベリーの赦免を拒絶し、否定している。しかし『カンタベリー物語』に否定的な見解は記さ

れていない。チョーサー自身が巡礼に参加することになっているのであるから。物語にはカンタベリーの権威や、カンタベリー巡礼による赦免、免償を否定する意図は見られない（Minnis74 参照）。

　チョーサーの場合、その区別（けじめ）は 'General Prologue'（以下 GP）冒頭部に示されている。GP 冒頭部の描写は、冬枯れた大地に新芽を誘う春の雨が注がれる情景である。大地に注がれた水は乾ききった地面に浸み込んでいき、その水が草木の根元に届く。するとその水が地下の根の先端から上に吸い上げられ、幹から大枝に、大枝から小枝に、新芽の出るべき先端にまで届く。これが若芽の出るべきいずこかを刺激し、浅緑の芽を吹き出させる。自然界における命の甦りを象徴する情景である。T. S. エリオットの描く "The Wasteland"（『荒地』）の元を辿れば聖杯伝説に描かれる荒地であるが、それが象徴するのは当時の精神的枯渇である。一方、チョーサーのそれは、魂の枯渇の比喩である。詩編が「涸れた谷に鹿が水を求めるように」（詩篇42、典礼聖歌版）とうたう言葉は、餓えた魂が「水」を求める情景である。「水」は魂にとっての命の水であり、神の恩寵である。聖書に譬えを求めるならば、モーゼ率いるイスラエルの人々に神が天から与えたマンナということになる。

　自然界の水に重ねて、人間の魂に命の水が描かれる。それを与えるものは神以外にない。水を与えられた自然界が芽吹き、花開き、実るように、命の水を与えられた人間は巡礼の旅に出かける。春の芽吹きが巡礼のときであるのは、桝井 1962; 1973（253）も触れているが、笹本（477）が示唆するように、復活の時期ということには意味があるかもしれない。自然界の命が甦る様に、巡礼の恩寵で魂の命が甦るときだからである。人は弥次・喜多同様、日々この世の塵芥に塗れながら生きている。その結果、魂は渇き、涸れた谷川で鹿が水を求めるように、時に、魂の命の水を求める。それに応えて神が恩寵を与え、魂を巡礼に向かわせる。春の訪れの描写は文学的コンヴェンションではあるが、比喩としても見事に美しい。しかし、そればかりでなくその本質的意味を見逃してはいけない。その意味で、チョーサーの『カンタベリー物語』GP 冒頭部は、チョーサーが物語を描く指針表明といえよう。

　作品の冒頭でこれほど確かな所信表明をしていながら、最後の説教に至るまで、巡礼者たちは弥次・喜多のように、俗に塗れて過ごす。最初と最後に区別（けじめ）を示し、その枠組みの中で人間世界の現実を描くチョーサーの洞察は、Pardoner の持つ人間の内面、心の奥深くにある本質的な毒を描きだす。

　これまで見てきたように、免償符／免罪符は印刷機の発明とともに、一気に、見逃すことのできない状態に進み、宗教改革の一原因になっていく。チョーサーの時代は、ウィクリフが世を去った時、問題なく埋葬が行われたことからも推察できるように、まだ、宗教改革を起こすほどの大きな問題にはなっていなかった時代と思われる。しかしチョーサーは、免罪符の実態の底に潜む悪の本質を洞察して Pardoner を描いた。それは、言ってみれば、PardT の話は、宗教改革前夜の象徴的予言的物語であったといえるのではなかろうか。

Notes

1. 「チョーサー『カンタベリー物語』の「免償符売りの話、以下 PardT」―日本の類話とその検討―」（多ヶ谷有子編著『チョーサー・アーサー・中世浪漫 III』ほんのしろ、127-75））その後、更にその改訂版を 2018 年 6 月中央大学における「アーサー王伝説研究」主催の講演会で発表した。
2. 春秋社の『ジャータカ全集』第一巻第 48 話にも翻訳があるが、その注・補注には対応する日本の類話への言及はない。補注には PardT の原拠である旨の記述がある。
3. 中央大学の渡邉浩司先生からハンス＝イェルク・ウター第二版と池田弘子氏について貴重なコメントをいただいたが、先の論文には紙面の関係で入れなかった。
4. 'Scalaseli' については現在調査中。
5. https://www.wul.waseda.ac.jp/TENJI/virtual/incunabla/incu03.html（2020/04/04）
6. 本論では森田氏の著書からではなく、Web 画像を掲載した。https://uplos.wiokimedia.org/wikipedia/commons/4/4a/The_Sele_of_Indulgenses%2C_by_Holbein_the_Younger.jpg（2020/04/04）
7. https://movie.walkerplus.com/mv12293/（2020/04/04）

多ヶ谷　有　子

Bibliography

アーウィン，ロバート 1998『必携アラビアンナイト―物語の迷宮』西尾哲夫訳．東京：平凡社.

秋月観暎 1987『道教と宗教文化』東京：平川出版社.

浅井了意『浮世物語』前田金五郎・森田武校注 1965；1983『仮名草子集』日本古典文学大系 90．東京：岩波書店．241-354.

浅井了意『浮世物語』谷脇理史・岡雅彦・井上和人校注訳 1999『仮名草子集』新編日本古典文学全集 64（東京：小学館）85-224.

池上惠子 1990『中世イギリス聖者伝『バルラームとヨサファトの物語』写本校訂と比較研究』東京：学書房.

伊藤千賀子 2014「『六度集経』と他経典とのかかわり―康僧会の経典作成の思考方法―」『印度學佛教學研究』第 62 巻第 2 号．平成 26 年 3 月．36-41.

上田敏 1929「菩薩由来物語」『上田敏全集』東京：改造社．176-87.

エーベルハルト，ヴォルフラム『中国昔話集2』馬場英子・瀬田充子・千野明日香編訳 2007『中国昔話集2』全 2 冊．東洋文庫 762．東京：平凡社.

王同軌『新刻耳談』万暦 30（1602）国立公文書館所蔵．全 3 冊．請求番号：309-0127．林羅山旧蔵．幕府紅葉山文庫旧蔵.

大江文坡『清誠談』安永七 [1778] 戊戌年正月吉日 京都書林（DVD 復刻シリーズ『国立国会図書館所蔵読本集 保存版 第 7-9 巻』2009．東京：フジミ書房．所収の第 7 巻.

王同軌『耳談』澤田瑞穂 1983『金牛の鎖―中国財宝譚』平凡社選書 83．東京：平凡社.

小野玄妙編纂 1933；1964 改訂；1977『仏書解説大辞典 第二巻』東京：大東出版.

大場正史訳 1966『バートン版 千夜一夜物語 2』東京：河出書房新社.

加藤耕義 2014「ハンス＝イェルク・ウター著『世界昔話話型カタログ』と池田弘子著『日本の昔花史話型カタログ』比較の試み」学習院大学外国語教育研究センター『言語・文化・社会』No. 12. 2014 年 3 月 31 日.

『カトリック大辞典』II.1942「贖宥」の項．東京：冨山房.

『新カトリック大事典』IV．2009「免罪符」、「免償」の項．2009 東京：研究社.

鎌田茂雄編 1981『中国仏教史辞典』東京：東京堂.

神山重彦『物語要素事典』（ネット、2015 年版、2014 年 12 月 25 日付け）の「二者同想」の項.

顏茂猷 崇禎四年（1631）（明末）序『廸吉録』

キップリング，ジョゼフ．ラドヤード 1975；1995「王様の象突き棒」『ジャングルブック』木島始訳．東京：福音館．303-350.

『合類大因縁集』国文学研究資料館 矢口丹波記念文庫、国文学研究資料館公開画像。http://base1.nijl.ac.jp/iview/Frame.jsp?（2020/04/04）
DB_ID=G0003917KTM&C_CODE=XYA8-02105&IMG_SIZE=&IMG_NO=34.（2017/10/09）

小泉弘・山田昭全・小島孝之・木下資本一校注 1993『宝物集』（平康頼 12C 後半）『宝物集』『宝物集 閑居友 比良山古人霊詫』新日本古典文学大系 40. 岩波書店. 1-353.

酒井忠夫 1999『酒井忠夫著作集 I』増補 中国善書の研究 上. 東京：国書刊行会.

笹本長敬訳 2002『カンタベリー物語』英宝社

康僧会訳 1924『旧雑譬喩経』高楠順次郎編集発行『大正新脩大蔵経』第四巻 本縁部下. 東京：大正一切経刊行会. 510-522. 旧雑譬喩経など大正新脩大蔵経所収の経典はネットの『大正新脩大蔵経テキストデータベース』で検索して見ることができる。

繁尾久訳注解 1985「免償説教家のプロローグ・話」『カンタベリ物語』フラグメント 6・グループ C329-966.『明治学院論叢』Dec. 1985. 通号 384『英語英文学』64. 1-24.

神保五彌・長谷川強校注・訳 1971；1990『仮名草子集浮世草子集』日本古典文学全集 37, 小学館.

孫晋泰・増尾伸一郎解説 2009『朝鮮民譚集』東京：勉誠出版.

高楠順次郎監修 1935『南傳大蔵経 第二十八巻』小部経典六. 東京：大蔵出版. 495-502.

多ヶ谷有子 2014「カンターベリー巡礼とお伊勢参り―『カンタベリー物語』と『東海道中膝栗毛』―」狩野晃一編『チョーサーと中世を眺めて―チョーサー研究会 20 周年記念論文集―』麻生出版. 169-84.

多ヶ谷有子 2018『チョーサー・アーサー・中世浪漫 III』越谷：ほんのしろ.

田中於菟彌・坂田貞二訳 1983『インドの笑話』東京：春秋社.

譚正璧主編・民国 50（1961）『中國文藝家大辭典』香港：香港上海印書.

張知甫『張氏可書』国立公文書館所蔵. 乾降四庫全書無板本. 請求番号：96-1. 昌平坂学問所写本.

張知甫『張氏可書』国立公文書館所蔵. 函海. 請求番号：371-42. 昌平坂学問所写本.

張知甫『張氏可書』国立公文書館所蔵. 函海. 請求番号：子 276-1, 308-193 昌平坂学問所写本.

道世撰 1928『法苑樹林』高楠順次郎編『大正新脩大蔵経』第 53 巻. 事彙部・外教部 上・目録部上. 東京：大正一切経刊行会. 269-1030.

中込重明 2004『落語の種あかし』東京：岩波書店.

西村正身・羅黨興訳 2013『壷の中の女―呉天竺三蔵康僧会旧雑譬喩経全訳』東京：渓水社.

『日本古典文学大辞典 第 1 巻』1983『日本古典文学大辞典 第 1 巻』編集委員会. 東 岩波書店.

パゾリーニの映画『カンタベリー物語』第 7 話.
https://movie.walkerplus.com/mv12293/（2020/04/04）

馬場英子・瀬田充子・千野明日香 2007『中国昔話集』第二巻（全二巻）東洋文庫 762. 東京：平凡社.

多ヶ谷 有 子

ハンス＝イェルク・ウター2016『国際昔話話型カタログ 分類と文献目録』加藤耕義訳，小澤俊夫監修．川崎：小澤昔ばなし研究所．

干潟龍祥 1954『本生経類照合全表』『本生経類の思想的研究』の別冊附編．東京：東洋文庫．

藤田宏達訳 1984「ヴェーダッパ前生物語」ジャータカ 48．中村元監修・補注『ジャータカ全集 1』東京：春秋社．292-96.

前田金五郎・森田武校注 1965；1988『仮名草子集』日本古典文学大系 90．東京：岩波書店．

桝井迪夫 1955「Chaucer 研究」『Anglica』Vol. 2, No. 3, Oct. 1955. 吹田：関西大学英語学会．69-108.

桝井迪夫 1962；1973（増補版）『チョーサー研究』東京：研究社．

目加田さくを 2010『世界小説史論』上下，福岡：木星舎．

森田安一 1999「宗教改革前夜の死のイメージ―スイスを中心にして―」『「生と死」の図像学』明治大学公開文化講座 XVIII．東京：明治大学人文科学研究所．1-54.

龍樹 1924『大智度論』高楠順次郎編『大正新脩大蔵経』第 25 巻．釈経論部 上．東京：大正一切経刊行会．57-522.

柳田國雄編 1943；1975 山口麻太郎『壱岐島昔話集』100.

『模範最新世界年表』（四訂新装版）三省堂編輯所．1911 初版；1938 四訂改版；1042 四訂新版．東京：三省堂．

Benson, Larry E. ed. 1987; 1991 *Riverside Chaucer.* Third Edition. Oxford: Oxford U. P.

Chavannes, Édouard 1962 *Cinq cents contes et apologues* extraits du Tripiṭaka chinois. Tome 1.

Clouston, W. A. 1886 "The Robbers and the Treasure-Trove: Buddhist Original and Asiatic and European Versions of the Pardoner's Tale," F. J. Furnivall, E. Brock, W. A. Clouston, eds., 1872-87 *Originals and Analogues of Some of Chaucer's Canterbury Tales.* London: Chaucer Society. 417-33.

Hamel, Mary & Charles Merrill 1911 "The Analogue of the Pardoner's Tale and a New African Version." *The Chaucer Review.* Vol. 26, No. 2, 1991. The Pennsylvania State University, University Park, PA. 176-83.

Hans Jörg Uther 2011 *The Types of International Folktales. A Classification and Bibliography. Based on the System of Antti Aarne and Stith Thompson. Animal Tales of Magic, Religious Tales, and Realistic Tales.* Turku: Academia Scientarium Fennica.

Ikeda, Hiroko 1971 *A Type and Motif Index of Japanese Folk-literature.* (FFC No. 209. Helsinki). Suomalainen Tiedeakatemia.

Ikeda, Hiroko 1984 *A Type and Motif Index of Japanese Folk-literature.* University Microfilm International. Mich: Ann Arbor. (Thesis (Ph.D.) Indiana University, 1956)

Ikegami, Keiko 1999 *Barlaam and Josaphat: A Transcription of MS Egerton 876 with Notes, Glossary, and Comparative Study of the Middle English and Japanese Versions.* New York:

AMS Press.

Jelien, de M. Stanislas. tr. 1860 *Contes et apologues indiens inconnus jusqu'à ce jour, suivis de fables et de poesies chinoise.* Tome 2. Paris: L. Hachette.

Jacobs, Joseph 1896 *Barlaam and Josaphat: English Lives of Buddha.* London: David Nutt.

Maxfield, David K. 1993 "St. Mary Rouncivale, Charing Cross: The Hospital of Chaucer's Pardoner." *The Chaucer Review.* Vol. 28, No. 2. 1993. The Pennsylvania State University. University Park. PA. 148-163.

Minnis, Alastair 2006 "Purchasing Pardon: Material and Spiritual Economies on the Canterbury Pilgrimage" *Sacred and Secular in Medieval and Early Modern Cultures.* Edited by Lawrence Besserman. New York: Palgrave Mcmillan. 63-82.

Skeat, Walter William 1894; 1900; 1972 *The Complete Works of Geoffrey Chaucer.* III. London: Oxford U. P.

Swanson, R. N. 2007 *Indulgence in Late Medieval England: Passports to Paradise?* Cambridge: Cambridge University Press.

Thompson, Stith 1934 *Motif-Index of Folk-literature.* Vol. 4. Indiana: Bloomington, IND.

画像「三人の破落戸と死神」
http://www.canterbury-tales.net/pardoners-tale/index.html（2017/10/13）

画像「ぬす人の事」『浮世物語』東京大学霞亭文庫所蔵
http://kateibunko.dl.itc.u-tokyo.ac.jp/katei/cgi-bin/gazo.cgi?no=109&top=49.（2017/10/13）

画像『1481 年贖宥状』（アウクスグルク、1481）
Werdenburg, Rudolfus, Graf fon, commissary, Indulgentia 1481. [Augsburg: Johann Baemler, 1481], Broadside. 1 lcaf. 135 × 224mm. Ref.: 595; GW, Einblattdrucke 1506; ISTC iw0011720. https://www.wul.waseda.ac.jp/TENJI/virtual/incunabla/incu03.html（2020/04/04）

チョーサーとオウィディウス
——Chaucer: 'The Legend of Thisbe' の典拠利用から

笹　本　長　敬

　Chaucer の *The Legend of Good Women*『善女列伝』は、キリスト教の信仰のためではなく、愛のために殉死し、その結果 "God of Love" のもとで、列聖になるのに打ってつけの 19 人の女性たちの物語を書く計画であった。『善女列伝』には、非常に楽しい 'Prologue'（F 版と G 版の二つの形で存在する）が付けられていて、当時の確かな史実を盛り込みながら、あまり技巧に走らない語り口と、哀感を効果的に利用した一連の善女（内容から言えば貞女）たちの物語詩を構成する作品になっている。

　チョーサーは、男に裏切られて捨てられる女性たち一人一人の身の上について語りながら、人の興味をそそるように物語をまとめ、楽しくこの物語を語り続けようとした。いや語り続けようとしたにちがいない。ところが、やがてチョーサー自身が書き続けることに興味をなくしたことをうかがわせることを言う（2454-55 行）。どの物語も駄作になってしまったとは考えにくいが、当初 19 名の女性を取り上げる計画が、結局 10 人の善女たちしか語られなくなった。最後となった第 9 話の 'The Legend of Hypermnestra' にいたっては未完に終わってしまっている。「プロローグ」F 版でそれとなく言っている（F496-7 行）ように、チョーサーは制作依頼されてこの作品を書いたもののようだが、物語が単調な繰り返しになったことは否めない。次第に制作熱は冷めていって、話の種は尽きてしまったのだろう。

　それはそれとして、チョーサーは『善女列伝』を創作するにあたって、典拠として利用したのは主に Ovid の作品である。すなわち、オウィディウスを利用していない第 1 話の 'The Legend of Cleopatra' は別として、これから考察する第 2 話の 'The Legend of Thisbe' は、大いにオウィディウスの影響をうけ、*Metamorphoses*『変身物語』巻 4. 55-166 行を利用してい

る。第3話の‘The Legend of Dido’では、1312-16行と最後の16行（1352-67行）においてオウィディウスの *Heroides*『名婦の書簡』第7書1-8行を付随的に使用している。特にディドの性格づけと動機づけはオウィディウスの影響をうけていると思われる。第4話の‘The Legend of Hypsipyle and Medea’はそのうちの「ヒュプシピュレ伝」ではオウィディウス『変身物語』巻7そして『名婦の書簡』第6書（第12書も？）を、「メデイア伝」ではオウィディウス『変身物語』巻7. 1-397行と『名婦の書簡』第12書を利用している。第5話の‘The Legend of Lucrece’は、オウィディウスの *Fasti*『祭暦』第2巻685-852行にほとんど忠実に従って書いている。ここではオウィディウスと共に、チョーサーは Livy の名を典拠として挙げているが、彼の作品を利用していない。リウィウスは古代ローマの歴史を書いた高名な大家ということで、ただ権威付けをするだけのためにリウィウスの名を使ったのかもしれない。第6話の‘The Legend of Ariadne’では、初めの部分はオウィディウス『変身物語』巻7. 456-58行と巻8. 6-176行から材を取っており、結論の部分はオウィディウス『名婦の書簡』第10書に基づいている。さらに2222-24行は『変身物語』巻8. 176-82行の部分から取っている。第7話の‘The Legend of Philomela’の主な典拠はオウィディウスの『変身物語』巻6. 424-605行である。第8話の‘The Legend of Phyllis’の主な原拠はオウィディウスの『名婦の書簡』第2書である。第9話の‘The Legend of Hypermnestra’も主な典拠はオウィディウスの『名婦の書簡』第14書である。

　さて、第2話の「ティスベ伝」について考察してみよう。さきほども述べたように、これはオウィディウス『変身物語』を典拠として巻4. 55-166行の‘Pyramus et Thisbe’「ピラムスとティスベ」の物語を取り上げて作成されている。それだけでなく、大変忠実に従って作成されている。しかし、適宜に改変したり付加したり、また短縮したり省略したりしたところも散見される。そのため、それらをどのように行なったか、典拠の利用の仕方に興味が引かれるので、典拠と比較しながらそういうところをこれから見ていきたい。

「ティスベ伝」は大変均整のとれた物語となっている。それはチョー
サーが筋を忠実に従ったオウィディウスの作品がそうなっていることもそ
の一因である。

「ティスベ伝」は、まず町の場面と野原の場面の二つの部分に分かれる。
それぞれの部分はさらに分割されている。前者の場面は、煉瓦の壁に囲ま
れて堀を巡らした都市バビロン（ただし町の名はここでは問題にならな
い）と石の壁に隔てられた貴族の両家の説明があり、隔てられた石の壁の
両側で、結婚を許されない両家の若い恋人同士のティスベとピラムスが頻
繁にあいびきする。しかし不自由な二人は町から逃げ出す計画をする。後
者の場面は、二人が町から逃げ出すべく、ティスベが先に、夜に月明かり
を利用して独りぼっちで野原に出かける。逢引場所の泉の辺でピラムスを
待つ。その時ティスベは口を血だらけにしたライオンが泉の水を飲みに来
たのを見つけ、怖くなって近くの洞窟に急いで隠れる。隠れる時にベール
を落としてしまう。水を飲み終わったライオンはティスベが落としたベー
ルを見つけ、血だらけの口でそれをずたずたに引き裂く。ライオンが去っ
た後、遅れてやってきたピラムスは血の付いたそれを見つけ、ティスベは
ライオンに殺されたと早合点し、ピラムスは自分の剣で自殺を図る。頃合
いを見計らって隠れ場所から出てきたティスベは、瀕死のピラムスを発見
するが彼は絶命してしまう。彼女は嘆きの告白をして、それからピラムス
の後を追って彼の剣で自殺する。

長くなったが物語の粗筋はこういうことであった。しかしチョーサーは
むやみにオウィディウスの猿真似をして、独創性を欠くような物語にしな
かった。彼は少し省略したり、拡大表現をしたり、さらに創作部分を付け
加えたりして独自の作品にした。

まずチョーサーが加筆して彼流の考えを述べているところを示そう。

まず、ピラムスとティスベの二人の名が広まっていったのは、近所にい
た女性たちが広めたためであった。つまりうわさ話好きの女性たちの口伝
えによるものとしているのである。評判の伝播の原因を説明したのは
チョーサーの加筆によるのである。彼はこう書き加えている。

The name of everych gan to other sprynge
By women that were neighebores aboute.
For in that contre yit, withouten doute,
Maydenes been ykept, for jelosye,
Ful streyte, lest they diden som folye.
This yonge man was called Piramus,
Tysbe hight the maide, Naso seyth thus;[1]
And thus by report was hire name yshove
That, as they wex in age, wex here love.[2] （719-727）

（それぞれの名前は、近所にいた女性たちの／口から広まって、相手に伝わった。／何しろ、もちろんのことだが、その国ではまだ、／娘たちは、愚かなことをするといけないからという、／警戒心の故に、厳重に守られていたからだ。／この若者はピラムスと呼ばれ、／娘はティスベと呼ばれたと、ナーソはかく言っている。／それから二人の評判は噂によって大いに広まっていき、／歳を重ねるにつれて、二人に恋心が募っていった。[3]）

　二人が恋仲になっていったことは、オウィディウスでは二人の両親しか知らないことになっているが、チョーサーではすでに世間に知られていることにしている。

　チョーサーは加筆によって現実的にあり得る状況に変えたようである。彼は噂や評判が速やかに伝わるものとして、The House of Fame でテーマとして取り上げている[4]。噂や名声の伝播に興味を持っていたようである。

　会うことを妨げられていたピラムスとティスベは、狭い壁の割れ目から小さな声で愛の言葉を交わす。オウィディウスは "murmure blanditiae minimo transire solebant"[5]（Met. Bk IV 70）（your loving words used to pass in tiny whispers）と表現するが、チョーサーはオウィディウスの「とても小さいささやき声」の代わりに、"And with a soun as softe as any shryfte / They lete here wordes thourgh the clifte pace,"（745-46）「告解の声に劣らぬ密やかな声で／彼らは割れ目から言葉を交わした」といって直喩を使って、教会の告解の密やかな声に譬える。愛の神聖さと二人の無垢を暗示する。そして時代錯誤的であるが、中世的雰囲気に変えて伝えている。

　もう一つは、オウィディウスもチョーサーも直喩表現を使ってピラムスの自刃場面を印象づけている。両者共使っている直喩はうまいが、チョーサーは直喩の表現を変えて簡潔に強く表現する。

　ティスベがライオンに殺されたと勘違いして、ピラムスは自分の剣を引き抜いてわき腹を突き刺す。そして死を早めようと、すぐに傷口から剣を引き抜く。オウィディウスではその時血潮の吹き出す様を、鉛管の痛んだ穴から水が高く吹き出す表現に譬える。

> non aliter quam cum vitiato fistula plumbo
> scinditur et tenui stridente foramine longas
> eiaculatur aquas atque ictibus aera rumpit.　　（Bk IV. 122-24）

（Just as when a pipe has broken at a weak spot in the lead and through the small hissing aperture sends spurting forth long streams of water, cleaving the air with its jets.）

　一方、チョーサーはピラムスが傷口から剣を引き抜く描写を省き、出る血を壊れた樋から水がほとばしり出る様子に譬えて、1行の直喩に変えて短く巧みに表現する。

> The blod out of the wounde as brode sterte
> As water whan the condit broken is.　　（851-52）

（血は傷口から、まるで樋が壊れた時の／水のように、どっとほとばしり出た。）

　話は戻るが、ティスベは家を捨てて夜に自分の家からひそかに抜け出して、ピラムスとの逢瀬を楽しみに行くという大胆な行動をとる。この無垢な娘ティスベの行動について、当時の乙女には禁じられていることだが、男であって人生経験を積んでいるチョーサーは、分別のある大人の目で見て、ティスベに皮肉っぽいが同情的な言葉をつけ加える。

> For alle hire frendes—for to save hire trouthe—

4

She hath forsake; allas, and that is routhe
That evere woman wolde ben so trewe
To truste man, but she the bet hym knewe,　（798-801）
（彼女は友達をすべて捨てたのだ―約束を守るために―／ああ、今まで女
が男を信頼して誠実でありすぎたということは、／たとえ男をもっとよく
知らなかったとしても、／なんと気の毒なことだろう。）

　ピラムスより早く逢瀬の場所である泉の辺に来たティスベは、水を飲み
に来た雌ライオンを目撃する。
　オウィディウスが語るティスベの恐怖の場面はこうである。

　　quam procul ad lunae radios Babylonia Thisbe
　　vidit et obscurum timido pede fugit in antrum,
　　dumque fugit, tergo velamina lapsa reliquit.　（Bk IV. 99-101）
（Far off under the rays of the moon Babylonian Thisbe sees her and flees with
trembling feet into the deep cavern, and as she flees she leaves her cloak on the
ground behind her.）

　この引用を見るとオウィディウスはただ状況を説明するだけで、ティス
べの恐怖の感情については語っていない、それに引きかえチョーサーの説
明は、ティスベがライオンの恐怖に脅えて洞窟に逃げて、彼女の逃げ果せ
た安堵の気持ちが伝わってくる。

　　And whan that Tisbe hadde espyed that,
　　She rist hire up, with a ful drery herte,
　　And in a cave with dredful fot she sterte,
　　For by the mone she say it wel withalle.
　　And as she ran hire wympel let she falle
　　And tok non hed, so sore she was awhaped,
　　And ek so glad that that she was escaped;
　　And thus she sit and darketh wonder stylle.　（809-16）
（ティスベはそれをみると、／恐ろしさのあまり、飛び上がり／脅えた足

取りで洞窟の中に逃げ込んだ。／実は月明かりでライオンがよく見えたか
らだ。／彼女は逃げる時ベールを落としてしまった。／それに気づかな
かったが、ひどく脅えていたので、／逃げ果せたことが大変うれしかった。
／こうして座って身じろぎもせず闇に隠れていた。）

　チョーサーはオウィディウスより細かく状況を説明する中で3行つけ加
えた。それは814-16行の雌ライオンにびっくりして、近くの洞窟に逃げ
込み安堵する箇所である。そこにおいてチョーサーはティスベの気持ちを
そのうちの1行ではっきり表現する。

　　　And ek so glad that that she was escaped;（815）
　　　（逃げ果せたことが大変うれしかった。）

　オウィディウスではティスベの感情は表現されていないが、チョーサー
のこの1行で読者も感情移入されてティスベに同情を寄せてしまう。
　なお、チョーサーは、オウィディウスの "timido pede"（＝with trembling
feet）（Bk. IV. 100）を "with dredful fot"（＝with frightened steps）（811）と訳し、
ティスベの心の内をより表す表現にしている。
　さらに、オウィディウスの話を拡大しているところもある。オウィディ
ウスではピラムスが家を出て泉のそばにやって来るまでの時間的経過中、
つまり、先に来たティスベがライオンを恐れて洞窟に隠れてピラムスを待
つ間のティスベのことは、オウィディウスでは説明されない。チョーサー
はその間彼女が考えたことや彼に話そうと思うことを披歴する。

　　　Now Tisbe, which that wiste nat of this,
　　　But sittynge in hire drede, she thoughte thus:
　　　"If it so falle that my Piramus
　　　Be comen hider, and may me not yfynde,
　　　He may me holde fals and ek unkynde."
　　　And out she cometh and after hym gan espien,
　　　Bothe with hire herte and with hire yen,

And thoughte, "I wol hym tellen of my drede,
Bothe of the lyonesse and al my deede." （853-61）

（さてこのことを知らないティスベであったが、／恐怖の中で座りつづけ
ながら、こう思った。／「ピラムス様がここに来られて、／私を見つける
ことがおできになれないなら、／私を嘘つきで不実な人とお思いになるか
もしれない」／そこで彼女は外へ出て、心を配り／目を配って、彼を探し
始めながら思った、／「雌ライオンが恐ろしかったことをお話しましょう、
／私のとった行動はびくびくものだったことも」）

　しかし、ライオンが去り、洞窟の外に出て泉の辺に来ると、ティスベは
自ら命を絶ったピラムスを見つける。その場面の叙述はオウィディウスも
素晴らしいが、チョーサーも異なる迫真の描写をする。両者を比べてみる。

dum dubitat, tremebunda videt pulsare cruentum
membra solum, retroque pedem tulit, oraque buxo
pallidiora gerens exhorruit aequoris instar,
quod tremit, exigua cum summum stringitur aura. （Bk IV. 133-36）

（While she hesitates, she sees somebody's limbs writhing on the bloody ground, and
starts back, paler than boxwood, and shivering like the sea when a slight breeze
ruffles its surface.）

And at the laste hire love thanne hath she founde,
Betynge with his heles on the grounde,
Al blody, and therwithal a-bak she sterte,
And lik the wawes quappe gan hire herte,
And pale as box she was, and in a throwe
Avisede hire, and gan hym wel to knowe,
That it was Piramus, hire herte deere. （862-68）

（ついに恋人を発見した。／彼は踵で地面をたたきながら、血だらけに
なって／倒れていた。それを見てはっと飛びのいた。／心臓は波のように
打ち、／黄楊（つげ）のように真っ青になったが、即座に／思いめぐらし、彼であ
ること、／愛する大事なピラムス様であることが分かった。）

　命を絶っているピラムスを発見して、びっくり仰天したオウィディウス
のティスベは、"tremit, exigua cum summum stringitur aura."「弱いそよ風が
海面を波立たせる時の海のように震えた」、一方、驚いて飛びのいたチョー
サーのティスベは、"lik the wawes quappe gan hire herte"「心臓が波打つ音の
ように鼓動した」と、両詩人とも海と波との似た語を入れて直喩を使って
いるが、チョーサーではティスベの驚きがオウィディウスと異なる。だが、
両者共ティスベは自らの行動によって愛において誠実であることを示した。
　オウィディウスはティスベの最期をこう表現する。冷たくなった恋人ピ
ラムスの亡骸をティスベは抱擁し、キスして悲嘆に暮れながらピラムスの
蘇生を訴え、それから父母に二人をひとつの墓に埋めてくれるように願っ
て、ピラムスの剣で自刃して果てるようにした。チョーサーも、筋書きは
オウィディウスに倣うが、ティスベが悲嘆の独白をする前に、ティスベの
悲痛の振舞いを、読者に呼びかけるように、修辞学の表現方法の一つであ
る疑問法を用いて、胸を打つ究極の表現へと高めていった。

> Who coude wryte which a dedly cheere
> Hath Thisbe now, and how hire heer she rente,
> And how she gan hireselve to turmente,
> And how she lyth and swouneth on the grounde,
> And how she wep of teres ful his wounde;
> How medeleth she his blod with hire compleynte;
> How with his blod hireselve gan she peynte;
> How clyppeth she the deede cors, allas!
> How doth this woful Tisbe in this cas!
> How kysseth she his frosty mouth so cold!
> "Who hath don this, and who hath been so bold
> To sle my leef? O spek, my Piramus!
> I am thy Tisbe, that the calleth thus."
> And therwithal she lifteth up his hed.　　(869-82)

（誰が書けようか、その時ティスベはどんな悲壮な／顔になったかを、ど
のように髪を引きちぎったかを、／どのように自分を責めさいなんだかを、

／どのように卒倒して地面に倒れたかを、／どのように彼の傷口に涙をいっぱい注いだかを、／どのように彼の血を掻き混ぜんばかりに嘆いたかを、／どのように彼の血で自分の身を朱に染めたかを、／どのように遺体をしっかり抱いたかを、ああ悲しい！／この場合悲嘆のティスベはどのようにするかを！／大変冷たい彼の凍る唇にどのようにキスをするかを！／「誰がこれをしたの、誰がこんなに大胆不敵だったの、／大事な人を殺すなんて、ああ、話して、ピラムス様！／こう呼びかけている私は、あなたのティスベよ」／そう言って、彼女は彼の頭を持ち上げた。）

　この物語の終わり近くになって、チョーサーは恋人たちと女性の側に立って祈願の言葉を挿入し、この列伝のテーマである女性は愛において男性よりも"trew(e)"（＝true）であることを訴える。

> "And ryghtwis God to every lovere sende,
> That loveth trewely, more prosperite
> Than evere yit had Piramus and Tisbe!
> And lat no gentil woman hyre assure
> To putten hire in swich an aventure.
> But God forbede but a woman can
> Ben as trewe in lovynge as a man!
> And for my part, I shal anon it kythe."　　（905-12）

（「そして正義の神様、願わくは真実愛し合っている／すべての恋人たちに、ピラムスとティスベが今まで／経験したより多くの幸せを授けて下さいますように！／そしていかなる高貴な女性にもこのような危険に／あえて身をさらすほどの羽目に陥らせませんように。／女は愛することにおいて、男よりも／誠実でないということは断じてございませんもの！／私はと言えば、それをすぐにお見せ致しましょう」）

　以上のように表現の仕方を探っていくと、チョーサーはオウィディウスよりも現実表現に徹しながら、登場人物の二人の性格化をより成し遂げ、読者に憐憫感情を催すような表現の道をすすめている。
　最後に、フェミニスト的チョーサーは、男性にも肩を持ち、ピラムスの

ように不実でない男もいることを主張してこの話を締めくくる。

And thus are Tisbe and Piramus ygo.
Of trewe men I fynde but fewe mo
In alle my bokes, save this Piramus,
And therfore have I spoken of hym thus.
For it is deynte to us men to fynde
A man that can in love been trewe and kynde.
Here may ye se, what lovere so he be,
A woman dar and can as wel as he.　　(916-23)

（こうしてティスベとピラムスはこの世を去った。／私のすべての書物の中を探してもこのピラムス以上に／誠実で心優しい男は、ほとんど見当たらない。／だから彼についてこうしてお話ししたのだ。／恋に真実で誠実のままいられる男を見つけることは／われら男にとって嬉しいことだから。／ここでお分かりだろう、男がいかなる恋人であろうと、／女は男に劣らず勇気があり、分別があるということを。）

　結びとして、この物語は、上述したように、オウィディウス『変身物語』巻4. 55 - 166 行におおむね従って忠実に書かれている。だが、これまで見てきたように、チョーサー自身の考えによってところどころ改変している。そして、ピラムスとティスベの逢引場所は、オウィディウスでは "busta Nini"（Ninus' tomb）に あ る "arbor ibi niveis uberrima pomis /（ardua morus）…"（a tree hanging full of snow-white berries,（a tall mulberry））（Bk. IV. 89-90）の陰であった。つまり、「ニノスの墓にある、雪のように白い実をいっぱいつけた木（高い桑の木）」の下であった。チョーサーでは "There kyng Nynus was grave under a tre"（785）「一本の木の下のニノス王が埋葬されている所」とした。チョーサーはオウィディウスの「桑の木」の代わりに、「一本の木」と言っているだけである。チョーサーは「桑の木」と言うのを言いそびれたか、あるいはその名称を省いたのかどちらかであろう。とにかく木の名称を記述していないのである。すなわち、その木のもとで起こった悲劇の証拠として、ティスベがこれから黒い実をつけるようにと

桑の木に頼んだことを、オウィディウスは書いているが、チョーサーは彼
女の臨終の言葉からそれを省いている。チョーサーは自分が桑の木の名を
出さなかったことを、ちゃんと弁えていたようである。

　チョーサーは、オウィディウスの『変身物語』から借用した物語ではい
つものことだが、主人公たちの大事な変身の部分を外している。ここでも
そうしている。チョーサーは虚構に関心をあまり示さないところがあり、
当時の一般の中世人よりも客観的な物の見方や考え方ができた人であろう。

注

1. Chaucer はここで "Naso seyth thus" といって、この作品の典拠が Naso であ
   ることを自ら認めている。なお、Naso は Ovid（Publius Ovidius Naso）のこ
   とである。
2. 以下、チョーサーの作品の引用は Larry D. Benson（gen ed.）（1987）による。
3. 'The Legend of Thisbe' の和訳はすべて論者による。
4. たとえば、*The House of Fame*, 349-52 参照。
5. 以下、オウィディウスのラテン語の引用は、Ovid III, *Metamorphoses I*（1916;
   rcpr. 1969）による。

参考文献

Benson, Larry D.（gen ed.）（1987）*The Riverside Chaucer*, 3rd ed. Boston: Houghton Mifflin.

Fisher John H.（ed.）（1977）*The Complete Poetry and Prose of Geoffrey Chaucer*. New York: Holt,
　　Rinehart and Winston.

Frank, Robert Worth.（1972）*Chaucer and The Legend of Good Women*. Cambridge Mass.: Harvard
　　University Press.

Gray, Douglas.（ed.）（1993）*The Oxford Companion to Chaucer*. Oxford: Oxford University Press.

地村彰之・笹本長敬訳、ジェフリー・チョーサー作『善女列伝・短詩集』（2020）広島：
　　溪水社。

Miller, Frank Justus（trans.）（1916; repr.1968）*Ovid III—Metamorphoses I*.（Loeb Classical
　　Library）Cambridge Mass.: Harvard University Press.

中村善也訳、オウィディウス作『変身物語』（上）（下）（1981）（文庫）東京：岩波書店。

田中秀央・前田敬作訳、オウィディウス作『転身物語』（1966）京都：人文書院。

「バースのおかみの話」における不条理は解決されたのか ——古典作品引用との関連を中心に*

狩 野 晃 一

1. はじめに

『カンタベリ物語』*The Canterbury Tales* 中「バースのおかみの話」'The Wife of Bath's Tale' は結婚の問題、フェミニズム、アーサー王伝説、そして loathly lady（醜い老婆）に関する種々のモチーフが含まれていることで知られている。ここに現れる loathly lady のモチーフは同時代の作品にも確認されるが、「バースのおかみの話」におけるそれは複雑さ、多層性において、これらとは一線を画す。[1] このモチーフはチョーサーよって自然な形でしっくりとくるように用いられ、（そのために、そしてアーサー王宮廷の「法」の規則によって）話はスムーズに進み、ハッピーエンドへと導かれる。非常に良いテンポで話が展開するのであるが、そこには人間の本性に由来する不条理なもの、何か不公平で未決着のものが報われない形で残されているようにも思われる。本論の目的は、「バースのおかみの話」にあらわれる登場人物たちによって引き起こされた人間の不条理を明らかにし、それに対するチョーサーの心理的態度について考察を深めることである。特にチョーサーが老婆に権威 auctoritas としての「古典作品」からの引用を語らせることと、不条理という困難な状況の打開がいかにして行われたのかということに注目して論じる。

2. 「バースのおかみの話」における不条理

ここで言う不条理とは、正当な筋や理屈が通らず（ロジカルでない）、本来あるべき（自然な）姿とは異なっている、またはかけ離れている、そして自らの力では如何ともしがたい外の力によって思い通りに事が進まな

い状態を示す。「バースのおかみの話」には、不条理であるとみなしうる状況が所々に見られる。まずそれらの不条理とはどのようなものであるのか、順を追って整理してみよう。

2.1. 若い騎士による乙女の陵辱行為という不条理

「バースのおかみの話」の舞台は、アーサー王宮廷のある世界に置かれている。話はアーサー王宮廷に出入りする若い騎士が鷹狩りの帰り道、ある乙女を犯してしまったところから始まる。これが、乙女が同意していない野蛮なレイプ行為であったことは、「無理矢理に」"by verray fors"（888）[2]や「彼女の意思に反して」"maugree hir heed"（887）といった表現から不条理であることは明らかである。この行為こそが、「話」の基点であり、最大の不条理なのである。なお、このエピソードは他の類話には見られず、チョーサーによる付け加えである。

2.2. 凌辱した騎士を救いたいと希望する不条理

騎士の犯したレイプという行為に対して、人々からは強固な抗議の声が上がり、死罪が求められた。それにも関わらず、王妃と宮廷の婦人らからは、騎士の犯した罪が万死に値することは重々承知しながらも、死罪だけは見逃すようにとの必死の懇願が出てくる。

> But that the queene and othere ladyes mo
> So longe preyeden the king of grace
> Til he his lif him graunted in the place,
> And yaf him to the queene, al at hir wille,
> To chese wher she wolde him save or spille. （894-8）

この若い騎士の命を死罪から救う理由はなんであるのかは本文には示されていない。わざわざ法律に反するようにしてまで、なぜ宮廷の貴婦人らは彼を救いたいと思うのか。通常考えれば、これはおかしい。これも不条理である。

2.3.　立場の違いに起因する不条理

　即刻死刑と死刑放免という意見の対立に対し、レイプされた乙女と同じ側の人間、すなわち女性にその決定権を委ねることになる。Biggs も指摘しているように、この場合レイプという犯罪は、男性の力の明らかな濫用であるから、「犯された側」the oppressed である女性にその決定権を委譲すべきであり、その決定権を得たのは王妃をはじめ宮廷の貴婦人らの「発言」によるものであった。[3] 確かにこの決定に至るプロセスは論理的（logical）である。そうではあるのだが、レイプされた乙女と王妃や宮廷の貴婦人たちとを同列に扱うことの可否については、疑問が残る。同じ女性といっても、貴婦人たちは罪を犯した若い騎士を擁護しているのである。また、後でも触れるが、災難にあった乙女は宮廷と関わりのある女性ではなく、階級そのものが異なっている。したがって、レイプされた乙女の側と、貴婦人らとでは、二重の意味で立場が違うと考えるのが妥当である。同列ではないのに同列にされてしまう。これもまた不条理として挙げられる。アーサー王は、その騎士の命を左右する権限を王妃に委譲する。決定権が法の執行者としての王から王妃に移る。[4] それと同時に誰が何を支配できるようになるのか、つまり支配権の問題についての輪郭が徐々にはっきりとしてくる。全ては「彼女の意思」"al at hir wille"（897）、すなわち王妃の采配にかかっている。同じ女性が裁くのには違いないが、ここでは凌辱された乙女からは完全に離れてことが進んでしまっている。

2.4.　自分本位、利己主義という不条理

　法の執行人としての権利を王から移譲された王妃は、騎士に対して「女性が最も望むものはなんであるか」"What thing is it that wommen mosst desiren"（905）という問いに答えられれば命を助けると約束する。即座に回答ができない騎士は12ヶ月と1日の猶予をもらい、その答えを探しに出かけることになる。結果として、騎士はしばらくの間、「死」からなんとか離れることができたのだが、物悲しく、そして切なくため息をつく。犯してしまった罪を悔いているのかと思いきや、そうではなく、彼は「好きなことが全くできない」"he may nat doon al as him liketh"（914）という身

勝手な理由のためにそうしていたのだ。反省の色が見えていない愚かで身勝手な若者の姿が印象付けられる。王妃の質問に対する回答にはならないオウィディウスの『転身物語』中の「ミダス王の話」の挿話がバースのおかみ自身によって挟まれる。騎士は鬱屈とした気分に苛まれ、答えが見つからない焦り、そしてそのために死刑になるのではないかという恐れが見て取れる。だが、こういった騎士のネガティブな気持ちは全く自分可愛さからくるもので、自分の犯した罪のことは一顧だにしない。自分は生き残りたい一心である。ここに最も不合理な人間の性が表出しているのを見てとることができる。

2.5. 合理的な不条理

騎士が、凌辱した乙女のことを顧みないのは、階級という社会的構造、あるいは騎士のもつ階層意識が密接に関わっているかもしれない。"A maide" と書かれたこの乙女はおそらく農民であったろう。若い女性で、一人で「歩いて」"walkynge"（886）いたことからそれとわかる。[5] 町から離れて道をひとり歩くということは宮廷人にはありえない。通常は馬に乗って行くはずだからだ。アンドレアス・カッペッラーヌス Andreas Cappellanus は『宮廷風恋愛について』De amore の 11 章において農民の少女に対する行為について以下のように述べている。

> Si vero et illarum te feminarum amor forte attraxerit, eas pluribus laudibus efferre memento, et, si locum inveneris opportunum, non differas assumere quod petebas et violento potiri amplexu. Vix enim ipsarum in tantum exterius poteris mitigare rigorem, quod quietos fateantur se tibi concessuras amplexus vel optata patiantur te habere solatia, nisi modicae saltem coactionis medela praecedat ipsarum opportune pudoris.[6]
>
> （De amore, Liber I, capitulum xi, 'de amore rusticorum'）

これを見ると、若い騎士が道すがら出会った乙女を凌辱したわけをある程度説明できるかもしれない。下線部「ちょうど良い場所を見つけたならば、

求めるものを得ること、力ずくの抱擁でそれを得ることを躊躇してはならぬ」は、若い騎士の行為と合致する。これが当時の恋愛指南書に記されているのであるから、騎士が正当化しようと思えば、その理由にもなりうる。賞賛にはまるで当たらない行為ではあるが、若い騎士は宮廷風恋愛の作法に則って行為に及んだ。ということは、ある意味で合理なのであるが、現実にはそこから不合理が生まれている。

2.6.　虚偽という不条理

　宮廷で「女性が最も望むものは何か」という難問を王妃から与えられてから、猶予の期限である一年が過ぎようとする直前、森の入り口で老婆と出会う。そして問に対する答えをある条件と引き換えに教えてもらう。騎士が答えを携えて宮廷に戻ると、王妃は法廷を開き、その裁判官となる。騎士は王妃と貴婦人らの眼前で、実際は自分で考えもせず老女からもらった答えを、あたかも自分でその解答を得たが如く「堂々と男らしい声で」"manly vois"（1036）答えるのである。これは虚偽であり、堂々と男らしくという言葉との乖離が大きい。

2.7.　因習的世界観の逆転による不条理

　老婆のスピーチが終わり、彼女が持ち出した3つの項目「真の高貴さ」「貧しさ」「老年」は、それまで若い騎士が浸かっていた因習的な世界—いわゆる貴族社会と呼ばれる皮相的な世界—を根底から覆した。騎士にとって道理の通った世界は突如として道理の通らない世界に変わり、今度は騎士自身が不条理の中に放り込まれる構図となる。

　見かけ上、ハッピーエンドで終わるように示されているが、今まで見てきた「話」の中に散見される不条理はいかに解決され整合性を保っているのか。あるいはそうでないのか。

3. 権威としての「法」と「古典作品」の表出と意味

　「バースのおかみの話」では権威に分類されるものが二つある。ひとつは法であり、もう一方は聖書の記述を含む古典作品とその作者である。法は社会のありようを規定するために存在するものであり、古典作品は経験と教訓であり、連綿と受け継がれてきた人間社会の知恵である。両者とも不条理と対立するものである。このセクションでは、それらがどのような描かれ方をしているのかまとめることにする。

3.1. 法と法廷のイメージ

　「バースのおかみの話」の舞台であるアーサー王の宮廷は、法廷という機能も持ち合わせている。王は法の保護者であり、さらにその執行者としての権限が与えられている。法廷のイメージは物語を通底しており、あちらこちらに「法」"lawe"や法律に関連する語彙が見られる。

　若い騎士による乙女の凌辱に対し、人々からは強い抗議の声が上がり、アーサー王の耳にまで届く。

> For which oppressioun was swich clamour
> And swich pursuite unto the kyng Arthour
> That dampned was this knygnt for to be deed,
> By cours of lawe, and shoulde han lost his heed —
> Paraventure swich was the status tho —　（889-93）

上記引用文の文脈において「凌辱、レイプ」という意味で用いられる "oppressioun" は *MED* によれば、わずか3例しか記録されておらず、珍しい用法であるが、宮廷＝法廷というセッティングがすでに含意されている。[7]さらに次行にあらわれる語「追求」"pursuite" も法律のニュアンスを含んでおり、場面設定に影響を与えている語である。当然、当時の法律に従って騎士は死罪を言い渡され、「それが当時の法律であった」"Swich was the statut tho"（893）という一文が置かれている。[8]

　老女が騎士に「この世で女性が最も望んでいるものは何か」という問い
に対する答えを教える前に、「誓ってください」"plight"と言ったり、法廷
が閉じる前に正義が行われるよう"do me right"と述べ、法廷での宣誓を連
想させ、法を常に意識させるような言葉が配置されている。

　老婆は自分が騎士に答えを教えたことを明かし、自分との約束—すなわ
ち彼女を妻に娶ること—を守るように要求する。ここでも「彼は私に誓っ
たのだから」"he plight me his trouthe there"（1051）と、再び plight を用いて
いる。騎士は「低い生まれの者と夫婦になることで家門を汚すことはでき
ない」"any of my nacioun / Sholde evere so foule disparaged be!"（1068-69）と
口にして、この要求を拒否する。婚姻は契約の問題である。契約には法的
な拘束力がある。契約を結んだ以上、有効な理由がない限り、本来この拒
否はできないものである。ここに先程あげた「堂々と男らしく」との大き
な対比が見られる。語 "manly" には、単純に「男らしく」という意味だけ
でなく、"noble, righteous, worthy" であることも含意されており、このよう
な特質を備えた人間は契約を反故にしたりはしないからだ。[9]「家族」「家
門」という意味で用いられている "nacioun" は、語源的にラテン語
nationem "breed, stock, race, nation"（nat- の部分は nasci「生まれる」の過去
分詞に由来）に遡り、騎士はここで階級、生まれの問題に立ち入っている。
チョーサーはこの語を意図的に脚韻部分に配置して、重みを持たせており、
この後で老婆によって引き起こされる世界観の逆転に大きな効果を与える
ことに成功している。しかし、騎士は生まれの問題を取り上げることもむ
なしく、主導権を得ることができないままでいる。

> But al for noght; the ende is this, that he
> Constreyned was; he nedes moste hire wedde,
> And taketh his olde wyf, and goth to bedde.（1070-72）

それでも騎士はこの状況を受け入れがたく、また「重々しい気分で悲嘆に
暮れるよりほかない（there nas but hevynesse and muche sorwe, 1079）ので
あった。新郎となった騎士の未成熟な態度に、新婦となった老女は、彼の

騎士道精神に疑義を投げかけながら、次のような厳しい一言を発する。

> ... 'O deere housbonde, benedicite!
> Fareth every knight thus with his wif as ye?
> Is this the <u>lawe</u> of king Arthures hous?
> Is every knight of his thus daungerous?
> I am youre owene love and eek youre wif;
> I am she which saved hath youre lif,
> And, certes, yet ne dide I yow unright.
> Why fare ye thus with me this firste night?
> Ye faren lik a man hadde lost his wit!
> What is my gilt? For Goddes love, tel it,
> And it shal ben amended, if I may.'　（1087-97）

この発話にも「これがアーサー王宮廷の法律なのですか。」"Is this the lawe of king Arthures hous?"（1089）の "lawe" や、「私に何の罪がありましょう。」'What is my gilt?'（1096）の "gilt" など法律に関する語があらわれ、この一連のやりとりもまた法廷での論争をイメージさせる。

3.2. 古典作品の引用

　上で挙げた法廷のイメージとともに、老婆はあたかも陪審員に雄弁に語りかける法律家のように、長いスピーチを始める。その約120行におよぶスピーチには、古典作品からの数多くの教訓的な引用が見られる。ウァレリウス、セネカ、ボエティウス、ユウェナリウス、さらに同時代のダンテなどがその代表である。[10]

　さて老婆のスピーチは、次に挙げた騎士の発言に対する反論である。

> Thou art so loothly, and so oold also,
> And therto comen of so lough a kynde,　（1100-01）

「醜さ」「老年」「身分の低さ」は、その人の本来的な性質には帰さない

もので、そのことを攻撃し、約束を無かったことにするための理由にする
ことなどあってはならないと、老婆は「生まれ持った高貴さ」"gentilesse"、
「貧しさ」"poverte"、「老年」"old age" の大切さを古典作品の過剰なほど
の豊富な引用とともに鋭く指摘する。これらのうち「生まれ持った高貴
さ」と「貧しさ」が、当時の類話に対するチョーサー独自の付け加えであ
る。[11]

　まず「生まれ持った高貴さ」の真の性質について説明が加えられる。こ
の部分はダンテ『饗宴』Il Convivio に多くを負っている。騎士が属してい
る社会階級について老婆は話を始めるが、高貴さというものが所属する階
級に当たり前に付随して現れるという考え方を真っ向否定する。そのよう
な思い上がりは「雌鶏一羽」"an hen" の価値もないという。

> But, for ye speken of swich gentilesse
> As is descended out of old richesse,
> That therfore sholden ye be gentil men,
> Swich arrogance is nat worth an hen.　（1109-12）

老婆は『神曲』「煉獄篇」第七歌および『饗宴』第四巻からの引用をする。
さらに著者（= acutor）ダンテの名前を出して、真の高貴さ "gentilesse" は
父祖の富 "olde richesse"（ダンテでは "antica richezza"）に由来するもので
はないと述べ、高貴さは生まれとは無関係であることを証明する。

> 'Ful selde up riseth by his branches smale
> Prowesse of man, for God, of his goodnesse,
> Wole that of hym we clayme oure gentilesse'　（1128-30）[12]

また『饗宴』第四巻でダンテが、gentilezza の源泉は神の恩寵であるといっ
ていることも、チョーサーと同じである。[13]「高貴さ」についての部分の
終わりに、老婆はウァレリウスやセネカやボエティウスといった古典作家
の名を挙げ、騎士が「高貴さ」を理解できるよう、騎士に対して彼らの作

品を読むことを勧める。ここでは物語中の騎士のみならず『カンタベリ物語』の聴衆や読者に対してもこれらの作品の内容に触れることを求めていると考えられる。「セネカ」"Senek"は『倫理書簡』*Epistulae* のことを指しており、特に書簡 44 に見られる記述に言及している。その内容は、我々を高貴そして高徳たらしめるのは魂のみであり、その出自ではないというものである。[14] ボエティウス『哲学の慰め』*De consolatione philosophiae*、さらにチョーサー自身による翻訳『ボエーセ』*Boece* では、貴族の称号はその血統に与えられていて、しかもそれは単に借り物ではないことが語られ、またその者の高貴さ、つまり真の立派さに由来する賞賛のことであるが、それが備わっていなければならないと説いている。[15]

　こうして矢継ぎ早に古典作家からの引用をし、その権威を借りて、老女は自分の主張である「高貴さとは何か」「高貴さが生まれではなく、徳や立派な行いから興るもの」を論理的に固めてゆく。そのような意味でいけば、彼女の結論「徳高く生き、罪を遠ざけている時、私は貴族なのです」"Thanne am I gentil, whan that I biginne / To liven vertuously, and weive sinne."（1175-76）は正しい。暴漢であり約束を反故にするような罪深い騎士は、いくら高い生まれであっても、彼には高貴さというものが全く内在していないことを示している。騎士と老婆を「高貴さ」"gentilessc" の観点から比較することで、その立場が逆転した状態となっている。

　次に語られるのは「貧しさ」についてである。騎士は生まれの卑しさに起因する貧しさを取り上げている。「貧しさ」とは無所有の状態を指し、とりわけ「喜んでする貧しさ」は所有欲肯定の否定である。「私たちが信仰する天の神様は、喜んで貧乏な生活をお選びになりました」"The hye God, on whom that we bileeve, / In wilful poverte chees to lyve his lyf."（1178-79）や「確かに喜んでする貧乏は敬うべきことでございます」Glad poverte is an honest thyng, certeyn（1183）などはこの考えを表している。生まれに起因する貧しさであろうが、進んでなる貧しさであろうが、それらはいかなる富にも勝るものであることが示されている。「貧しさ」のセクションはまた後半部分の論理的補強材料にもなっている。ここでは「コリント人への手紙 2」、セネカ、ユウェナリウスが主な典拠として用いられている。老

婆はこのセクションを通して、騎士の生まれながら所有する富を再び否定し、自らの常の状態、すなわち貧しさの肯定が達成されている。

　最後に「老年」について語られる。老いは人間にとり、あらゆる生物にとり、避けられないことである。最後の瞬間には死が訪れる。これは絶対的な真理である。この絶対真理に対し、老婆はもはや古典の作者からの引用に頼ることはしないで、自分と同じ考えの作者を容易に見つけることができると言い、このトピックに数行加えるに留めている。

> . . . ye gentils of honour
> Seyn that men sholde an oold wight doon favour,
> And clepe hym fader, for youre gentillesse. （1209-1211）

ここに込められたメッセージは明らかである。つまり歳をとっている老婆は丁重に扱われるべきであると。歳をとり、死ぬということは真理であり、老人を大切に扱うべきであるということは当然の行い、あるいは当然持つべき心的態度である。言い換えれば常識ということになろうか。この常識に対してわざわざ権威的な古典作家からの引用をする必要もないという判断だろう。老婆によるスピーチの最後の部分は、老婆と騎士が最初に出会った時に発せられた言葉「年寄りは多くのことを知っているのじゃよ」"Thise olde folk kan muchel thyng"（1004）を思い起こさせる。「年寄り」"olde folk"、"oold wight"は古い人であり、その示すところは古からの知恵、すなわち古典作品である。年寄りの知恵は古典作家の書いた作品の内容と同等であると考えられる。

4. 不条理と古典作家、不条理と条理のねじれ

　騎士が生んだ不条理、そしてそのために自らに降りかかった不条理は、彼の特権階級意識に全て由来することが上に示した通りである。

　老婆の古典作品をふんだんに取り入れたスピーチによって血統や出自といった彼がしがみつき、また信じてきた人為的に作られた「立派に見え

る」伽藍は崩れ堕ちた。騎士の世界を崩すことは、どのような意味があったのか。以下で検証する。

　騎士がそれまで浴していた世界が否定されることは、アーサー王宮廷などの現世の否定にも繋がるようにも思える。アーサー王宮廷は絶対的な階級社会である。それはチョーサーのいた社会も同じであった。確立された階級に抗うことは当時は危険を伴った。1381年のワット・タイラーの乱の際、聖職者ジョン・ボールは「アダムが耕しイヴが紡いだとき、誰がジェントリだったのか」と述べたとされるが、それに対する権力者の意思表明は明らかであった。つまり「首をつっこむな、知ろうとするな、今ある階級社会に疑問を呈するな」ということで彼は刑に処された。特に老婆が主張する「真の高貴さ」についての言説は、社会のヒエラルキー構造を脅かす危険すらある。

　ここではスピーチのタイミングに注目したい。老婆のスピーチが行われたのは、騎士と結婚をしてからのことである。結婚をするということは家庭をもつということで、それは社会を構成する最小単位であり、外と内の二つの異なる社会が形成されることを意味する。この限られた環境で騎士の世界観を覆す行為があったことが鍵であろうと思う。老婆が口にしたことは騎士と老婆の夫婦の間だけでのことで、それ以外の場所や社会には影響がない。そしてアーサー王宮廷にも変化が及んでおらず、家庭の外の世界はそのまま以前と変わらない価値観で続いていることになる。つまり現実にはねじれたままの状態が続いている。

　この世の富が移ろい易いものであることは、中世ラテン詩 *Cur mundus miliat* や Trinity College, Cambridge MS. 181 に残るその中英語訳などのチョーサーと同時代に広く読まれた詩のテーマとも重なっている。[16] 現世の富は儚いものであるからそれらを手放せと教える。「貧しさ」というものはまさに絶えず変化する世界──名声や権力や富や所有といった無常のもの──から距離を置くことである。言い換えれば、現世的に価値が高いと思われるものとともに存在しないこと、あるいはそれらに依存しないことである。それでも現実に存在する一人間としては、それら現のものを超越する何かに絶対的な価値を置く必要がある。では、何に、あるいはどこにそ

狩　野　晃　一

の絶対的な価値を見出すのか。

　騎士はひとり道を歩いていた乙女を陵辱した人間である。同時にそのような法に反する行為をしても、自分の命を失いたくないと思う人間である。彼が真に高貴な人間として見做すことができない事実は老婆のスピーチによって暴露される。老婆によって二者択一を迫られるが、もはや騎士にとっては選択の余地はなかった。しかしここで深く考え込むのだ。考え込んでいるように見えるのは、二つの選択肢の間で揺れているなく、自分がどのような人間であるかという否定し得ない事実を目の当たりするのみにであった。

> "My lady and my love, and wyf so deere,
> I put me in youre wise governance;
> Cheseth yourself which may be moost pleasance
> And moost honour to yow and me also.
> I do no fors the wheither of the two,
> For as yow liketh, it suffiseth me."（1230-35）

老婆による支配権 "governance"（1231）の行使は老婆にとっても騎士にとっても喜び "pleasance"（1232）であるという。脚韻に用いられたこれら二つの語がともに響きあい、そこに調和が生まれている。チョーサーはまた、騎士に再び「力」"fors" という語を使わせている。ここでは「力を行使しない」"I do no fors"（1234）、すなわち「構わない」という意味になる。「力ずくで」'by verray fors' 乙女を陵辱した騎士が、自らの口から力を行使しないと言い、全てを女性の判断に委ねる変化を遂げている。この言葉から、騎士が婚姻関係における主導権を手放していることがわかる。アーサー王宮廷で法廷が開かれた時、答えは老婆に教えてもらったものではあるが、「おとこらしく堂々とした声で」"manly vois" 答えを言い放った騎士とはもはや同じではない。彼は完全に婚姻における支配権を老婆に委ね、自分を賢明に導くよう懇願している。この時点で、騎士はエゴセントリックな存在を捨てた。その代わりに老婆を精神的支柱として認知し、老婆の

古典作品の引用を含む言説がもつ精神に価値を置くことで彼はこの世に存在し続けることが可能となったのではないだろうか。

5.　むすび

　老婆は古典作品や聖書からの引用で騎士の既存の立場を転覆させ、騎士は自分の行為の結果としての不条理を否が応でも受け入れる結果となる。確かに、老婆の言い分は論理的で反論のしようのないほど正しいものであるから、騎士は老婆の導きに一切を任せてしまっている。否、任せることを強いられる。チョーサーは人間世界の不条理を認めるのである。チョーサーは騎士に自らの行いに起因する結果を不条理として負わせている。ダンテは、真の高貴さ gentilezza は神の恩寵である徳に存すると言った。セネカは高貴なことは実行に移すことが肝要であると述べた。若い騎士は自らの支配権を手放した時に自己の存在を証明することができたように思える。しかし、老婆がうら若き乙女に変身することによって男性支配の世界が再び戻ったように解釈することも可能であろうが、[17] それまでの自分の世界を捨てるという苦渋の決断をした騎士は、以前の男性優位の世界が戻って来ることを求めているのではない。はじめ騎士は老婆から「女性が最も求めるものはなんであるか」との問いに対して答えを教えてもらい、それを「知った」が、老婆との約束を守ることによって本当の意味でその答えの意味を「理解した」のである。知ることから理解することへの成長こそが、ねじれを解消できた一因であろう。騎士と老婆の関係においては、ねじれた状態は修復されるが、この婚姻関係の外では元の世界はそのままである。犯された乙女は法廷での騎士の回答によって報われたのか。騎士の死罪を求めた人々の不満は解消されたのか。王という男性から女妃という女性への決定権の委譲によって一見、権力構造が中和されたように描かれているが、果たしてそうなのだろうか。「醜い老婆」の類話と「バースのおかみの話」が決定的に違うのは、類話では、例えば『ラグネル妃の結婚』では、魔法によって乙女が醜い老婆に姿を変えられていたのが、元に戻るのだが、チョーサーの老婆はそうではない。あるいは犯された乙女が

森のところで老婆に姿を変えたのだろうか。異界譚的な考え方をすればそ
れも可能であろうが、「バースのおかみの話」の場合、そのことは明示さ
れていない。残念ながら、チョーサーの諸作品では、すべての不条理が救
済されるとは限らない。そのいくつかは偶然によって救済され、残りは救
済されないままである。「バースのおかみの話」を通して理解されるのは、
人間の弱さと愚かさに由来する破滅的な行為と悲劇的な意思決定、人間社
会のねじれた姿、そして全てを救済することのできない不完全と不平等が
厳然と存在することである。それをチョーサーは経験豊かなバースのおか
みに語らせたのではないだろうか。

注

＊．本論文は 2019 年 7 月に英国リーズにて開催された International Medieval
   Congress での発表原稿に大幅に加筆修正を施したものである。発表原稿に
   ついて関東学院大学名誉教授の多ヶ谷有子先生より有益なご助言をいただ
   いたことに対し、ここに感謝の意を表するものである。

1. 同時代の類話として *The Tale of Florent* および *The Weddyng of Syr Gawen and
   Dame Ragnell* などが挙げられる。Correale and Hamel（2005: 405-441）を参照。

2. チョーサー『カンタベリ物語』の原文は、全て Benson（gen. ed.）, *The
   Riverside Chaucer*（1989）から引用した。引用語句の後の括弧は行数を示す。

3. Biggs（2017）, p. 185.

4. Turner（2019）, p. 71 は 'It was an archetypal scene of queenly intercession of the
   type that monarchs often staged, and that would be played out again and again in
   Chaucer's works（the 'Knight's Tale' and the 'Wife of Bath's Tale' stage exactly this
   scene of make kingly violence being neutralized by queenly abjection and pleas for
   peace).' といっている。

5. Biggs（2017）, p. 183.

6. Trojel（ed.）. *De amore*, p. 236 を参照。以下に瀬谷による邦訳を付しておく
   「しかし、万一農民の女と恋をすることでもあったら、大いに誉めそやすこ
   とを忘れるな。そして恰好な場所があったら、ためらうことなく激しく抱
   いて念願のものを手に入れるがよい。何故なら、少なくともある程度まで
   強制的な治療法を駆使して、彼女たちの羞恥心に巧みに機先を制しなければ、
   大人しく抱擁されたり、念願のものを赦し与えたりするほど、あの頑固に
   思える態度を懐柔することは大変困難であろうから。」（瀬谷, 1993, p.

138)

7. *MED* oppressioun (n.) 定義 (c) を参照。

8. Pollock and Maitland (1952), vol. 2, pp. 490-1. によれば、13 世紀イングランドの法学者ブラクトンによるレイプの罪に対する処罰は以下の通りであったという。すなわち「上控訴人が処女を奪われた事件に対しては、目潰しと去勢という最も重い刑罰を留保しており、それ以外の場合には、手足を失うにいたらないほどの体罰を与えるべき」と。さらに、それを逃れようとした場合には、死罪が言い渡されることもあったと加えている。レイプに対してはおよそ同様の処罰であり、いずれにせよかなり重いものであったと言って良いだろう。

9. *MED* manli (adj.) 定義 (4a) を参照。

10. チョーサーは、個々の古典作品から独自に引用をしてきたのではなく、おそらくコンピレーションやアンソロジーといったものから材源をとっている。用いられた可能性が最も高いのが、フランシスコ会の神学者ジョン・オヴ・ウェールズ John of Wales (?-c.1285) によって 1260 年ごろに編纂された *Communiloquium* である。これは聖職者が説教をするときなどの手引き書、ネタ帳として用いられたもので、144 の写本が現存していることからかなり流布していたものと推定される。しかし、上に挙げた作家の内、ダンテは含まれておらず、権威として「話」にダンテを加えたのはチョーサーのオリジナルである。

    John of Wales の作品の流布と影響については Swanson (1989) , p. 204 に詳述されている。

11. Mann (2005), p. 899 を参照。

12. ダンテ『神曲』「煉獄篇」では以下の通り。

    Rade volte resurge per li rami

    l'umana probitate; e questo vole

    quei che la dà, perché da lui si chiami. (Purgatorio 7: 121-3)

    （人間の美質が、枝分かれした子孫の中に蘇ることはまれです。美質をお与えになる方が、それは自らに由来すると人々に言わせるため、こうお望みだからです。(原，2014，「煉獄編」p. 115))

13. Dante, *Convivio*, vol. 4, chapters 20-21 を参照。

14. Seneca, *Epistles*, XLIIII, 2-5 を参照。特に 5 'Non facit nobilem atrium plenum fumosis imaginibus. Nemo in nostram gloriam vixit nec quod ante nos fuit, nostrum est; animus facit nobilem, cui ex quacumque condicione supra fortunam licet surgere.'

15. Boethius, *Consolation*, III, prose 4 を参照。

16. Brown (1952), pp. 237-38.

17. Noji (2017), p.100 を参照。

狩 野 晃 一

参考文献

一次資料

Larry D. Benson（gen. ed.）. *The Riverside Chaucer*, 3rd ed.（Houghton Mifflin, 1987; Oxford University Press, 1988; rpt. 2008）

Mann, Jill（ed.）*The Canterbury Tales*. Penguin Classics. 2005.

二次資料

Alighieri, Dante. *Convivio: A Dual-Language Critical Edition*（ed. and tr. by Andrew Frisardi）, （Cambridge University Press, 2017）

Alighieri, Dante. *La Divina Commedia*（ed. G. H. Grandgent, rev. Charles S. Singleton, 1972. Tr. Charles S. Singleton）, 3 vols.（Princeton University Press, 1970-73）［邦訳　原基晶訳『神曲』全 3 巻（講談社学術文庫，2014）］

Biggs, Frederick. M. *Chaucer's Decameron and the Origin of the Canterbury Tales*（D. S. Brewer, 2017）

Boethius, *Theological Tractates. The Consolation of Philosophy*, translated by H. F. Stewart, E. K. Rand, and S. J. Tester.（Loeb Classical Library 74, 1973）

Brown, Carleton（ed.）. *Religious Lyrics of the XIVth Century, 2nd ed.*（Oxford: Clarendon Press, 1952）

Copeland, Rita（ed.）. *The Oxford History of Classical Reception in English Literature, vol. I: 800-1558.*（Oxford University Press, 2016）

Correale, Robert M. and Mary Hamel（eds.）*Sources and Analogues of the* Canterbury Tales*, vol. II*（D. S. Brewer, 2005）

MED: Middle English Dictionary.（https://quod.lib.umich.edu/m/middle-english-dictionary/dictionary）

Mann, Jill. *Feminizing Chaucer*（Cambridge University Press, 2002）

Noji, Kaoru, *Eloquence of Chaucer's Women: the Wife of Bath, Criseyde and Prudence*（Hon-no-Shiro, Otowa-shobo Tsurumi-Shoten, 2017）

Pollock and Maitland, *The History of English Law Before the Time of Edward I*（Cambridge University Press, 1952）

Seneca. *Epistles, Volume I: Epistles 1-65*, translated by Richard M. Gummere（Loeb Classical Library 75, 1917）［邦訳　兼利琢也，大西英史（訳）『セネカ哲学全集〈5〉倫理書簡集 I』（岩波書店，2005 年）］

Swanson, Jenny. *John of Wales: A Study of the Works and Ideas of a Thirteenth-Century Friar*（Cambridge University Press, 1989）

Trojel, E.（ed.）. *Andreae Capellani regii Francorum De amore libri tres.*（München : Fink, 1972）［邦訳　瀬谷幸男（訳）『宮廷風恋愛について―ヨーロッパ中世の恋愛術指南の書』

（南雲堂，1993）〕

Turner, Marion. *Chaucer: A European Life*（Princeton, Oxford: Princeton University Press, 2019）

Revisiting Hoccleve and Isidore of Seville

Hisashi Sugito

1. Introduction

As "My Compleinte," the first item of the *Series*, nears its end, Thomas Hoccleve consults a "book" which he borrowed from his friend. Hoccleve, labeled as a mad man by those around him, literally complaints about the situation throughout the poem and finally finds consolation in the book, which was identified as Isidore of Seville's *Synonyma* by A. G. Rigg's 1970 article.[1] According to Rigg, the extant manuscripts containing "My Compleinte," except for the holograph manuscript in Durham, MS Cosin V. iii. 9, come with Latin quotations which are written in the margins or between the stanzas.[2] These four manuscripts have mostly identical Latin texts after line 309, where Hoccleve's borrowed book appears, and from the quotations Rigg concludes that the "book was without question the *Synonyma*, subtitled *De lamentatione animae dolentis*, by Isidore of Seville (d. 636)."[3] Later in 1998, J. A. Burrow revised Rigg's suggestion, stating that the *Synonyma* Hoccleve could have consulted was a shortened version, or "*Synonyma* epitome," which was widely circulated in the age of Hoccleve. After examining MS Bodley 110, which contains a shorter *Synonyma*, Burrow suggests that Hoccleve's Latin glosses are very close to this version.[4]

Although *Synonyma* has thus been established as the source text for Hoccleve's "book," its thematic impact on Hoccleve's poems has not been fully discussed. This essay tries to reconsider the intertextual effect brought by Hoccleve's reference to *Synonyma* and argues that the reference affects how we read "My Compleinte" in relation to the entire compilation, the *Series*.

2. *Synonyma* and the Idea of the Book

We should first note that the thematic impact of the reference to *Synonyma* is highlighted by the formal structure of "My Compleinte." *Synonyma*'s text appears in a book which Hoccleve reads in the poem, and the image of a poet reading a book is one of the signature traits of Chaucerian dream visions. In the *Book of the Duchess*, for instance, the insomniac narrator requests a book to read on bed: "Upon my bed I sat upright / And bad oon reche me a book, / A romaunce, and he it me tok / To rede and drive the night away."[5] This book is about the story of Ceyx and Alcyone, and the source is most possibly Ovid's *Metamorphosis*. Chaucer repeats this literary device in the *Parliament of Fowls*, in which the narrator eagerly reads a book to learn "a certain thing."

> For out of olde feldes, as men seyth,
> Cometh al this newe corn fro yer to yere;
> And out of olde bokes, in good feyth,
> Cometh al this newe science that men lere. (22-25)

Chaucer's poems make good use of the theory represented here; Chaucer refers to the "old books" to produce new literary ideas.[6] In the *Parliament* he takes a look at "Dream of Scipio," the sixth book of Cicero's *De re publica*, and meets Scipio the Elder in his dream, suggesting a thematic resonance between the book and what he sees after falling asleep. In the *Book*, too, both Ovid's book and the dream deal with the subject of bereavement, and our reading experience is enriched by this intertextuality. This is a literary device characteristic of Chaucer, who depicts himself as a bookish man. In the *House of Fame*, the eagle reports how Chaucer, like a hermit, silently enjoys reading after work (652-60).

Thomas Hoccleve is also a reclusive bookworm just like his master. In "A Dialoge," the second item of the *Series*, the friend visits Hoccleve's room and sees the poet for the first time in three months: "Me thinketh ful ȝore / Sithen I the sy.

What, man, for Goddis ore / Come oute, for this quarter I not the sy, / By ouȝt I woote" (4-7).[7] Also, the friend famously attributes Hoccleve's mental illness to his overstudy: "Of studie was engendred thy seeknesse, / And þat was hard" (379-80). Hoccleve well understands the conventional image of a bookish poet developed by Chaucer, and the act of reading in "My Compleinte" can safely be considered in light of this convention. In fact, it is noteworthy that the opening of "My Compleinte," although it involves no dreaming, resembles that of the *Book of the Duchess*; in both works, the narrator is sleepless and explore his own melancholic state of mind. Only a few scholars, however, have tried to pay due attentions to the dream-vision elements found in Hoccleve's poems. Christina von Nolcken rightly states that "[t]he opening parts of the *Series* direct us to read it as we would a Chaucerian dream poem, therefore, with its old books very much in mind."[8] And how Isidore of Seville's *Synonyma* as an old book can affect the structure and theme of the *Series* can be further explored by reading the entire text. *Synonyma*'s main argument is Boethian by nature, reminding the reader of mutability and contingency of the material world as opposed to spiritual eternity. This accords well with Hocceve's concern throughout the *Series*.

First, Isidore of Seville himself does not claim the authorship of *Synonyma*, reporting that he came across the book by chance:

> Isidore to the Reader: greetings. Recently there came into my hands a certain book which they call *Synonyms*. Its form convinced me, in a certain mind, to put together for myself, or for miserable people, these lamentations.[9]

The contingent nature of reading is shared by Hoccleve's reference to *Synonyma*, which was a borrowed book and had to be returned to the owner:

> Lenger I þouȝte reed haue in þis book,
> But so it shope þat I ne miȝte nauȝt.
> He þat it ouȝte aȝen it to him took,

Me of his hast vnwar. (372-75)

Hoccleve only partially reads the book, meanwhile Chaucer, in the *Book of the Duchess*, reads Ovid in detail: "What I had red this tale wel / And overlooked it everydel ..." (231-32). Hoccleve's world is entirely dominated by chance; the consolation is only gained from the unfinished reading.

Also it should be considered that "My Compleinte" does not start with the act of reading a book, but ends with it. As I have explained, Chaucerian dream vision was unique because the books he reads anticipate some of the subjects explored in the following dreams, hence producing a highly metafictional framework. In the case of Hoccleve, however, this framework is inverted. Without falling asleep, Hoccleve sets out to write a complaint about his situation, and at the end of the poem he is finally consoled by reading a book. Consolation is usually gained in a dream through dialogue with an allegorical character; but Hoccleve does not experience a dialogue, merely reading what he would have experienced in a dream world. Hence in "My Compleinte," in terms of form and function, dreaming is replaced by reading. In fact, Reason's words in *Synonyma* are truly effective to Hoccleve:

> This othir day a lamentacioun
> Of a wooful man in a book I sy,
> To whom wordis of consolacioun
> Resoun ʒaf spekynge effectuelly,
> And wel esid myn herte was therby,
> For whanne I had a while in þe book reed,
> With the speche of Resoun was I wel feed. (309-15)

Here Reason's words in the book ease and nourish Hoccleve's heart. Although those words are of course directed to the lamenting man in *Synonyma*, Hoccleve reacts as if he experienced the dialogue with Reason. It is remarkable that John Stow, a seventeenth-century antiquarian who owned Hoccleve's holograph manuscript,

Durham University Library Cosin V.III.9, added a marginal note "Thomas" on fol. 7ᵛ, which identified the lamenting man with Hoccleve.[10] According to Stowe's reading, the spiritually troubled man in *Synonyma* is Hoccleve's *alter ego*, and this produces an illusion in which Hoccleve the narrator jumps into the book he is reading and assimilates himself with the character. This can be generically called a "pseudo-dream vision," where philosophical dialogue and enlightenment we expect in a dream world are offered in the form of reading, and the poet goes into the text and can bring back the knowledge. He is not a true dreamer, but at least in part shares a dream-like experience with other dreamer-poets.

After this reading, Hoccleve finishes "My Compleinte" with spiritual satisfaction:

Farwel my sorowe, I caste it to the cok.
With pacience I hensforþe thinke vnpike
Of suche þou3tful dissese and woo the lok,
And let hem out þat han me made to sike. (386-89)

The patience to deal with one's difficulty is exactly what Reason exhorts to in the quotation from *Synonyma*, and importantly, this advice improves Hoccleve's chief problem in "My Compleinte": his mental illness and people's skeptical eyes. Traditionally, as we read in the *Consolation of Philosophy* and Dante's *Commedia*, dreams and visions provide spiritual answers to the poets' problems. In a largely twisted manner, "My Compleinte" develops the structure of traditional dream-poems.

3. *Synonyma's* Thematic Effect on the *Series*

Now I would like to see how *Synonyma* deals with Hoccleve's troubled situation. First it would be helpful to notice that Hoccleve's complaint is resonant with the woeful man's account of his life; Stow's attempt to identify the man with Hoccleve, therefore, is not farfetched. The anguished man in the book is tormented by the sense of guilt, and his spirit is always vexed: "Vexacioun of spirit and torment / Lacke I ri3t noon. I haue of hem plente / Wondirly bittir is my taast and sent" (323-25). Earlier in "My Compleinte" Hoccleve tells us about his similar inner trouble. People around him still doubt the recovery of his mental breakdown, and his mind is "vexed" by this estrangement: "I oones fro Westminstir cam, / Vexid ful greuously with þou3tful hete" (183-84). Also, the woeful man longs for his death (330-31), just as Hoccleve is ready to die (261, 266). Finally, both protagonists perceive the endless nature of their agony. The woeful man sees "no end" of his sorrow (335), and Hoccleve asks himself how he could bring rest to his spirit (173-74).

Reason's advice is, of course, directed to the man in the book, but also tailored to fit Hoccleve's situation. Reason stresses patience with mutability and says that the hardship helps to purify one's guilt. In the dialogue Reason refers to "God's stroke," an idea Hoccleve discusses throughout "My Compleinte" : "To hem þat ben suffrable / And to whom Goddis strook is acceptable / Purueied ioie is, for God woundith tho / That he ordained hath to blis to goo (354-57). We can find a similar passage in *Synonyma*, but the idea of "God's stroke" is clearly Hoccleve's addition.[11] In "My Compleinte" Hoccleve attributes his mental breakdown to the work of God, but the reason of his complaint is people's doubt against this mystical account of madness. Hoccleve starts "My Compleinte" with the story of God's visitation, and tells how God restored Hoccleve's wit, which had been away from the poet. People, however, reject the spiritual understanding. As Hoccleve says, people around him talk about the possibility of recurrence after the apparent recovery (85-93). Their focus is mainly on Hoccleve's outer appearance: his head moved like a buck, and he restlessly walked like a roe deer (120-33). Hoccleve's exasperation, then, derives from people's misunderstanding of the nature of his illness; what he insists to be a spiritual event is interpreted as a psychosomatic problem.[12] Reason's advice, however, provides a spiritual context which justifies Hoccleve's complaint. Before reading *Synonyma*, Hoccleve's mind is preoccupied with how to stop the unjust imagination of his audience: "I may not lette a man to ymagine / Fer aboue þe mone, if þat him liste" (197-98). But after he was eased by Reason's lesson, people's imagination became less afflictive: "For euere sithen sett haue I the lesse / By the peples ymaginacioun" (379-80). This moment is crucial not only to "My Compleinte" but also to the ensuing item, "A Dialoge." In the dialogue with his friend, who still doubts his full recovery, Hoccleve confidently tries to argue for the mystical interpretation of the illness by borrowing Reason's key phrase. The friend advises Hoccleve not to publish the complaint, but his answer is that one should not be ashamed of "God's stroke" (54-55). He was not noted for doing vicious acts, and again he insists that his malady was "the strook of God" (79), for which there is no reason to withdraw "My Compleinte." Hoccleve's attitude toward the skeptical audience has clearly changed after the act of reading. By drawing on the idea of "God's stroke" he encountered in the Reason's discourse, Hoccleve, who used to be troubled by the uncontrollable interpretation, now provides a reading more meaningful to the author himself.

Synonyma not only changes our reading of "My Compleinte" and "A Dialoge"; it also echoes the theme we can see in "Ars Vtillissima Sciendi Mori" or "Lerne for to Die" in English, the fourth item of the *Series*. In "My Compleinte," what Reason mainly tells in the book is that God's stroke as a hardship finally leads to cleansing one's guilt. This idea of inner purification thematically anticipates the three other parts of the *Series*. The two Roman stories focus on the confession and conscience of the characters, and "Ars Vtillissima" is a treatise about how to prepare for death by looking into one's own heart. Here the connection between *Synonyma* and the "Ars" is especially noteworthy in terms of structure: they both proceed through dialogues, and, moreover, if we read the entire *Synonyma*, Reason's argument is strikingly resonant with that of Sapience in "Ars Vtillissima." These two texts have not been closely studied together in Hoccleve criticism, but we largely benefit from their thematic integrity for our better understanding of the structure of the *Series*.[13] Reason in *Synonyma*, outside Hoccleve's reference, directs our attention to the inner part of man and invites repentance. She tells the woeful man to acknowledge his own sin by exploring his inner world:

Examine your conscience, listen to your mind, question yourself, let your heart speak to you, consider your merit.[14]

The idea of dealing with one's conscience drives Hoccleve's project of translating "Ars Vtillissima." In "A Dialoge" Hoccleve declares his intention to translate "Lerne for to Die" to purify not only his soul but also interiority of the readers. He wishes his readers to examine their conscience and reflect upon their lives while they have time (218-224). This is also what the text of "Ars" tries to tell the readers. In the "Ars," the disciple character has an inner dialogue with the image of a dying man, who repents, on the verge of death, his unclean spirit and the corruption of heart. The disciple, after the image disappears, receives Sapience's advice to correct his life (826). According to Sapience, many folks are spiritually blind, and fail to search in their mind to know how they should live (869-75); they do not open their ears to correct themselves, either (876-78).

True repentance comes from the recognition of death. Both *Synonyma* and "Ars Vtillissima" focus on the imminent nature of the last hour to invite the reaction of the readers. *Synonyma*'s Reason tells the woeful man that people are approaching death every moment:

Look daily at the end of your life, have death before your eyes every hour, let the coming of darkness dwell always before your eyes. Think about your death every day, always consider the end of your life, recollect always the obscure day of death. Be anxious lest you are suddenly seized. Every day the last day approaches, daily we head toward the end, daily we pass over the road of life, daily we hurry to death, daily we head toward the end of life, we are led to the end as moments hasten by.[15]

Meanwhile, in "Ars Vtillissima," the image of a dying man provides an even more relentless view of one's death preparation.

"And so with al thyn herte it is the beste

Keepe thee foorth as þat thow this day right,
Or tomorwe or this wike atte fertheste,
Sholdist departe fro this worldes light,
And therwithal enforce thow thy might,
As Y shal seyn, in thyn herte to thynke,
And thow shalt it nat reewe ne forthynke. (484-90)

The thematic culmination of the *Series* lies in this message: we always need to be aware of our mortal nature, and conscience can be purified by remembering death. Hoccleve's "book," read in its entirety, intertextually corresponds to other parts of the *Series*, contributing to the integrity of the poem. The disciple figure in "Ars Vtillissima" learns how to die by experiencing the lesson in his mind; likewise, Hoccleve's act of reading functions as an inner experience which offers the poet with a thematic overview of his compilation.

Notes

1   A.G. Rigg, "Hoccleve's *Complaint* and Isidore of Seville," *Speculum* 45 (1970): 564-74. For Isidore of Seville himself, see Stephen A. Barney, W. J. Lewis, J. A. Beach, and Oliver Berghof, trans., *The Etymologies of Isidore of Seville* (Cambridge: Cambridge University Press, 2006), pp. 7-10.
2   The manuscripts are Bodley Selden Supra 53, Bodley 221, Bodley Laud misc. 735, and Coventry City Archives PA 325. See Rigg, "Hoccleve's *Complaint*," pp. 564-65 and Roger Ellis, ed., *'My Compleinte' and Other Poems* (Exeter: University of Exeter Press, 2001), pp. viii-ix.
3   Rigg, "Hoccleve's *Complaint*," pp. 565-66.
4   Burrow, "Hoccleve's *Complaint* and Isidore of Seville Again," *Speculum* 73 (1998): 424-28.
5   The *Book of the Duchess*, lines 46-49. All the citations from Chaucer's texts are taken from Larry D. Benson, ed., *The Riverside Chaucer*, 3rd ed. (Oxford: Oxford University Press, 1987), with line numbers given in the text.
6   For how old books beget new poems, see Piero Boitani, "Old Books Brought to Life in Dreams: the *Books of the Duchess*, the *House of Fame*, the *Parliament of Fowls*," Boitani and Jill Mann, eds., *Cambridge Chaucer Companion* (Cambridge: Cambridge

University Press, 1986), pp. 39-57.

7   All the citations from Hoccleve's works are taken from Roger Ellis, ed., *'My Compleinte' and Other Poems* (Exeter: University of Exeter Press, 2001).

8   Von Nolcken, "'O, why ne had y lerned for to die?' : *Lerne for to Die* and the Author's Death in Thomas Hoccleve's *Series*," *Essays in Medieval Studies* 10 (1993): 27-51, at 32. Also see my article about Hoccleve's dreamless visions: Hisashi Sugito, "Reality as Dream: Hoccleve's Daydreaming Mind," *The Chaucer Review* 49 (2014): 244-263.

9   Priscilla Throop, trans., *Isidore of Seville's* Synonyms (*Lamentations of a Sinful Soul) and Differences* (Charlotte: MedievalMS, 2012), p. 10. The original Latin text reads: "Isidorus lectori salute. Venit nuper ad manus meas quaedam scedula, quam Sinonimam dicunt, cuius formula persuasit animo quoddam lamentum mihi uel miseris condere." See Jacques Elfassi, ed., *Synonyma* (Turnhout: Brepols, 2009), p. 5.

10 See also J.A. Burrow and A.I. Doyle, eds., *Thomas Hoccleve: A Facsimile of the Autograph Verse Manuscripts* (Oxford: Oxford University Press), 2002.

11 In *Synonyma* we can read: "Here God always wounds those whom he prepares for eternal salvation." See Throop, trans., *Isidore of Seville's* Synonyms, p. 20.

12 The nature of Hoccleve's illness has attracted much critical attention. See for instance: Penelope B. R. Doob, *Nebuchadnezzar's Children: Conventions of Madness in Middle English Literature* (New Haven: Yale University Press, 1974); Matthew Boyd Goldie, "Psychosomatic Illness and Identity in London, 1416-1421: Hoccleve's *Complaint* and *Dialogue with a Friend*," *Exemplaria* 11 (1999): 23-52; Lee Patterson, " 'What is Me?' : Self and Society in the Poetry of Thomas Hoccleve," *Studies in the Age of Chaucer* 23 (2001): 437-70.

13 Studies on "Ars Vtillissima" include: John Bowers, "Hoccleve's Two Copies of *Lerne to Dye*: Implications for Textual Critics," *Papers of the Bibliographical Society of America* 83 (1989): 437-472; Steven Rozenski, Jr., " 'Your Ensaumple and Your Mirour' : Hoccleve's Amplification of the Imagery and Intimacy of Henry Suso's *Ars Moriendi*," *Parergon* 25. 2 (2008): 1-16; Robyn Malo, "Penitential Discourse in Hoccleve's *Series*," *Studies in the Age of Chaucer* 34 (2012): 277-305.

14 Throop, trans., *Isidore of Seville's* Synonyms, p. 23. "Discute conscientiam tuam, intende mentem tuam, examina te, loquatur tibi cor tuum, considera meritum tuum." Elfassi, ed., *Synonyma*, p. 29.

15 Throop, trans., *Isidore of Seville's* Synonyms, p. 28. "Vitae tuae cotidie terminum intuere, omni hora habeto mortem prae oculis, ante oculos tuos tenebrarum semper uersetur aduentus. De morte tua cotidie cogita, finem utiae tuae semper considera, recole semper diem mortis incertum. Esto sollicitus ne subito rapiaris. Cotidie dies

ultimus adpropinquat, cotidie ad finem tendimus, cotidie uiam transimus, ad mortem cotidie properamus, ad utiae terminum cotidie tendimus, momentis decurrentibus ad finem ducimur." Elfassi, ed., *Synonyma*, pp. 38-39.

聖人伝を読む——聖人伝の女性たち

池 上 惠 子

1. 聖女とは

　中世ヨーロッパに流布したキリスト教の布教文書である聖人伝（saints' lives）は、キリストの生涯を語る教会歴（Temporale）と狭義の聖人伝（Sanctorale）から成り、とくに後者は殉教者伝（martyrology）とも言われるように、キリスト教信仰を護り異教徒の迫害と拷問によって殉教した人たちの生涯を書き綴るのが原則である。そこに登場する女性たちは、その凄惨な拷問による殉教のありさままで人々によく知られ、彫像や絵画の主題となり文学作品に再話されてすでに多くの関連書物が存在する。しかし、聖人伝に登場する女性は、その様な殉教者だけではない。なお、聖人は女性も指すが、本小論ではローマ教会によって聖別（consecrate）された女性に聖女という名称を用いる。また、聖人伝でキリスト教徒と対立した異教徒とは、イスラム教徒やときに本来同じ起源をもつユダヤ教徒を指すと思われがちであるが、一部の聖人伝を除いて、キリスト教成立および布教の初期に対立したローマの偶像崇拝の者たちである。

　15 世紀に編纂された散文聖人伝 *Gilte Legende*（以下 *GiL*）全編 179 章（1 章重複）のうち Temporale を除く章および追加 3 写本（*ALL*）の 31 章を主要な対象として、[1] すでに殉教者として有名な聖女たちに限らず、聖人伝にさまざまな立場や役割で登場する女性を含めて、彼女たちがどのように描かれているのかを広く見ていきたい。典型的な聖女として一般に理解されている人物像とは異なる例も取り上げる。殉教に到る事情もさまざまであり、拷問による殉教ではなく自然死で帰天する聖女もいるように物語の内容は多岐にわたり複雑である。聖人伝を詳細に読むとき、それは「物語」であり、主要聖人の章に含まれる逸話に登場する女性たちの生き様も

語られている。聖女には歴史的に実在した女性と伝承にのみ存在する場合
があり、実在の場合も聖人伝の形式に沿うため史実ではない記述が多い。
聖書に書かれている人物の場合も聖人伝なりの改作が施されている。本小
論ではすべて *GiL* に書かれた「物語」の人物として扱い、特別な場合を除
き区別しない。

　聖女の主要条件を、ほぼ次のように定義することは否めない。聖女はし
ばしば異教徒の位の高い家に生まれた若い美貌の持ち主で、異教徒との結
婚を強いられて拒むか形式的に承諾しても処女性を護り、物語が始まる前
にすでにキリスト教徒となっているか物語中で改宗し、異教徒の神々への
拝礼、供香、捧げ物などを拒んで責め苛まれ、残酷な手段の拷問により殉
教する女性である。人々を改宗させるのも聖女の役割である。聖人の常と
して、聖女も各種の職業や人々の体験の守護聖人となる。殉教後に生じる
奇跡や教会奉献にも聖女は関わる。しかし、画一的に語られるとは限らな
い。本小論では *GiL* と *ALL* に書かれている内容に限定する。

　典型的な殉教者である聖マルガレータ（87. St. Margaret）[2] は、異教徒の
族長テオドシエンの娘で乳母に育てられ、密かに受洗してキリスト教徒と
なっていた。15歳の時乳母の羊の世話をしていて異教徒の長官オリブリ
ウスに見初められ「自由民なら妻に、そうでなければ妾にする。身分と美
しさは申し分ないが、キリスト教を信じることは認めない」と言われる。
父親は意のままにならない娘を牢に入れ、手下の者たちに打擲させる。彼
女は「肉体は痛め付けられても魂は神のもの」と言い健気に堪え忍ぶ。オ
リブリウスはその凄惨な姿を見るに堪えず衣で目を被う。彼女は再び投獄
され、竜が現れ彼女を呑み込むが、十字を切ると竜は砕けてしまう。彼女
は人間の男の姿で近づいた悪魔の髪を掴み地面に打ち付け右足で頸を踏み
つける。地面が揺れ、狂おしい大気が満ちても彼女は無傷で、神に祈る時
間を求めたのち斬首でこの世の生を終え殉教する。か弱い少女が強くなり、
数回に及ぶ拷問に耐えるという聖マルガレータ伝は人々に好まれたようで、
多数ある図像では竜を踏みつけている。

　生前の生き方が神の嘉するものでなく、ふしだらあるいは傲慢なつみび
とであったが回心して聖女となった例としては、エジプトの聖マリア（52.

St. Mary of Egypt）や聖タイース（145. St. Thais）がよく知られている。エ
ジプトの聖マリアは 12 歳でアレキサンドリアに移り、そこで娼婦として
17 年を過ごし、エルサレムに行く男達に同行し彼らの意のままになって
いた。エルサレムの門を入ることを禁じられたが、聖母マリアに祈って許
された。その後ヨルダン河を渡り砂漠で 47 年人に会わずに悔悛の日々を
送り、衣服は腐ってなくなった。ある日修道士ゾジマスが河を渡って来て、
全身日焼けし変り果てた裸の彼女に出会った。彼女は修道士に衣服を求め、
生涯を語り、聖金曜日に聖餅を受けた。翌年再び来て欲しいと頼まれた修
道士が訪れると、彼女は死んでいた。修道士はライオンの助力で墓穴を掘
り埋葬し、庵に戻って彼女の生涯の物語を書いた。聖タイースもまた、現
世での放埒な生き方を悔いた女性であった。平民の娘で美しく、多くの男
が彼女を求めて競い、財を失い血なまぐさい争いも起こした。修道士ペイ
ン（Payn; *GiL* のグロッサリーでは Pannutius, *Legenda Aurea* では Pafuntius）
は神を信じる敬虔な修道士であったが、世俗の姿で彼女を訪れ 12 シリン
グ渡し、彼女は誰の目にも触れない奥の部屋へと彼を寝室に誘う。神はす
べてをご存知ですと言う彼女にペインは、「神がすべてご存知なのを知っ
ているならば、神が地獄の苦しみで人を罰し神を信じる者は天国の恵みに
与ることを知らないのか」と続ける。鉤括弧のペインの言葉は *GiL* での用
心深い加筆であり、ペインが聖職者でありながらタイースの色香に迷う男
ではなく、信仰へ導く修道士であることが強調されている。タイースは男
達から得た財宝を町の人々の前で燃やし、ペインによって尼僧院の庵に閉
じ込められ入り口は鉛で塞がれた。ペインは口先だけで神や三位を語る彼
女を戒める。3 年経過し、修道僧アントニーの弟子たちの夢で、彼女の罪
が赦されたことを知ったペインが庵を開け神の赦しを告げ、彼女は 15 日
生きて帰天した。タイースの聖人伝は、アナトール・フランスの小説及び
マスネーの歌劇に脚色され、そこでは聖職者がタイースに対して抱く恋慕
が強調されている。

　聖テオドラ（86. St. Theodora）の場合は、神を信じる夫のある身なのに
不義を犯した過ちを悔い、男装して家を出て僧院に入った。物語では、テ
オドラの信仰心を妬んだ悪魔に唆されて金持ちの男を受け容れてしまった

池 上 惠 子

と書かれるが、悪魔は他者ではなく、自らの心の迷いと読める。世俗の華美な生活を悔いた女性の例としては、聖ペラギア（143. St. Pelagia）他がある。いずれも罪を悔いて聖女となっている。

2.　婚姻

2.1.　異教徒の求婚を拒絶する

　高貴な生まれの女性には財産が伴い、それを含めて美しい娘がしばしば異教徒の権力者の目にとまり婚姻を求められる。前出の聖マルガレータのように異教徒の父親が娘を有力者に嫁がせようとする例も多々ある。後述の聖クリスティーナの場合は、言うことを聞かない娘を父親が塔に閉じ込め、自ら手を下して拷問する。キリスト教を信じる女性は、異教徒との婚姻を拒んで捕らわれ、多くは拷問により殉教する。

2.2.　形式的結婚

　形式的に結婚するが夫を拒み処女性を護り、夫を改宗させる女性にはキリストの花嫁という思想が根底にある。[3] 聖セシリア（124. St. Cecilia 1; 126. St. Cecilia 2）は夫となったヴァレリアンに、あたかも愛する人がいるかのように語り、夫は猜疑心に悩むが、それがキリストと知って彼も改宗する。なお、聖アグネス（23. St. Agnes）は、異教徒の長官の息子に見初められるが、愛する人がいると言って断り、この若者は病に伏してしまった。

　夫から逃れた聖マルガレーテ・ペラギア（144. St. Margarete Pelagia）や夫が死んで自由になった聖アナスタシア（6. St. Anstasia）もいる。夫から逃げる手段として奇異なのは聖ブライド（ALL 7. St. Braide; Brigid of Ireland）である。父の命令で結婚するが、顔を醜く変えるよう神に願い、夫に嫌われ尼僧院へ行くことになった。

2.3.　キリスト教徒としての結婚

　生涯結婚しない女性は多数いるが、聖女が必ずしも未婚女性とは限らず、結婚して夫とともにキリスト教徒として生きた聖女もいる。平安な生活を

送り子どもを生み育てた聖女の例は稀であるが存在する。ハンガリーの聖エリザベト（161. St. Elizabeth of Hungary）はハンガリー王の娘として高貴な生まれながら世俗の華やかさを避けて信仰心篤く育った。5歳で教会へ行き始めたが同じ身分の子ども達と遊びつつも常に主の祈りや聖母崇敬を忘れなかった。父の願いで同じく身分の高い男性と結婚しても、みすぼらしい衣服をまとい、食事も慎ましくして貧者や病人の世話をした。夫も協力して貧者のための家を建てた。妻に頼まれて聖地を訪問した夫は死に彼女は財産を得たが、3人の子どもをそれぞれ人に預け、再び貧者への施しの生活を続けた。貧しくなった彼女に司教である伯父は再婚を勧め、父は家に戻るよう諭したけれど、彼女は清貧を望み慈善に専念し、病で帰天した。聖パウラ（28. St. Paula）にも夫と5人の子どもがあった。4人の娘を生んだ後、跡取りとして夫が望む男子を産んでいる。女児二人は夭折したが、娘の一人は母の最期まで行動を共にしている。夫の死後相続した財産を子どもたちには分け与えず、貧者や病人への施しに専念し、修道院も建てた。

　今回対象の聖人伝に登場する女性たちより時代は下るが、第三者による口述筆記または書きドろしの The Book of Margery Kempe で知られるマージェリーは、15世紀に生きた市井の商人の妻であり、8人の子どもがいた。行動力に富み財力があり聖地へも行き、たびたび発作を起こして幻視体験をしている。聖女となることを切に望んでいたのは彼女の妄想であったのか、神秘家（mystic）として認められる可能性があったのか、議論の余地がある。しかし、少なくとも結婚して子どもをもった上記の聖女たちの例と通底する部分がある。[4]

　聖ジェローム（ヒエロニムス）が語った聖マルコスの物語（66. St. Jerome on St. Malchus）では、聖マルコスとその妻となった女性はともに異教徒に捕らわれていて、雇い主に強いられて結婚するが、霊的夫婦として互いに助けあい異教徒から逃れ、老いて聖ジェロームに出会った。聖人伝では聖女となっていないこの女性は、夫を良く助ける賢明な妻として書かれている。

　生涯結婚しない聖女は多数いる。聖マグダラのマリア（90. St. Mary

Magdalen）について *GiL*（ll. 358-67）は、使徒聖ジョン（ヨハネ）が彼女
と結婚したという者がいるが、主は彼を婚礼の場から呼び戻したと書いて
この説を否定している。

3. 男装の聖女

　男装する女性は章のタイトルとなる聖女以外の章にも登場する。男装に
到る事情はさまざまで、自主的に男性と同等の修道生活を送るためという
近年のジェンダー論者の好みそうな理由ではないのが聖マリナ（77. St.
Marina）である。[5] 母親が死に、父親が修道院に入る際に娘マリナを一人残
せず、男装させて伴ったのである。自らの不義が原因とはいえ夫との婚姻
関係を拒み、男装して修道院へ逃れる例は、前出の聖テオドラがいる。マ
ルガレーテ・ペラギア（144. St. Margarete Pelagia）は婚礼の夜に髪を切り
男装し、男子修道院へ逃れた。男装した女性が、修道院近くに住む世俗の
娘の不義による妊娠の相手とされ、冤罪を堪え忍んで生まれた子を育て、
死んで初めて女性と判明するという構図は、聖マリナだけではなく、聖マ
ルガレーテ・ペラギアと聖テオドラも同様である。

　聖ペラギア（143. St. Pelagia）はマルガレーテと呼ばれ豊かな生まれで
着飾り贅沢の限りを尽くしていたが、司教ノイロン（Noyron）の導きで受
洗した。隠棲者の姿、つまり男の姿になって小さな庵に籠った。後日司教
はペラギアを訪ねるが変貌した姿から彼女と判らず、死んではじめてマル
ガレーテだったと知った。144章との類似および名前の重複はあるが、別
の人物として語られている。

　127. Sts. Protus and Hyacinthe に登場するユージニー（Eugeni）は男装して
修道士となったが、巷の娘が「彼」に言い寄られたと訴えた。ユージニー
は乳房を見せて、冤罪を晴らした。この章は、表題の2名というよりユー
ジニーの物語であるが、聖女にされていない。同様に異教徒に捕らわれた
夫とその仲間への差し入れのため、男装して獄を訪れるエピソードに登場
する妻（後出の聖エイドリアンの妻ナタリー）もいる。

　異装について、聖人伝はとくに異論を差し挟まない。男装はやむを得な

い事情があった、あるいは女性であることを隠す必要があったと分類できる。なお、男性が女装する場合は、悪魔が聖人あるいは聖女を誑かすために女の姿を取るので、好ましくないという評価が読み取れる。

4.　殉教あるいは帰天の経緯

　殉教にいたる拷問は、冒頭で述べたように、聖人伝の必須要素で猟奇的と言うべきであろうが、これをもって聖人伝を悪趣味と蔑むことは可能である。しかし、今回は言及しないが、神の力によって聖人や聖女が生前あるいは多くは帰天後に起こす種々の奇跡譚とともに拷問も類型的に語られ、神・キリストの力を示す布教文書の形式の一つと考える。奇跡については慎重な考察が必要であるとはいえ、人々の願望の現れと考えることもできる。

　拷問の典型はピッチ、タール、油その他金属を溶かした高熱の釜茹である。車輪型の刑具に張り付け引き裂く車刑は聖カテリーナの場合が有名で、車輪は彼女を表象するアトリビュート（表徴：attribute）となっている。ここに粗筋を書くことすら躊躇う *GiL* で最も残酷極まりない例は、聖クリスティーナ（92. St. Christina）の父親とその手下による拷問である。父親は娘を金銀財宝とともに 12 人の侍女を付けて塔に閉じ込めた。彼女は異教徒の神々への拝礼を拒んだ。父親の手下の 12 人の男が、彼女を裸にし、鞭打ち、鉤付き刑具で柔肌を裂いた。彼女は肉片を掴み父親に投げつけ、食べろと叫んだ。車輪に繋がれ火あぶりの後、重い石を頸に結びつけられて海に投げ入れられたが、天使ミカエルに救われた。さらに熱したピッチやタールの鉄桶に入れられ、髪を剃られ市中を引き回され、乳房を切られ矢で心臓と脇腹を射られついに絶命した。この極端な拷問を聖職者は人々に読み聞かせたであろうか、あるいは聴き手や読み手はこれでも神の救いを信じたであろうか。あるいは、残酷物語、つまりフィクション、として受け取ること、敢えて言うならば楽しむことがあり得たであろうか。

　聖アガタ（38. St. Agatha）も両乳房を切り取られ、乳房を乗せた皿を持つ図像がある。異教徒の実父による拷問は聖ジュリアナ（43. St. Juliana）、

聖バーバラ（*ALL* 31. St. Barbara）、前出の聖マルガレータ、その他の例が
あり、異教徒の残酷さを示そうとの意図が明らかである。

どのように過酷な拷問でも、神の助けで傷ついた肉体が元に戻ることも
あり、しばしば天使が現れて、拷問から救われる。しかし、その場合も最
終的にこの世の生を終わるのは斬首である。ただし斬首の試みは三回まで
との定めがあり、聖セシリアの場合、三回目を三日間生き延びて帰天した。
斬首が強調される聖女はウエールズの聖ウィニフレッド（*ALL* 2. St.
Winifred; Gwenfrewi）である。男に襲われ切り落とされた首が転げ落ちた
ところに水が湧き、今日 Holywell という地名の聖地となっているのは周
知のことである。なお、この聖女の聖遺物は特筆する聖人をもたなかった
シュロスベリー（Shrewsbury）に移葬（translate）され、町興しを担った。

拷問を受けず病死で帰天する聖女も少なからずいる。前出の聖タイース
のように現世を悔いた場合は拷問を受けていない。聖マグダラのマリアは
祭壇の前に横たわって、聖マルタは熱病で、帰天している。使徒ペテロの
娘とされている聖ペトロニーラ（71. St. Petronilla）は、熱病に冒されてい
て結婚を断り、絶食して帰天と書かれている。

5. 聡明な女性たち

聖人伝に登場する女性たちは、それぞれの立場で賢明に生きた聡明な女
性と読み取れる。とくに異教徒との議論で異教徒の学者たちを論破した聖
カテリーナ（165. St. Catherine）が、その典型である。コールの家系でセス
タ王の娘カテリーナは 14 歳で学校へ行き、7 人の学者から七芸を学んだ。
父の死後、母と家臣たちは彼女が結婚してその相手を王にと望むが、主イ
エスを理想の夫と考える彼女は拒絶する。エイドリアンに伴われ、砂漠で
聖母と殉教者たちに会い、エイドリアンがキリストとカテリーナの結婚を
司るが、キリストは指輪を残して消えた。[6] キリスト教徒が死を怖れて異
教の神々に供物をするのを見たカテリーナは、皇帝マクセンティウスが招
集した学者たちと激しく論争し、彼らを改宗させた。皇帝の求婚を拒絶し
た彼女は車刑ののち斬首で殉教した。物語の始め弱々しく描かれる前出の

聖マルガレーテも、獄に現れて彼女を傷めつけようとする竜の姿の悪魔つまり異教徒の男の表象を、踏みつけるだけでなく、雄弁な言葉でやり込めて追い払う。

　聖マルタ（99. St. Martha）はキリスト受難後に使徒たちと別れ、ある島に聖母の教会を建て女性たちと清貧で敬虔な日々を過ごした。彼女の説教を聞くために島に泳いで渡ろうとした男が溺れたのを助けたというエピソードが加わる。男装の聖女の一人のユージニーは、男装し修道士となる以前は、127章表題にあるふたりの男性聖プロヘトゥスと聖ヒアキントゥス（ヒアシンス）と共に学び、学芸に秀でていた。聖女たちの識字について具体的に言及のあるのは前出の聖パウラである。彼女は聖書の知識を持ち、ラテン語の影響の少ないヘブライ語を話し、ギリシャ語も使えたと書かれている。28章の聖パウラは修道女として多くの修道士や修道女を育てた。

　聖女たちの教育については、学校へ通っていたという記述が多数ある。たとえば聖フリーデスウィーデ（*ALL* 9. St. Frideswide）はオックスフォードの人で両親はキリスト教徒だった。5歳で学校へ行き信仰心ある女性たちと過ごした。前出 *ALL* 2章の聖ウィニフレッドが襲われたのは、いつも登校していたのに病で家にいたときのことだった。

　主要な聖女として語られるのではなく、男性の聖人伝に登場する女性にも強く聡明な女性がいる。聖エイドリアン（125. St. Adrian）の妻ナタリー（Nataly）は、迫害を怖れて密かにキリスト教徒となっていた。夫が投獄されたと知り嘆くが、その理由がキリストを信じたためと知り喜ぶ。夫は殉教の前に、獄吏に物を与え一時帰宅したが、妻は殉教を逃れたのだと思い家の戸口を開けない。夫は結婚してわずか14ヶ月の妻に別れを告げるために戻って来たのだった。これを知った妻は夫とともに牢に行き投獄されている仲間の傷の手当をした。帝は女性たちが牢にいるキリスト教徒の慰問に来ることを禁じたので、ナタリーは髪を切り男装し、他の女性たちもこれに倣った。殉教し切断されたエイドリアンの手をコンスタンチノープルへ運び、エイドリアンの遺体に手を戻し、帰天。異教徒の妻が、夫にキリスト教徒の助命を促した例もある。96. Sts. Nazarius and Celsus では、

ガリア（*GiL* では France）の裁判官が二人のキリスト教徒を投獄し翌朝拷
問すると知った妻は、無実の者を殺すのは正しくないと人を介して夫に助
言し、彼は説教をしないことを条件に二人を釈放した。

　聖人伝には、賢い女性だけでなく、よくありそうな口の軽い女も登場す
る。47. St. Benedict に、高貴な生まれながらお喋りな尼僧二人が戒められ
るエピソードがある。

　上記のように聖カテリーナ、ユージニー、その他女性が教育を受けてい
た例は複数書かれている。これが、たとえば聖母の図像でしばしばマリア
が書物を手にしている場合と同様女性の理想像なのか、どのような事実と
符合するのかは、本小論の域を超えて別途考察が必要である。信仰への導
き手としての修道士・聖職者が、聖女たちの教育を担っていたと考えられ、
学びの場は教会や修道院にあったと読み取れる。

　なお、女性による教育について、13 世紀に修道女の教養書として書か
れた *Ancrene Wisse*（または *Ancrene Riwle*）8 章の記述がある。[7] 修道女の生
活規範の一つとして、他者を教育することを禁じている。それは、神以外
に注意を逸らしてはいけないからだ、とある。少女たちが男性に教えられ
る際の危険を避けるならば、修道女に仕える女性にそれを任せよ、とある。
しかし、写本によって加筆箇所に、指導者の助言があれば、他者の学びの
助力をしてもよい、とあることも注目しておきたい。[8]

6.　聖人伝の受容と女性観

　女性蔑視（misogyny）が中世ヨーロッパに広く行き渡った思想であると
考えられている。その観点で *GiL* に例を拾えば、男性の女性蔑視の態度は、
おもに異教徒の男の態度として、少なからず読み取れる。しかし、前章で
述べた聡明な聖女に留まらず、女性は賢い存在として書かれていることが
多いのである。俗世にあって物欲に溺れ不義を犯した女性であっても悔悛
で救われるのは聖人伝の型であるとは言え、現実にありうる女性の生き様
を書きながら、一方的な蔑視ではないのである。

　聖女たちの評価の基本には、聖母マリア崇敬という中世キリスト教にお

ける絶対的な価値観があった。[9] 聖母マリアは穢れなく、美しく慈愛に満ちた女性である。しかし、*GiL* には興味深い挿話がある。聖母マリアの生涯を語る章のうち、123. Nativity of Virgin, ll. 305-32 には、聖母マリアがいわば普通の女性のように描かれている。聖母を崇敬し日々祈りを捧げていたある男が妻を娶ることになり忙しさに聖母への祈りを怠った。教会の前を通りふと思い出して聖母に祈ろうとしたとき聖母が現れ、「愚か者、そなたの愛する妻である私から離れて別の女を娶るのか」と男を叱責した。ここの聖母はあたかも嫉妬する普通の女のように描写されている。男は悔いて表向きは結婚を継続するふりをしながら修道会に入り生涯聖母に心を捧げ尽くした。この挿話は聖人伝の形式で終わるとはいえ、当時の読者あるいは聴者の女性たちはここをどのように読んだあるいは聴いたのであろうか。マリア様も自分たちと同じ女性だったと思うことは許されたであろうか。

　GiL に多数ある加筆には、目的語 "the whiche fulfilled the fader and the moder"（75. Sts. Vitus and Modestus, l. 19）や主語 "he receiued baptime and his wyff and his meyne and many other"（104. St. Peter in Chains, l. 101）など「女性」を追加した箇所（下線部）が複数ある。*GiL* のコロフォン（MS Oxford Bodleian Douce, f. 163vb）で "synfulle wrecche" と匿名で名乗る書き手が、女性聴者および読者も意識したのは確かである。

　GiL がどのように利用されたのか問わねばならない。15 世紀半ばに差し掛かる頃すでに一般平信徒の男性にはかなりの母語つまり英語の識字力があったと推定される。女性にも聖人伝の女性の生き方を聞き取り理解する能力のみならず平易な英語散文を読める人もいたであろう。それは、*GiL* の冒頭（MS BL Harley 4775, f. 1ra）にこの聖人伝の目的として "... to excite and stere simple lettrid men and women to encrese in virtue bi the often redinge and hiring of this boke." と記されていることから明白である。*GiL* は、文意や構文を判りやすくする修正を加えた散文体で書かれている。それは読み手や聴き手を「簡単な読解力の男女」を想定してのことであるのは確かである。[10] すでに 13 世紀に母語の英語で書かれた *Ancrene Wisse* の匿名の著者は、社会の上層部出身という限定はあるが、修道女が読むことを大前提として

いる。教会の制度や規範が変化する直前の時代のイングランドにおける *GiL* の受容については、客観的エヴィデンスを得ることが今後の研究に望まれる。

　GiL には今回対象の女性に限らず、人々が体験する諸々の社会現象や世相が描かれている。[11] 聖人伝の評価は、理性の時代と言われる 16 世紀に、ローマ教皇庁を離れイギリス国教成立に到る時代変化とともに著しく低下した。聖人伝を saints' legend とも言うが、17 世紀初めには、この'legend'に虚偽の物語という定義が加わったことを *Oxford English Dictionary* [12] は記録している。聖人伝のいわば終焉とも言える時代になった。

　しかし、*GiL* の原文を精読して読み取れる内容は、当時の実社会を彷彿とさせる。さらに、今日の歴史・文化を異にする人々にも通底する人間の生き様が書かれているとも言える。聖人伝が聖人を信仰の手本とし、奇跡も殉教も神そしてキリストの御業と解釈し、聴き手あるいは読み手の信仰心を高める宗教書であるとの大前提を超えて聖人伝を読んで良いのかと問わねばならないが、卑近な話題の例え話を用いるのも宗教書あるいは説教の常套手段である。我が国にも仏教説話から発展し物語性をもった説経節と言うジャンルがある。書き残された聖人伝を、聖と俗に二分することを避けて改めて「物語」（narrative）として再評価することを提案したい。

注

1. Richard Hamer and Vida Russell（2006, 2007, 2012）. *GiL* の追加として成立した写本のうち主要 3 写本 *Additional Lives*, Hamer and Russell（2000）は *ALL* と略記される。*GiL* に先行し、その成立に深く関わった中世フランス語 *Légende dorée* およびその元となった *Legenda Aurea*、さらに *GiL* の約 50 年後にこの 3 点を利用して成立した *Caxton's Golden Legend* は、一般にそれぞれ先行する聖人伝の「翻訳」と言われるが、言語の変更に留まらず、加筆修正、聖人伝各章の削除追加、章の配列も異なり、単なる翻訳とは言えないのである。前田敬作（1979, 1987）が *Legenda Aurea* 邦訳の際、第一巻凡例で Caxton を挙げて「英語版はほとんど役に立たなかった」と記しているが、各種聖人伝集の成立過程および伝播の実態を知れば、異本の存在は当然である。
2. 聖女その他の固有名詞のカタカナ表記は、*GiL* の表記をそのまま読む場合

と一般に通用していると思われるものを用いる場合がある。聖人伝の固有
名詞の表記はさまざまである。聖女名初出の後に括弧で *GiL* および *ALL* の
章番号と、そのタイトル表記を加える。

3. Mango Museum, Glasgow は世界各地の宗教関連資料をやや雑多に集めている
   が、1900 年台に、3 人の女性がキリストとの結婚のため花嫁衣装を着て修
   道院に入る写真があった。

4. Stanford Brown Meech and Hope Emily Allen eds. *The Book of Margery Kempe.*
   EETS 212（1940）. マージェリーについては、神秘主義の聖女と扱うなど過大
   な評価もあるが、聖別はされていない。世俗での生活も含めて、聖地へも
   赴き、聖女になるという望みを遂げようと逞しく生きた女性には違いない。
   ローマ教皇庁の聖別とは異なる基準で祝日を認める英国国教会の日課表で
   は、November 9, Margery Kempe, Mystic, c.1440 とされている。*The Lectionary* ,
   SPCK 参照。

5. 聖マリナ伝は英文学を学んだ芥川龍之介が *Legenda Aurea* の英語訳で知り、
   それを一つの原典として『奉教人の死』を書いた。Ellis ed. *Golden Legend* を
   見たという説があるが、近代文学館収蔵の彼の蔵書には、George V. O'Neill
   ed. *The Golden Legend*, Cambridge UP（1914）もある。
   Ikegami Keiko, "The Medieval Roots of Akutagawa Ryunosuke's *The Martyr*: 'De
   Sancta Marina Virgine' Transformed", in *In Geardagum*: *Essays on Old and Middle
   English* XV, The Society for New Language Study（1994）, pp. 31-51. 参照。

6. *GiL* の聖カテリーナ伝は 877 行と長いが、Hamer（2012）の注によれば、エ
   ディションで l. 544 までの出典は不明、l. 545 以下は *Légende dorée* に依る。

7. Bella Millett（2009）, p. 161. Kubouchi & Ikegami et al（2005）, p. 198; A 114v20-25.

8. Bella Millett（2009）, pp. 274-75.

9. 本小論では扱わないが、聖母マリアの生涯は 5. Nativity およびイエスキリス
   トの章の他、以下の Tempolare の章で語られる。章の配列は教会歴順である。
   123. Nativity of the Virgin, 177. Conception of the Virgin, 36. Purification of the
   Virgin, 112. Assumption of the Virgin.

10. *GiL* の加筆修正について：池上惠子「中英語散文 *Gilte Legende* の言語的特
    徴」第 33 回日本中世英語英文学会全国大会、2017 年 12 月 3 日、立教大学、
    研究発表。

11. 池上惠子（2019）, pp. 31-46;（2020）, pp. 214-31.

12. *OED*, legend 6a. An unauthentic or non-historical story, esp. one handed down by
    tradition from early times and popularly regarded as historical. 1613.（1989: printed）.
    池上惠子「中世イギリス聖者伝：隆盛と終焉」第 84 回日本英文学会招待発
    表、2012 年 5 月 26 日、専修大学生田校舎。

池 上 惠 子

主要文献

Hamer, Richard, and Vida Russell eds. *Supplementary Lives in Some Manuscripts of Gilte Legende.* EETS 315, 2000.

Hamer, Richard, and Vida Russell eds. *Gilte Legende*, Vol. I. EETS 327, 2006; Vol. II. EETS 328, 2007; Vol. III. EETS 339, 2012.

参照文献

Dunn-Lardeau, Brenda ed. *Jaques de Voragine: La Légend dorée.* Paris: Champion, 1997.

Ellis, F. S. ed. *The Golden Legend or Lives of Saints as Englished by William Caxton,*7 vols, London: 1900.

Graesse, Th. ed. *Jacobi A Voragine; Legenda Aurea, Reproductio Phototypica editionis tertiae 1890.* Osnabrück: Otto Zeller Verlag, 1969.

Kubouchi, Tadao, and Keiko Ikegami et al eds. *The* Ancrene Wisse: *A Four-Manuscript Parallel Text, Parts 5-8 with Wordlists.* Frankfurt am Main: Peter Lang, 2005.

The Lectionary, Society for Promoting Christian Knowledge.

Millett, Bella. *Ancrene Wisse: Guide for Anchoresses: A Translation.* University of Exeter Press, 2009.

Simpson and Weiner, *The Oxford Dictionary of English*, Scond Edition, Volume VIII. Oxford: Clarendon Press, 1989 [printed].

Taguchi, Mayumi and John Scahill with Satoko Tokunaga eds. *Caxton's Golden Legend,* Vol. 1, EETS o.s. 355, Oxford UP, 2020. Introduction, pp. xvii-lxxvi.

池上惠子「中世後期イギリス聖人伝を読む」『英米文学 Rikkyo Review: Arts & Letters』No. 79. 立教大学文学部英米文学専修、2019、pp. 31-46.

池上惠子「聖人伝を読む―聖人伝に見る世相」菊池清明、岡本弘毅編『中世英語英文学研究の多様性とその展望―吉野利弘先生・山内一芳先生 喜寿記念論文集』2020：春風社、pp. 214-31.

前田敬作・今村孝訳『ヤコブス・デ・ヴォラギネ黄金伝説 1』人文書院（1979, 1987）.

Fairies in the Middle English Romance *Sir Orfeo*
as the *Daoine Maithe* of Irish Folk Tales

Kanako Arisaka

1. Introduction

The Middle English romance *Sir Orfeo* was recorded in the form of manuscripts from the first half of the fourteenth century to the beginning of the fifteenth century. The author is unknown. *Sir Orfeo* has 602 lines and is classified into the "Matter of Britain," particularly into Breton lays, which incorporates Celtic motifs.[1]

Sir Orfeo owes its origins to the Greek myth of Orpheus and Eurydice[2] even though its "Other World" is very different from the one depicted in *Sir Orfeo*.[3] "The Other World" in the Greek myth is a dark and terrifying world of the dead, while in *Sir Orfeo* it is described as a magnificently luxuriant and picturesque Celtic fairyland. The two stories are similar in plot, but fairies or beings as vital manifestations do not appear in the Greek myth. The fairy is indispensable for understanding the nature of the poem.

This paper aims to clarify the significance of the fairy in *Sir Orfeo* by comparing it with the *daoine maithe* in Irish folk tales, which provides an essential background for a better understanding of the fairy depicted in *Sir Orfeo*.

2. Dead or Alive?: Heurodis in *Sir Orfeo*

In *Sir Orfeo*, Heurodis, the wife of Orfeo, happens to fall asleep one day, "Vnder a fair ympe-tre" (68), or "under a fair grafted tree," and the King of Fairies appears in her dream along with his knights and damsels. He spirits her away with him and shows her around his realm. He then bids her return to the place where she is dreaming at the same time the next day so she can go away with him forever.

Heurodis is distraught and almost driven to insanity when she awakens. She ultimately informs Orfeo that she must part from him.

The next day, Orfeo tries to protect her by forming an impenetrable bodily shield around her along with a thousand knights. The events are put into verse:

Ac ʒete amiddes hem ful riʒt
Þe Quen was oway ytuiʒt,
Wiþ fairi forþ ynome,
Men wist neuer wher sche was bicome.

(*Sir Orfeo*, 189–192)

However, the plan to save her is ineffective and despite the best efforts of Orfeo and his knights, Heurodis is "ytuiʒt"[4] away with the mysterious and powerful "fairi."[5] According to the *Oxford English Dictionary*, the word *fairy* has several meanings, and the word in *Sir Orfeo* (191) can be construed as "enchantment" or "magic." The *fairi* makes it possible for Heurodis to "dis-appear" faster than the human characters could understand or react. After the loss of his wife, Orfeo, spends his life wandering in the primeval forest until he finally reaches his destination, fairyland. Here he sees Heurodis lying within the castle walls. She is not the only one who has been brought there. The poet depicts the scene:

Sum stode wiþouten hade,
And sum non armes nade,
And sum þurch þe bodi hadde wounde,
And sum lay wode, ybounde,
And sum armed on hors sete,
And sum astrangled as þai ete,
And sum were in water adreynt,
And sum wiþ fire al forschreynt:
Wiues þer lay on child-bedde,
Sum ded, and sum awedde;

And wonder fele þer lay bisides,

Riȝt as þai slepe her vndertides;

(*Sir Orfeo*, 389–400)

In *Sir Orfeo*, the fairyland appears to be filled with beauty; however, the sights that Orfeo witnesses in the castle do not fit its magnificence.

Line 389 quoted above, "sum stode wiþouten hade" suggests a hideous death and those that follow until 391 seem to describe a scene akin to the aftermath of a cruel war. The people described in line 389 are still standing even though they have lost their heads, suggesting that the knights were killed so suddenly in an intense war experience that they remained unaware of their own deaths. The postures of these dead knights bear testimony to their exemplary bravery and sincerity.

Some "lay wode, ybounde" (392) or "lay mad, bound." Seen from the perspective of warfare, these people were possibly taken prisoners since they are "ybounde." If people are placed in such a terribly desperate situation, they would be "wode." Some "armed on hors sete" (393), but it is not clear whether these people are dead or wounded. They do not appear to suffer difficulties, but it is unknown whether they continue in good health: the scene could signify their last living moment. The line, "Sum astrangled as þai ete" (394) does not evince a direct connection to war; instead, it describes people who died while eating, or choked to death. To continue "sum were in water adreynt" (395) or drowned; these people could also be knights if a war is being described. They could have "adreynt" as they tried to cross a moat. There are also "sum wiþ fire al forschreynt" (396), or shrunken by fire, a common way people are killed and structures destroyed in times of war. Finally, there are "wiues" who "lay on child-bedde" (397) embodying the women who often died at childbirth in medieval England.

All the people are described as appearing to be dead or it may at least be said that the number of the dead would outnumber that of the living. The poet of *Sir Orfeo* seems to have difficulty explaining their true state. He speaks of "Sum ded and sum awedde" (398), which is inconsistent with the expression of "And þouȝt dede and nare nouȝt" (388). In other words, the poet says that they are thought to be dead but are not actually not dead (388), then 10 lines later he acknowledges that some are dead and some are mad (398). However, the poet himself cannot be certain about the exact condition of the people. He can only describe people dying from his own general experience.

Orfeo finally observes that many people are sleeping at "vndertides," or "around noon" (400), and finds his wife Heurodis among them. The profile of a sleeping person sometimes resembles that of a dead person and whether the "sleeping" people in this scene are alive or dead remains unclear. Most of the people described in the scene seem to be fatally wounded or dead. Thus, it is difficult to regard Heurodis' sleep as ordinary.

Importantly, Heurodis is not described as being dead in the fairyland in *Sir Orfeo*; rather, she is temporarily asleep. In the original Greek myth, Eurydice accidentally treads on a serpent that bites her and she dies from its venom. Similarly, in the Japanese myth of Izanagi and Izanami, Izanami also dies from a burn caused from birthing the Fire God.[6] As they die, the souls of Eurydice and Izanami separate from their bodies and travel to the world of the dead. Thus, both the traditional myths describe death, while *Sir Orfeo* differs in keeping Heurodis alive and merely asleep.

Although death and sleep convey discrete meanings, they are also related. For example, Hypnos, son of Erebos and Nyx, is the god of sleep in Greek mythology. His twin brother Thanatos is the god of death. Thus, the close relationship between death and sleep has been recognized, and both phenomena have been personified in mythology. To cite a literary example, William Shakespeare refers to the relationship between death and sleep in *Hamlet* as "To die, to sleep—No more, and by a sleep to say we end...." Percy B. Shelley also exhibits the intimacy of death and sleep in "To Night": "Thy brother death came, and cried, / Would thou me? / Thy sweet child sleep, the filmy-eyed, ..." The poet of *Sir Orfeo* accepts that Heurodis is asleep and describes it as such; nevertheless, whether her condition in the fairyland should be regarded as sleep or death remains open to question.

3. The Similarity Between the Folk Tale "The Coffin" and *Sir Orfeo*

As George L. Kittredge points out, *The Wooing of Étaín,* an early Irish legend reflecting Celtic thought,[7] greatly influences *Sir Orfeo.*[8] Some other Irish folk tales are also related to *Sir Orfeo* including "The Coffin," a story collected by Kevin Danaher,[9] a prominent Irish folklorist. Danaher inscribed a folk story memorized and narrated to him by John Herbert in 1967 in county Limerick in Ireland where Danaher was born. A scrutiny of this folk tale leads to a deeper understanding of the fairy of *Sir Orfeo.* The plot of "The Coffin" may be outlined as follows:

> Long time ago, there was a young married man. One night, when he was sitting by the fire in the kitchen with his wife and some other people, the door of his house opened, and four men came in with a coffin. They laid it down in the middle of the house without uttering a single word and then turned and walked out. These four men were strangers to the people of the house.
>
> After a while, the young man plucked up his courage and lifted the coffin's cover. There was a young girl lying in it. She was not dead but breathing, as if she were asleep. She woke up in about half an hour. She told them that she went to bed, as always, at home and the next thing she knew was to wake up in this house.
>
> The next day they started off for Newtown, which was the girl's home. It was a journey of about 15 miles. According to her parents, they thought their daughter was dead in her sleep a few days ago, and they held a wake and buried her. Later, they sent a few men to the churchyard to open the grave and found the coffin in the grave empty.

It is apparent from the story that the parents accept the sad fact of their daughter's death and do not doubt its veracity because they hold a wake for her and bury her. If they had any hope of her being alive, they would not have completed her last rites. In other words, the tale clearly conveys her clear death in terms of general human knowledge.

The death of the girl during her sleep one night in "The Coffin" corresponds to the series of the scenes in *Sir Orfeo* describing Heurodis falling asleep under a fair grafted tree (68), her madness, and her final conversation with her husband (178). "The Coffin" does not include a section alluding to the circumstances of the girl's death; however, *Sir Orfeo* details what happens to Heurodis. Heurodis is not herself when she awakens from her sleep and returns to consciousness in this world. Two maidens discover her near madness. Not knowing what to do, they rush to the Orfeo's palace to seek help, and Heurodis is carried back to the castle. Although she is a beautiful woman, she suddenly changes after waking from her sleep. Orfeo, seeing his wife, says:

> "O lef liif, what is te
> Þat euer ȝete hast ben so stille,
> And now gredest wonder schille!
> Þi bodi, þat was so white ycore,
> Wiþ þine nailes is al totore!
> Alas, þi rode, þat was so red,
> Is al wan as þou were ded!
> And also þine fingers smale
> Beþ al blodi and al pale!
> Allas! þi louesum eyȝen to
> Lokeþ so man doþ on his fo!
> (*Sir Orfeo,* 100-110)

Orfeo is surprised at the change in her demeanor. Heurodis "euer ȝete hast ben so stille," or "has been ever so still," but now "gredest wonder schille," or "cries frantically loud." She used to have "white ycore" skin. According to the *OED*, the word "ycore" is "chosen, fair, comely," but now "al totor" or "all torn" by her nails. She scratches herself until she bleeds. Her beautiful complexion is completely dull, and she looks almost dead. Orfeo further bewails that his wife used to have lovely eyes that now look like they are gazing at enemies: "þi louesum ey3en to / Lokeþ so man doþ on his fo." Thus, after her re-awakening, Heurodis becomes a very different woman than the one introduced at the beginning of *Sir Orfeo*: "Þe fairest leuedi for þe nones / Þat mi3t gon on bodi and bones, / Ful of love and godenisse / Ac no man may telle hir fairnize" (51–54). In brief, these lines confirm that she is so much the fairest lady that no one can describe her beauty. It is difficult to judge whether her appearance remains as graceful after her experiences. However, her madness and the contrasts in her conduct and looks suggest that she must be dying.

In the next sequence in *Sir Orfeo*, the fairies appear and take Heurodis away to the fairyland using their mysterious powers. Although "The Coffin" does not have a corresponding event, the story does describe four men mysteriously carrying a coffin that holds the girl to a house that is not hers. The girl in the coffin wakes up in a stranger's home after she goes to bed one night at her own home. The information offered in the entire story can only yield the inference that the four men took her body from inside the coffin that was buried in the grave and placed her in another coffin which they brought to the kitchen of a house 15 miles away from her home. A power beyond human knowledge and understanding is thus implied from the events that have unfolded. Unlike the appearance of the fairies in *Sir Orfeo*, however, the four men in "The Coffin" appear without any omen. The nature of these men is examined in the next section.

4. The *daoine maithe* of Irish folk tales

Dorena Allen's article[10] specifically attends to the ambiguous expression from *Sir Orfeo* cited above "they are thought to be dead, but actually, they are not dead" (388). Her commentary on this line is noteworthy:[11]

> .....less than a hundred years ago an Irish or a Scottish countryman would have recognized in them the echo of his own convictions: "Very few die at all, most are *taken*. When a man dies, he does not die at all, but the *daoine*

maithe take him away. No-one dies, but the *daoine maithe* take him away, and leave something else in his place.[12]

She thus illuminates that people in some regions of Ireland or Scotland believed not so long ago that their dead were not completely dead, merely taken away by the *daoine maithe*. According to the *Irish-English Dictionary*, the term *daoine* signifies "the people, everybody, the public," and *maithe* means "good, kind, appropriate, useful, skillful, happy, wholesome, well." The dictionary entry on *maithe* incorporates the compound *daoine maithe* or "the good people, the fairies."[13] The fairies in *Sir Orfeo* and the four men in "The Coffin" can hence be considered *daoine maithe*.

The moment of death suddenly visits the girl in "The Coffin" one night. Her body is left behind as a sleeping figure and she hence appears dead to her family. However, she is saved shortly after her burial by the four "good people." After she returns home alive, the girl's surprised family sends people to check her grave, only to find an empty coffin. In the end, she remains alive to everyone. She is too young to die. The four men deserve appreciation.

As per *Sir Orfeo*'s source, the Greek myth of Orpheus and Eurydice, the latter is accidentally bitten by a serpent. She dies and goes to Hades, a dark and terrifying world of the dead. Given this context, it may be assumed that *Sir Orfeo*'s Heurodis is meant to suffer the same misfortune as Eurydice. The very moment when Heurodis is to die, however, the King of Fairies and his knights appear, and using their mysterious power, they spirit her safely away to their land before she expires completely. Although the King of Fairies in *Sir Orfeo* is described as her merciless abductor and is blamed because he forcibly separates Heurodis from her husband, he may not be culpable. The fairyland in *Sir Orfeo* is depicted as a brightest and extremely beautiful realm, a quality that could symbolize the virtuous aspect of the goodness of the King of the Fairies.

In *Fairy and Folk Tales of the Irish peasantry*, Yeats described some other facets of the *daoine maithe*: "Do not think the fairies are always little. Everything is capricious about them, even their size. They seem to take what size or shape pleases them."[14] The size or shape of both the fairies in *Sir Orfeo* and the four men in "The Coffin" seem human in proportion. Orfeo must learn the size and shape of the fairies to defeat the King of Fairies and his people, but the poet of *Sir Orfeo* does not offer any special physical markers about the fairies, perhaps because the size and shape were not remarkable and the fairies in *Sir Orfeo* were the same size and shape as humans. In "The Coffin," the four men are also big enough to carry a coffin between them.

Yeats also comments, "Witness the nature of the creatures, their caprice, their way of being good to the good and evil to the evil, having every charm but conscience – consistency."[15] In "The Coffin," the four men are quick to act in transporting the coffin with the girl to a human habitation without any advance notice and thus they save the girl from her destiny. The girl's temperament is not described in the story, but there is no indication that she is evil. In *Sir Orfeo,* similarly, no heralds announce the coming of the King of Fairies. He chooses to take Heurodis at a whim. Although the King of Fairies deprives Heurodis of her happy life with her husband, he bears her no malice. The fairies merely perform a good deed for Heurodis, "the fairest lady with full of love and goodness" (51-54). The caprice of the King of Fairies ends up sustaining her life.

What appears to be death to humans is not death to both the fairies in *Sir Orfeo* and the four men in "The Coffin." In both narratives, the mysterious powers of "good people" are harnessed to save young lives on the verge of death. They show up unpredictably and do good to the good. Being the same size as human beings, they seem human at first glance, but they are not humans by nature. Arguably, they are the *daoine maithe*, who appear as fairies in *Sir Orfeo*.

5. "Fairy" and "Fate"

The term *fate* is intimately related to the word *fairy*. The *OED* explains the origin of the word fairy as "*faerie*," "*faierie*," or "*fae*" in Old French, which originates in the Latin *fata* (plural of *fatum*), meaning fate. The word evolved into *fay*, equivalent to fairy. Thus, the *OED* explains that the English word fairy is derived from the Latin *fatum*.

In the context of the traditional myths, the sudden deaths of Eurydice and Izanami make their lives irrecoverable. They die completely and there is thus no hope for their return to the world of human existence. Their sudden deaths are so unexpected that their husbands deeply mourn their absence. Their deaths are ascribed to fate. Fate represents destiny that is beyond human power, and that cannot be changed; even the god of the underworld, Hades, cannot interfere with fate. Eurydice and Izanami go straight to the world of the dead, to Hades and the land of Yomi, respectively.

Yeats states in his work, "[the *daoine maithe*] will do best to keep misfortune away from you."[16] The *daoine maithe* in "The Coffin" come to the girl and the fairies in *Sir Orfeo* appear to Heurodis capriciously, just in time for them to avoid their encounter with the fatality. The sudden appearance of the *daoine maithe* is indispensable for Heurodis and the girl to overcome the sudden death that is to befall them. These stories thus explain the essence of fate: invisible but described in these narratives as visible and magical fairies. Thus, the *fairy* could be an anthropomorphization of *fate*.

6. Concluding Remarks

The poet of *Sir Orfeo* may find it impossible to offer adequate explanation for Heurodis' physical condition in fairyland: is she merely asleep or actually dead? From the above cited depiction of the other fatally wounded or dead observed in *Sir Orfeo*'s fairyland, it would be natural to interpret her state as dead in a manner similar to Eurydice in the Greek myth or Izanami in the Japanese myth. In "The Coffin," too, the girl is perceived to be dead by her family members.

However, one cannot easily accept the death of a beloved. People universally desire their loved ones to remain alive regardless of time or place. Certainly, the thoughts, emotions, and desires of the Irish people of yore created the *daoine maithe*, as reflected in the Irish folk tale, "The Coffin."

This paper has evinced that the fairies in *Sir Orfeo* are equivalent to the *daoine maithe* or the "good people" of Irish folklore who rescue the virtuous who are destined to die from misfortune. The compound term *daoine maithe* encompasses the connotation of supernatural phenomena that transcend human knowledge. These supernatural "good people" are comparable to the English *fairy*, a word that is etymologically derived from the Latin *fate*. The *daoine maithe* who spirit Heurodis away in *Sir Orfeo* just before her death do not appear in the Greek source; they materialize as fairies in the Middle English adaptation of the Greek myth, perhaps to reflect the innermost desires buried within the minds and hearts of the romance's audiences. This universal human hope over countless generations for loved ones to stay alive has crystallized into the *daoine maithe* who appear as fairies in *Sir Orfeo*.

Notes

1 Walter H. French and Charles B. Hale, eds., *Middle English Metrical Romances*. 2 vols (1930; repr., New York: Russell and Russel, 1964). The numbers of the quoted lines in this paper correspond with this edition.

2 The classical legend of Orpheus and Eurydice, found most prominently in Virgil's *Georgics* IV, Ovid's *Metamorphoses* X, and Boethius' *Consolation of Philosophy*, forms the primary source of *Sir Orfeo*.

3 Howard R. Patch refers in his work *The Other World* to a variety of worlds that people imagine. What Patch designates as "the Other World" can represent something that potentially exists in the human mind. The concept of "the Other World" includes fairylands and countless imagined worlds that poetry, music, and other arts can create. The concept also includes the place where the dead stay when their worldly lives are over; it also includes Heaven, where God and deities live. This paper adopts his concept of "the Other World." See Howard. R. Patch, *The Other World according to Descriptions in Medieval Literature* (Cambridge: Harvard University Press, 1950), 1. In this paper, "the Other World" contrasts with "this world." In the stories dealt with here, the world that contrasts with "this world" is always "the Other World," not "another world."

Kanako Arisaka

4   The word "ytuiʒt" is the past participle form of "twig." According to the *Oxford English Dictionary*, in the medieval period "twig" was defined: "Twig, v3 [Of obscure origin; perh. merely an imitative word of the same type as Twick, tweag, Tweak, and Tug.] ... 2. To pull, pluck, twitch. It is considered to be a sudden pull." Readers refer to *The Oxford English Dictionary*. 2nd ed. 20 vols. (1989; Oxford: Oxford University Press). All quotations from the *OED* are based on this version. According to the *Collins Dictionary of the English Language,* edited by Patrick Hanks (London: Collins, 1979), "twitch" means "1. to move or cause to move in a jerky spasmodic way. 2. to pull or draw (something) with a quick jerky movement."

5   Interestingly, the informal British phrase "away with the fairies" describes a person who seems insane or abstracted, as if in a dreamworld.

6   The myth of Izanagi and Izanami is included in the *Kojiki* (『古事記』) (712) and the *Nihon-Shoki* (『日本書紀』) (720).

7   George L. Kittredge, "*Sir Orfeo*," *American Journal of Philology*, vii (1886), 176-202.

8   Kittredge believes that *The Wooing of Étaín* greatly influences *Sir Orfeo*, although Alan J. Bliss disagrees with this view. For details, see G. L. Kittredge, "*Sir Orfeo*," *American Journal of Philology* vii (1886), 191-193, and A. J. Bliss, ed., *Sir Orfeo* (1954; repr., London: Oxford University Press, 1961), xxxiii-xxxv.

9   Henry Glassie, ed., *Irish Folktales* (1985; repr., Suffolk: Penguin Books, 1987), 142-143.

10   Dorena Allen, "Orpheus and Orfeo: The Dead and the *Taken*," *Medium Aevum* 33 (1964), 102-111.

11   Allen, "Orpheus and Orfeo," 104.

12   Allen notes: "Quoted from material in the possession of the Irish Folklore Commission, Dublin, by kind permission of Professor J. Delargy. These remarks were recorded in this century by collectors working in Gaelic-speaking Ireland." See Allen, "Orpheus and Orfeo," 104.

13   Patrick S., Dinneen, comp. and ed. *Irish-English Dictionary* (1927; repr., Dublin: The Educational Company of Ireland, 1975).

14   William B. Yeats, ed., *Fairy and Folk Tales of the Irish Peasantry* (1888; repr., New York: Dover Publications, 1991), 2.

15   Yeats, *Fairy and Folk Tales of the Irish Peasantry,* 1.

16   Yeats, *Fairy and Folk Tales of the Irish Peasantry,* 1.

"Chevalier sans cheval"
——Tryamour の馬の死に対する無関心について

貝 塚 泰 幸

1.

Sir Tryamour は 14 世紀後期に成立したとされる中英語騎士物語である。[1]
この物語を完全な形で収録している写本は Cambridge University Library Ff.
2. 38 写本だけであるが、いわゆる Percy Folio 版や 16 世紀の印刷本が複数
現存していることから、物語が長く人々に親しまれていたことが窺い知れ
る。中英語ロマンスの多くが古フランス語あるいはアングロ・ノルマン語
で書かれた作品を原典に持つが、この作品のフランス語原典や類似する作
品は見つかっていない。[2] おそらく、中世イングランドにおいて創作され
た物語なのであろう。[3]

　この騎士物語が研究者の関心を集めているとは言い難いが、[4] "popular
romance" に分類される作品であるにも拘らず、その評価は低くない。[5] 前
半は *The Man of Law's Tale* や *The Clerk's Tale* を想起させる聖女伝的な筋書
きで、主人に寄り添う忠犬の挿話が架け橋となって、[6] 若者の成り上がり
と社会的成功を描く後半部分へと展開していく。とりわけ、主人が死して
なお寄り添い続け、その敵を討つ忠犬 True-love の復讐譚は他の中英語騎
士物語にはなく、強い印象を残す。また、その名前が英語化された主人公
の名前と対応していることも興味深い。[7] これに加えて、*Sir Tryamour* には
現代の読者の好奇心を刺激する場面がもう一つある。それは、決闘の最中
に主人公が相手の馬を過って殺してしまう場面である。騎士物語には同じ
ような場面が少なくないものの、他の騎士物語とこの作品をわかつ特異な
点が主人公の態度にある。本稿では、この中英語騎士物語のなかにある騎
士と馬との関係を描いた場面の特異性を明らかにし、作者が人馬一体とい
う中世における騎士のアイデンティティーの構築に不可分な馬を主人公に

放棄させ純粋な力の行使だけで、馬を必要としない人間中心主義の騎士の
アイデンティティーを獲得する過程を描いていることを示したい。

2.

　フランス語の騎士を意味する語彙が示すように、騎士と馬とは不可分な
関係にある。Jeffrey J. Cohen は、騎士のアイデンティティーについて論じ
た章のなかで、14 世紀初期に成立したロマンス *Beues of Hamtoun* のある場
面を引用している。そこでは主人公 Beues が監禁されていた城から逃走す
る際に奪った馬 Trenchefis が巨人に頭を割られてしまう様子が描かれてい
る。それを目の当たりにした Beues は激怒し、その行為を不名誉だとして
相手を激しく非難する。

> 'O,' queþ Beues, 'so god me spede,
> þow hauest don gret vileinie,
> Whan þow sparde me bodi
> And for me gilt min hors aqueld,
> þow witest him, þat mai nouȝt weld. (ll. 1890-94)[8]

Cohen は、Beues の言葉を現代の読者にとっては理解し難いが中世の騎士
にとって馬はなくてはならないものだと解説を加え、次のように続けてい
る。

> Bevis, his mount, and their numerous analogues in the romances allow us to
> add that, even if the genre offers a powerful vision of individuality, such
> coherence of form ultimately rests on a blending of species, on a body that in
> its movements is in fact no longer human. (55)

彼はロマンスというジャンルが描き出す登場人物の個性の重要性を認めな
がらも、個性が騎士と馬との関係の表象に関連性はないと考えているよう
だ。Susan Crane もまた同じ場面について考察し、この場面に Beues の倫理

観の変化を認めている。[9] 彼女は、馬を消耗品として認識することをやめ、自らの意思を抑えて騎士に仕える馬は守られるべきだと Beues が考えるようになったのだと指摘している。

　2 人の考察にはいくつかの問題点がある。Beues の倫理観が変化したと指摘する Crane の考察は、それまでの Beues の愛馬 Arondel から逃走途中に追手から奪った Trenchefis という馬に変わっている事実を無視して考えてはならない。彼女がこの違いについて理解しているのは明らかだが、それを考慮して Beues の倫理観の変遷を追っているようには思えない。[10] とりわけ、Cohen の用いた表現は問題である。彼は "numerous" という形容詞や "coherence of form" といった表現を用いて同様の場面がたくさんあるかのように述べているが、少なくとも中英語騎士物語に関するかぎり、彼は間違っている。物語文学や年代記において、戦闘中の馬の死への言及は少なからずある。しかし、馬を殺されて騎士が怒りを露わにする場面は "numerous" と表現できるほど多くはない。[11] 管見の限りでは、*Beues of Hamtoun* の例を含めても 5 ないし 6 例ほどしか確認できていない。[12] そしてその数少ない用例の一つが、*Sir Tryamour* のなかに描かれている。

　ハンガリー皇女 Helen が伴侶を探し求めて開催した馬上試合において、主人公 Tryamour はドイツ皇帝の嫡子 Sir James を殺してしまう。それに怒った James の父親はその場にいたと報告されたアラゴン王 Ardus への戦争を計画する。Ardus 王はドイツ皇帝の計画に気づくと一騎討ちを提案、Tryamour とドイツ皇帝一番の騎士 Moradus の決闘が始まる。その最中、Tryamour の狙いが外れ槍が Moradus の馬を貫いてしまう。

> He faylyd of hym, hys hors he hytt—
> To hys herte hys spere can byte.
> Moradas seyde, 'Hyt ys grete shcame
> On a hors to wreke thy grame!' (ll. 1220-3)

騎乗する馬を殺された直後の Moradus の台詞は、まさに Beues が Trenchefis を殺された直後に発したそれと酷似している。Lisa J. Kiser は騎

士の行動規範が相手の馬への意図的な攻撃を禁じしていると解説して Moradus のこの台詞を引用しているが、[13] 残念なことに騎士の行動規範について具体的に説明するものはない。例えば、Chrétien de Troyes の Yvain の物語において見られる "Et de ce firent mout que preu, / Qu'onques lor chevaus an nul leu / Ne navrerent ne anpirierent; / Qu'il ne vostrent ne ne deignierent; / Mes toz jorz a cheval se tindrent, / Que nule foiz a pié ne vindrent; / S'an fu la bataille plus bele."（ll. 855-861）という語り手の解説があるが、[14] これは彼が想定していた 12 世紀の聴衆の価値観を示唆するものであろう。騎士の手引書と評される 14 世紀のフランス人騎士 Geoffroi de Charney が "joust" や "tournament" などについて語った著作にはそのルールが明示されているわけではなく、読者に質問する形式で馬への攻撃について触れられているに過ぎない。[15] また 1466 年 Sir John Tiptoft が公示した馬上試合での騎士の評価システムには、失格要件として「馬への攻撃」が挙げられているが、その理由について、詳細な解説はない。[16]

Sir Tryamour のこの場面もまた Chrétien の語りなどと同様、馬を傷つけることについて中世の騎士がどのように考えていたかを知るための史料的価値がある。しかし、この場面に描かれているのは Kiser のいう意図的な攻撃ではない。"faylyd of him" とあるように、Tryamour は馬を狙っているわけではない。騎士が意図して相手の馬を狙う姿がはっきりと描かれている例は、13 世紀古フランス語ロマンス *L'Atre Perilleux* の主人公以外に私は知らない。[17] したがって騎士の馬への意図的な攻撃について考察するのであれば、この場面を引用することは適切ではない。この場面の持つ史料的価値は、偶発的な事故で馬を傷つけた場合でも、騎士の行為は卑劣かつ不名誉な行為と見なされた可能性があったいうことにある。

この場面を歴史的な資料としてだけではなく、文学作品として正しく評価するためには、Moradus と Tryamour の言動は作品の文脈から切り離すことなく考察されるべきである。この場面のみを文脈から切り離して見れば、Kiser が利用したように、数少ない騎士の行動規範を後世に伝える資料としての価値を見出すことができよう。また Moradus は馬への攻撃を卑劣かつ不名誉な行為と誹る Beues のような模範的な騎士の姿のようにも映

る。そのため Cohen や Crane の議論を援用して、この場面を解釈すること
ができるかもしれない。しかし、これには重要な視点が欠落している。す
なわち、模範的な騎士の台詞を述べる登場人物 Moradus が、Beues とは異
なり、この作品の主人公ではないという点である。もし、馬を殺され騎士
道精神に基づき相手を非難する Moradus が主人公であれば、騎士の理想像
が投影された人物造形だとして物語を読み進めることもできよう。ところ
が作者は、不当な対アラゴン王国戦争をもくろむドイツ皇帝の臣下、簡単
に言ってしまえば敵役の騎士に、Beues のような主人公に相応しい役柄と
台詞を配しており、結果として主人公 Tryamour は卑劣かつ不名誉な行為
の実行者になりさがっているのである。この主人公と敵対する登場人物の
間にみられる期待される役割の逆転こそ、この場面を中英語騎士物語にお
いて極めて特異なものにしている。[18]

　Moradus の叱責の言葉に続く Tryamour の返答はさらに重要である。中
英語騎士物語に限ってみても、主人公の騎士が過って相手の馬の命を奪っ
てしまう場面は多からず描かれている。[19] しかし、Moradus のように主人公
を誹るような敵役はまずいない。したがって主人公が卑劣かつ不名誉とみ
なされる行為を顧みることもない。そもそも Tryamour が返答すること自
体珍しい。Tryamour の言葉は挑発的であり、騎士と馬との関係を考慮す
ると、自ら騎士としてのアイデンティティーの一部を放棄するかのような
内容であり、強烈な違和感を覚えさせる。

> Tryamowre seyde, as tyte,
> ʼLevyr y had to have hyt the!
> Have my hors, and let me bee—
> Y am lothe to flyte.ʼ（ll. 1224-27）

この作品の TEAMS 版編者 Harriet Hudson はこの Tryamour の返答を"rejoinder"
と表現している。一見すると、彼は当意即妙の受け答えをしているようだ
が、騎士が自分の馬を無条件に差し出すようなことをふつうはしない。例
えば、*Sir Tristrem* や *Sir Degare* では相手に馬から降りるよう要求されて、

主人公たちはその求めに応じている。*Amis and Amiloun* では主人公の一人が、馬に乗らない相手と戦うことを潔しとせず、自ら馬を降りている。また主人公が相手の馬を攻撃した例ではないものの、*The Awntyrs off Arthure* の Galeron の対応についても触れておく必要がある。Arthur 王によって不当に奪われた領地を取り返すべく Galeron は Gawain との決闘にのぞむが、その際 Galeron は相手の乗る馬の首を切り落としてしまう。馬を殺された Gawain は哀しみと怒りで我を忘れんばかりであったが、Galeron はこのとき自分の連れてきた馬を一頭譲ることを申し出ている。その類例自体が限定的であるため過度な一般化は危険であるものの、これらの類似する場面から相手の馬の命を奪った際の騎士の行動規範が推察できる。相手の馬を殺してしまった場合、騎士は馬から降り、対峙する相手と同じ条件にすることで対等に戦うことを選択する。さもなければ、複数連れている馬のなかから一頭を選ばせるという方法で、相手とのバランスを取ろうとする。馬への攻撃を卑劣かつ不名誉な行為とみなす騎士の規範からすれば、これらの行動は実に理にかなっている。

　騎士にとって必要不可欠な馬を放棄するという愚かな行為を自発的にするのだとすれば、Tryamour の返答は確かに滑稽である。しかし 2 人の騎士の様子は鬼気迫るもので、場面の雰囲気や調子もまた重々しさを帯びている。そこで発せられる Tryamour の言葉に知性やユーモアを読み込むことはできない。むしろ押問答を避けるために自分の馬を差し出すという提案は、馬を降りて戦うという手段をすぐに選べない Tryamour の冷静さや騎士としての経験の欠如を露呈させてしまっている。Tryamour の無知蒙昧な放言に対して、Moradus は最後まで理想的な騎士として振る舞い続けている。

> Moradas seyde, 'Y wyll hym noght,
> Tyll thou have that strok boght,
> And wynne hym wyth ryght.' (ll. 1228-30)

Moradus は Tryamour の申し出を断り、正当な手段によって馬を手に入れ

ることを宣言する。直後 Tryamour は馬を降り、再び 2 人の戦いが始まるのだが、結局のところ一連の場面は騎士の価値観を重視する Moradus の模範的な姿を強調する一方で、主人公である Tryamour の騎士道的価値観に対する無知と騎士としてのアイデンティティーの自発的な放棄を描き出してしまっているのである。未開の森から Arthur 王の宮廷にやってきたばかりの Perceval のように、精神的な未熟さや騎士としての経験不足を理由に、Tryamour を情状酌量することはできない。Tryamour はすでに馬上試合の経験があるだけでなく、文明から離れて育った Perceval とは異なり、Sir Barnard という騎士のもとで不自由のない生活を謳歌している。

　Tryamour の騎士道的価値観とは相入れない行為はもう一つある。Moradus との決闘の後、Tryamour は潜伏していたその兄弟たちと戦闘になる。彼が容易にそのうちのひとりを倒してしまうと、もう 1 人は剣を手に Tryamour に襲いかかる。

　　　Wyth hys swerde to hym he yede,
　　　And slwe Syr Tryamowres stede──
　　　Full mekyll was hys mayne.
　　　Syr Tryamowre faght on ffote. (ll. 1435-37)

Tryamour の馬は殺された。しかし Moradus が咎めたように、Tryamour が彼の兄弟を非難することはない。多くの騎士物語において、馬を殺された騎士は馬の死への配慮や関心を示さないことが一般的である。そのため、ここだけを見れば Tryamour の態度におかしなところはないようにも見える。状況を考慮しても Tryamour が何も言わないことに不自然さはないが、決闘の際の Moradus の言動を思い返してみると、相手に馬を殺された Tryamour の反応は物足りなくもあり、理想的な Moradus の姿によって Tryamour の姿は矮小化されてしまうような印象さえ受ける。

　作品の主人公はあくまで Tryamour である。馬上試合や決闘などでの勝利は主人公の "prowess" を最大限に前景化させる。しかし主人公の運命を決める重要な場面で騎士の価値観に反するような行動をとり、非難を受

け、自省することがない。Kiser が解説しているように、Moradus の台詞
は馬への攻撃が中世の騎士の行動規範のなかでどのように判断されていた
のかを示す史料的価値がある。しかし、この場面を作品のコンテキストに
戻して常にスポットライトを浴びる主人公に視点を合わせると、物語のな
かで Tryamour と Moradus が対立しているように、主人公の姿と理想的な
騎士の姿は相入れないことが鮮明になってくる。

3.

　意図的でないにしても相手の馬を殺し、さらには自分の馬を自発的に相
手に差し出す提案をする Tryamour の言動は、騎士物語の主人公としては
やはり問題である。特に人間と馬とが一体化した集合が騎士のアイデン
ティティーだとすれば、Tryamour の言動は深刻な問題を引き起こす。そ
の問題の本質は、局所的とはいえ現代の読者に違和感を覚えさせるかもし
れない中世の騎士の価値観とは相入れないはずの主人公の人物造形にある。
　この問題を解決する上で鍵となるのは、「現代の読者に違和感を与える」
かもしれないという点である。この作品が含まれる写本のファクシミリ版
の序文を書いた Frances McSparran は、この写本が読者の利益と喜びを目
的としてデザインされているのは明らかであると述べている。[20] Tryamour
の言動は騎士の行動規範を体系的にまとめた著作や多くの騎士道ロマンス
などから理想的な騎士を思い描いている現代の読者を落胆させ、作者の意
図や騎士の倫理観に対する認識について疑念を懐かせる。しかし、写本が
読者の要求を満たしているものだとすれば、そこに収録されている作品が
中世の人々を満足させていたことはおそらく間違いないのだから、現代の
読者の側に誤解があると考えるべきである。完全な形で残っているのは1
写本内のみだが複数の写本にその断片が残っており、16 世紀には印刷本
も出版されている。これは作品の成立直後からその人気が衰えていなかっ
たことを示しており、Tryamour の馬と騎士との関係を断つような言動は、
現代的な視点から見れば奇異な言動と認識されうるものだが、当時の読者
あるいは聴衆はそれについて少しの違和感も抱くことはなかったのであろ

う。だからこそ、成立以降 200 年以上もの間、人々に親しまれる物語であり得た。

　しかし、馬は騎士のアイデンティティーを形成する必要不可欠な構成要素である。馬そのものが騎士のアイデンティティーを象徴する存在であろうと、馬の背に乗る騎士という人馬一体の集合が騎士のアイデンティティーであろうと、自らの意思を抑えて背中に乗る騎士に尽くそうとする馬は守られるべきとする倫理観があったとすれば、意図的でないにしろ相手の馬を殺し、自分の馬さえ差し出そうとする Tryamour の言動は馬と騎士との関係を断絶させるものであり、そこに文学的にも文化的にも極めて重要な意義を見出すことができる。

　その意義とはなにか。それは、騎士のアイデンティティーの表象としての馬を放棄することで、あるいは一体化した騎士と馬との集合体が瓦解することで人間単体で騎士としての「個別性」と新たな騎士のアイデンティティーを主人公が獲得したことである。いわば騎士の馬からの独立である。それはルネサンスを迎えようとする中世イングランドにおける人間中心を謳う人文主義の萌芽とも捉えることができるかもしれない。

　歴史的に見れば、この騎士と馬との関係の変質は、実戦におけるイングランドの騎馬戦術が 13 世紀末から 14 世紀初期にかけて大きな転換期を迎えていることに関連があるように思う。[21] 人馬一体となって戦う騎士の姿は、長弓部隊の登場と新たな戦術と兵器の導入によって、影を潜めつつあった。経済的な損失を恐れ状況に応じて馬の派遣を控えることがあったにせよ、[22] 14 世紀半ばまでは戦場での馬の損失は王室が補償していた。この補償制度は 1370 年を境に終了しているようだが、Andrew Ayton によれば、これは馬の補償が財政を圧迫したからというわけではなく、そもそも重騎兵の戦略上の重要性が著しく低下したからである。[23] この制度の終了は、戦術や騎兵の役割の変化を示すだけでなく、騎士と馬との関係を考える上でも示唆に富んでいる。Ayton はこの点について次のように述べている。

　　　For the Englishman of the mid-late fourteenth century, the association of

knight and warhorse was as strong as it had ever been. The tactical changes
which helped to bring unparalleled successes and prestige to English arms on
the continent do not appear to have shaken this association. (p. 31)

　Cohen もまた Luttrell Psalter にある Geoffrey Luttrell の挿絵を例に Ayton と
同様の指摘をしているが、[24] 中英語騎士物語に見られる描写に関していえ
ば、騎士の馬に対する無関心な態度が圧倒的である。Chrétien の Yvain の
物語を比較的忠実に翻訳したことで知られる中英語ロマンス *Ywain and
Gawain* から、先に引用した馬上で戦い続ける騎士の様子を賛美した語り
手の言葉が、その本来の意味を読み取ることができないほどに簡略化され
ていることは象徴的である。[25] 想定された読者あるいは聴衆の社会的な地
位が、作者による騎士の人物造形に影響を与えた可能性も十分にある。[26]
戦略上の騎兵の重要性の低下と騎士とは異なる社会階級の人々の視点から
みた騎士像の変化の相関性が、中英語騎士物語における騎士と馬との描写
の傾向に反映されているのではないだろうか。実戦における騎兵の衰退は、
空想の世界で描かれる騎士の姿に少なからず影響を与えていたとしても不
思議はない。
　文学的な視点から見れば、作者の意図が大きく関わっていることは間違
いない。作者の意図は、中英語ポピュラー・ロマンスの特徴でもある過度
に様式化されたモチーフの構成のなかだけでなく、主人公の人物造形のな
かにもその独自性を認めることができる。池上忠弘は、同じ写本にも収録
されている *Sir Eglamour* に関する論考で、作者の意図を「作品の娯楽性」
を強調しながらも「理想化された主人公」を通して作者の "sens" を伝える
ことだと指摘している。[27] 中英語騎士物語は、かつてのテレビ時代劇のよ
うに、定型表現や慣習化したモチーフの組み合わせによって構成されてい
る。これらパターンからの僅かな逸脱や主人公の人物描写は作者のオリジ
ナリティーとなり、そこに作者の "sens" を見出すことができるはずだ。
問題の場面は、Beues や Oliver、Richard といった主人公たちが馬を殺され
た時にみせる怒りを描いた場面としては見かけ上同一であるが、怒りを露
わにするのが主人公ではない点において騎士物語のパターンから外れた特

異な例である。言うまでもなく、物語の主人公は Tryamour である。彼は
Beues や Oliver、Richard のように馬を殺されて理想的な騎士の振る舞いを
することはないが、それでも作者の「理想化された主人公」である。そう
であれば、Tryamour の言動にこそ作者の理想的な騎士像が映し出されて
いると考えるべきだ。伝統的な騎士の行動規範に則った振る舞いをする
Moradus と対比させるように描かれる Tryamour は、唯一その武勇におい
てのみ物語に登場するいかなる騎士をも凌駕している。この他を圧倒する
肉体的な強さは、宮廷風の礼儀作法や騎士の規範という時として難解な基
準によって騎士としての価値を測ることから―特にその文化に通暁してい
ない人々を―解放する概念であり、他の騎士との優劣を判断する上でもっ
とも単純かつ明確な物差しでもある。この作者による徹底した力の賛美は、
物語のクライマックスで Sir Burlonde を嫌悪感を抱かせるような嘲りの犠
牲者にし陰惨な最後を迎えさせ、一つの家族を根絶やしにすることにつな
がった。美しい花嫁を手に入れ、王となり、離散していた家族が再会する
という Tryamour のハッピーエンディングとは対照的である。それでも
Tryamour こそが主人公であり、作者が描く騎士の理想像なのである。

　Moradus との決闘の場面における主人公の言動は、現代の読者が抱く騎
士の理想像という基準に照らし合わせると、彼自身に対する心証を悪くし
ているように思える。おそらく「現代の読者が抱く騎士の理想像」とは中
世文学を正しく評価する上では独善的な物差しに過ぎないのかもしれな
い。[28] 作者によって「理想化された主人公」が作者の "sens" を読者や聴衆
に伝えているのであれば、たとえ伝統的な騎士と馬との関係を踏襲してい
ない言動をする主人公であったとしても、中世の人々にとってはその主人
公こそ理想的な騎士に違いない。そして主人公というだけで、その騎士が
体現する価値観に読者や聴衆は自然と感情移入していくことになるだろう。
この物語に描かれている理想の騎士とは、伝統的に騎士にとって不可欠だ
とされる馬の束縛から解放された、自律した一個の人間としての騎士であ
る。Crane は中世文学に見られる騎士と馬との提示法として "a mechanism
coordinating multiple bodies and technologies" と "a partnership that attributes
courage, nobility, and initiative to both knight and horse" との 2 つを指摘してい

るが、[29] どちらのカテゴリーにも分類することのできない騎士が馬を必要
としない第3の提示法—"un chevalier sans cheval"—の存在を指摘すること
ができるかもしれない。Cohen は騎士のアイデンティティーに個性を認め
ることに懐疑的であるが、やはり騎士のアイデンティティーの表象にも個
性が存在するとみなすべきであろう。そして、騎士のアイデンティティー
に必ずしも馬が必要ではないと考えていた中世の人々がいたことが、
Tryamour の個性的な言動からは推察できるのである。

4.

　Sir Tryamour の作者が造形した理想的な騎士の姿は、現代の読者が考え
る騎士の理想像とは乖離しているようにも思える。肉体的な強さと宮廷風
の礼儀作法が一人の騎士のなかで調和し、騎士が騎士であるために不可欠
な存在として馬がいる。時として両者の結びつきは、その馬が騎士の愛情
の対象となるほどに強固であった。中世文学における理想的な騎士といえ
ば、私たちはこのような騎士の姿を思い浮かべることだろう。これに対し
て、Tryamour の人物像の背後には、力こそ正義であり、勝利こそすべて
という浅薄な価値観しか見えてこないが、それもまた私たちには思いつき
もしないような騎士の理想像であり、中世の読者や聴衆はこれを受け入れ
歓迎さえしている。

　作品そのものの評価は低くはないものの、研究者の関心を引きつけるま
でにはないこの作品は、現代の読者が思い描く騎士の理想像と中世の人々
が認めうる騎士の理想像とが必ずしも一致しないことをまざまざと見せつ
ける。このような乖離の原因のひとつに、中英語の canon とされる作品を
絶対視するような潜在意識が考えられるのではないか。Geoffrey Chaucer
や the *Gawain*-poet といったいわゆる中英語の canon とされる作品だけに目
を向けさせればいいという考え方があるとすれば、賛同できない。私は
canon の重要性を否定するわけではない。それとそれに関連する著名な研
究者らの先行研究を盲目的に信頼することによって視野が狭まる可能性を
危惧しているのである。この作品は私たちを戒めているようにも思える。

なおざりにされてきた中英語ポピュラー・ロマンス研究を通して、そのような警告に耳を傾けて、先入観を捨て、作品と誠実に向き合うことが求められているのではないだろうか。

　確かに *Sir Tryamour* を含む中英語ポピュラー・ロマンスの評価は低い。Stephen Knight がこれらの作品を指して用いた "the ugly ducklings" という表現は衝撃的である。[30] しかし、その存在を軽視していいほど取るに足らない作品だとは思えない。確かに中英語ポピュラー・ロマンスは、Derek Pearsall が "grammar of romance" と呼んだ慣習的に繰り返し用いられる定型のモチーフによって構成されているため、[31] ともすればテレビ時代劇を見るかの如く、その単調さに嫌気がさしてしまうこともあるだろう。それでもやはり、特に外国語文学として中英語文学を研究する私たちにとって "grammar" は重要である。文法を理解していなければ外国語の読解に支障をきたすように、欧米の研究者と比較して圧倒的に中世ヨーロッパの文化に馴染みの薄い私たち日本の研究者が中英語ロマンスの "grammar" を理解していなければ、不利益が生じることは明白である。中英語文学の基礎を修得するという目的のためだけでも、中英語ロマンスの鑑賞や研究には十分な価値を見出すことができるはずだ。私たちは決して、巡礼者たちを聖トマスのもとへと導く Harry Bailly の言葉に惑わされてはならないのである。

注

1.　引用はすべて *Of Love and Chivalry: An Anthology of Middle English Romance*, edited by Jennifer Fellows（J. M. Dent, 1993）に拠る。
2.　Fellows, xvi.
3.　Rhiannon Purdie によれば、14 世紀後期以降に北部地域で創作された脚韻ロマンスの大部分が、イングランド固有の作品であると指摘している（*Anglicising Romance: Tail-Ryhme and Genre in Medieval English Literature*（D.S. Brewer, 2008）, 144.）。
4.　Fellows, xvi.
5.　Lilian Herald Hornstein, "Sir Triamour", *A Manual of the Writings in Middle English*

1050-1500, Fascicule 1: I. Romances, edited by Jonathan Burke Severs and Albert E. Hartung（Connecticut Academy of Arts and Sciences, 1967）, 130.

6. Harriet Hudson, "Sir Tryamour: Introduction," *Four Middle English Romances*: *Sir Isumbras, Octavian, Sir Eglamour or Artois, Sir Tryamour*, edited by Harriet Hudson（Medieval Institute Publications, 2006）.《https://d.lib.rochester.edu/teams/text/hudson-sir-tryamour-introduction》19 Oct. 2020 accessed.

7. "Sir Tryamour" in *The Encyclopedia of Medieval Literature in Britain*（2017）, 1731-2.

8. *The Romance of Sir Beues of Hamtounn*, edited by Eugene Kölbing（Kraus Reprint, 1978）.

9. Susan Crane, *Animal Encounters: Contacts and Concepts in Medieval Britain*（University of Pennsylvania Press, 2013）, 162-3.

10. *Beues of Hamtoun* において描かれているのは、主人公の倫理観の変遷ではなく、騎士と馬との関係が相互的な信頼関係へと成熟していく過程を描いたことにあると私は考えている。ただし、これは中英語の翻案者の功績ではないように思う。

11. 拙論「中英語騎士物語における騎士と馬との関係についての初期研究」『千葉商大紀要』56:1（2018）, 53-69.

12. *Sir Ferumbras* では Oliver が彼の馬を殺した Ferumbras を非難している（ll. 588-99）。また *Richard Coer de Lyon* では混戦のなか馬 Fauvel を殺された Richard が激怒してサラセン人を次々と倒していく様子が描かれる（ll. 7101-17）。*The Romance of Otuel* では Roland が Otuel の馬を殺してしまい、それに対して Otuel が怒りを露わにするという場面がある。一方別のヴァージョン（*Romance of Duke Rowlande and Sir Ottuell of Spayne*）では、Ottuell は馬を殺されても怒らない。これらの例に、南部版 *Octovian* を加えることも可能であろう。

13. Lisa J. Kiser, "Animals in Medieval Sports, Entertainment, and Menageries", *A Cultural History of Animals in the Medieval Ages*, edited by Brigitte Resl（Berg, 2007）, 111.

14. Chrestien de Tryoes, *Yvain*（*Le Chevalier au Lion*）: The Critical Text of Wendelin Foerster, introduction, Notes and Glossary by T.B.W. Reid（Manchester UP, 1952）.

15. Geoffroi de Charny, *Jousts and Tournaments: Charny and the Rules for Chivalric Sport in Fourteenth-Century France*,（Chivalry Bookshelf, 2002）, p. 28 and 102-3.

16. Richard Barber and Juliet Barker, *Tournaments*: *Jousts, Chivalry and Pageants in the Middle Ages*,（The Boydell, 1989）, 192.

17. *L'Atre Périlleux*, edited by Brian Woledge（Champion, 1936）, ll. 2326-35.

18. Thomas Chestre の作品とされる南部版 *Octavian* にも馬を殺された一騎討ちの

相手が主人公のひとりを非難する場面がある。この場面では、主人公を厳しく叱責するのがサラセン人であり、シャルルマーニュ・ロマンスに登場する異教徒の騎士 Otuel（Ottuell）とは異なり、このサラセン人の騎士はキリスト教徒に改宗することもないため、非常に興味深い例であるといえる。（*Octovian Imperator*, edited by Frances McSparran（Carl Winter, 1979）, ll. 1094-1108.）

19. 例 え ば、*Amis and Amiloun*, ll. 1321-44; *Sir Tristrem*, ll. 1028-67; *Ywain and Gawain*, ll. 1877-80; *Sir Degare*, ll. 920-49; *Sir Ferumbras,* ll. 3383-88, 5585-98; *Ipomadon*, ll. 4384-4404; 7880-7915 などがある。

20. *Cambridge University Library MS Ff. 2.38*, introdcution by Fracnes McSparran and P. R. Robinson（Scolar Press, 1979）, xii.

21. Andrew Ayton, *Knights and Warhorses*: *Military Service and the English Aristocracy under Edward III*（The Boydell Press, 1994）, 26; Ann Hyland, *The Warhorse 1250-1600*（Sutton Publishing, 1998）, 34-5, 41-45.

22. Ayton, 213.

23. Ayton, 120-2.

24. Cohen, 70.

25. *Ywain and Gawain*, edited by Albert B. Friedman and Norman T. Harrington（Oxford UP, 1964）, ll. 655-5.

26. フランス語の著作を含む写本の構成や *Sir Tryamour* の成立時期を考慮すると、読者や聴衆が必ずしも庶民や新興階級だけであったと断定するのは早計だろう。個別の作品についてはともかく、写本全体としては貴族階級が読者として想定されていた可能性もあるように思う。ロマンスの読者や聴衆に関する議論については、Carol M. Meale, 'gode men / Wiues maydnes and alle men' : Romance and Its Audiences," *Reading in Medieval English Romance*, edited by Carole M. Meale（D. S. Brewer, 1994）, 209-225 を参照。

27. 池上忠弘, "Sir Eglamour of Artas の 'Sens'"『ガウェインとアーサー王伝説』（秀文インターナショナル , 1988）, 102.

28. Cohen は騎士道には地域差があり普遍的な価値観を完全に共有していたわけではないと指摘している（70）。騎士道には地域差だけでなく、時代や階級間の認識の差異もあったに違いない。

29. Crane, 137.

30. "The Social Function of the Middle English Romances," *Medieval Literature: Criticism, Ideology and History*, edited by David Aers（Harvester Press, 1986）, 99.

31. "The Development of Middle English Romance," *Studies in Medieval English Romance*: *Some New Approaches*, edited by Derek Brewer（D.S. Brewer, 1988）, 11.

Ipomydon (*B*) とその Wynkyn de Worde 版の 「初期 R 消失」を示すライム

池　上　　　昌

1.　はじめに

1.1.　*Ipomydon* (*B*) と Wynkyn de Worde

Ipomydon (*B*) というのは現在 London, British Library 所蔵の写本 Harley 2252、ff.54-84 に納められている *The Lyfe of Ipomydon* の通称である。この作品は、Hue de Rotelande による Anglo-Norman 語の *Ipomédon* (ca. 1190) を基にした韻文ロマンスであるが、他にも二つこの同じ Anglo-Norman 作品を種本とした中英語のイポミドン物語が存在する。それらを区別して、およその制作年代順に A,B,C という符号をつけて呼ばれているのである。ここで取り上げる B 版は 2346 行からなる four-beat couplets である。作者は不詳だが、使用された方言のタイプは North-East Midland, おそらく 15 世紀後半の作品と思われる。[1]

Wynkyn de Worde (歿年 1535) は William Caxton の印刷工房を引き継いだイングランド第二世代の印刷出版業者である。de Worde が入手したのはこの B 版である。Meale 1982 の研究で、de Worde が印刷用原稿 (exemplar) として使用したのはまさにこの Harley 写本の *The Lyfe of Ipomydon* (以下これを H と略す) であったことが突き止められている。[2] 彼の刊本が二編現存している。一つは British Library, Bagford Ballads, Vol. i, No. 18 の一葉 (*STC*, No. 5732.5, c.1522) で、全部で 56 行分しかない。H の ll. 261-288、ll.293-320 に対応する (以下 BL と略す)。もう一つは New York, Pierpont Morgan Library 20896 の 38 葉 (*STC*, No. 5733, c.1527) である。全部で 2028 行分、冒頭が欠けているが、H の 193 行目から最後の 2346 行までに対応している (以下 PML と略す)。奥付に "Enprynted at London in the Fletestrete at the synge of the Sonne by Wynkyn de Worde" とあるので、この書物は de

Worde がロンドンのフリートストリートの太陽印工房で印刷した物である
ことが確認できる。de Worde の刊本二部、BL 版 56 行分とそれに対応する
PML 版の行であるが、この部分を比べてみると印刷用原稿 H には無い読
みを共有しているので、どちらかが他方を基に再版した物であることが想
像できる。[3]

1.2. Wynkyn de Worde 工房の本文の修正

de Worde の印刷用原稿の本文の扱い方は、作品によって異なるようであ
る。チョーサーの「カンタベリー物語」出版（1498 年）にあたっては、
「本文は手を加えることなく、できるだけ著者が意図したままに残す」と
いう編集方針（ヘリンガ・徳永、146-47）を実現させた。[4] しかし韻文ロマ
ンス *Ipomydon* は違う。印刷出版するなら、売れない物は困る。想定され
る読者にうまく受け入れてもらえるように工夫した。本文が分かりにくい
と思えば、より良いと思う表現に変える、馴染みの薄い地方言や野卑と感
じられる言葉は別の言葉に入れ替える、古めかしい感じの言い回しは現代
風に改める。[5] スペリングは de Worde 工房で平素使っているものにして統
一を図る。[6] 行末のライムの部分で原稿 H のスペリングが異なっている場
合は修正の第一標的となったようである。ライム部分は同じスペリングで
綴るほうが確かに見栄えが良い。かなり周到に改訂されている。この結果、
H の原作者の言語上の特質は de Worde 版でほとんど消えた。[7]

しかし、修正されずにそのまま残ったライムもある。その中で興味深い
ものの一つが、子音の前の R 音が発音されなくなったことを示唆するラ
イムである。この R 消失は、後に英国英語で一般的になった R 消失と区
別して、「初期」の R 消失として知られているものである。このタイプの
ライムを de Worde 工房がスペリングの異なりにもかかわらずそのまま
使ったということは、この位置の R 音は *Ipomydon*（*B*）を創作した詩人の
言語で発音に存在しなくなっていたばかりでなく、de Worde 工房でこの書
物の編集や印刷に関わり、何らかの形で字句の修正の機会を持ち得た 16
世紀初頭のロンドンの人々も同様に、この R はスペリングにあっても無
音であると認識していたためではないか。

　この作品には子音の前にRがある語が全部で21のライムに使われてい
る。このうち3つはHの冒頭192行の中にあるので、de Worde版に対応
しない。BLがカバーする56行分の中には用例がない。従って以下で記述
するのは印刷原稿Hと de Worde版 PMLの対比である。
　この比較可能範囲にR＋子音を持つ語を使用したライムが18例ある。
このうちR消失を示すライムは4例である。3例がPMLの修正を免れた
ライムで、あと1例はPMLの修正を被っている。残り14例はRについ
てはself-rhyme、つまりR＋子音を持つ語とR＋子音を持つ語がライムし
合うもの（e.g. ME /ar/ ＋m, 1463-64 H barme（n.）'lap'（OE bearm）: harme
（n.）'harm'（OE hearm）; PML arme（n.）'arm'（OE earm）: harme（n.））、R音
が発音上存在するか、しないか、について何ら証言するものではない。
　本稿でベースにしたテクストは Tadahiro Ikegami ed., *The lyfe of Ipomydon,*
Vol. I（1983）, Vol. II（1985）である。

2.　子音の前の R 音「初期消失」を立証するライム

2.1.　de Worde 版 PML の修正を免れた三つのライム

　次の三つのライムを見て欲しい。原稿Hと de Worde版 PMLのライム部
分のスペリングを見ると、1では〈-us/-ous〉が〈-ours〉と、2では〈-ord〉
が〈-od〉, それから3では〈-on〉が〈-orn〉と組になっている。各組の一
方にRが含まれているのに相手方にはそれが無い。

（1）539-40 H victoryus（adj.）'victorious'（AN victorious）: cours（n.）'charge
　　in tourney'（OF cours, cors, curs & L cursus）; PML victoryous : cours.
（2）1655-56 H bord（n.）'board, dining table'（OE bord）: wode（adj. pred. sg.）
　　'insane'（OE wōd）; PML borde : wode.
（3）2299-30 H on（pron.）'one'（OE ān）: befforne（adv.）'before'（OE
　　beforan）; PML one : here-beforne.

　Hのライムは（1）が victoryus の接尾辞 -yus と cours、（2）が bord と

wode、それに（3）が on 'one' と befforne の第二音節、語幹部分 -orne である。PML は（1）の接尾辞 H の〈-yus〉を〈-yous〉に変更し、（2）の bord 語末に〈-e〉を加え、（3）の on も〈-e〉付きにし、befforne の〈ff〉を〈f〉にした。de Worde 工房のスペリングに合わせたのであろう。これらの変更はライムの発音に関わりない。H のライムをそのまま踏襲したのである。私は（1）が ME /u: s/,（2）が ME /o:d/,（3）は ME /ɔn / に基づくライムと考える。各組の〈r〉を持つ語、（1）の cours,（2）の bord(e)、（3）の bef(f)orne の〈r〉は、発音には存在しないと考えないとライムは成立しない。

ライムから発音を推定するという作業は、ライムとして組み合わされている一組の語それぞれの当初の発音が、それぞれの変遷をたどる中で、同じ発音になり得るのはどんな発音かを見極める作業である。

（1）のライム -yus/-yous : cours に共通する母音は ME /u:/ と推定する。そのように推定したのは、接尾辞 -ious を Gower が長母音 /u:/ とライムさせているので（e.g. *Confessio Amantis*, 7. 1229-30 hous（n.）'house'（OE hūs）: glorious（adj.）（AN glory(o)us, OF glorieux））、この接尾辞は ME で長母音 /u:/ で発音されても良いと思えることと、相手の語 cours の OF, AN の /u/ は ME で通例長母音 /u:/ で表されていたことが知られている（Wright, §201; Jordan, §229）という理由による。

（2）のライム bord/borde : wode の母音は間違いなく ME close /o:/ である。bord/borde の長母音 /o:/ は、OE の短母音 o が母音の長音化を起こさせた子音群 -rd の前で伸張されて /o:/ になったのがそのまま残った例で、それが wode の OE ō とライムしている。

（3）のライム、on/one（pron.）: bef(f)orne には短母音 /ɔ/ を想定したが、これには前提として両方の語にそれぞれ次の変化があったとしなければならない。

（i）on/one: ME /ɔ:n/ の /ɔ:/ ＜ OE ā は短縮されて /ɔ/ になった。このような単音節語の母音が単独子音の前で短縮されるという音韻変化は 15 世紀初頭に最も活発に起こったものである（Dobson, II, §24; §33, note 2）。ここで想定した on/one（pron.）の ME /ɔn / と言う発音は、今の英語の *one* の

発音［wʌn］の短母音 /ʌ/ に直接つながるものではない。この /ʌ/ は ME
open /ɔː/ の異音、ME close /oː/ に遡る。[8]

　(ii) bef(f)orne: ライムの -f(f)orne（OE -foran）の o は ME の開音節伸張
（open syllable lengthening）で ME open /ɔː/ となってもよいのだが、このラ
イムでは伸張が無かった短母音 /ɔ/ が使われている。ME の開音節伸張は
一律の結果をもたらす規則的な音韻変化ではなく、長音化を逃れた場合が
ある。ここはその一つの例で、問題の母音の後に続いて -el, -en, -er（ある
いは syllabic l, n, r）があると、伸張は起こる場合と起こらない場合とある
（Ekwall, §22; Dobson, II, §13, (a)）。[9] *LALME, I, Dot Maps* の 365 BEFORE
adv/pr には、'(-)forn(e)' type, incl rare -ffoorn' とある。ここの「まれな
-ffoorn」の〈oo〉というスペリングは ME の長母音 /ɔː/ を表すと思われる
が、*LALME, IV* の 78 BEFORE の項で見る限り、この〈oo〉が存在するの
は BL の Harley 写本 2390 の一例 a-ffoorn のみで、他にこの語の -n で終わ
る形には〈oo〉の綴りはない。

　'Before' の -forne 型、beforne/byforne はこの作品の中で他に三回ライム
に現われる。そのうちの一つ、1227-28 のライムは H 詩人の発音では
-forne は短母音の /ɔ/ を持っていたことを示していると解釈出来ると思う。

1227-28 H byforne（prep.）: corvyn（p.ppl.）'carved'（OE corfen, p.ppl. of
ceorfan）; PML dout（n.）'doubt'（OF dote, dute）: out（adv.）（OE ūt）

　H のライム byforne : corvyn の過去分詞 corvyn の発音は ME /kɔrvən, kɔrvn/
が普通であったと思うが、ここで詩人が使ったのは /v/ が無い形 /kɔrn/ で
あったと推察する。/v/ の消失は過去分詞の接尾辞 -en の -e- が脱落した
ため /v/ が子音 /n/ の前にきた形 /kɔrvn/ から説明できる。この位置の /v/ が
消 失 し た（kɔrvn ＞ kɔrn）（Jordan, §216, 2）。こ う し て 生 じ た corn
（＝corvyn）の母音 /ɔ/ は長音化される理由がないので、ライム相手の
byforne の -forne の母音も短母音 /ɔ/ でなければならない。意図されたライ
ムは両語の /ɔrn/ に基づいている。この H のライムはスペリング上ではま
るで発音の合っていない欠陥ライムに見えるので、PML はこの二行を書

き換えて、脚韻を dout : out に改めた。[10]

残り二つの beforne を含むライムは 1219-20 H horne（n.）'horn'（OE horn）: beforne（prep.）; PML horne（n.）: beforne（prep.）と、1987-88 H borne（p. ppl.）'carried'（OE boren, p.ppl. of beran）: therebeforne（adv.）'previously'（late OE þǣr-beforan）; PML borne（p.ppl.）: therebeforne（adv.）である。1219-20 では beforne とライムする horne が OE o が母音の長音化を起こさせた子音群 -rn の前にあるので長母音の OE ō になっていて、この ō に由来する ME close /o: / が beforen（＞ -forn）の ME open /ɔ: / の異音 ME /o:/（cf. 注 8）とライムしていると解釈するのも可能である。従って -forne の短母音を立証することは出来ない。1987-88 は開音節にある ME /ɔ / 同士の self-rhyme である。Self-rhyme はライムの発音について何の証言もしない。この二つのライムについては、PML はそのままの形を残している。

2.2.　R 音の後続子音への同化

現代の英語では、子音の前にある R の発音は方言のタイプによって異なる。「容認発音」（Received Pronunciation）と R 音は発音しない 'non-rhotic' な英国発音（ロンドンを中心とした南部イングランド地域の発音）では、この位置の R は無音になった（Wells, *LPD*, p. 577）。R は発音の仕方が時代を経るに従って次第に変わってきたようである。OE ではどの位置でも trill（舌先を歯茎に数回たたきつける、ふるえ音）であったが、ME や初期 ModE 期には trill は語頭には残ったが、語中や語末では post-alveolar fricative（舌先を歯茎の後部に近づけて調音する摩擦音）になったとされている（Ekwall, §129; Dobson II, §370; Gimson, §8.8）。上に挙げた三つのライムが示唆する R 音消失は、このように発音されるようになった R が後続の子音に同化（assimilation）されて生じたものと説明できる。

　この強勢のある音節にある R の後続子音への同化について Jordan §§166、302 は、1300 年頃から R は後続の子音 /s/ に同化されるようになり、やがて /s/ に加えて他の後続子音への同化も現われるようになったと述べている。又、Hill（1940）は R は、/ʒ/ を除くすべての「広い意味での dentals」/d, t, n, l, θ, ð, s, ʃ, dʒ, ʧ/ に同化されたと報告している。Wyld, *Rhymes*

ではもっとも古いライムとして Bokenam の *Lives of Saints*（1443）の adust 'in the dust'：wurst 'worst' を挙げ、R の子音の前での消失は遅くとも 15 世紀に始まったもので、かつては上品な 'respectable antiquity' であったと述べている（p.113）。Wyld, *Coll. Eng.*, pp.298-300 では、R の他の子音との同化は 15 世紀半ばまでに Essex や Suffolk で起こり、R 無しの発音はその 100 年後には London の庶民間に、やがて上流階級へと広まっていったと記している。この同化による「初期」R 消失タイプの発音の名残は、今日の容認発音にいくらか残っているが（e.g. bass [bæs] 'fish'（OE bærs）; worsted [wʊstɪd, -əd] 'cloth'（OE Wurþestede, later Worthstede, now Worstead（a name of a parish in Norfork））、「後期」R 脱落との直接のつながりは無い。

　　上記三つのライムで子音の前で R 音が無くなっていると示唆された語は 1 の cours, 2 の bord, そして 3 の bef(f)orne である。ここでは R の後続子音は 1 が /s/, 2 が /d/, そして 3 が /n/ である。母音の発音は cours が ME /u:/、bord が ME /o:/、bef(f)orne が ME /ɔ/ と推定した。Wells, *LPD* は cours と bord の現代の 'non-rhotic' な英国発音を次のように記している：course [kɔ:s], board [bɔ:d]。Bef(f)orne のような -n 付きの before は *LPD* に記載は無いが、*OED* には 17 世紀の古風な形として beforen, biforn がある。もしこの -n 型が現代に残っていれば、bear の過去分詞 born [bɔ:n]（OE boren）と同様に [*-fɔ:n] と発音されるに違いない。母音はどれも /ɔ:/ である。

　　これら三つの語の母音が ME では別物であっても、今の英国発音ではすべて同じ母音 /ɔ:/ になり得たのは、後続の R のおかげである。15 世紀以降、イングランド南東部の教養ある人々が母音の後の R 無しの発音を受け入れるようになった 18 世紀末（Gimson, § 8.8）に至るまで、R は母音の発音にさまざまな影響を与え続けた。[11] これらの語の現在の発音 /ɔ: / は、ME で母音の後の R が発音されていた形（course ME /ku:rs /, board ME /bo:rd /, beforne ME /-ɔrn /）から発達したものと考えなくてはならない。「初期」R 脱落が介在するものではない。

2.3.　de Worde 版 **PML** に修正されたライム

　　PML では修正されているが、H に「初期」R 脱落を示すライムがもう

Ipomydon（B）とその Wynkyn de Worde 版の「初期 R 消失」を示すライム

一つある。

637 - 38　H glad（adj. pred. sg.）（ OE glæd ）: herd（p. sg.）'heard'（OE hērde
＞ late OE herde）; PML glad : had（3 pt. sg.）（OE hæfde, early ME hædde）.

このライムが使われた 637-38 行は下記の文脈である：

H　　　　Ipomydon in hert was full **glad** ／ Whan that he the tythyngis **herd**
PML　　Ipomydon in herte was full **glad** ／ Whan that he the tydynges **had**

　印刷原稿 H 写本の 638 行には、tythyngis と herd の間に挿入のマークが
入れられ、その上に had と書き込みがある。この had が、写本の地の部分
よりずっと黒みの濃いインクの色で残っているので、この修正は写本本体
を書き写した人物とは明らかに別人の手によるものと分かる（ Ikegami,
Vol I, p. xv; Vol II, p.xliii）。Meale（19 82）はこれを de Worde 工房の編集者に
よる修正で、印刷に回す前に原稿に手を加えた例の一つとして挙げている
（p. 167）。Kölbing（1889）の edition ではこの had を採用し、Sánchez-Martí
（2009）§1.10 では、PML は脚韻語 herd を had に入れ替えることだけで、
明白な corrupt rhymes の一つを簡単に修正した（p. 512）と述べている。
Ikegami も H の glad : herd はテクストの伝承過程で生じた corrupt rhyme と
取っていたが（ Ikegami, vol. I, p.liv）、他の解釈ができるのではないか：即
ち herd 'heard' の ME /er/ の /ar/ への変化を前提とすると、ライムは glad :
hard になる。ここで R の「初期」消失を hard に認めると、H の意図した
ライムは両語の ME / ad / に基づくライムとして成立する。
　道徳劇 *Everyman* の同じタイプのライムに注目したい：759-60 bad（adj.）
（ME badde（OE bæddel））: harde（p.ppl.）'heard'（A. C. Cawley, ed., *Everyman*,
1978）。この組み合わせも不完全ライムと見なされてきたが、ここでも同
様に harde 'heard' の ME /er/ ＞ /ar/ への変化と R の脱落を想定すると、
ME /ad/ のライムであると正当化出来る。*Everyman* は 15 世紀末か 16 世紀
初めにロンドンで書かれた作品とされている（*Manual*, 5 [30]）。

2. 4.　ME /er/ ＞ ME /ar/

　ME の短母音 e が続く R 音の影響を受けて ME a へと変化したのは、14世紀の音韻変化である。この変化は 14 世紀初頭北部方言に始まりこの世紀末には南部方言にも現われるようになったが、新しい発音 /ar/ はなかなか受け入られず、古い発音 /er/ も共存していた（Dobson II,§ 64; Jordan §§ 67, 270）。Heard については Wyld, *Coll. Eng.*, p. 218 に 15 世紀から 18 世紀にかけての ME /ar/ を示すライム（herde : farde, *Siege of Rouen,* c.1420）やスペリング〈harde, hard〉が挙げてあるのだが、de Worde 工房にはこの語の /ar / 型は馴染みがなかったのであろう。そこで、原稿 H の glad : herd に代えて、書き加えられた had を採用して 見た目の良い glad : had へと躊躇無い修正に至ったに違いない。PML のこのライムの修正は、herd の R 音の有無と直接の関係はない。

　Herde（p., p.ppl.）‘heard’（OE herde（p.）, herd（p.ppl.））と言う語は、このライムの他、三つのライムに用いられている。このうち二つは ME /-erd/ を持つ OE fēran の過去単数 fēr(e)de ＞ late OE ferde との self-rhyme である（1629-30 H herde（p. sg.）: ferde（p. sg.）‘proceeded’; PML herde（p. ppl.）: ferde （p. sg.）. 2175-76 H herde（p. sg.）: ferd（p. sg.）happened’; PML herde（p. sg.）: ferde（p. sg.）。残りの一つが、H の詩人は heard の ME /ar /（＜ ME /er/）発音を知っていたこと、一方 de Worde 工房はそれを好まなかったことを示すライムである：

2229-30 H　herd（p. pl.）: thedyrward（adv.）‘towards that place’（OE þiderweard）; PML　herde : thyderwerde.

　ここで H は herd を接尾辞の -ward ＜ OE -weard とライムさせている。接尾辞 -ward は今の英語の発音では unstressed form の /-wəd/ であるが、toward（prep.）（OE tōweard）のように -ward に stress をうけると /-wɔːd/ である（*LPD* が記している英国発音は［təˈwɔːd, tu- ; tɔːd]）。Thither, -ward は Jones の *EPD*（14ᵗʰ edn.）に記載があって、接尾辞の部分には -wəd と共に、広く使われているが -wəd より一般的ではない発音として［-wɔːd]を挙げ

ている。H がライムに使用した -ward は stressed form に違いないから、現
代の /-wɔːd/ の直系の祖先、ME /-ard/（Dobson II, §§ 49, 195 参照）を持っ
て発音されていたはずである。従って、H の herd : -ward のライムは、
herd は 〈-er-〉を使って書き表されているが、H 詩人がここで使った発音
は -ar- 型、/hard/ であったとするのが妥当であると思える。一方 PML は、
herd の 〈er〉はそのまま置いて、それに合わせて -ward にも 〈er〉のスペ
リングを使い、見かけ上申し分のないライムに直している。

　実際、PML がよく使ったもっとも安直なライムの修正術はスペリング
を操作することである。特に固有名詞のライム部分のスペリングを必要に
応じて自在に操る手法は一部の ME 詩によく見られるものである。PML
の例を挙げる：

919-20　　H　man（n.）（OE man(n), mon(n)）: Ipomydon;　PML　man : Ipomydan

941-42　　H　Ipomydon : þan（adv.）'then'（OE þanne, þonne ）; PML　Ipomydan :
　　　　　than

459-60　　H　tane（p.ppl.）'taken'（taken の 短 縮 形）: Ipomydon;　PML tane :
　　　　　Ipomydane

　ここでは主人公の名前 Ipomydon の末尾の音節 -don をライム相手によっ
て 〈-dan〉,〈-dane〉とスペリングを代えている。

　しかし、ME er ＞ ar の変化について PML は全く知らなかったのではな
い。H の dwerf / dwerffe（n.）'dwarf'（OE dweorg, dweorh）1741, 1749, 1770,
1810, etc. の 〈-er-〉に対して、PML は規則的にすべてを 〈-ar-〉に改めて
dwarfe にしている。一方、H のほうは、スペリング 〈-ar-〉は決して使わな
い。99-100 smert（p. sg.）'caused pain'（OE *smeart; 13th c. smart（p. sg.）（*OED*
s.v. smart v.））: hert（n.）'heart'（OE heort）のライムでは作者の hert の母音の
発音は ME er ＞ ar の変化を経た /ar/ であったに違いないが、H 写本のスペ
リングは 〈-er-〉である。この 99 － 100 行は de Worde 版に対応するもの
がないが、'heart' が使われているもう一つのライム 1073-74 は ME /er/ の
self-rhyme, H hert（n.）'heart': smerte（inf.）（OE smeortan）; PML herte : smerte

では、H と PML 共にスペリングは〈-er-〉である。

3.　おわりに

　2.2 で触れた Hill（1940）の論文では、R 音の子音の前での「初期消失」を示すもっとも早いスペリングが 11 世紀の写本にあるとして、'cress'（植物・クレソン）（OE cresse, cerse）と 'gorse'（植物・ハリエニシダ）（OE gors, gorst）がそれぞれ cesena tācen 'the sign of cress'（ces ＜ cers + ena（gen. pl.））、gost（＜ gorst）と書かれていることを挙げている（pp.320-21; 326, 330）。この例は少なくともこれら二つの語の R は、11 世紀にすでに発音されなくなっていたことを示している。ライムが英語の詩の構成要素として用いられるようになったのを 12 世紀初頭とすると、それ以降、この R 消失を証明するライムが ME 詩に自由に使われ始めても良いのだが、それがなかなか無い。

3.1.　*Kyng Alisaunder* と *Havelok* のライム

　G.V. Smithers は自身の校訂本 *Kyng Alisaunder* と *Havelok* の注で「初期 R 消失」を示すライムを数例挙げている。[12] この中で明確に R 消失を現わしていると思えるライムの一つは *Kyng Alisaunder*, Vol. II の 5089 行への注にある 6954-55 tache（1 pr. sg.）'teach'（OE tǣcan（ǣ^2））: Marche（n.）'March'（OF marche）である。このライムは tache の /aːʃə/ と Marche の /arʃə/ とのライムである。Tache の ME /aː/ は OE ǣ の特別の発達で、Essex-London 地域に現われたものである。この ME /aː/ が Marche の /ar/ とライムして間違いなく Marche の R 音消失を立証している。[13] Smithers はこのタイプのライムは 'admitted at least in ME. Romances' と述べて *Havelok* 1038-9 のライム stareden（p. pl.）'stared'（OE starian（wk.v. II）＋ -odon（p. pl.））: ladden（n. pl.）'serving-men, young fellows'（ME ladde, of unknown origin）を挙げている。

　Smithers は *Havelok,* 1038-9 には注をつけて、1038 の stareden には stadden への修正が提案されているが、それはふさわしくない、として退け、ここで意図されたライムまさに starden : ladden である、と主張している。そう

であるならライムは /ardən/ : /adən/ であるから、star(e)den からの R 脱落を
示していることになる。更に、このような R 音の弱化の形跡は 'occasionally
traceable in ME writings' として Mannyng の *Chronicle* 15659-60 fled : wyþsperd
と 13393-4 pres : trauers を挙げている。この *Chronicle* は Northeast Midland
方言で書かれ 1338 年に完成された作品（*Manual*, 8 [8]）である。

　Kyng Alisaunder は 14 世紀初頭の London 方言で書かれた作品である
（*Manual*, 1, [64]）。*Havelok* はおよそ 1280 年から 1300 年の間に Lincolnshire
の方言で書かれた作品である（*Manual*, 1, [5]）。いずれも上掲 2.1 と 2.3 の
Ipomydon（*B*）とそれを踏襲した Wynkyn de Worde 版 PML のライム、ある
いは 2.2 で触れた Wyld, *Rhymes* の 1443 年のライムより、150 年から 200 年
程前の R の「初期消失」を示唆するものである。これらがこのタイプの
ライムの一番早い用例であろうか。

3.2. *Eger and Grime* と Skelton の *Phylyp Sparrowe* のライム

　実際、子音の前の R 音消失を示唆するライムはなかなか見つからない。
私が今まで調べた限りでは、本稿の *Ipomydon*（*B*）とその de Worde 版以外
では、いずれも 1400 年以降の popular verse と分類されるような作品の中に、
それぞれ大概は一作品につき一個限りの用例を見たにすぎない。Chaucer
や Gower, Hoccleve, Lydgate, それに Henryson など高名な中世詩人達の作品
には無かった。

　ところが最近、French and Hale の *Middle English Metrical Romances,* Vol. II
に納められた *Eger and Grime* という韻文ロマンスに *Ipomydon*（*B*）と同種
の R 音消失、つまり子音 /s/, /d/, /n/ の前にある R 消失、を示すライムが、
一作品の中に揃って現れるのを見つけた。それをここに付け加えたい。上
記 2.1 と 2.3 に挙げた *Ipomydon*（*B*）のライムは決して特異なものではなく、
同種の用例は他の作品にも存在することの実例である。

　Eger and Grime は 15 世紀半ば、スコットランドのフォース湾沿いの
Linlithgow あたりの北部方言で書かれた作品で（*Manual*, I, [100]）、1474
行の couplets からなる。R 消失を立証するライムは下記の四つである。各
組の語の組み合わせが *Ipomydon*（*B*）によく似ている。ライム誂えに関す

る同一の伝統を持ち合わせていたようである。

374 worse（adj. comp.）（= werse < ON verri（*wersi）; *OED* s.v. worse, adj. and
　　sb.; B-forms: 2-6 werse）: distresse（n.）'distress'（OF destrece, destresse）
985 word（n.）（OE word）: woode（adj. pred. sg.）'mad'（OE wōd）
1028 sworde（n.）'sword'（OE sword）: childhood（n.）（suffix -hood < OE -hād）
1065 borne（p. ppl.）'born'（OE boren）: one（pron.）（OE ān）

　　R が発音されないのは /s/ の前で 374 の worse（詩人が意図したのは -ers-
型、werse）、/d/ の前で 985 の word と 1028 の sworde、そして /n/ の前で
1065 の borne である。374 worse（= werse）: distresse のライムは ME / es / に
基づく。985 word : woode は ME / o:d / に基づく。Word の OE o + rd は長母
音 OE ō を維持、ME で /o:/。1028 sword : childhood も ME / o:d / に基づく。
Sword の ME /o:/ は word 同様 < OE ō < OE o + rd。Cildhood の接尾辞
-hood には ME open /ɔ: / < OE ā から ME close /o:/ への変化がある（本論の
注 8 参照）。1065 borne : one は ME / -ɔn / に基づく。Borne の短母音 /ɔ / は
ME の開音節伸張を受けなかったもの、one の /ɔ / は ME /ɔ: / < OE ā の短
縮形（*Ipomydon（B）*の on : befforne 上記 2.1 参照）。

　　最後に、John Skelton（c.1460-1529）の *Phylyp Sparowe* のライムを付け加
えたい。これは de Worde 版 PML が原稿 *Ipomydon（B）* の R 消失を意味す
るライムをそのまま残した（上記 2.1）のは、スペリングの異なりを見落
として修正しそびれた結果ではなく、実際に R 無しの発音が当時のロン
ドンで普通であったからではないかと思わせるライムである。それは次の
二つである。

122 wormes（n. pl.）'worms'（OE wyrm, later wurm）: crommes（n. pl.）'crumbs'
　　（OE cruma）
684 further（inf.）'promote'（OE fyrþr(i)an）: other（pron.）（OE ōþer）:

　これらのライムでは 122 の wormes から /m/ の前の R、684 の further から /ð/ の前の R が発音されない。ライムの stressed vowel は共に /u/ である。前者の wormes, crommes の ME /u/ ＞ early ModE /u/, 後者の other の ME/o:/ または early ModE /u:/ は短縮されて /u/ となり（Dobson, II, § 4）、それが further の early ModE /u/（＜ ME /u/＜ OE y）とライムしている。

　Skelton（? 1460-1529）は古典を修め 'laureate' の称号を与えられた宮廷詩人である。*Phylyp Sparowe* はおそらく 1505 年の作とされもので、全部で 1382 行 の 'Skeltonic verse' で あ る（John Scattergood ed., *John Skelton: The Complete English Poems,* 1983）。Skelton のライムに現われた発音は、まさに 15 世紀後半から 16 世紀前半のロンドンの、宮廷やその周辺の教育のある人々の、英語の発音であろう。de Worde 工房の人々もこのタイプの発音に親しんでいた筈である。1498 年秋に書かれた Skelton の *The Bowge of Courte* はその翌年 de Worde が出版している（Scattergood, p.16）。Skelton と de Worde 工房の近さを感じる。

注

1.　Tadahiro Ikegami, ed. *The Lyfe of Ipomydon*, Vol. I（Tokyo: Seijo U. 1983）, lx -lxiv.
2.　Carol M. Meale, 'Wynkyn de Worde's Setting-Copy for "Ipomydon".' *Studies in Bibliography,* vol. 35（1982）, 156-171.
3.　BL, PML が印刷された年代について *STC* は BL が c.1522、PML が c.1527 としてきたが、Sánchez-Martí（2005）では PML が初版本で 1520 から 1524 の間に印刷されたもの、BL は PML 版に基づいて印刷された後発本であるとしている。
4.　ロッテ・ヘリンガ著、徳永聡子訳　高宮利行監修「初期イングランド印刷史―キャクトンと後継者たち」雄松堂書店（2013）。特に pp. 139-155、"ド・ウオード、出版業者として独立する（1496〜1535 年）"。
5.　Sánchez-Martí（2009）では de Worde 工房が原稿 H の読みに加えた多様な変更を分類し記載している。この記載方法は Nicolas Jacobs（1995）が本文批判（textual criticism）の視点から示した手法に沿ったものである。Jacobs は、韻文ロマンス *Sir Degarre* が *Auchinleck* MS（c. 1300）に最初に現われてから、16 世紀半ば de Worde など印刷業者の手を経て、17 世紀半ば *Percy Folio* で哀れな姿に終わるほほ 300 年の間に、どのように写し替えられていったか、

作品が書き写されるたびに生じる variants を分析、分類して記述した。

6. de Worde 工房で用いたスペリングについては Mark Aronoff（1989）で論じられている。

7. この例を二つ挙げる。（i）885-86　H　Ipomydon to his maister **camme** / He found hym and his houndis **anone**; PML Ipomydon to his mayster came **soone** / And founde hym and his greyhoundes **anone**. ここでは PML は H の camme（p. sg.）'came' の後に soone（adv.）'soon'（OE sōna）を付け足して、それを anone（adv.）'at once'（OE on ān(e)）とライムさせた。元の H のライム camme : anone は原作者の言語では 'to come' の過去形に ME /oː/ を持った OE cōm に由来する形（coom/ come ）が残存していたことを立証するものだが、それは PML で無くなった。PML の 'to come' の過去形は <came> に統一されている。

（ii）1495-96　H　In his sadille þey sette hym **bakwarde** / And bound hym **faste with a cord**; PML　In his sadle they set hym **backewarde** / And bound hym **with a cord full harde**. H は bakwarde の接尾辞 -ward（OE -weard）の ME /ard/ と cord（n.）（OF corde）の ME /ɔrd/ をライムさせている。これは H の cord の発音に ME /ɔ/ から ME /a/ への変化があったこと（Dobson, II, §§ 87, 194, n.3; Jordan, § 272）を匂わせるものだが、PML は cord を含むフレーズを書き直し -ward と見合う harde（adv.）'hard'（OE hearde）をライムに据えたので、それは全く分からなくなった。

8. ME の long open vowels /ɛː/ と /ɔː/ に対する異音 long close vowels /eː/ と /oː/ の発達は、一般に後に続く子音 dentals が及ぼした combinative change によるものとされてきたが、Dobson はこれを independent change とし、北部や東部の地方言に顕著であった発音だが、やがて London の教育ある人々にも受け入られていったとしている（II, §§ 121-25; 148-52）。

9. なお、syllabic consonant の発達については Dobson, II, §§ 318-26 参照。

10. 1227-28 は PML が H の本文を書き直して、平凡なライムを捻出した：H And hyr leman **hyr byforne** / Scantly had þey **the mete corvyn**; PML And her lemman, **without dout**; / Scantly had they **mete set out**　ここでも PML の修正によって、文意の表現方は平板になり、元著者の意図したライムの発音は全く分からなくなった。

11. RP /ɔː/ については、Gimson, 7. 9. 8.（4）；ME /uː, oː, ɔ / + R に関する発達については、特に Dobson, §§ 165, 207, 218 を参照されたい。

12. これは私の友人、*Kyng Alisaunder* 研究者の松沢絵里さんにご指摘いただいたもので（2019 年 12 月 6 日）、これが私のこの小論のきっかけになった。

13. Smithers は他に二つ *Kyng Alisaunder* から R 消失を示すと解釈可能なライムを挙げている：5089-90 þurst（n.）'thirst'：for-þrest（p.ppl.）（cf. OE -þræstan 'to crush'（OED, s.v. threst, thrast v. obs.）；1341-42 werst（a. super.）'worst'：to-brest

Ipomydon（B）とその Wynkyn de Worde 版の「初期 R 消失」を示すライム

（inf.）'burst'。更に「14 世紀宗教詩集」に納められた 'Vernon Lyrics' から一つ、*RLFC*,104, 39 bast（inf.）'burst, be broken suddenly'。この語は hast（2 pr. sg. of 'have'）, wast（n.）（in ～ 'wastefully'）, a-tast（imp. sg.）'put to test' とライムしている。ただし、各ライムの中で R 消失を想定される語は、それぞれ R の音位転換（metathesis）による異形を持つ語なので、R 消失を確実に立証するとは言えない。*Kyng Alisauder* 5089 の þurst（n.）に対して Smithers は詩人の意図した形として þerst を呈示しているが、これには r が e の前にある þrest がある（*OED*, s.v. thirst（sb.））。次の *Kyng Alisaunder* 1342 の to-brest（inf.）の -brest と Vernon Lyric の 39, bast（inf.）は同じ語で、今の英語の 'burst' である。この語にはさまざまな異形が共存し brest/berst（OE berstan）、brast/ barst（OE p. sg. of berstan, bærst）は ME で不定詞として機能していた（*OED*, s.v. burst（v.））。

参考文献

Primary Sources

Brown, Carleton, ed. 1924. *Religious Lyrics of the XIVth Century*. 2nd edn. rev. G. V. Smithers. 1952, 1957, 1965, 1970. Oxford: Clarendon Press,.

Cawley, A. C., ed., 1961, rpt. 1978. *Everyman*. Manchester: Manchester U. P.

French, Walter Hoyt and Charles Brockway Hale, eds. 1964. *Middle English Metrical Romances*. Vol. II. New York: Russell & Russell.

Ikegami, Tadahiro, ed. 1983. *The Lyfe of Ipomydon. Vol. I Text and Introduction*. Seijo English Monograph, No. 21. Tokyo: Seijo University.

Ikegami, Tadahiro, ed. 1985. *The Lyfr of Ipomydon. Vol. II. The Two Imperfect Early Printed Editions of 'The Lyfe of Ipomydon' With an Introduction*. Seijo English Monograph, No. 22. Tokyo: Seijo University.

Macaulay, G. C. ed. 1900-01. *John Gower's English Works: Edited from the Manuscripts, with Introduction, Notes, and Glossary*. Vol. 1（1900, rpt.1963）EETS ES 81. Vol. 2（1901, rpt. 1957）EETS ES 82. London: Oxford University Press.

Scattergood, John, ed. 1983. *John Skelton: The Complete English Poems*. New Haven and London: Yale U. P.

Smithers, G. V., ed. 1952. *Kyng Alisaunder. Vol. I: Text*. EETS OS 227. London: Oxford University Press.

Smithers, G. V., ed. 1957. *Kyng Alisaunder. Vol. II: Introduction, Commentary and Glossary*. EETS OS 237. London; Oxford University Press.

Smithers, G. V., ed. 1987. *Havelok*. Oxford: Clarendon Press.

Secondary Sources

Aronoff, Mark. 1989. "The Orthographic System of an Early English Printer: Wynkyn de Worde." *Folia Linguistica Historica* 8, 1-2, 65-97.

Dobson, E. J. 1968. *English Pronunciation 1500-1700.* 2nd edn. 2 vols. Oxford: Clarendon Press.

Ekwall, Eilert. Trans. and ed. Alan Ward. 1975. *A History of Modern English Sounds and Morphology.* Oxford: Basil Blackwell.

Gimson, A. C. 1962. *An Introduction to the Pronunciation of English.* 4th edn. Rev. Susan Ramsaran. 1989. London: Edward Arnold.

Hartung, Albert E. gen. ed. *A Manual of the Writings in Middle English 1050-1500. [Manual].* Vol. 5, 1975 . New Haven, Connecticut: The Connecticut Academy of Arts and Sciences. Vol. 8, 1989. New Haven, Connecticut: Archon Books for The Connecticut Academy of Arts and Sciences.

Hill, Archibald A. 1940. "Early Loss of [r] Before Dentals." *PMLA* 55: 308-59.

Jones, Daniel. 1917. *Everyman's English Pronouncing Dictionary.* 14th edn. rev. and ed. A. C. Gimson, 1977. [*EPD*]. London: Dent & Sons.

Jacobs, Nicolas, ed. 1995. *The Later Versions of 'Sir Degarre': A Study in Textual Degeneration. Medium Aevum Monograph*, New Series XVIII. Oxford: The Society for the Study of Medieval Languages and Literature.

Jordan, Richard. Trans. and rev. Eugene Joseph Crook. 1974. *Handbook of Middle English Grammar: Phonology.* Hague: Mouton.

Kölbing, Eugen, ed. 1889. *The Lyfe of Ipomydon.* Breslau.

McIntosh, Angus, M. L. Samuels, Michael Benskin. 1986. *A Linguistic Atlas of Late Medieval English.* 4 vols. [*LALME*]. Aberdeen: Aberdeen University Press.

Meale, Carol M. 1982. "Wynkyn de Worde's Setting-Copy for 'Ipomydon'." *Studies in Bibliography*, vol. 35: 156-171.

Pickeles, J. D. & J. L. Dawson, eds. 1987. *A Concordance to John Gower's 'Confessio Amantis'.* Cambridge: D. S. Brewer.

Pollard, A. W., & G. R. Redgrave. *A Short-Title Catalogue of Books Printed in England, Scotland, & Ireland, and of English Books Printed abroad 1475-1640.* 2nd edn. Rev. and Enlarged by W. A. Jackson, F. S. Furguson & Katharine F. Pantzer. 1986. Vol. 1. [*STC*]. London: The Bibliographical Society.

Sánchez-Martí, Jordi. 2005. "Wynkyn de Worde's Edition of 'Ipomydon' : A Reassessmnet of the Evidence." *Neophilologus* 89: 153-63.

Sánchez-Martí, Jordi. 2009. 'The Textual Transition of the Middle English Verse Romances from Manuscript to Print: A Case Study.' *Neuphilologishe Mittenlungen* : 497-525

Severs, J. Burke, gen. ed. 1967. *A Manual of the Writings in Middle English 1050-1500. [Manual].* Vol. 1. New Haven, Connecticut: The Connecticut Academy of Arts and Sciences.

Wells, J. C. 1990. *Longman Pronunciation Dictionary.* ［*LPD*］. Harlow: Longman.

Wright, Joseph and Elizabeth Mary Wright. 1923, 2nd edn. 1928, rpt. 1962. *An Elementary Middle English Grammar.* Oxford: Clarendon Press.

Wyld, Henry Cecil. 1920, 3rd edn. 1936, rpt. 1956. *A History of Modern Colloquial English.* ［Wyld, *Coll. Eng.*］. Oxford: Basil Blackwell.

Wyld, Henry Cecil. 1923, reissued 1965. *Studies in English Rhymes from Surrey to Pope: A Chapter in the History of English.* ［Wyld, *Rhymes*］. New York: Russell & Russell.

ロッテ・ヘリンガ著、德永聡子訳、高宮利行監修. 2013. 「初期イングランド印刷史―キャクストンと後継者たち」東京：雄松堂書店

ヘルシンキコーパスの後期中英語から初期近代英語における二項句の変遷 ——テキストタイプ、頻度、語源の観点から[1]

谷　　明　　信

1.　はじめに

　近年 time and tide のような A and/or B 形式の binomials（二項句）が再注目されている。二項句は "coordinated pair of linguistic units of the same word class which show some semantic relation" と、Kopaczyk & Sauer（2017: 3）に定義されている。この二項句は中世作品には頻出し、例えば、（1）のように、公文書では現代英語まで使用される定型的な二項句も存在し、（2）のように William Caxton はこれを多用する。なお、以下の引用例で、二項句には下線を、多項句（multinomials）には破線下線を、筆者が施した。

（1）Pleas it therfore yo=r= most noble Grace by thadvyce and assent of the lordes sp~uall and temporall in this p~sent parliament assemblid and by auctorite of the same, in consideracion of the p~mysses to ordeyn establissh and enacte, that the seid Acte and orden=a=nce in the seid last Parliament made and ordeyned may alwey stand contynewe and endure in p~fite strenght and effecte[2].　（ME4: CMLAW）

（2）Thus endeth this boke which is named the boke of Consolacion of philosophie whiche that boecius made for his comforte and consolacion he beyng in exile for the comyne and publick wele hauyng grete heuynes & thoughtes and in maner of despayr（ME4: CAXTPRO）[3]

　このような二項句の歴史的研究として、後期近代英語と現代英語についての Mollin（2014）が、さらに古英語から現代英語までを網羅した歴史的研究の論文集 Kopaczyk & Sauer（2017）が出版された。しかし、Archer Corpus と COHA により 1600-2000 年までの二項句を調査した Mollin

（2017）、Helsinki Corpus により古英語から初期近代英語の二項句を含む "apposition with an explicit markers" を調査した Pahta & Nevanlinna（1997）、同コーパスにより後期中英語から初期近代英語の二項句を調査した谷（2017）を除いて、二項句の史的変遷を扱った研究は少ない。また、後者 2 つの研究は Helsinki Corpus での二項句の変遷についての明確な結論を出していない。

　本研究は Helsinki Corpus の後期中英語から初期近代英語期である ME3（1350-1420）、ME4（1420-1500）、EModE1（1500-1570）、EModE2（1570-1640）、EModE3（1640-1710）の 5 期を対象に、時代とテキストタイプの分類に基づき、A and B 形式の二項句の頻度と語源の史的変遷を調査する[4]。また、英語の語彙の変遷との関連と、Helsinki Corpus の問題点についても議論する。なお、本研究で対象とする二項句は A and B であり、接続要素が & また or, nor, either, oþþe などの用例は含めない。なお、本研究が対象とする Helsinki Corpus には、時代・テキストタイプ・方言などのパラミターが付加されており、*KWIC Concordance for Windows Ver.5* を用いて、その情報を利用し検索した[5]。

2.　二項句の頻度

2.1.　二項句の実頻度

　二項句の頻度を調査した結果、コーパス全体でのタイプ頻度は 5786、トークン頻度は 8255 である。そのうち、繰り返し使用される二項句は 885 タイプ、3354 トークンで、全体の 40.6％ を占める。二項句が 300 以上のトークン頻度を示すテキストタイプは以下の通りである。

> LAW（971）, REL TREAT（777）, SERMON（725）, HISTORY（588）, PHILOSOPHY（488）, HANDB OTHER（434）, EDUC TREAT（410）, FICTION（405）, BIBLE（384）, DOCUM（366）, LET NON-PRIV（366）, TRAVELOGUE（306）

このうち、SERMON, HISTORY と FICTION のみが全 5 期のテキストを含み、REL TREAT と DOCUM は ME3, ME4 のみで存在し、その他のテキストタイプは 3 ないし 4 期のテキストを含んでいる。このリストによれば、説教や聖書でも生起数は多い。しかし、テキストの総語数に相違があり、例えば、総語数が LAW は 4 時代で 47990 語、REL TREAT は 2 時代で 78170 語、BIBLE は 4 時代で 66860 語である[6]。従って、時代によるテキストタイプの語数に違いがあるため、実頻度による比較は困難である[7]。

　次に、トークン頻度 100 以下のテキストタイプは以下の通りである。

DRAMA COMEDY（99）, RULE（67）, BIOGR AUTO（66）, HOMILY（54）, HANDB ASTRONOMY（53）, BIOGR LIFE SAINT（25）, PROC DEPOS（16）, HANDB MEDICINE（0）

喜劇、自叙伝、説教、聖人伝、天文学・医学手引きなどであるが、これらのテキストタイプは喜劇を除いて、トークン頻度の高いテキストタイプよりも存在する時代が少ない傾向にある。

2.2.　テキストタイプによる二項句の正規化頻度

　上記の理由により、テキストタイプによる二項句の全時代での 1000 語あたりの正規化頻度を検討する。計算の結果、コーパス全体の二項句の正規化頻度は 8.7 であった。テキストタイプと二項句の関連性をより理解するため、ここでは時代に関わりなくテキストタイプ全体での正規化頻度が、コーパス全体の正規化頻度 8.7 と隔たりが大きいテキストタイプを考察する。

　正規化頻度がきわめて高いテキストタイプには、LAW 20.2, PREFACE/EPIL 20.0, DOCUM 14.1, LET NON-PRIV 14.1 があり、それぞれ法文書、（書物の）序文・終章、文書、非私的（＝公的）書簡である。一方、正規化頻度が低いテキストタイプは BIBLE 5.7, PROC TRIAL 5.6, DIARY PRIV 5.4, SCIENCE OTHER 5.2, LET PRIV 5.0, BIOGR AUTO 4.3, HANDB ASTRONOMY 3.3, DRAMA COMEDY 2.8, HANDB MEDICINE 0 で、それぞ

れ聖書、弁論記録、私的日記、他の科学、私的書簡、自伝、天文書、喜劇、医学書である。

LAW と DOCUM は Statutory という同一の上位カテゴリーに集約され、また、LET NON-PRIV も公的書簡で、これらの文書は公的性質の強いテキストである。一方、正規化頻度が低いテキストタイプは聖書や、私的な日記と私的書簡、科学文書、さらに弁論記録や科学である。正規化頻度の点で最も対照的であるのは、同じ書簡でありながら公的な LET NON-PRIV と私的な LET PRIV である[8]。

ここで、上記のいくつかのテキストタイプの用例を見てゆく。LAW については（1）で、また、PREFACE/EPIL については（2）で見た。（3）は DOCUM から、（4）は BIBLE から、（5）は LET PRIV から、（6）は SCIENCE OTHER からの引用である。

(3) For the furst article of theire grevous compleyntis the saide Maier and Cominalte seyn that there as where the tenantis and inhabitants of the saide Bysshop with ynne the sayde Cite and suburb of the same ben cessable and chargable . . . （ME4: CMDOCU4）

(4) Blessed bee Abram of the most high God, possessour of heauen and earth, （EModE2: CEOTEST2）

(5) Right worshipful Sir, in my most harte wyse I recommend me unto you, desiring to here of your welfare and good speed in your matters. （EModE1: CEPRIV1）

(6) . . . the difference of Longitude whereof we shall speake hereafter more at large when we come to treate of the Longitude and Latitude of the earth . . . （EModE2: CESCIE2B）

これらの用例を見れば明らかだが、同じ二項句といえども、その構成要素の語源や音節数などが明らかに異なり、テキストタイプの特質を反映している。

2.3.　コーパス全体での正規化頻度と品詞の割合の変遷

　ここでは実頻度に基づき 1000 語あたりの正規化頻度を時代毎に計算した。なお、先に述べたように全体での正規化頻度は 8.7 である。さらに、この正規化頻度を品詞に分類し、その変遷を図 1 にまとめた。

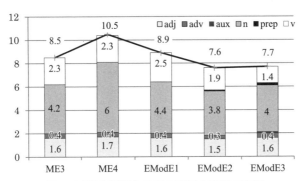

図 1：正規化頻度と品詞の正規化頻度の変遷

　まず、コーパス全体での二項句の正規化頻度を時代別に観察すると、ME3 での 8.5 から正規化頻度が上昇し、ME4 の 10.5 でピークに達し、EModE1-2 と減少、EModE2-3 はほぼ横ばいで推移する。ただし、EModE1 の正規化頻度は ME3 より若干高い。品詞で分類し頻度を検討すると、動詞、形容詞、副詞の二項句の頻度はほぼ変化がないため、ME4 での正規化頻度の高さの要因が名詞二項句の増加であることが判明した。なお、この増加は後述するように、借用語の増加と関連する可能性がある。ただし、動詞の二項句は EModE2-3 の時代に減少し、同時代に前置詞は 0.1, 0.2 に増加し、助動詞も EModE3 で 0.1 に増加する[9]。

2.4.　テキストプロトタイプでの正規化頻度の変遷

　ヘルシンキコーパスは全 22 のテキストタイプを設定し、それを包括する上位カテゴリーとして、次の 6 つのテキストプロトタイプ（以下、プロトタイプ）を設定する。(1) statutory (STA), (2) secular instruction (IS), (3)

religious instruction（IR）,（4）expository（EX）,（5）non-imaginative narration
（NN）,（6）imaginative narration（IN）。後述するように、テキストタイプに
は時代的に不連続が存在する場合があり、すべてのタイプでの比較が困難
である。一方、プロトタイプでは不連続がほぼ存在しないが、分類不能
（XX）と言うカテゴリーがある。そのため、プロトタイプもテキストタイ
プも調査で用いるには一長一短があるが、まず、プロトタイプごとの二項
句の生起化頻度の変遷を考察する。その調査結果を、それぞれの正規化頻
度を付加し、図2にまとめた[10]。

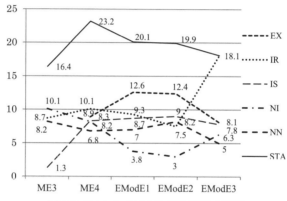

図2：プロトタイプの生起化頻度の変遷

　STA（LAW と DOCUM を含む）は正規化頻度がプロトタイプの中で一
番高く[11]、図1で見たコーパス全体の頻度と同様の推移パターンを示して
いる。なお、ME3 での正規化頻度は他の時代と比較して低いが、STA の
ME3 のテキスト総語数は 1520 語で、同テキストタイプの他の時代、また、
他のプロトタイプと比較し 1/10 以下であることを勘案する必要がある。
一方、NI や NN では時代とともに低下する。IS は ME3 での頻度が非常に
低く、ME4 で頻度が上昇し、その後、EModE1-3 期はほぼ横這いである。
SERMON, HOMILY, REL TREAT, RULE を含む IR は、ME3 から上昇し ME4
でピークに達し、EModE1, 2 期に減少しコーパス全体の頻度パターンに合

致するが、EModE3 のみが 2 倍以上に上昇し、非常に不自然である。これは、EModE3 の HOMILY のテキスト選択の影響と考えられる。

　最後に、EX の正規化頻度は、コーパス全体の正規化頻度 8.7 よりも高く、STA 以外のプロトタイプよりは高いが、STA の半分以下である。ME4 よりも EModE1, 2 に正規化頻度が上昇し、EModE3 で減少する。プロトタイプでの正規化頻度の変遷から、STA の頻度は高いが、図 1 で見たような変遷の傾向は見られない。

　さて、説明が主目的である EX（＝解説文）において、二項句の頻度がそれほど高くないことは示唆的である。二項句の使用目的として難解な借用語を本来語で解釈を示すという説（Jespersen（1982: 89-90））があるが、その目的が主要なものであれば、二項句は解説文においてこそ利用されると期待される。しかし、そうではない。言い換えの意味のある or ではなく、and を本調査が対象として調査することに起因する可能性もあるが、EX での頻度は解釈が二項句使用の主要因ではないことを間接的に示しているのではなかろうか[12]。

2.5.　テキストタイプでの正規化頻度の変遷

　時代によりテキストが欠如するテキストタイプがあるため、ここでは全 5 時代のうち、4 ないし 5 時代が存在するテキストタイプでの二項句の変遷を比較する。対象とするのは次の 5 つのテキストタイプである。すわなち、LAW、LET NON-PRIV、LET PRIV、BIBLE、SERMON である。これらのテキストタイプでの二項句の生起数から正規化頻度を時代ごとに求め、結果を二項句全体の数値（Avg.）とともに図 3 にまとめた。

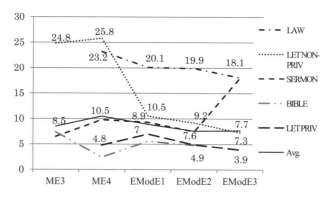

図3：テキストタイプによる正規化頻度の変遷

　全体では、BIBLE を除いて、ME3 から ME4 にかけて正規化頻度が増加して、それ以降は減少するという傾向が見られ、第2.3節で確認した二項句全体の傾向と合致する。なお、BIBLE の ME4 での減少と SERMON の EModE3 での上昇については後述する。

　まず、LAW は ME4 においては、LET NON-PRIV よりも頻度が低いものの、テキストタイプの中では頻度が高く、全正規化頻度8.7の倍以上の数値を示す。頻度は ME4 から漸次減少し、二項句全体の傾向に合致する。

　次に、LET NON-PRIV は ME3, 4 で頻度（24.8, 25.8）が顕著に高く、テキストタイプ中最高の正規化頻度を示し、この時代は LAW よりも正規化頻度が高い。その一方で、ME4 から EModE1 の正規化頻度（10.5）の減少の度合いは1/2以下と非常に大きい。これは ME4 から EModE1 で非私的（＝公的）書簡の書き方が変化した可能性を示唆する[13]。ただ、EModE1 以降の減少は比較的少ないが、EModE3 では正規化頻度3.9で二項句全体の正規化頻度よりも低くなる。ただし、LET NON-PRIV に関しては、他のテキストタイプと比べ総語数が少ないことに留意する必要がある。ME3 から EModE3 までの総語数は各々5010, 3140, 6300, 5660, 5870 語で、LAW や LET PRIV の約半数である。

　公的書簡と対照的なのが私的書簡 LET PRIV で、その正規化頻度は

EModE1 を除いて、二項句全体の正規化頻度 8.7 よりかなり低い。また、ME4 で増加し、EModE1 から減少するという二項句全体の傾向より、一時代遅れてずれている。EModE1 において正規化頻度 7 でピークに達し、それ以降減少する。

　次に BIBLE では正規化頻度が元々低いが、ME3 から全時代でさらに下落し続ける。なお、ME4 で正規化頻度が突然下落するが、これはテキスト選定の問題と考えられる（第 3.3 節で論じる）。同じ宗教的文書である SERMON では ME3 から EModE2 の間は二項句全体の変遷の傾向と合致し、正規化頻度も類似している。しかし、EModE3 での頻度が突然上昇し LAW と同じ 18.1 に達するのは不自然で、テキスト選定の問題と考えられる。また、BIBLE と比較して、SERMON は ME3 を除いて、正規化頻度が倍近い。

　5 テキストタイプの正規化頻度は、数値の違いや不自然な部分もあるものの、基本的に二項句全体の変遷の傾向と類似している。

　ここでの正規化頻度と第 2.2 節での考察から、二項句が公的で改まった文書において使用される傾向があること、一方、私的な場面では使用されない傾向があることが確認できる。また、客観性が求められる弁論の記録や科学文書では使用されない傾向があることも確認した。

3.　二項句の語源構成

　二項句の構成要素の語順と語源構成として主要なものは、OE（本来語）＋OE, OE＋OF（フランス語借用語）、OF＋OE、OF＋OF、その他である。もちろん、古ノルド語やオランダ語からの借用語の構成要素もあるが、全体の割合が少ないため、その他として扱う。

3.1.　全期でのテキストタイプによる二項句の語源構成
　二項句の語源構成の中で、割合が高い 2 つのタイプは OF＋OF, OE＋OE の語源構成であるため、これら 2 タイプの語源構成の割合に注目し分析を行う。コーパス全体で、OF＋OF あるいは OE＋OE の割合が 50％以上の

テキストタイプを抽出し、表1にまとめた。

表1：OF + OF か OE + OE の割合が **50%** を超えるテキストタイプ

	OF + OF	OE + OE	OE + OF	OF + OE	Others
DOCUM	51.9%	8.7%	18.3%	15.3%	5.7%
EDUC TREAT	51.7%	14.4%	19.0%	11.0%	3.9%
LAW	50.7%	17.5%	17.0%	8.9%	6.0%
DRAMA COMEDY	16.2%	52.5%	12.1%	10.1%	9.1%
HANDB A STRONOMY	11.3%	52.8%	17.0%	9.4%	9.4%
ROMANCE	8.9%	55.3%	16.3%	9.8%	9.8%
DRAMA MYST	12.6%	55.7%	9.3%	7.7%	14.8%
HOMILY	9.3%	63.0%	7.4%	7.4%	13.0%
BIBLE	11.5%	69.8%	8.6%	7.6%	2.6%
全体	32.4%	30.0%	17.4%	12.7%	7.5%

　表1から OF + OF の割合が高いテキストタイプは LAW、公文書関係の DOCUM と教育的論説の EDUC TREAT である。一方、OE + OE の割合が高いテキストタイプは BIBLE とそれに関連する HOMILY や DRAMA MYST（奇跡劇）である[14]。また、この OF + OF あるいは OE + OE の割合の高いテキストタイプは、それぞれ、第2.2節で確認した正規化頻度の高いテキストタイプと正規化頻度の低いテキストタイプの多くに重複することが確認できる。さらに、表1から、OF + OF の割合が高いテキストタイプでは OE + OE の割合が低く、一方、OE + OE の割合が高いテキストタイプでは OF + OF の割合が低くなる傾向があることが確認できる。つまり、あるテキストタイプでの OF + OF と OE + OE の割合は反比例する傾向があることを意味する。また、OE + OE の割合が高いテキストタイプでは、OE + OF と OF + OE の割合が低い傾向にあることも確認できる。

3.2.　コーパス全体の語源構成の割合の変遷

　上記の二項句構成要素の語源構成とその語順の分類に基づき、ME3 から EModE3 までの語源構成の割合の変遷を調査し、図 4 にまとめた。まず、全 期 間 の 語 源 構 成 の 割 合 は、OE + OE 30.0%, OE + OF 17.4%, OF + OE 12.7%, OF + OF 32.4%, その他 7.5% である。

　図 4 から明らかなように、OF + OF の割合は ME3 から継続的に増加し、対照的に OE + OE の割合は ME3 から継続的に減少する。また、OF + OE の割合は ME3 から継続的が減少する一方、変動があるものの OE + OF の割合はほぼ一定しており、OF + OE よりも OE + OF の方が全時代で割合が高い[15]。また、OF + OE はその割合が全期で徐々に減少する。全体では、OE + OE と OF + OF の割合が大きく変化し、特に ME4 から EModE1 の間に、割合の一番高い語源構成が OE + OE から OF + OF に逆転する。

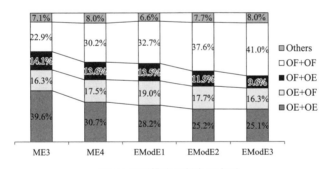

図 4：語源構成の割合の変遷

　なお、正規化頻度で語源構成の変遷を再考すると、OE + OE は ME3 から EModE2 まで減少し続け、一方 OF + OF は、ME4 で OE + OE と同じ正規化頻度に上昇したあと、ほぼ一定になる。このため、割合においては OF + OF が増加し続けているように見えるのである。

　二項句全体の語源構成の正規化頻度の変遷に関しては、ME4 でフランス語借用語の二項句構成要素が増加し、それが EModE 期に定着し、一方、

本来語の構成要素が減少する様子が読み取れる。なお既に指摘したように、ME4 での正規化頻度の上昇は、名詞二項句の増加が要因であるため、ME4 で増加した OF 要素の多くに名詞が関与している。

　モセ（1963: 89-90）によれば、フランス語借用語の英語への流入は 1350-1400 年にピークに達し、それ以降は急速に減少する。このピークの時代はヘルシンキコーパスの ME3（1350-1420）にあたる。フランス語借用語流入期のピークと、二項句での OF 要素の増加の時期（＝ME4）の間に時間的ズレはあるものの、二項句での OF 要素の増加は、英語語彙におけるフランス語借用語の増大と英語語彙の再編成を反映すると言えるであろう。さらに、EModE 以降での OE＋OE 二項句の減少については、後期中英語の語彙中でフランス語借用語が増加し、それらが元々の本来語と交替したためと、更にフランス語借用語が高い文体価を持つようになり、相対的に本来語の文体価が低下したために、文飾のために利用される二項句の中で、OE＋OE 二項句が減少したのではなかろうか。

3.3. テキストタイプによる二項句の語源構成の変遷

　テキストタイプにより二項句の語源構成に大きな差があることは既に確認した。ここではテキストタイプによる二項句の語源構成の変遷を、第 2.5 節で調査した 5 つのテキストタイプ LAW, LET NON-PRIV, LET PRIV, BIBLE, SERMON を対象に調査する。

　はじめに、LAW の二項句の語源構成の変遷を調査し、結果を図 5 にまとめた。

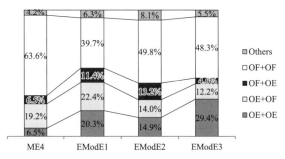

図 5 ：LAW での語源構成の割合の変遷

　注目すべき事は、LAW での語源構成の変遷傾向が、二項句全体の変遷
傾向と正反対である事である。つまり、変異はあるものの、LAW では、
ME4 と比較して EModE1-3 では OF + OF の割合が減少し、一方で OE + OE
の割合が増加する。すなわち、LAW では他のテキストタイプと対照的に、
二項句の脱フランス語化、つまり本来語化あるいは土着語化（＝
vernacularization）が進んでいると言えよう。二項句に見られる、この傾向
は、法文書自体の土着化を反映するものだろう。ノルマン人の征服以後、
法文書は元々ラテン語、次にフランス語で書かれていたが、それが英語に
移行した。英語の法関係の専門用語は、ほぼフランス語借用語で（Baugh
and Cable 2002: 158）、翻訳されずに用いられ、翻訳がある場合も直訳で
あった（Tiersma 2012: 22）。当初は二項句もフランス語に基づいていたも
のが大多数だった中に、第 3.4 節で見るような shall and may や by and with
のような本来語を持つ二項句が漸次増加したことも一因であろう[16]。
　次に、正規化頻度において対照的である LET NON-PRIV と LET PRIV を
検討する。まず LET NON-PRIV の二項句の語源構成の変遷を調査し、図
6 にまとめた。

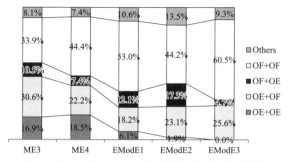

図6：LET NON-PRIV での語源構成の割合の変遷

LET NON-PRIV においては、全二項句の変遷傾向と合致し、OF + OF 二項句の割合が ME4 から顕著に増加する。EModE3 では OF + OF の割合は、60.5% と顕著に高い。その一方、OE + OE の割合は減少し続け、EModE3 では 0 となる。ただし、二項句全体の語源構成の変遷傾向と異なり、OE + OF の割合が高い。

　次に LET PRIV の語源構成の変遷を図 7 にまとめた。

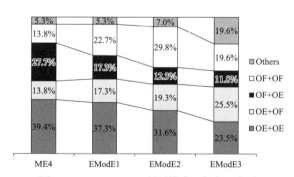

図7：LET PRIV での語源構成の割合の変遷

LET PRIV においても、OE + OE は継続的に減少し、一方で OF + OF の割合は ME4 から EModE2 まで増加し、EModE3 で減少する。また、OE + OF は継続的に増加し、反対に OF + OE は継続的に減少する。なお、EModE3

では OE + OF の割合が語源構成の中で最も高いが、これはテキストタイプ中では稀な現象である。OE + OE の減少という点ではコーパス全体と同じ傾向を示す。一方で、OE + OE と OF + OF のうち、前者の方が全期において割合が高いが、この点はこのテキストタイプの特徴で、LET NON-PRIV と対照的である。この 2 テキストタイプは正規化頻度の変遷で対照的であるが、語源構成の変遷においても同じ事が言える。さらに、このことから、正規化頻度の多寡が、主要な語源構成が OF + OF か OE + OE ということと相関することが改めて確認できる。

次に、BIBLE の二項句の語源構成の変遷を調査し、図 8 にまとめた。

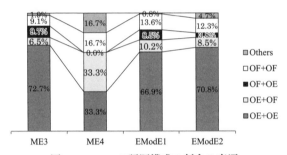

図 8：BIBLE の語源構成の割合の変遷

BIBLE での語源構成の変遷の特徴は、ME4 を除いて、語源構成は基本的に OE + OE が 70% 前後で一定し、他の語源構成の割合も変化が少ないことである。ただし、OF + OF は ME4 を除いて、EMod1, 2 においてわずかに増加している。OE + OE の割合の高さは、本来語を重視する聖書の翻訳方法の伝統のためと考えられる。BIBLE の ME4 は語源構成が他の時代と較べ不自然で、これは第 2.5 節で指摘した不自然な正規化頻度と同様である。当該のテキストは Richard Rolle の *The Psalter or Psalms of David* で、旧約聖書の一部の翻訳でラテン語本文を含み、翻訳方法も聖書翻訳と異なる可能性がある。また、旧約聖書であるため繰り返し度の高い answered and said も見られない。従って、テキストの選択の問題が影響を与えてい

ると考えられる。

最後に、SERMON の二項句の語源構成の変遷を調査し、図 9 にまとめた。

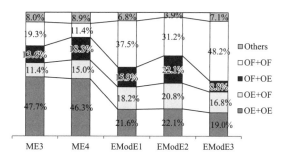

図 9：**SERMON** での語源構成の割合の変遷

SERMON では ME4 を除いて OF＋OF の増加傾向と、ME3 以降で OE＋OE の継続的減少が見られる。また、第 2.5 節で見た正規化頻度と同様に、EModE3 での OF＋OF の増加の仕方は、個別テキストの影響が疑われる。BIBLE と同じ宗教テキストであるとは言え、BIBLE と異なり、話し言葉に基づく SERMON において OF＋OF の割合が拡大しているのは、英語語彙の変遷を反映しているといえよう。

3.4. 繰り返し度の高い二項句とその語源構成

時代・テキストタイプを考慮せず、繰り返し度の高い二項句を抽出した。これらとその語源構成を検討する。抽出した二項句の中で生起数 20 以上のものを検討すると、テキストタイプでの分布の観点から、宗教関係と法文書関係とその他に属するものに分類できる。そのうち、その他に属する二項句は分布が特定のテキストタイプに限定されない[17]。これら 3 つに分類し、総生起数と頻度の高いテキストタイプとともに、頻度の高い二項句を現代化綴り字で示す。

宗教関係：answered and said（99: BIBLE 77）; day and night（35: BIBLE

10, TRAVELOGUE 8）; father and mother（34: BIBLE 16, SERMOM 6）; heaven and earth（22: BIBLE 9, SERMON 6）; male and female（20: BIBLE 17）; man and woman（62: REL TREAT 18, SERMON14）; body and soul（29: REL TREAT 9）

法文書関係：spiritual and temporal（48: LAW 35, DOCUM 6）; lands and tenements（34: LAW 24, DOCUM 8）; manner and form（21: LAW 11, DOCUM 7）; shall and may（20: LAW 20）; mayor and commonality（20: DOCUM 18, LAW 1）

その他：up and down（24）; by and by（22）; meat and drink（22）

　宗教関係の二項句は male and female を除いて、OE＋OE から構成される。一方、法文書関係の二項句は lands（and tenements）と shall and may を除いて、フランス語借用語から構成される[18]。「その他」に分類した二項句も、宗教関係のものと同様、OE＋OE から構成される。既にテキストタイプと語源構成の関連は検討したが、これら繰り返し度の高い二項句の語源構成もそのテキストタイプの性質を反映している。

　ここに、幾つかの繰り返し度の高い二項句を引用する。

（7）Iesus <u>answered, and said</u> vnto him, Verily, verily I say vnto thee, . . . （EModE2: CENTEST2）[19]

（8）Nether shall sowynge tyme and harvest, colde, and hete, somere & wynter, <u>daye and nyghte</u> ceasse, as longe as the erth endureth. （EModE1: CEOTEST1）

（9）if any thinhabytaunt~ of suche <u>land~ and tenement~</u> doo sufficientlie repaire and pave before theyre mansions and dwelling places the saide Streates lanes and hiegh waies　（EModE1: CELAW1）

（10）Be it enacted by the Kings most Excellent Majesty by and with the Advice and Consent of the Lords <u>Spirituall and Temporall</u> and Commons in this present Parliament assembled and by Authority of the same That from and after the Five and twentieth Day of March One thousand and seaven hundred all and every Person and Persons who shall apprehend and take one or more Popish Bishop Priest or Jesuite

and prosecute him.（EModE3: CELAW3）
（11）Ey, how ＋ge turne ＋te erth <u>wppe and down</u>!（ME4: CMMANKIN）

　これらの二項句の構成要素間の意味関係の全調査はできていないが、繰り返し度の高い二項句に関する限り、語源構成と同じように意味関係もテキストタイプにより大きく異なり、従って、その相違はテキストタイプに依存すると考えられる。BIBLE など宗教的テキストの二項句では、構成要素間の意味が反意的であるものが多く、二極を表現することでその全体を指示する二項句が多い[20]。一方で、LAW などの法文書や公的書簡 LET NON-PRIV では Contiguity（近接）や同義的な意味の二項句が多いと言える[21]。

3.5. 品詞による二項句の語源構成の変遷

　二項句構成要素の主要な品詞は、次例のような名詞、動詞、形容詞、副詞である。

（12）and sir Launcelot smote hym evyn thorow the shylde # and his sholdir, that <u>man and horse</u> wente to the erthe, ...（ME4: CMMALORY）

（13）And J <u>requyre and byseche</u> alle suche that fyndc faute or errour / # that of theyr charyte they <u>correcte and amende</u> hit（ME4: CMCAXPRO）

（14）And ＋te haly men sal ay syng omang, With <u>delitabel</u> voyces <u>and clere</u>;（ME3: CMPRICK）

（15）[I] and there walked <u>up and down</u> to the Queen's side　（EModE3: EDIAR3A）

このような品詞別に二項句の語源構成を調査し、語源構成の割合の変遷を図 10-12 にまとめた。

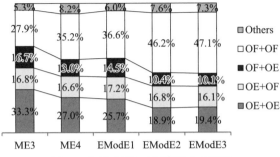

図 10：名詞二項句の語源構成の変遷

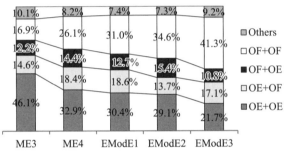

図 11：動詞二項句の語源構成の変遷

　図 10 と図 11 に示すように、名詞と動詞の二項句においては、OF＋OF
は ME3 から増加し続け、一方 OE＋OE は減少し続ける。ただし、OF＋OF
と OE＋OE の割合が逆転する時期が異なる。OE＋OE に対して OF＋OF の
割合が高くなるのが、名詞二項句では ME4 であるのに対し、動詞二項句
では EModE1 である。ここでは示さないが、形容詞二項句も動詞二項句と
同じ変化傾向を示す。従って、OF＋OF の拡大に関して、名詞二項句が動
詞・形容詞二項句に先んじることを示す。これは、図 1 で確認したように、
ME4 における二項句の増加が名詞二項句に依拠するものであることと合
致する。
　一方、図 12 で示すように、副詞は、名詞・動詞・形容詞と異なる傾向

を示す。ME3 から EModE3 まで、減少傾向は示すものの、語源構成の中で、常に OE＋OE の割合が一番高い。ただし、副詞二項句は図 1 で示したように、全体の中で生起数は非常に少ないため、全体への影響はほぼないと言える。

　副詞二項句を調査すると、OE＋OE の割合の高さは副詞の種類が原因であることが判明した。副詞二項句 196 例中 43 例だけが、-ly 副詞の構成要素から構成されている。このような -ly 副詞は様々な語源の形容詞から生産されうる。しかし、ここで副詞と分類するものの大多数は、-ly 副詞ではなく、by and by, here and there, more and less, up and down のような古くから存在する本来語の副詞構成要素を含む二項句であった。このような副詞二項句は語彙化が進んでおり、汎用性が高いが、意味の特定性に欠け、名詞などの二項句のようにテキストの必要性により創造される（可能性がある）ものとは大きく異なる。

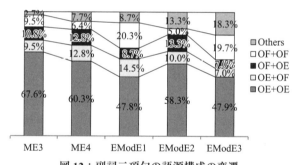

図 12：副詞二項句の語源構成の変遷

　品詞に分け、二項句の語源構成の変遷を考察したが、フランス語借用語による英語の語彙再編成に関して、OF＋OF と OE＋OE の二項句の割合の逆転時期を勘案すると、フランス語借用語が、始めは名詞で、そのあと遅れて、動詞や形容詞で増加していったと考えられる。

3.6.　正規化頻度と語源構成の関連

　ここまで、二項句の正規化頻度と語源構成を別々で考察してきたが、これら二要素に関連はないのだろうか。全時代の正規化頻度と語源構成の割合を比較すると、そこには関連があることが判明した。各テキストタイプの全語源構成のうち OF + OF の割合の一番高いものから並び替えたリストと、各テキストタイプの全時代の正規化頻度の一番高いものから並び替えたリストを結合し、表 2 に示す。

表 2：OF + OF 二項句の割合と正規化頻度

	OF + OF		正規化頻度
DOCUM	51.90%	**LAW**	20.2
EDUC TREAT	51.70%	PREFACE/EPIL	20
LAW	50.70%	**DOCUM**	14.1
PROC TRIAL	49.20%	**LET NON-PRIV**	14.1
LET NON-PRIV	44.30%	**PHILOSOPHY**	12.8
PHILOSOPHY	44.10%	**EDUC TREAT**	12.4
DIARY PRIV	40.10%	SCIENCE MEDICINE	11

　表中の下線・太字で示すテキストタイプでは、正規化頻度と OF + OF 二項句の割合の両方が高いテキストタイプである。従って、二項句の正規化頻度が高いテキストタイプは、OF + OF の割合が高い傾向があることは、表 2 から明らかである。このような傾向を示すのは、公文書や法文書である。また、OF + OF 二項句の割合の高さを勘案すると、二項句の高い正規化頻度も改まり度（formality）に貢献する。一方で二項句の正規化頻度が低いテキストタイプでは OE + OE の割合が高い傾向があるが、これほどきれいな対応関係は見られない。

4. まとめ

　後期中英語から初期近代英語での二項句の変遷を、頻度と語源構成とテキストタイプの点から、考察した。調査結果を要約すると、(1) 正規化頻度においては ME4 でピークに達し、それ以降は低下していく。(2) 正規化頻度に関して、平均では LAW が一番高く、LET NON- PRIV がそれに続く。また、聖書・宗教関連文書、私的な文書、科学系文書では正規化頻度が低い。(3) 語源の点で、ME4 から OE＋OE よりも OF＋OF の二項句が増加し、一方 OE＋OE 二項句は減少し続ける。(4) このような語源の傾向に反するのが LAW と BIBLE で、LAW では逆に OE＋OE 二項句が ME4 以降で増加、OF＋OF 二項句が減少傾向で、一方 BIBLE では ME4 を除いて、OE＋OE 二項句の割合が一番高く、その他の語源構成も一定である。(5) OE＋OE 二項句と OF＋OF 二項句は反比例の関係があり、特定テキストで OE＋OE の割合が高ければ、OF＋OF の割合は低くなる。(6) 高い正規化頻度と OF＋OF 二項句の割合の高さが文書の改まり度と関係する。

　今回の考察から Helsinki Corpus の ME3-EModE3 の二項句については、次のことが明らかになった。(1) 二項句が公的で改まった文書で使用される傾向があり、逆に私的な文書では使用されない傾向があること。また、客観性が求められる弁論記録や科学文書でも使用されないこと、(2) このような考察を通して、二項句使用の目的が難解語の解釈ではないこと、(3) 二項句の構成要素間の意味がテキストタイプにより異なり、二項句の機能がテキストタイプにより異なる可能性があり、さらには、二項句の使用目的とその出自が単一ではないことを示唆すること、(4) ME4 での二項句の増加が名詞のフランス語借用語の増加によるもので、これはフランス語借用語による英語語彙の再編成に関わる現象であること。

　さて、二項句の正規化頻度は 1420-1500 年の ME4 期にピークに達し、それ以降減少する。この変遷は Written Standard English の発達とも関係すると考えられる。Samuels (1963) によれば、Written Standard English は Type IV の "Chancery Standard" と呼ばれる公文書の伝達手段として 1430 年頃に出現した。この時期は Helsinki Corpus の ME4 とちょうど重複し、

しかも Written Standard English の起源となる公文書において二項句の頻度
は高い。英語の公文書は、フランス語やラテン語の形式的特徴を持つ公文
書（Burnley（1986）が言う curial prose）の影響を受けて発達したため、書
き言葉の標準語の成立期に、そのような特徴の一つである二項句の頻度が
高くなり、OF＋OF 二項句の割合が高くなるのは当然と言える。

注

1. 本稿は英語コーパス学会第 45 回大会（令和元年 10 月 5 日（土）、高知県立
   大学）での口頭発表「Helsinki Corpus ME3-EModE3 での binomials の史的変
   遷 － 特に頻度と語源から」の一部に基づき、執筆した。
2. 谷（2021 出版予定）は by thadvyce and assent of the lordes sp~uall and temporall
   などのように、公文書の二項句の中に、フランス語の二項句や定型句に基
   づいているものがあることを指摘する。
3. 以下 Helsinki Corpus からの引用は時代とテキスト名を示し、引用中の下線
   は筆者によるものである。なお、Helsinki Corpus からの引用例における、＝
   は原典での肩付き文字（superscript）を示し、～（＝tilde）は省略を示すもの
   で、原典ではチルダや文字上のダッシュ、飾り線の文字やアポストロフィー
   で表され、引用中の ^...^ は原典で斜体、太字、ゴチックなどの活字等での
   変化を表す（Kytö 1996）。例えば、コーパス中の y=t= は原典の yᵗ を、
   co~mau~dyd は commaundyd の省略を示す。また、＋t と ＋g はそれぞれ þ（＝
   thorn）と ȝ（＝yogh）を示す。
4. ME1, EModE2 などのアラビア数字は元のコーパスでは I, II などローマ数字
   であるが、本論ではアラビア数字に変更した。
5. ヘルシンキコーパスの詳細な情報とその検索方法については、西村（2005）
   を参照のこと。
6. REL TREAT は 2 時代にもかかわらず、4 時代の BIBLE よりも頻度が高いこ
   とは、このテキストタイプでの語数が不釣り合いに多いためと言える。古
   英語から中英語の連続性の確保のために宗教関係のテキストタイプの語数
   が多いことはある程度致し方ないが、それでも不釣り合いであることは否
   めない。
7. 時代毎の全語数はほぼ同じになるようにヘルシンキコーパスでは調整され
   ているが、各時代の各テキストタイプについては総語数が 1810 語から
   22190 語と、かなりばらつきがある。
8. 同様のことについては、Paston Letters の家族間とそれ以外での間の書簡で

の二項句使用の違いを示した Tani（2008）を参照のこと。

9. 谷（2021 出版予定）は、法文書での EModE2, 3 における助動詞、前置詞の二項句の増加を論じている。

10. 分類不能の XX は図 2 では見やすさのために省略したが、総数 2522 で全二項句の約 3 割を占めている。そのため、XX というこの分類項目は分析の正確さを損ねる。

11. LAW は ME3 でテキストが欠如、DOCUM は ME3, 4 でしかテキストがないため、STAT 全体としての正規化頻度の信頼性は不確実である。なお、LET NON-PRIV は XX（＝その他）に分類されている。

12. 今回の対象コーパスと接続要素 and の二項句に関しては、解釈が二項句使用の主目的ではないと主張するのであって、二項句が解釈目的で用いられる可能性を否定している訳ではない。例えば、Sir Thomas Elyot の "education or bringing up of children" のような or を含む二項句が "a self-interpreting pair" であることを Baugh & Cable（2002: 215）は指摘し、Tani（2011: 194）も *Reynard the Fox* での中オランダ語の構成要素を含む二項句の目的が解釈目的である可能性を指摘する。ただ、何れにせよ、主要な目的とは言えない。

13. ME3-4 と EModE1-3 で、なぜ私的書簡の書き方に大きな差が出たか。考察するために、ME4 と EModE1 の書簡から、その冒頭部を引用する。

   （7）Right worthy and worshepefull ser, I recomaunde［{me{］to # yow, preyeng
         yow to wite ＋tat I haue resceyued yowr goodly lettres . . .［ME4:
         CMOFFIC4］

   （8）Plese it your Grace to undirstond that besids al other maters contenyd in our
         Lettres jointly written t thys tyme to your Grace, oon is in them untowchyd by
         cause. . .［EModE1: CEOFFIC1］

   （7）は William Paston から Master John Urry への書簡、（8）は Cuthbert Tunstall から Henry 8 世への書簡である。それぞれの to wite と to undirstond までの本題に入るまでの丁寧な儀礼的表現の違い、特にその長さと定型的な二項句使用に大きな違いがある。書簡の本文中の二項句使用の変化というよりも、書簡冒頭部などでの儀礼的な書き方が簡素化したのが、一つの要因と言える。

14. HANDB ASTRONOMY での OE＋OE の割合の高さに関しては、OE＋OE の二項句は 57 例で、ME4 の CMMETHAM（*Works of John Metham Including the Romance of Amoryus and Cleopes* 中の *Days of the Moon*）で to bye and to selle が 9 回、wyse and trwe が 2 回繰り返され、内容と関連するとはいえ、このテキストが二項句の語源構成の割合をゆがめていると言えよう。また、ROMANCE に関しては、ME3 と EModE3 で OF＋OF が高く、OE＋OE が低いが、その間の時代は割合が一定していず、確たることは言えない。

15. 全時代で OF＋OE よりも OE＋OF の割合が高いことは、通常 OF 要素は OE

要素よりも音節数が多いため、フレーズにおける短＋長という傾向を指摘する Behagel's Law に合致していると、一般論として言える。

16. 谷（2021 出版予定）は LAW の EModE2, 3 で OE＋OE の前置詞、助動詞の二項句が増加したことと、法文書が土着化する過程を論じる。

17. その他に属する二項句については、*OED2* は up and down, by and by を見出し語に挙げ、同様に meat and drink も語彙化が進んでいることを示す（*meat* n. 1a, b の記述を参照）。つまり、その他に属する二項句は、語彙化しており、テキストタイプと関わりが弱く、あまり制限なく使用されることを示唆する。

18. *OED2*（*tenement* 2 b）は lands and tenements をフレーズとしてあげ、英語の初出例の前に括弧入りでフランス語の用例を次のようにあげる。［1292 Britton i. xix. §4 Et ausi <u>des terres et des tenementz</u> alienez par felouns.］つまり、lands and tenements が実はフランス語の terres et tenements の翻訳借用か、フランス語の影響を受けていることを示唆する。従って、lands は本来語であるが、フランス語の影響を考慮する必要がある。

19. 本来語二項句の answered and said が実は "A Hellenism of the N.T." であると、*OED2*（*answer* v. 13）は指摘する。

20. 一番生起数の多い answered and said については、古英語から存在するものの、注 19 で示したように、その起源が新約聖書のギリシア語の影響ということを勘案する必要があるのではなかろうか。

21. 二項句の構成要素間の意味関係については、主要なものに synonymy, antonymy, contiguity があげられる（Kopaczyk & Sauer（2017: 12）を参照のこと）。

引用文献

Baugh, A. C. and T. Cable.（2002）*A History of the English Language*. 5th Ed. London: Routledge.

Burnley, D.（1986）"Curial Prose in England." *Speculum* 61（3）, 593-614.

Jespersen, O.（1982）*Growth and Structure of the English Language*. 10th Ed. Oxford: Basil Blackwell.

Kopaczyk J. and H. Sauer（eds.）（2017）*Binomials in the History of English*. Cambridge: Cambridge University Press.

Kytö, M.（comp.）（1996）*Manual to the Diachronic Part of the Helsinki Corpus of English Texts: Coding Conventions and List of Source Texts*.（http://icame.uib.no/hc）

Malkiel, Y.（1959）"Studies in Irreversible Binomials." *Lingua* 8, 113-160.

Mollin, S.（2014）*The（Ir）reversibility of English Binomials*. Amsterdam: John Benjamins.

Pahta, P. and S. Nevanlinna.（1997）"Re-phrasing in Early English: The Use of Expository Apposition with an Explicit Marker from 1350 to 1710." In M. Rissanen（ed.）*English in*

Transition: Corpus-based Studies in Linguistic Variation, 121-183. Berlin; New York: Mouton de Gruyter.

Samuels, M. L.（1963）"Some Applications of Middle English Dialectology." *English Studies* 44, 81-94.

Simpson, J. A. and E. S. C. Weiner.（prepd.）（1989）*The Oxford English Dictionary, Second Edition on CD-ROM*（v. 1.13, 1994 & 4.0.0.3, 2009）. Oxford: Oxford University Press.

Tani, A.（2008）"The Word Pairs in *The Paston Letters and Papers* with Special Reference to Text Type, Gender and Generation." In Amano, M., M. Ogura & M. Ohkado（eds.）. *Historical Englishes in Varieties of Texts and Contexts*, 217-231. Frankfurt am Main: Peter Lang.

Tiersma, P. M.（2012）"A History of the Language of Law." In Tiersma, P. M. & L. Solan（eds.）, *The Oxford Handbook of Language and Law*, 13-26. Oxford: Oxford University Press.

谷明信（2017）「中英語における定型表現―binomials の場合」 *Conference Handbook* 35（日本英語学会）, 206-211.

谷明信（2019）「Helsinki Corpus ME3-EModE3 での binomials の史的変遷 ― 特に頻度と語源から」英語コーパス学会第 45 回大会（高知県立大学）（口頭発表）

谷明信（2021 出版予定）「後期中英語から初期近代英語の法文書の定型性 ― 特に二項句（binomials）について」 柴崎礼士郎、渡辺拓人編『英語史における定型表現』（仮題）ページ未定. 東京：開拓社.

西村秀夫（2005）「第 8 章 コーパスに基づく英語史研究」齊藤俊雄他編『英語コーパス言語学：基礎と実践』改訂新版. 162-182. 東京：研究社.

モセ、フェルナン（郡司利男、岡田尚訳）.（1963）『英語史概説』東京：開文社.

A New Approach to the Manuscripts and Editions of *The Canterbury Tales*: With Special Reference to Thynne's Edition*

Akiyuki Jimura

1. Introduction

This paper surveys the textual variations found in the nine texts of *The Canterbury Tales*. Our project has been to make a computer-assisted comprehensive textual comparison among the Hengwrt (Hg) and Ellesmere (El) Manuscripts of *The Canterbury Tales* by Geoffrey Chaucer and the two edited texts based on them, Blake (BL: 1980) which is faithfully reconstructed from Hg, and Benson (BN: 1987) which is mainly based on El. The other editions are Caxton's editions (X1 [1476] and X2 [c1482]) and his successors: Pynson's edition (1492) and de Worde's edition (1498). William Thynne's edited text (1532) is added in this textual comparison. This project is expected to contribute a great deal to the textual criticism of Chaucer. We would like to investigate the ways in which the linguistic features of these two manuscripts have been transmitted through the printed texts of Chaucer's works. We will explore some of the systematic differences between the two manuscripts and the edited/printed texts by means of statistical methods. Our comparative concordance, we hope, will be able to offer data of first class importance in this international scholarly field.

Since 1993, the project team have dealt with Blake's, Benson's, and Caxton's texts as well as the two manuscripts mentioned above. At the 19th congress of the New Chaucer Society in 2014, the team reported that Caxton's two editions are linguistically distant from the two manuscripts and from each other. The team read the paper: "The Manuscripts and Editions of *The Canterbury Tales*: Textual Variations and Readings" at the 20th congress of the New Chaucer Society in 2016, working on Caxton's successors' texts, i.e. Pynson's and de Worde's. Now this time, the team have digitized *The General Prologue* and *The Knight's Tale*, with William Thynne's edited text (1532) added in this textual comparison. A sample of our parallel text is quotation (1), which shows the difference among the nine texts plainly.

It is difficult to deal with the problems of textual transmission of Chaucer's manuscripts and printed texts, but it would be easier to trace the linguistic connection between earlier manuscripts and edited texts as objectively as possible. It is said that "while Thynne's edition presents a considerable number of modifications to Chaucer's language, it also retains certain of the marked Chaucerian linguistic forms identified above" (Horobin 2003: 87). The third person plural pronouns 'they', 'her' and 'hem' are preserved in Thynne's edition. The archaic forms of the verb BE 'ben' and the archaic <y-> prefix in past participles are some examples.

It is generally said that the Hengwrt MS, on which Blake's edition (BL) is based, was commenced while Chaucer was alive. As is well known, this manuscript gives a different impression from the Ellesmere MS, which has beautifully coloured ornate initials, and is carefully written and decorated. The Hengwrt MS scribe seemingly wrote Chaucer's works in a great hurry. Benson's edition (BN) is treated as a standard text of Chaucer's works, ascribable mainly to the Ellesmere MS, which is thought to have been written about ten years later by the same scribe as the Hengwrt MS. BN has also been said to be an eclectic text, since it has been scrupulously edited, consulting the Ellesmere MS and checking the other manuscripts and texts. Both BL and BN are thought to be the printed texts betraying historically the last stage of the textual transmission, while Caxton's first (X1) and second (X2) editions are the firstly edited texts printed soon after the introduction of the printing in England. Our present project of comprehensive textual comparison would be a unique and meaningful investigation, because our nine parallel texts include the earliest scribed manuscript (HG), the first and second printed editions (X1 and X2), the faithful transcription of the Hengwrt MS (BL) and the scrupulously edited text (BN) showing probably the last stage of our printed editions.

First, we would like to know what kind of manuscripts Caxton was based on, editing his favourite Chaucer's *Canterbury Tales*. Second, we would like to investigate what kind of linguistic features in the history of English Caxton's editions reflect. Then we would like to recognize the textual transmission from Caxton's editions to the later printed editions such as Richard Pynson's (1492), Wynkyn de Worde's (1498) and William Thynne's (1532). Finally, we would like to survey the long history of textual criticism of *The Canterbury Tales* from the sixteenth century up to the present.

It would be amazing that a computer-assisted approach to Chaucer's textual criticism should provide us with plentiful and abundant data as quickly as possible, but we should be careful in reading the data closely and discriminatingly, depending on our intuitive judgement and intelligent understanding. Thus our computer gives us a quantitative research, while we should have to be flexible enough to make a qualitative research in order to achieve a comprehensive textual comparison. This will lead to our scrupulous and sensitive text reading of *The Canterbury Tales*. We would like to see some examples in the following.

2. Some of the Examples in 'General Prologue' to *The Canterbury Tales*

The line number is based on our data, and the underscores show the missing letters or other elements as against the Hengwrt manuscript. The abbreviations "HG," "EL," "BL," "BN," "X1," "X2," "PY," "WY" and "TH" stand for the Hengwrt and Ellesmere manuscripts and Blake's, Benson's, Caxton's (two versions), Pynson's, de Worde's and Thynne's editions respectively.

We are able to print the complete line in the Hengwrt MS, but only the differing word forms and other elements from this as regards the Ellesmere MS, Blake's text, Benson's text, X1, X2, PY, WY and TH. However, in the following (1), (2) and (3), we have listed every complete line of the nine texts, in order to catch the differences clearly and distinctly. The under-bars show that the letter, word, or other element is missing in the manuscript or text.

(1)

18

HG: That hem hath holpen whan þᵗ they weere seeke

EL: That hem hath holpen / whan þᵗ they we_re seeke

BL:That hem hath holpen _whan that they weere seeke.

BN:That hem hath holpen _whan that they we_re seeke.

X1: That them hath holpyn _when _they we_re se_ke

X2: That them hath holpyn _when _they we_re se_ke

PY: That theym hath holpyn _when _they we_r_ se_ke

WY: That them hath holpe_ _whan _they we_re se_ke

TH: That them hath holpen _whan _they we_re se_ke.

(2)

127

HG: At mete / wel ytought⁷ was she with alle

EL: At mete / wel ytaug_ħt⁷ was she with alle

BL: At mete _wel ytaught_ was she with_alle.

BN: At mete __wel ytaught_ was she with alle;

X1: At mete __wel _taught_ was she with al__

X2: At mete __wel _taught_ was she wyth al__

PY: At mete __wele taught_ was she with alle

WY: At mete __well taught_ was she wyth all_

TH: At meate was she wel ytaught_ w_____ith_al__

(3)

270 HG: Somwhat he lypsed / for his wantownesse

EL: Somwhat he lipsed / for his wantownesse

BL: Somwhat he lypsed _for his wantownesse

BN: Somwhat he lipsed_, for his wantownesse,

X1: Somwhat he lispyd _for his wantownesse

X2: Somwhat he lispyd _for hys wantownesse

PY: Somwhat he lisped _for his wantownesse

WY: Somwhat he lysped _for his wantonnesse

TH: Somwhat he lysped _for his wantounesse

In (1), while HG, EL, BL and BN use the third person plural objective *hem*, X1, X2, PY, WY and TH use Present-day pronoun *them*. We can notice that X1, X2, PY, WY and TH do not use the pleonastic *that* after the conjunction *whan*.

However, we should pay attention to the disappearance of the pleonastic *that* in the extract of (1), although the pleonastic *that* is used in all nine texts (including X1, X2, PY, WY and TH) in the beginning of "General Prologue" to *The Canterbury Tales*, like "Whan that April with his shoures soote," to be more precise, the very beginning of the *Tales*, which might have been necessary to make the audience have a strong impression on *The Canterbury Tales*.

In (2), while the prefix *y-* such as *ytaught⁷* is used in HG, EL, BL and BN, we cannot find the prefix *y-* in X1, X2, PY and WY. But it is interesting that TH has the past participle with the prefix y-. Present-day English has a few fossilized forms such as *yclept* or *yclad*, although the prefix *y-* was supposed to be revived in the sixteenth century temporalily by William Thynne.

In (3), we have found metathesis of /p/ and /s/ in the verb lipsen: HG, EL, BL and BN have the forms *lypsed* and *lipsed*, while X1, X2, PY, WY and TH have the metathesized form *lispyd*, which leads to Present-day English.

3. Nine Text Files

This section will show the statistical data based on the quantitative analysis. The data cover replacements, insertions, deletions, and missing lines. We have counted the frequencies of those variants among the nine texts, and tried to visualize the relative distances among them. It is noted that the analytical software calculates the relative approximation among the texts by counting the number of steps in which a letter sequence of a word in HG is changed to that of the corresponding word in each of the later texts. The software, which does not have a dictionary, also judges that *helpith* and *helpyth* in (4) are different although they are merely variant forms of the same word. The edited texts are inevitably different from the manuscripts because the former have punctuation marks and quotation marks. The raw data are in the appendix.

(4)

796	797
HG: Euerich of hem / heelp_ for to armen oother	HG: As frendly / as he weere / his owene brother
EL: Euerich of hem / heelp͞ for to armen oother	EL: As freenly / as he we_re # his owene brother
BL: Euerich of hem _heelp for to armen oother	BL: As frendly _as he weere _his owene brother.
BN: Everich of hem _heelp for to armen oother	BN: As freendly _as he we_re _his owene brother;
X1:Euerich of hem _he_lpith other to arme_____	X1: As frendly _as he we_re _his owen_ brother
X2:Euerych of hem _he_lpyth other to arme_____	X2: As frendly _as he we_re _hys owen_ brother
PY: Eueriche of them _he_lp_ith to arme_ o_ther	PY: As frendly _as he we_re _his owen_ brother
WY: Eueryche of them _he_lp_yth to arme_ o_ther	WY: As frendly _as he we_re _his ow_ne brother
TH: Everyche of hem helpeth for to arme_ o_ther	TH: As frendly / as he we_re _his owene brother

4. Correspondence of Nine Lines and Distances among the Nine Works Based on *Levenshtein distance*

First, we have summarised the data concerning the replacements, insertions, and deletions in Figures 1 and 2. Figure 1 is shown by Dendrogram based on hierarchical clustering method. Figure 2 is shown by scatter plot based on classical multi-dimensional scaling method.

In the two figures (Fig. 1 and Fig. 2), we have tried to visualize the distances between nine works. Figure 1 is shown by Dendrogram based on hierarchical clustering method. Figure 2 is shown by Scatter plot based on classical multi-dimensional scaling method. Both figures show that BL and BN are close and the cluster is near that composed by HG and EL. Furthermore, the cluster by X1 and X2 is far from other two clusters (PY and WY). And the cluster TH is different from both two clusters (HG, EL, BL and BN; X1, X2, PY and WY).

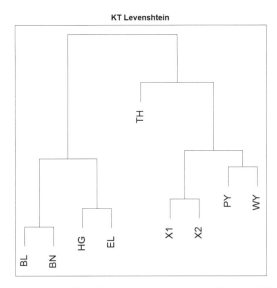

Fig. 1   Dendrogram Based on Replacements, Insertions, and Deletions

Akiyuki Jimura

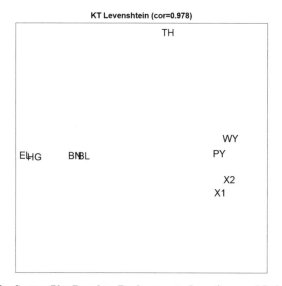

Fig. 2　Scatter Plot Based on Replacements, Insertions, and Deletions

Now we would like to visualize which clusters are nearer to the cluster TH, the clusters (BL, BN, HG and EL) or the clusters (X1, X2, PY and WY), using cutoff point in Levensthein distances. See Figure 3.

KT: cutoff point in Levenshtein distances = 11632

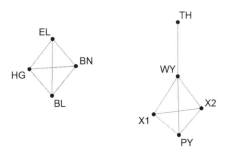

Fig. 3 Undirected graph based on adjacency matrix of which cutoff value is the minimum Levenshtein distances of TH in Table 1.

In Table 1 of Appendix, the minimum distance between TH and WY is 11632, which is cutoff value. The lower number than 11632 is regarded as the value 1 and the higher number than 11632 is regarded as the value 0. Then we have an adjacency matrix given in Table 2 according to Table 1.

Figure 3 is the undirected graph based on the adjacency matrix, where nine works are vertexes and the nodes of two works show a numerical value 1 of adjacency matrix.

This figure (Figure 3) indicates how close TH is to the other clusters of works. Three figures show that BL and BN are close, that the cluster of the two editions are near to that of HG and EL, and that the cluster of X1 and X2 is far from the two foregoing ones. The cluster of PY and WY is relatively near to that of X1 and X2. However, the cluster of TH seems to be far from that of HG and EL, though that of TH is a little near to that of PY and WY.

5. Visualizations and Distances among the Nine Works Based on *Missing Lines Information*

Now we have tried to visualize the missing lines information, one example of which is shown in quotation (6) below. Figures 4 and 5 are shown in the same way as Figures 1 and 2. We visualize the nine works. Figure 4 is shown by Dendrogram based on hierarchical clustering method. Figure 5 is shown by Scatter plot based on classical multi-dimensional scaling method. Both figures show that the cluster HG and BL is very close to that of EL and BN. X2, PY, and WY are far from those two clusters and X1 is quite different from the others. But the cluster TH is rather near to that of HG and EL.

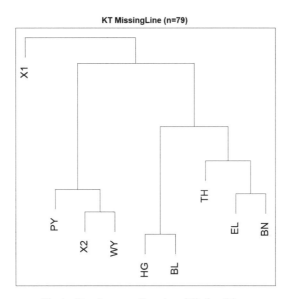

Fig.4   Dendrogram Based on Missing Lines

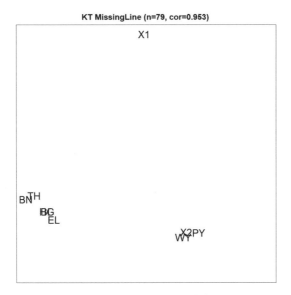

Fig. 5   Scatter Plot Based on Missing Lines

According to these two figures, the cluster of EL and BN is very close to that of HG and BL, while X2, PY, and WY constitute another cluster, which is far from the two foregoing ones. The figures also show that X1 is quite far from the other texts. However, this time the cluster TH is relatively close to that of HG and EL.

6.   Linguistic Features of Nine Texts

6.1.   Similarities

Although it is said that Pynson's and de Worde's editions are based on Caxton's second edition and the previous section supports it statistically, they are different in many cases. For example, quotation (4) above shows that the two editions emend the collapsed rhyme in X1 and X2, which have *arme* at the end of line 796.

Quotation (5) may show their closeness to HG and EL: the two editions have the different word order with *be* before *brought* in the latter half of line 1701.

(5)

1700	1701
HG: And he ___ᵖᵗ is at meschief / shal be take	HG: And noght slayn / but be broght vn to the stake
EL: And he / that is at meschief / shal be take	EL: And nog_ht slayn / but be broght⁷ vn to the stake
BL: And he that is at meschief __shal be take	BL: And noght slayn_, but be broght vn_to the stake
BN: And he that is at meschief __shal be take	BN: And noght slayn_, but be broght un_to the stake
X1: And he that is at myschief __shal be take	X1: And no__t slayn . but b___rought ___to the stake
X2: And he that is at myschyef __shal be take	X2: And no__t slayn / but b___rought to be the stake
PY: And he that is at myschief __shal_be take	PY: And n__at slayn __but be brought ___to the stake
WY: And he that is at myscheyf __shall be take	WY: And no__t slayn __but be brought ___to the stake
TH: And he that is at misch_efe / shal be take	TH: And no__t slayne / but be brought ___to the stake

The word order appears to avoid the contextual or syntactic defect observable in Caxton's second edition, in which *be* is put between the preposition *to* and the noun phrase *the stake*. At the same time, it is closer to the order of HG and EL, although they do not have the preposition *vn to*. It is also noted that their forms of the negative *nat* and *not* are different from those in the earliest manuscripts.

A third example of this kind is quotation (6). Pynson and de Worde have the line which is missing in Caxton (marked with "!NULL").

(6)

1804 HG: Vn to the folk⁷ / that foghten thus echon	1805 HG: He cryde / hoo namoore / for it is doon
EL: Vn to the folk_ / __ᵖᵗ foghten thus echon	EL: He cryde / hoo namoore / for it is doon
BL: Vn_to the folk_ __that foghten thus echon	BL: He cryde: 'Hoo, namoore_, for it is doon.
BN: Un_to the folk_ __that foghten thus echon	BN: He cryde, ";Hoo! namoore_, for it is doon!
X1: !NULL	X1: !NULL
X2: Vn_to the folke __that foughten thus echone	X2: !NULL
PY: Vn_to the folke __that foughten thus echone	PY: He cryed than hoo nomo_re __for it is done
WY: Vn_to the folke __that foughten thus echone	WY: He cryed then ho / nomo_re __for it is done
TH: He _cryed hoe: no more _/ for it is __don.	TH: Ne _none _shal lenger to his felowe go_n

It is noteworthy that in the quotation they have the adverb *than* or *then*, which is not contained in the earliest manuscripts. Especially, quotations (5) and (6) may show that Pynson and de Worde relied also on a source different from Caxton's second edition.

6.2. Peculiarities

In comparison with Caxton's second edition, Pynson's and de Worde's editions also have their own peculiarity in spelling, word order, and other linguistic features. Here are some examples. First, Pynson tends to use the present tense for the past, which is known as "historical present" or "dramatic present." As far as we have counted, there are five examples of the historical present transcribed only by Pynson (In lines 1065, 1066, 1095, 2384, and 2806 in BN) while there are two opposite examples. (In lines 1682 and 1815 in BN.) In quotation (7) Pynson uses the present *duellith* (l. 1953), *felith* (l. 1954), *Dussheth* (l. 1955), and *fayleth* (l. 1955), while the earliest manuscripts have the past tense, the fact which corresponds to Thynne.

(7)

1952

HG: Oonly   the Intellect⁷ with~oute_ moore

EL: Oonly / the intellect⁷ with=outen moore

BL: Oonly __the intellect_ with_oute moore

BN: Oonly __the intellect, with_outen moore,

X1: Saue only __the intellectis with_outen mo_re

X2: O_nly __the intellectis with_outen mo_re

PY: O_nly __the intel_ectys with_outen mo_re

WY: O_nly __the Intellectes wyth_outen mo_re

TH: Saue onely __the intellecte / with_out_ mo_re

1954

HG: Gan faillen / whan the herte felte deeth

EL: Gan faillen / whan the herte felte deeth

BL: Gan faillen __whan the herte felte deeth.

BN: Gan faillen __whan the herte felte deeth.

X1: Gan fayl_e_ __whan the herte felith de_th

X2: Gan fayl_e_ __whan the herte felyth de_th

PY: Gan fayl_e_ __whan the herte felith de_th

WY: Gan fayl_e_ __whan the herte felyth de_th

TH: Gan fayl_en / whan the herte felte de_the

1953

HG: That dwelled in his herte / syk and soore

EL: That dwelled in his herte / syk and soore

BL: That dwelled in his herte __syk and soore

BN: That dwelled in his herte __syk and soore,

X1: That dwellith in his herte __sike and so_re

X2: That dwellyth in hys herte __syke and so_re

PY: That duellith in his hert_ __syke and so_re

WY: That dwelleth in his herte __syke and so_re

TH: That dwelled in his herte __sycke and so_re

1955

HG: Dusked hise eyen two / and fayl_ed breeth

EL: Dusked hise eyen two / and failled breeth

BL: Dusked hise eyen two __and fayled breeth.

BN: Dusked his_ eyen two_, and failled breeth,

X1: Dusshid his_ _yen ___ __and fayleth his bre_th

X2: Dusshyd hys_ eyen t_o __and to fayleth hys bre_th

PY: Dussheth his_ eyen t_o __and fayleth his bre_th

WY: Dusshyd his_ eyen two __and faylleth his bre_th

TH: Dusked his_ eyen two / and fayled bre_the

The present tense can help to describe more vividly the last breath of Arcite, who had won the battle against Palamon for Emelye but fell off from his horse when the infernal fury came abruptly out of the ground.

Hellinga says that Pynson made "no attempt at improving Caxton's version (as De Worde later did), and in fact quite a few new errors were introduced" (117). However, Pynson's alterations in these quotations appear to be more than errors.

De Worde's text also has its peculiarity. In quotation (9), for example, line 428 has *syn*, while Caxton's and Pyson's editions have *say*.

(8)

428	429
HG: Thow mayst⁷ syn thou hast wisdom / and manhede	HG: Assemblen / al__ the folk⁷ # of oure kynrede
EL: Thou mayst⁷ syn thou hast wisdom # _⁷ manhede	EL: Assemblen / alle the folk_ / of oure kynrede
BL: Thow mayst, syn thou hast wisdom __and manhede,	BL: Assemblen __al the folk_ __of oure kynrede
BN: Thou mayst, syn thou hast wisdom __and manhede,	BN: Assemblen alle the folk_ __of oure kynrede,
X1: Thou mayst_ say thou hast wisedom _ _⁷ manhede	X1: Assemble_ alle the folk_ __of our_ kynrede
X2: Thou mayst_ say thou hast wysedom _ _⁷ manhede	X2: Assemble_ alle the folk_ __of our_ kynrede
PY: Thou mayst_ say thou hast wisdom_e and manhede	PY: Assemble_ alle the folke __of oure kynrede
WY: Thou mayst_ syn __t} hast wysdom ⁷ ____manhede	WY: Assemble_ __all the folke __of our_ kynrede
TH:Thou maist / sith t}u hast wysd e ⁷ ____m_ hede	TH: Assemble_ __all the folke __of our_ kynrede

In the quotation the clause beginning with the conjunction *syn* is parenthetic so that the auxiliary *mayst* governs the infinitive *Assemble* (*n* in line 429. If the word *say* is the infinitive and not a variant form of the conjunction *syn*, (Note: Neither the *OED* (s.v. *sin*, adv., prep., and conj.) nor the *MED* records the form *say*.) the three texts will have an awkward reading in the two lines. It may be reasonable to think that de Worde does not follow the three texts and eventually comes close to the Hengwrt and Ellesmere manuscripts. Thynne's text uses a more reasonable variant form *sith*.

7.　Some characteristics of Thynne's text

We would like to consider some outstanding features of Thynne's text from the following three points:

7.1.　Considering the similarities and differences of the nine texts, the following four texts: HG, EL, BL and BN constitute one group, which should be called Group 1. Here are a couple of instances where the texts of Group 1 (HG, EL, BL and BN) are closely related to TH.

1033

HG: ¶ This passeth   yeer by yeer / and day by day

EL: ¶ This passeth / yeer by yeer / and day by day

BL: _This passeth _yeer by yeer _and day by day

BN: _This passeth _yeer by yeer _and day by day,

X1: _THus passe_d _yeer be yeer _ _d_ay be day

X2: _THus passe_d _yere by ye_r_e _ʒ day by day

PY: _tHus passe_d _yere by yere _and day by day

WY: _THus pass_yd _yere by ye_r_e _ʒ day by day

TH: _THus passeth _yere by yere / _ʒ day by day

1034

HG: Til it fil ones / in a morwe of May

EL: Til it fil ones / in a morwe of May

BL: Til it fil ones _in a morwe of May

BN: Till it fil ones_, in a morwe of May,

X1: Tyl it fyl oues _in a mornynge of may

X2: Tyl it fyl ones _in a mornyng of may

PY: Tyl it fel ones _in a mornyng of May

WY: Tyll it fell ones _in a mornynge of may

TH: Tyll it fell ones _in a morowe of May

7.2.　Considering the similarities and differences of the nine texts, the following four texts: X1, X2, PY and WY also constitute one group, which should be called Group 2. Here are a couple of instances where the texts of Group 2 (X1, X2, PY and WY) are closely related to TH.

1055 HG: And as an Aungel / heuenysshly she soong⁷

EL: And as an Aungel / heuenys_hly she soong⁷

BL: And as an aungel _heuenysshly she soong.

BN: And as an aungel _hevenysshly she soong.

X1: And as an aungel _heuen____ly she so_nge

X2: And as an aungel _heuen____ly she so_nge

PY: And as an aungel _heu_y_nly she so_ng_

WY: And as an _angel_l heuen____ly she so_nge

TH: And as an _angeli / heuen____ly she so_nge

1077 HG: He caste his eye / vp=on Emelya

EL: He caste his eye / vp_on EmelyA

BL: He caste his eye _vp_on Emelya

BN: He cast_ his eye _up_on Emelya,

X1: He cast_ his _ye_n vp on Emelia

X2: He cast_ hys eye_n vp on Emelia

PY: He cast_ his eye_n vp_on Emelya

WY: He caste his eye_n vp_on emelia

TH: He caste his eye_n vp_on Eme

7.3.　Now I would like to show some instances where TH is different from both groups (Groups 1 and 2). This group would be called Group 3. Here are a couple of instances where TH is different from both groups (Groups 1 and 2).

1056

HG:¶ The grete tour/ Þᵗ was so thikke and stro_ng⁷	1060 HG: Was euene ioynant⁷ to the gardyn wal
EL: The grete tour/ Þᵗ was so thikke and stroong⁷	EL: Was euene ioynant⁷ to the gardyn wal
BL: _The grete tour that was so thikke and strong,	BL: Was euene ioynant_ to the gardyn wal
BN: _The grete tour, that was so thikke and stroong,	BN: Was evene joynant_ to the gardyn wal
X1: _The grete tour that was so thicke and stronge	X1: Was euene ioynant_ to the Castel wall
X2: _The grete tour that was so thycke and stronge	X2: Was euene Ioynant_ to the gardyne wall
PY: _The grete toure that was so thicke and stronge	PY: was euyn_ ioynaunt_ to the gardyn walle
WY: _The grete tour that was so thicke and strouge	WY: Was euen_ Ioynaunt_ to the gardyne wall
TH: _The great tour / ₁ᵗ was so thicke _₇ stronge	TH: Vvas euyn_ ioynaunt_ to the garden wall

8. Summary

Our investigation remains much to be done. Our findings through this research are the following:

(1) Blake and Benson are close to the Hengwrt and Ellesmere manuscripts.

(2) Caxton's 1st (X1) and Caxton's 2nd (X2) are far from Pynson's and Wynkyn de Worde's.

(3) Thynne's is different from both two clusters (HG, EL, BL and BN; X1, X2, PY and WY).

(4) Caxton's 1st and Caxton's 2nd are found here distanced a great deal from each other. In short, the cluster of EL and BN is very close to that of HG and BL, while X2, PY, and WY constitute another cluster. Caxton's 1st edition is quite far from the other texts.

(5) We have also noticed some peculiarities of Pynson's and de Worde's texts and tried to explain how they are close to, near to, or different from the Hengwrt and Ellesmere manuscripts. However, the cluster TH is relatively close to that of HG and

EL.

Let us conclude our presentation by hoping that our present report will be useful for developing the digitally based Chaucerian and medieval textual and linguistic studies. This research is significant in that it has also discovered the possibility of advanced and closer investigations on various syntactic items, such as the impersonal construction and the tense, and on the manuscripts of *The Canterbury Tales*. Much more digital data and much more references will certainly enable us to continue further researches on the textual criticism of Chaucer.

Appendix

Table 1   Distances among Nine Works Based on Levenshtein Distance

	HG	EL	BL	BN	X1	X2	PY	WY	TH
HG	0	4728	5646	8308	16338	16460	16340	16798	15349
EL	4728	0	8402	7863	17080	17288	17084	17588	15892
BL	5646	8402	0	3371	12747	12755	12554	13217	12694
BN	8308	7863	3371	0	13832	13977	13567	14307	13561
X1	16338	17080	12747	13832	0	5412	8705	9002	14046
X2	16460	17288	12755	13977	5412	0	7791	6065	13368
PY	16340	17084	12554	13567	8705	7791	0	7788	12500
WY	16798	17588	13217	14307	9002	6065	7788	0	11632
TH	15349	15892	12694	13561	14046	13368	12500	11632	0

Table 2 Adjacency matrix among Nine Works Based on Levenshtein Distance

	HG	EL	BL	BN	X1	X2	PY	WY	TH
HG	0	1	1	1	0	0	0	0	0
EL	1	0	1	1	0	0	0	0	0
BL	1	1	0	1	0	0	0	0	0
BN	1	1	1	0	0	0	0	0	0
X1	0	0	0	0	0	1	1	1	0
X2	0	0	0	0	1	0	1	1	0
PY	0	0	0	0	1	1	0	1	0
WY	0	0	0	0	1	1	1	0	1
TH	0	0	0	0	0	0	0	1	0

Table 3 Distances among Nine Works Based on Missing Lines Information

	HG	EL	BL	BN	X1	X2	PY	WY	TH
HG	0	0.286	0	0.429	0.974	0.722	0.765	0.706	0.533
EL	0.286	0	0.286	0.2	0.973	0.643	0.692	0.615	0.364
BL	0	0.286	0	0.429	0.974	0.722	0.765	0.706	0.533
BN	0.429	0.2	0.429	0	0.972	0.786	0.846	0.769	0.222
X1	0.974	0.973	0.974	0.972	0	0.958	0.971	0.972	0.972
X2	0.722	0.643	0.722	0.786	0.958	0	0.222	0.111	0.786
PY	0.765	0.692	0.765	0.846	0.971	0.222	0	0.125	0.846
WY	0.706	0.615	0.706	0.769	0.972	0.111	0.125	0	0.769
TH	0.533	0.364	0.533	0.222	0.972	0.786	0.846	0.769	0

*This paper was read at the 21st Congress of the New Chaucer Society at University of Toronto, Canada on 12 July, 2018. This is a joint research of Hideshi Ohno, Hiroshima University, Yoshiyuki Nakao, Fukuyama University, Noriyuki Kawano, Hiroshima University and Kenichi Satoh, Shiga University. This work is in part supported by Grants-in-Aid for Scientific Research, Japan Society for Promotion of Science (No. 18K00400).

Akiyuki Jimura

Select Bibliography

Editions

Benson, Larry D., ed. *The Riverside Chaucer.* 3rd ed. Boston: Houghton Mifflin, 1987.

Blake, Norman, ed. *The Canterbury Tales by Geoffrey Chaucer: Edited from the Hengwrt Manuscript.* London: Edward Arnold, 1980.

Bordalejo, B., ed. *Caxton's Canterbury Tales: The British Library Copies.* London: British Library, 2003.

Edmonds, D., ed. *Electronic Edition of Benson's The Riverside Chaucer (1987).* Oxford: Oxford University Press, 1992.

Pynson, R., pr. *Canterbury Tales.* 1492. Web. Early English Books Online.

Ruggiers, Paul G., ed. *The Canterbury Tales: A Facsimile and Transcription of the Hengwrt Manuscript with Variants from the Ellesmere Manuscript.* Norman: University of Oklahoma Press, 1979.

Stubbs, Estelle, ed. *The Hengwrt Chaucer Digital Facsimile.* Leicester, UK: Scholarly Digital Editions, 2000.

Thynne, William, ed. *The workes of Geffray Chaucer.* 1532. Web. Early English Books Online.

de Worde, Wynkyn, pr. *The Boke of Chaucer Named Caunterbury Tales.* 1498. Web. Early English Books Online.

Secondary sources

Bordalejo, B. "Notes on the Caxton *Canterbury Tales* Editions and Their Place in the Textual Tradition of the *Tales.*" *Caxton's Canterbury Tales: The British Library Copies.* London: British Library, 2003.

Crystal, David. *A Dictionary of Linguistics and Phonetics.* 6th ed. Oxford: Blackwell, 2008.

Elmer, Willy. *Diachronic Grammar: The History of Old and Middle English Subjectless Constructions.* Tübingen: Niemeyer, 1981.

Hellinga, Lotte. *William Caxton and Early Printing in England.* London: British Library, 2010.

Hanna III, Ralph, intro. *The Ellesmere Manuscript of Chaucer's Canterbury Tales: A Working Facsimile.* D.S. Brewer, 1989.

Horobin, Simon. *The Language of the Chaucer Tradition.* Cambridge: D. S. Brewer, 2003.

Horobin, Simon. *Chaucer's Language.* New York: Palgrave/Macmillan, 2007.

Hutmacher, William F. *Wynkyn de Worde and Chaucer's* Canterbury Tales*: A Transcription and Collation of the 1498 Edition with Caxton² from the* General Prologue *through* The Knight's Tale. Amsterdam: Rodopi, 1978.

Furnivall, F. J. A., ed. (1967) *A Six-Text Print of Chaucer's Canterbury Tales in Parallel Columns*

A New Approach to the Manuscripts and Editions of *The Canterbury Tales*: With Special Reference to Thynne's Edition

from the Following MSS.: 1. The Ellesmere. 2. The Hengwrt 154. 3. The Cambridge Univ. Libr. Gg. 427. 4. The Corpus Christi Coll., Oxford. 5. The Petworth. 6. The Lansdowne 851. London: Chaucer Society, 1868. Rpt., New York: Johnson Reprint.

Jimura, Akiyuki, Yoshiyuki Nakao and Masatsugu Matsuo, eds. *A Comprehensive List of Textual Comparison between Blake's and Robinson's Editions of* The Canterbury Tales. Okayama: University Education Press, 1995.

Jimura, Akiyuki, Yoshiyuki Nakao and Masatsugu Matsuo, eds. *A Comprehensive Textual Comparison of Troilus and Criseyde: Benson's, Robinson's, Root's, and Windeatt's Editions.* Okayama: University Education Press, 1999.

—, eds. *A Comprehensive Textual Collation of Chaucer's Dream Poetry.* Okayama: University Education Press, 2002.

Jimura, Akiyuki, Yoshiyuki Nakao, Masatsugu Matsuo, Norman F. Blake and Estelle Stubbs, eds. *A Comprehensive Collation of the Hengwrt and Ellesmere Manuscripts of* The Canterbury Tales: *General Prologue.* The Hiroshima University Studies, Graduate School of Letters. Vol. 62, Special Issue, No. 3. 2002.

Jimura, Akiyuki, Yoshiyuki Nakao and Masatsugu Matsuo, eds. *"General Prologue" to* The Canterbury Tales*: A Project for a Comprehensive Collation of the Two Manuscripts* (*Hengwrt and Ellesmere*) *and the Two Editions* (*Blake* [*1980*] *and Benson* [*1987*]). The Hiroshima University Studies, Graduate School of Letters. Vol. 68, Special Issue. 2008.

Jimura, Akiyuki. "On the Decline of the Prefix y- of Past Participles." Tomonori Matsushita et al. ed. *From Beowulf to Caxton: Studies in Medieval English Languages and Literature, Texts and Manuscripts.* Frankfurt: Peter Lang, 215–28, 2011.

Jimura, Akiyuki, Yoshiyuki Nakao, Noriyuki Kawano, and Kenichi Satoh. "A Computer–Assisted Textual Comparison among the Manuscripts and the Editions of *The Canterbury Tales*: With Special Reference to Caxton's Editions." *Kotoba de Hirogaru Chisei to Kansei no Sekai: Eigo, Eigokyouiku no Shinchihei wo Saguru.* Ed. Y. Yanase and T. Nishihara. Hiroshima: Keisuisha, 2016. 68–85.

Kurath, Hans, et al., eds. *Middle English Dictionary.* Ann Arbor: The University of Michigan Press, 1952–2001. [*MED*]

Manly, John M. and Edith Rickert. *The Text of The Canterbury Tales: Studied on the Basis of All Known Manuscripts.* 8 vols. Chicago: The University of Chicago Press, 1940.

Masui, Michio. *Studies in Chaucer.* Tokyo: Kenkyusha, 1962

Nakao, Yoshiyuki, Akiyuki Jimura and Masatsugu Matsuo, eds. *A Computer–Assisted Comprehensive Textual Comparison between the Hengwrt Manuscript and the Ellesmere Manuscript of* The Canterbury Tales *by Geoffrey Chaucer.* [A Report of a Grant-in-Aid (No. 12610494) for Scientific Research from the Ministry of Education, Science and Culture.] 2002.

—, eds. "A Project for a Comprehensive Collation of the Hengwrt and Ellesmere Manuscripts of *The Canterbury Tales: General Prologue.*" *English Corpora under Japanese Eyes.* Ed. J. Nakamura, N. Inoue and T. Tabata. Amsterdam/New York: Rodopi, 2004. 139–50.

—, eds. *A Comprehensive Textual Comparison between the Hengwrt and the Ellesmere Manuscripts and the Edited Texts of* The Canterbury Tales*:* The Cook's Tale, The Wife of Bath's Prologue and Tale, The Friar's Tale *and* The Summoner's Tale. [A Report of a Grant–in–Aid (No. 18520208) for Scientific Research from the Ministry of Education, Science and Culture.] 2008.

—, eds. "A Project for a Comprehensive Collation of the Two Manuscripts (Hengwrt and Ellesmere) and the Two Editions (Blake [1980] and Benson [1987] of *The Canterbury Tales*)." *Hiroshima Studies in English Language and Literature* 53 (2009): 1–22.

Nakao, Yoshiyuki, Akiyuki Jimura, and Noriyuki Kawano. "Choice and Psychology of Negation in Chaucer's Language: Syntactic, Lexical, Semantic Negative Choice with Evidence from the Hengwrt and Ellesmere MSs and the Two Editions of *The Canterbury Tales.*" *Hiroshima Studies in English Language and Literature* 59 (2015): 1–34.

Ohno, Hideshi. *Variation between Personal and Impersonal Constructions in Geoffrey Chaucer: A Stylistic Approach.* Okayama: University Education Press, 2015.

Ohno, Hideshi, Akiyuki Jimura, Yoshiyuki Nakao, Noriyuki Kawano, and Kenichi Satoh. "Textual Variations and Readings among the Manuscripts and Editions of *The Canterbury Tales*: With Special Reference to *The Knight's Tale,*" *Hiroshima Studies in English Language and Literature* 62 (2018): 1–13.

Partridge, Stephen. "Wynkyn de Worde's Manuscript Source for the *Canterbury Tales*: Evidence from the Glosses." *The Chaucer Review* 41 (2007): 325–59.

Simpson, J. A. and E. S. C. Weiner, eds. *The Oxford English Dictionary.* 2nd ed. CD–ROM, ver. 4.0. Oxford: Oxford University Press, 2009. [*OED*]

Tokunaga, Satoko. "Wynkyn de Worde's Lost Manuscript of the *Canterbury Tales*: With New Light on HRC MS 46." *The Chaucer Review* 50 (2015): 30–54.

White, Jack Hammons. "A Collation of Richard Pynson's 1492 Edition of *The Canterbury Tales* and William Caxton's 1485 Edition, with a Study of Pynson's Variants." Unpublished Dissertation. Texas Tech University, 1978. Web. 5 May 2016.

"The Three Ravens"（Child 26）と異版 "The Twa Corbies" に みる、民衆の視点

原　田　英　子

　西洋の口承文学のジャンルには、大きく分けて叙事詩、ロマンス、伝承バラッドなどがある。叙事詩やロマンスは、もともと口承のみで伝わっていたものが後世において筆録され、読み物として保存された。一方、伝承バラッドは 18 世紀に至るまで「読む」「書く」の手段を持たない民衆の間で音声のみによって伝承されてきた。

　発するそばから消えてしまう音声を介して作品が何世紀もの間伝承されることが可能なのは、時代を超えてなお人々が共感できる要素を含んでいるからだと考えられる。その要素のひとつとして、後世に語り継ぐべき英雄の偉業が例に挙げられ、叙事詩はこれに当てはまる。またロマンスにおいても、アーサー王と円卓の騎士たちが優れた英雄として登場する。伝承バラッドには、スコットランドとイングランドの辺境地方での貴族間の戦闘を歌った Border Ballads があり、民衆が登場人物たちを英雄視していたことが認められる。しかし、伝承バラッドは、叙事詩のように戦いや英雄の偉業を、国を挙げた歴史として伝えて保存することを目的としているのではない。伝承バラッドには、主人公となる人物の描写に加えて、その人物の周辺にいる者たちや敗者、思いがけず命を落としてしまった者といった、叙事詩やロマンスにはない弱者や脇役の視点が重要な要素となっているのではないだろうか。本稿では、Francis James Child 編纂の *The English and Scottish Popular Ballads* の 26 番 "The Three Ravens" とその異版 "The Twa Corbies" を中心に、伝承バラッドに見られる民衆の視点について考察をする。

　初めに、二つのバラッドの内容を整理する。Child は 26 番 "The Three Ravens" に、ヴァージョンＡとＢを収録している。彼は "The Twa Corbies" を "The Three Ravens" のヴァリエーションのひとつとしてでは

なく異版として、26 番 "The Three Ravens" の頭注に収録している。"The
Three Ravens" のヴァージョン A は最もよく知られており、1611 年に出版
された Thomas Ravenscroft の版[1] の "Country Pastimes" の章 20 番として収
録されていたものを Joseph Ritson が *Ancient Songs and Ballads, from the Reign
of King Henry the Second to the Revolution* に収録したものである。Ritson は、
"The Three Ravens" の古さについて、Ravenscroft の版が出版された 1611 年
より古いだけでなく Ravenscroft の版に収録されているどのバラッドより
も古いものだと説明しており[2]、William Chappell はヴァージョン A が彼の
時代においても民衆の間で人気だと述べている[3]。このことから、ヴァー
ジョン A は 17 世紀初頭以前のおそらく中世から 19 世紀においても人気
であり続けてきたことがわかる。また、ヴァージョン B は William
Motherwell の *Minstrelsy: Ancient and Modern: With an Historical Introduction
and Notes* の Appendix にバラッドの最初のスタンザが収録されている版で、
Motherwell はスコットランドでとても人気だと述べている[4]。

　Child は Appendix に "The Three Ravens" のもうひとつの異版を載せてい
る。Child は Appendix の頭注で、その版を歌った人物が住んでいるイング
ランド東部の Lincolnshire の地区には Ea、Ee、もしくは Hay と呼ばれる、
小川に続いた草地があり、そこがバラッドの悲劇の舞台になっているのだ
という解説付きでこの異版を受け取ったことを説明している。ヴァージョ
ン A では、何らかの事情で殺された騎士を、お腹を空かせた三羽のカラ
スが狙っているが、忠実な鷹と猟犬が守っているがためにカラスたちは近
づけず、鹿に姿を変えた恋人が騎士を埋葬して自らもなくなる様子が描か
れている。Appendix の版には口承による欠落部分はなく、ヴァージョン
A とは若干の違いがみられる。まず、殺されるのは騎士ではなく騎士見習
いで、年齢が若いことが見て取れる。またヴァージョン A では、殺され
た騎士を猟犬が傍らで守り、空では鷹が飛び回ってほかの鳥が近づかない
ように警戒している様子が描かれているのに対し、Appendix の 4 スタン
ザ目では、彼の死体を守っている動物のうち鷹は馬となっていて、「彼が
起き上がって乗るのではと思って彼の脇にずっと立っている[5]」（'His
Horse all standing by his side, / thinking he'll get up and ride.）と歌われる。猟犬

は、警戒のために傍らにいるというより、主人が負った深手をなめること
で忠誠心が表現されている。そしてヴァージョン A では妊娠してお腹の
大きな牝鹿が恋人の化身として登場し、騎士を葬った後に自らも亡くなる
が、Appendix では妊娠した女性が鹿に変身することなく悲しみに暮れた
様子で登場し、騎士見習いを埋葬することなしに傍らで亡くなる。この
Appendix の 版 に つ い て Child は、"It has already been noted that traditional
copies of 'The Three Ravens' have been far from infrequent. When a ballad has
been nearly three hundred years in print, and in a very impressive form, the chance
that traditional copies, differing principally by what they lack, should be coeval and
independent amounts at most to a bare possibility. Traditional copies have, however,
sometimes been given in this collection on the ground of a very slight chance; and
not reasonably, I think, considering the scope of the undertaking.[6]" と説明してい
る。

　"The Three Ravens" がイングランドのバラッドであるのに対し、"The
Twa Corbies" はスコットランドのバラッドであり、スコットランド方言で
歌われている。"The Twa Corbies" のヴァージョン A は Sir Walter Scott の
Minstrelsy of the Scottish Border で初めて紹介され、Charles Kirkpatrick Sharpe
がある婦人から採録して Scott に提供した版で、もっとも有名なヴァー
ジョンである。Child が "The Twa Corbies" を "The Three Ravens" の頭注
に収録したのは Scott が「もう一方の写しというより同じ要素を持つ別物
（"rather a counterpart than copy of the other[7]"）」と評価したことを尊重してい
るからである。Child は Scott の版の他に 3 つのヴァージョンをあげている
が、C と D のヴァージョンはごく短い断片である。

　Child 版の "The Twa Corbies" ヴァージョン A では、"The Three Ravens"
同様に 2 羽のカラスが食事をどこで取るかの相談から始まっているが、物
語の結末は正反対である。"The Three Ravens" で忠実だった騎士の鷹と猟
犬はそれぞれ狩りに出かけ、恋人は別の男性の許へ行ってしまう。今や騎
士に注目するのはご馳走として狙っているカラスたちだけで、多くの人が
悲しむが誰も彼の居場所がわからない。最後には、「彼の白い骨がむき出
しになると / その上を風が吹き抜ける」（Oer his white banes, when they are

bare, / The wind sall blaw for evenmair.）と歌われる。Motherwell の *Minstrelsy* には、スコットランドのバラッドとして "The Twa Corbies" が収録されているが、Child はヴァージョンに挙げていない。Motherwell の版では、2スタンザ目のカラスの食事の相談の中で、難破して打ち上げられた船で食事をするという一羽に対し、3スタンザ目では相手のカラスが「もっといいものを見せる」と人気のない峡谷（lonsome glen）で殺されたばかりの騎士を示す。その後の展開は Child 版のヴァージョン A とよく似ているが、「騎士の剣は半分抜かれ、矢は放たれていない」（His sword half drawn, / his shafts unshot）と、反撃する間もなく急襲されて騎士が亡くなったことが語られている。そして4、5スタンザでは Child 版のヴァージョン A と同じく鷹、猟犬、恋人の不忠が語られる。カラスたちのおしゃべりとは対照的に、Motherwell 版の最後のスタンザでは騎士の遺体がひっそりと自然に溶け込む様子が描かれている。

O cauld and bare will his bed be,
When winter storms sing in the tree;
At his head a turf, at his feet a stone,
He will sleep, nor hear the maiden's moan,
O'er his white bones the birds shall fly,
The wild deer bound and foxes cry.
（"The Twa Corbies", 6）

　Child 版のヴァージョン B は、スコットランドの南東部、イングランドとの辺境にある Jedburgh で採録されたものだ。ヴァージョン B の3スタンザ目ではヴァージョン A 同様に騎士の目や髪をどのようにするかの相談をしているが、4スタンザ目以降は "The Three Ravens" のヴァージョン A とも "The Twa Corbies" のヴァージョン A とも内容が大きく異なり、カラスの生い立ちと巣立ちが歌われている。
　次に、それぞれのバラッドに登場するカラスたちを指す *raven* と *corbie* の語源と、カラスが伝統的にどのようなイメージで扱われてきたかについ

て見る。英語 *raven* は、語源が古英語であり、現代英語では動詞で「がつ
がつ食う」の意味を持つ。古英語や古ノルド語の文学作品においても、
raven は鷲や狼と共に戦場で死肉をあさる動物として常套的に登場する。
古英語詩 *The Battle of Maldon* では、ヴァイキングとの戦いのときが近づい
てきたことを告げるとともに、戦士が倒れるべき時が来たとも述べられる。
そして空を飛び回る大鴉（*hræfn* = raven）や鷲（*earn* = eagle）の存在が、
その戦いでたくさんの死者が出ることと、その遺体がカラスや鷲の餌とな
るであろうことを予感させている。

> Þā wæs feohte nēh,
> tīr æt getohte. Wæs sēo tīd cumen
> þæt þæt þǣr fǣge men   feallan sceoldon.
> Þǣr wearð hrēam āhafen,   hremmas wundon,
> earn ǣses georn.
>   (lines 103b-107a)[8]

Beowulf においてもカラスが戦いで出た死者を餌とすることが言及されて
いる。詩の終盤でウィーイラーフから送られた伝令が、ベオウルフの竜と
の闘いと死を人々に伝える。そしてベオウルフの死が知れ渡ればフランク
人、フリジア人との戦いが再発するかもしれないと伝令が懸念を呈する言
葉の最後に、戦いで死者が出ることについて、「大鴉は狼と競って遺体を
食べる自分の様子を、鷲に得意げに語るだろう」と表現している。

> ac se wonna hrefn
> fūs ofer fægum   fela reorrdian,
> earne secgan,   fū him æt æte spēow,
> þenden hē wið   wulf wæl rēafode."
>   (lines 3024-3027)[9]

Frederich Klaeber は、*Beowulf* の 3024 行 から 3027 行 に 関 し て、"The bold
and brilliant picture reminds us … of 'The Twa Corbies' ('The Three Ravens')

…."と述べている[10]。また、古英語や古ノルド語の作品においては、百戦
錬磨の戦士の強さを表現するために、「カラスを喜ばせる者」という常套
句も多用される。*Corbie* は、スコットランド方言で *raven* よりも小柄なハ
シボソガラスを指す。語源は古仏語の *corb* (*corp*)、さらにラテン語の
corvus に遡る。古仏語の作品では、戦闘の場面にカラスがついてまわる表
現はほとんど無い。しかし、バラッドでは *corbie* も *raven* 同様に餌として
騎士の死体を狙っている。

　カラスが餌として死体を分け合う様は文学に限った表現ではなく、むし
ろ現実の経験に基づく表現と言える。イングランド西部のシュロップ
シャー（Shropshire）には、一羽が見つけた餌をもう一羽が山分けしたがる、
二羽のカラスのユーモラスな会話の詩が伝わっている[11]。

> First Crow, 'All glor, all glor !'
> Second Crow, 'W'eer is it? W'eer is it?'
> First Crow, 'Down i' the moor, down i' the moor.'
> Second Crow, 'Shall I come alung? shall I come alung?'
> First Crow, 'Bar bwuns, bar bwuns!'

この詩の最後の1行 "bar bwuns (＝bare bones)" の解釈については、「（餌
に近づいてみたら）むき出しの骨だ」と解釈するか「（すっかり平らげて）
骨だ」と解釈するかに余地がある。しかしここで明らかなのは、骨では食
べる価値がない、もしくは骨になってしまえば食事が終了するという意味
にとれることだ。死体の側からすると、カラスにつつかれて骨だけになる
と、生前の姿を奪い取られてアイデンティティを奪われる。つまりは誰だ
かわからなくなることでその人物の遺功も伝えることが叶わなくなるので、
野ざらしで放置されることは避けるべきだ。

　ふたつのバラッドでは、亡くなった騎士の遺体は周囲からどのように認
知されているだろうか。"The Three Ravens" では、忠実な猟犬と鷹が亡く
なった主人を守っているが故にカラスが手を出す余地がなく、そしてその
後子供を身ごもった牝鹿が現れ、騎士の傷にキスをして遺体を背に載せて

運び、埋葬した後に自らも死ぬ様子が歌われる。Child 版の "The Three Ravens" ヴァージョン A の最後のスタンザは、後世に付け足されたものだと言われているが、「神様は高貴なものに贈るのです、このような鷹と猟犬と恋人とを。」（God send euery gentleman, / Such haukes, such hounds, and such a leman.）と歌っていることから、聴衆は、埋葬した騎士の傍で死ぬ牝鹿については、leman つまり恋人が変身した姿なのだと理解し、gentleman である騎士がなぜ殺されるに至ったのかと想像を掻き立てられる。また最後のスタンザが付加されていないとしても、聴衆は牝鹿の正体について、騎士の恋人であり、かつ騎士の子を身ごもっていると想像する。"The Twa Corbies" では、カラスたちの会話で殺された騎士が土塁の陰に横たわっていることが示される。しかし、その騎士がそこに倒れていることは鷹と猟犬と恋人しか知らない。そして "The Three Ravens" では忠実に主人を守っていた鷹、猟犬、恋人は騎士のもとを離れて不誠実な振る舞いをし、今や騎士に注目するのはご馳走として狙っているカラスたちだけ、多くの人が、騎士がいなくなったことを悲しむけれども、誰も見つけられないという様が描かれている。

　英雄叙事詩では、クライマックスでその生き様や活躍の集大成として英雄の死が語られる。そうすることで英雄の存在を後世まで残すことを目的とするが、ふたつのバラッドのどちらの場合も、固有名詞は何も語られず、猟犬や鷹を従えていることから、狩りの途中であったこと、また Motherwell の版に見たように、剣を抜いたり矢を放ったりと反撃の間もなく殺されたことがわかるが、騎士がなぜ命を落とすに至ったのかについての詳細は何も語られない。妊娠した恋人の登場で、聴衆は例えば "Douglas Tragedy"（Child 7B）のような恋愛に関したいざこざの末の殺人と想像することもできる。"The Three Ravens" では、騎士がどのような事情で命を落としたのかはわからないものの、忠実な鷹や猟犬、あるいは馬が主人を忘れることなく守り、恋人が埋葬しに現れることで騎士がカラスに啄まれて身元不明になること、つまりアイデンティティを失うことが避けられている。一方、"The Twa Corbies" では、騎士の死の現場に居合わせた動物たちはその場を離れ、恋人が他の男性に心変わりする様はもはや、敢えて騎

原 田 英 子

士の存在を知らせようとするものが居なくなったことを意味する。Child
のヴァージョン A の 1 スタンザ目では、「私がたった一人で歩いている時
に / 二羽のカラスの内緒話を聞いた」(As I walking all alane, / I heard twa
corbies making a mane;) と、「私」がたまたまカラスの前を通りその会話を
聞くことがなければ騎士の遺体の存在が明らかになることはない。民衆は
展開される不条理を知りながら何度も何度もそのバラッドを聴き、もしく
は歌った。歌に固有名詞が何もなく、騎士の死ぬに至る事情が語られない
ということは、それだけバラッドは聴衆に想像をする余白を与えていると
言える。その余白は聴衆一人一人の経験を当てはめて補充させることがで
き、バラッドの内容を身の回りのよく似た内容の出来事を重ね合わせて想
起させる働きをする。聴衆が重ねる個人の経験は、バラッドの主人公と、
その周りのものについてだといえる。Sir Patrick Spens (Child 58) のヴァー
ジョン B の 15、16 スタンザ目を例に挙げると、難破した船の乗組員の妻
たちが船の帰りを待ち続けている。

> Lang, lang may our ladies wait
> Wi the tear blinding their ee,
> Afore they see Sir Patrick's ships,
> Come sailing oer the sea.

> Lang, lang may our ladies wait,
> Wi their babies in their hands,
> Afore they see Sir Patrick Spence
> Come sailing to Leith Sands.
> (Child 58B, 15-16)

聴衆は、バラッドで展開される物語の中心となる優秀な船乗りの Sir
Patrick Spens と彼の船に同乗して命を落とした者たちの死に同情するが、
彼らの帰りを待ち続ける物語の外側の者たちにも深い同情を寄せるのでは
ないだろうか。"Sir Patrick Spens" のバラッドの挿絵には、荒波にもまれ
る船の様子を描いたものが多いが、スコットランドの画家 Robert Burns

（1869-1941）の作品 *The Ballad of Sir Patrick Spens*[12] や同じくスコットラン
ドの画家 James Archer（1823-1904）の作品 *The Legend of Sir Patrick Spens*[13]、
ラファエル前派の作品の多くでモデルを務め、自身も画家だった Elizabeth
Siddal（1829-1862）の作品 *The Ladies' Lament from the Ballad of Sir Patrick
Spens*[14] では、それぞれの作品で岸から海を眺める女性たちが主題として
描かれている。このことからも、物語の外側の者たちを描写することが
人々の心を打つ要素になることがわかる。

　最後に、正反対の内容の異版がなぜどちらも人気であり得るのか考察を
する。Scott は "The Twa Corbies" が "The Three Ravens" の counterpart だと
表現していることから、お互いが影響し合ってはいるけれども独立した存
在だということが考えられる。Scott は "In order to enable the curious reader
to contrast these two singular poems, and to form a judgement which may be the
original…[15]" とどちらの版がオリジナルか明言しないが、Ritson の版の
"The Three Ravens" を載せるとともに、1611 年に出版された Ravenscroft の
版に収録されているどのバラッドよりも古いものだとする Ritson の説明
も紹介している。伝承の段階でつけ足されたり欠落したりで出来た新しい
ヴァージョンではないとすると、ある時代の特定の出来事を反映して意図
的な変更が行われたと考えられる。しかし、バラッドの特徴のひとつとし
て、おそらく初めは特定の個人の物語だったとしても、伝承が繰り返され
るうちに人物の個性がはぎとられ、個人の名前が大きな意味を持たなくな
る傾向がある。ふたつのバラッドが 19 世紀になってもなお人気だったこ
とを考えると、伝承の段階で変更された片方も歴史上の特定の出来事とは
受け取られてはいなかったであろう。

　もう一つの可能性は、片方のバラッドがもう片方のパロディだというこ
とだ。パロディの語源はギリシャ語の παρωδια（paroidia）で、最も古い例
では、紀元前 4 世紀の哲学者アリストテレスの『詩学』で「再現」、「模
倣」を表すミメーシスの対象の違いを説明する 2 章に、叙事詩をもじって
滑稽な内容にした詩を意味してパローディアという語を使っている[16]。山
中光義氏は『バラッド詩学』の 5.4. parody の項で、"The Twa Corbies" が
"The Three Ravens" の完全なるパロディだと述べ、ロビン・フッドが時代

を追うごとにパロディ化される例と、19世紀以降のバラッド・リバイバルとして伝承バラッドを模して作られたバラッド詩とそのパロディの例を挙げている[17]。ロビン・フッドが伝承バラッドか、一つの作品が長いことから純粋な伝承バラッドではないのかの点については意見が分かれることもあるが、時代が新しくなるごとに滑稽な内容に変容していく様は、山中氏が述べる通り民衆の英雄がパロディ化されていると言える。バラッド・リバイバルの時代のバラッド詩は、連綿と受け継がれてきた元の伝承バラッドを客観的に模して作られた個人の作品であり、それらの作品が同時代的に揶揄され、パロディ化していることがわかる。

　では、"The Twa Corbies"は"The Three Ravens"のパロディと言えるだろうか。食事の相談をするカラスが騎士の死体の存在を明らかにするという設定は同じだが、騎士の死体の扱われ方は全く異なり、騎士を取り巻く忠実なものたちは不実なものとして描かれている。パロディの意味は、もとは必ずしも作品を嘲笑的に変更することを指してはいなかったが、現在に至るまで概ね意図的に滑稽さや皮肉を付け加えて作り替えられた作品を指すので、内容がより不条理な展開をする"The Twa Corbies"が"The Three Ravens"のパロディだと考えるのが自然である。しかし、"The Twa Corbies"に滑稽さや風刺が感じられるかというと、聴衆には別の感情が沸き起こるのではないだろうか。"The Twa Corbies"は、立派な騎士が死んでしまったら誰にも見向きもされなくなったと滑稽に描いたものではなく、いなくなった彼を悲しむ多くの人々の存在がある。このバラッドが心に訴えかける点は、行方不明を悲しむ者たちがが大勢いるにもかかわらず、一番身近な存在の者たちの不忠義によって誰にも見つけてもらえずに自然に帰るという、騎士の身に起こった不条理さである。

　"The Three Ravens"では騎士にまつわる不幸に終始し、恋人が埋葬に訪れて傍らで亡くなることで物語の完結がみられる。一方、"The Twa Corbies"は、殺された後にひっそりと人知れず自然に帰るという、主人公の身に起こる悲劇性と、騎士の行方を突き止められないという周りの者にとっての悲劇性をもはらんでおり、騎士の死体が見つからないために物語は完結しない。アリストテレスは悲劇を「悲劇とは…あわれみと恐れを

通じて、そのような感情の浄化（カタルシス）を達成するものである」と
定義しており、そのあわれみと恐れはお互いに関連している[18]。もちろん、
伝承バラッドを歌い継いできた民衆は読み書きもままならず、アリストテ
レスについての知識もなかったが、バラッドの中で騎士の身に起こった人
知れず死んでゆく不幸、もしくは大切な者が突如行方知れずになる不幸に
ついて感じるあわれみは、聴き手自身の身に将来起こるかもしれない恐れ
から生じ、また逆にこのバラッドで生じる恐れは騎士や周りの者へのあわ
れみから生じている。"The Three Ravens" の方が早い時代のものと仮定し
ても、"The Three Ravens" と "The Twa Corbies" のどちらも廃れることなく、
ある時から民衆に同時進行的に受け入れられ歌い継がれてきた。それを踏
まえると、死体をむさぼるカラスたちの会話が引き金となるふたつの伝承
バラッドを通して、民衆はその悲劇性を鋭敏にとらえ、主人公となる騎士
だけでなく騎士の周りの者という脇役をも悲劇の中心に据え、いつの時代
においても自らの経験に照らし合わせて心を動かす普遍的なものに昇華し
て歌い継いできたのだ。

注

1. Thomas Ravenscroft, *Melismata, Musicall Phansies, Fitting the Court, Citie, and Countrey Humors. to 3, 4, and 5 Voices.*
2. Joseph Ritson, *Ancient Songs and Ballads, from the Reign of King Henry the Second to the Revolution.* p. 193.
3. William Chappell, *The Ballad Literature and Popular Music of the Olden Time*, p. 59.
4. Motherwell, Appendix, p. xviii, No. xii.
5. カギかっこ内のバラッドの和訳は全て筆者による。Child 版のバラッドの引用は全て以下のテクストを使用している。Francis James Child, ed. *English and Scottish Popular Ballads.* 5 vols., Loomis House Press, 2001（1882-1898）
6. Child 26, Appendix の頭注参照。
7. Sir Walter Scott, *Minstrelsy of the Scottish Border*, Vol. II, p.210. the other は、"The Three Ravens" を指す。
8. 本稿では、*The Battle of Maldon* の引用は次のテクストを使用した。Donald Scragg, ed., *The Battle of Maldon.* Manchester: Manchester University Press, 1981.
9. *Beowulf* からの引用は Klaeber 版を使用した。Friedrich Klaeber, ed. *Beowulf and*

the Fight at Finnsburg. 3rd ed. New York and London: D.C. Heath and Company, 1941.

10.　Ibid. p. 225.

11.　Georgina Frederica Jackson, Shropshire Word-book, a Glossary of Archaic and Provincial Words, etc., Used in the County. London: Trübner & co, 1879., ʻglorʼ の項参照。

12.　Robert Burns, The Ballad of Sir Patrick Spens, 1902, oil on canvas, 113 x 198cm（44 1/2 x 77 15/16in）. https://www.bonhams.com/auctions/17985/lot/642/　参照（閲覧日：2020 年 11 月 10 日）

13.　James Archer, Legend of Sir Patrick Spens, 1870, oil on canvas, 115.6 x 208.9cm（45.5 x 82.2in）, Auckland Art Gallery.

14.　Elizabeth Siddal, The Ladies' Lament from the Ballad of Sir Patrick Spens, 1856, Watercolor on paper, 241 × 229 mm, Tate Gallery.

15.　Sir Walter Scott, op. cit., p. 210.

16.　松本仁助、岡道男訳『アリストテレース「詩学」ホラーティウス「詩論」』岩波文庫、1997 年、p. 25 および p. 121。

17.　山中光義、『バラッド詩学』、pp. 79-82.

18.　松本仁助、岡道男訳、前掲書、p. 34 および p. 137。

参考文献

第一次資料

【Ballads】

Chappell, William. The Ballad Literature and Popular Music of the Olden Time: A History of the Ancient Songs, Ballads, and of the Dance Tunes of England, with Numerous Anecdotes and Entire Ballads: also, a short Account of the Minstrels. 2 vols., New York: Dover Publications, 1965（1859）.

Child, Francis James. English and Scottish Popular Ballads. 5 vols., Loomis House Press, 2001（1882-1898）.

Motherwell, William. Minstrelsy: Ancient and Modern, with an Historical Introduction and Notes. Glasgow: John Wylie, 1827.

Ravenscroft, Thomas. Melismata, Musicall Phansies, Fitting the Court, Citie, and Countrey Humors. to 3, 4, and 5 Voices. London: William Stanby, 1611.

Ritson, Joseph. Ancient Songs and Ballads, from the Reign of King Henry the Second to the Revolution. London: Reeves and Turner, 1877.

Scott, Walter. Minstrelsy of the Scottish Border, 3 vols., Edinburgh: Longman, Hurst, Rees and Orne, 1810.

"The Three Ravens" (Child 26) と異版 "The Twa Corbies" にみる、民衆の視点

【Old English】
Klaeber, Friedrich, ed. *Beowulf and the Fight at Finnsburg*. 3rd ed. New York and London: D.C.
　　Heath and Company, 1941.
Scragg, Donald, ed., *The Battle of Maldon*. Manchester: Manchester University Press, 1981.

第二次資料
Bold, Allan. *The Ballad*. The Critical Idiom 41. New York: Methuen, 1979.
Jackson, Georgina Frederica. *Shropshire Word-book, a Glossary of Archaic and Provincial Words,*
　　etc., Used in the County. London: Trübner & co, 1879.
オング、W. J. 著、桜井直文、林正寛、糟谷啓介訳『声の文化と文字の文化』藤原書店、
　　1993 年
加藤憲市『英文学動物物語』松柏社、1978 年
松本仁助、岡道男訳『アリストテレース「詩学」ホラーティウス「詩論」』岩波文庫、
　　1997 年
山中光義『バラッド詩学』音羽書房鶴見書店、2009 年

試論：ジョージ・エリオットのジェフリー・チョーサー作 『カンタベリー物語』「騎士の話」の受容 ——心の語り：思想文学的語りと東洋仏教異文化の自然観

高 野 秀 夫

1. 愛、悲しみ、同情の思想文学的語り

　ジョージ・エリオット（1819-1880）には、30才を過ぎて自分が本格的に作家になるきっかけを作り、ヴィクトリア朝を代表する自然主義女流作家になる手助けをした、人生の最良の伴侶ジョージ・ヘンリー・ルイスが身近にいた。エリオットはその心から愛する人を亡くした時、シェイクスピアではなくジェフリー・チョーサー（1340-1400）の『公爵夫人の書』、英文学史上、最初の三大悲哀歌のひとつの一節を日記に書き込んでいる。その一節は、詩人の夢のなかに登場する黒衣に身を包んだ王族の騎士が、心から愛する妻を亡くして嘆き悲しんでいる行である。エリオットによる死線を越えて妻を愛した黒衣の騎士への思い入れ（sympathy）は、よっぽど深いものであったことが分かるであろう。チョーサーの愛、悲しみ、同情の表現が、シェイクスピアよりもエリオットに深く心を打つものがあったのであろうか。親愛なるルイス亡きあと 2 年後には、自分自身の人生を閉じる年に、「騎士の話」の語り手の騎士が登場する『カンタベリー物語』の「総序」[1] を読んでいる。悲しみと愛の関係は、死と生、光と影のように、ワンセットであり、どちらが欠けてもその存在は、不完全で分かりにくい。まさに時空を越えた、切っても切れない深いものである。エリオットは、心から愛するルイスとの出会い、その愛の本質を知る前は、心がしっかり定まらず、過去の辛い気持ちで記憶が満ちていた。エリオットは、今まで春よりも秋のほうが好きだったし、一年中秋を巡って過ごしたい、とも思っていた。だが、作家の道が拓け、春が好きになったのである。エリオットは、作家として生きて行く心が定まったことで、自然観までもが大

きく変わった。チョーサー文学の傑作『カンタベリー物語』「総序」[1]の冒頭に語られている美しい春の自然描写による心の表現に魅了され続けて来たのは間違いないであろう。エリオットは、思いもよらない自分の心の様変わりに気が付いた。自分自身の心が定まらない、未来も定まらない、過去の紆余曲折の辛い記憶ばかりが独り歩きして自分で自分を苦しめてきたのである。私たちの心の存在は、今しか確かめられないであろう、その現在の心を大切にするエリオット文学の誕生である。

　なぜエリオットが、長い間、最後までユーモアとペイソスのチョーサー文学で心が癒され続けて来たのか、またなぜ女流作家のエリオットが、生涯最後まで男性名の「ジョージ」という筆名を使い続けてきたのかも分かるであろう。ジョージ・エリオットの筆名には、時空を越えた、死線を越えた今を生きる愛についての思い入れが含まれているからである。つまり、エリオットの作家人生にとって最も大切な人は、内縁の夫ジョージ・ヘンリー・ルイスなのである。作家になる決心がついてからは、長年抱いてきた過去の記憶に深く根ざしていた自然観、人間観、世界観も大きく変わっていくのである。特に、チョーサー文学のような春の美しい自然が好きになったのも、ルイスの愛のお蔭で、人生の指針に迷うことなく心が定まったからであろう。エリオットが英国文壇に彗星のごとく現れた作品『アダム・ビード』に、"心の言語、最高の言語"についての"語り"がある。

That is a simple scene, reader. But it is almost certain that you, too, have been in love — perhaps, even, more than once, though you may not choose to say so to all your feminine friends. If so, you will no more think *the slight words, the timid looks, and the tremulous touches* , by which two human souls approach each other gradually, like *two little quivering rain-streams,* before they mingle into one—*you will no more think these things trivial than you will think the first-detected sign of coming spring trivial* , though they be *but a faint indescribable something* in the air and in the song of the birds, and the tiniest budding on the hedgerow branches. *Those slight words and looks and touches* are part of *the soul's language*; and *the finest language* , I believe, is chiefly made up of *unimposing words* , such as "light," "sound," "stars" "music"—words really not worth looking at, or hearing, in themselves, any more than "chips" or "sawdust." It is only that they happen to be the signs of *something unspeakably great and beautiful*. I am of opinion that love is a great and beautiful thing too, and if you agree with me, the smallest signs of it will not be chips and sawdust to you: they will rather be like those slight little words "light," and "music," *stirring the long-winding fibres of your memory and enriching your present with your most precious past.*[2] (Italics, mine)

　読者のみなさん、それは、単純なシーンです。しかし私は、あなた方も、多分、一度だけでなく人を愛したことがあることをほとんど確信しています。だが、すべての女友だちのみなさんには、その事を話したいとは思わないでしょう。もしそうであったとしたら、二人の心は、震える可愛い雨粒の二つの流れが互いに一つの流れになる前のように、軽い言葉や内気な目つき、そしてわずかな手の震えの感じで、しだいに近づいていくのです。だが、あなた方はそれらの言葉、目つき、感じが、やがて最初に目にする春の訪れのきざしのように、もはや、つまらないものとは思わないでしょう。しかしそれらは、大気の中に、小鳥の歌声の中にもありますし、さらに生け垣の枝の最も小さな芽の中にもあるのです、だが、それらは、ただの何か、言葉にならないかすかなものでしかないのです。それらのちょっとした言葉、目つき、触れ合いが、心の言語の一部なのです。もっとも素晴らしい言語は、私の信じるところでは、おもに"光"、"音"、"星"、"音楽"などの目立たない言葉にしか過ぎないのです。つまり、本当にそれらは、それら自体、"木っ端"や"おが屑"以上に見聞きしたりする価値がないのです。だが、それらが、たまたま、筆舌に尽くしがたいほど素晴らしく、美しいものの記号になるのです。私は、愛が崇高な、美しいものであると思っています。もし同意して頂けるのでしたら、愛の最も小さな記号は、あなた方にとって"木っ端"でも"おが屑"でもないでしょう。むしろ、その愛の最も小さな記号は、ちょっとした可愛い"光"や"音楽"の言葉のようでしょう。そしてその目立たない言葉で、あなたがたの曲がりくねった長い記憶の素質は、揺さぶられて、あなたがたの

現在は、最も大切な過去で豊かになるのでしょう。

エリオットの"あなたがたの現在は、最も大切な過去で豊かになるのでしょう"の言葉には、過去、現在、未来のそれぞれの人生が、一対であり、その一連の時の言葉は切っても、切っても切り離せないものである。だが、その時の連鎖の中で最も大切なのが現在であることの"語り"であり、東洋仏教文化の現在を大切にする精神、お茶の"一期一会"の考えにも通じる。最も美しい過去の記憶を忘れずに、その記憶を永遠の現在の記憶として時空を超えて心に留めることで人生が豊かになる。これが、エリオットの"語り"による"心の言語"である。わたしたちの語りの一語一語は、未熟な心には、木っ端のようだが、心の持ちようで、瞬時に、一語一語が宝石以上の美しい輝きを放つのである。一語一語の時空を越えた美しい心を込めようとする詩人の原点をエリオットはチョーサー文学からも受容していたのであろう。

エリオットは、産業革命のお蔭で、大工の身から上流階級の豪族で大地主の土地差配人[2]になった父を持ち、ディケンズと同じく庶民階級の人生の悲哀にも精通していた作家である。ジェフリー・チョーサーも、酒屋の息子で、町民文化の色濃い作家である。彼にとって最も身近に居て大切な人たちのなかには、貴族の英国王ヘンリー4世の父ジョン・オブ・ゴーント公爵と、その公爵の第三夫人の妹、つまりチョーサーの妻もいる。中世ヨーロッパにおいて3分の1の人口がペストの悲しい犠牲になった、世界史上の大惨事で、そのゴーント公爵の妻が、亡くなっている。チョーサーが本当にお世話になっていたゴーント公爵の心から愛する妻が、そのペストで命を落としたのである。その心から愛されていた亡き妻の胸の内と愛する妻の死で嘆き悲しんでいる公爵自身の胸の内を書いたのが、処女作の『公爵夫人の書』である。またチョーサー自身も、晩年、妻を亡くした年に、一気に『カンタベリー物語』における「総序」と「騎士の話」を含めた前半部を書いている。王族宮廷風恋愛、騎士道精神の神髄も描かれている。チョーサーが、英国のレディー・ファーストの騎士道精神を体現し、その神髄まで知り、語り尽くすことが出来たことや、チョーサーが"愛の

詩人"とも呼ばれるようになったのは、身近な妻のおかげもあるであろう。全く予想も付かない世界的規模の天災が起きる現実の無常の世の中で、長年苦楽を共にしてきた人生の最良の伴侶の死ほど悲しいものはない。チョーサーの作家人生における最後の大作である『カンタベリー物語』、そのなかの「騎士の話」にも処女作のように、瑞々しい言葉では言い尽くせない騎士の深い愛と悲しみの心情の"語り"がある。シェイクスピアの『ロメオとジュリエット』に見られるロマンチックで燃えるような激しい愛の思いに繋がって行くのであろう。だが、その「騎士の話」は、老境に達したチョーサーの人生の集大成とも思われる。王妃となる姫の心を射止めようとするアーサイトとパラモンの青年騎士たちの愛の女性観や人生観が展開される。東洋仏教異文化の人生の無常観を思わせる「騎士の話」の語り手である中年騎士、セーセウス王である熟年騎士、老公である騎士の"語り"がある。だが、とりわけ、生まれてから絶えず生死を彷徨う運命を歩み続けてきた老公の騎士による、より真に迫った盛者必滅、諸行無常の人生観、世界観が読み込める"語り"もあるし、チョーサーによる『カンタベリー物語』の巡礼の心も分かるであろう。

　人生における愛と悲しみの心の本質が、エリオット自身の"語り"で、『アダム・ビード』において述べられている。

　　　Let us rather be thankful that our sorrow lives in us as an indestructible force only changing its form, as forces do, and passing from pain into sympathy － the one poor word which includes all our best insight and our best love.[3]

　　　有難いことに、私たちの悲しみは、怒涛の力で心に生き続けて、形だけを変えて、苦しみを通して、同情に変わるのです。だが、その同情の一つの貧弱な言葉には、最高の叡智と愛が含まれています。

　悲しみの"最高の叡智と愛"の光が、わたしたちの心の闇を照らし、私たちは癒されるのであろう。悲しみの心の変遷が、時間軸で述べられてい

る。そして悲しみそのものが、生き物であるかのように、悲しみは、その形を変えて、苦しみへ、さらに、同情へとなって、その本来の姿を現す、という“語り”である。私たちは、自分自身の心の持ちようで瞬時に鬼のイメージから神のイメージへと変身・心するのである。まさにその私たちの心の変化は面白い、人生は面白いほど変わってゆくのである。そこにエリオット文学の言葉そのものの本質、ユーモアとペイソスの本質が潜んでいるのである。私たちは、“悲しみ”の言葉を日常なんとなく使っている。だが悲しみが我が身に降りかかった時は、その時こそ、その悲しみで大きく人生が変る時でもある。

　わたしたちの“語り”の言葉、そのものの本質は何か。言葉は、見方を変えれば、単なる文字、目で見て読み、手で書く記号であり、また耳で聞く単なる音にしか過ぎないし、また、時に道端の石ころのように取るに足らないものにもなる。だが、心の持ちようで“悲しみ”は瞬時に最高の叡智にも愛にも悟りにもなり得る一つの文字の言葉なのである。その心の文字を操る作家の文学には論理的、哲学的思考の深まりは欠かせない。言語は私たちの心の無意識とも深く係る人間の本質の表現であるからだ。エリオットは、異文化言語の理解、修得には、異文化の人たちの人生観、世界観の理解が欠かせないことも知っている。エリオットはチョーサーと同様に宗教哲学書の翻訳で心の本質の理解を深め、自分自身の言葉の理解も深めた。より活動的で、包括的で幅広い国際的な視野で、人間の存在そのもの、言葉そのものの、さらに心と言葉そのものの関係に迫り、言葉の本質の理解に努めた。またエリオットは、ラテン語、ギリシャ語、ドイツ語、フランス語、イタリア語を学び、ヘブライ語も習い、さらに仏教経典のサンスクリットにも関心がある。言語は心、精神、文化、人間が連動するものであり、私たちの人間の世界観でもある。“同情心が欠けると知も鈍る”とも言われているが、この文の言葉の意味は、異文化の人たちにも理解できるであろう。どの国の人の思いも同じである。“知情意”の認識の“心”はみな同じで、知、情、意は、それぞれが、一体の言葉としてしっかり連動しなければならないのである。19世紀英国の第一線級の急進派主義者、ジャーナリストでもあるエリオットは、国境を超えた国の人たちの心にも

訴える "the soul's language:「心の言語」"、"the finest language:「最高の言語」" についてもしっかり語っているのである。

そして、エリオットは、ひどい女性差別の男尊女卑のヴィクトリア朝社会で、女性であるということだけで思うようにならないで苦しんでいる多数の女性たちの心の内にも思いを馳せている。彼女たちに共感してもらい、彼女たちの論理的思考を深めるための手助けになるような "語り" の必要性を感じた。またエリオットは自分自身女性であるのになぜ男性名にしなければならなかったのか？　それは多くの読者に読んでもらうためである。さらに彼女はそのような辛い社会の現状を変えたいと願い小説を書いた。それは彼女が社会改良主義の作家と呼ばれる所以である。エリオットは女性名の作家が軽視されている世間のなかで、彼女自身、まだ自由に愛することも許されない社会故に、絶えず自分と内縁の夫のルイスへ向けられている世間の冷たい目に晒されていた。だがその世間の冷たい目こそ、エリオットにとって物事の真実を追求する論理的思考の深まりの手助けとなっている。まだまだ社会は不完全であり、人も自分もさらに言葉も、不完全であるので万人の心を理解し語る愛の "心の言語" があれば、世間の目も穏やかになり、苦しんでいる社会弱者の女性たちも救われ、世間も明るくなるのである。間違いなくエリオットの "心の言語" は、彼女がフェミニストの作家であることの証であろう。

エリオットは、チョーサーのように新時代の要求に答え、国際的視野に立ち、世の中を見ている。産業革命後の大英帝国の 19 世紀は、言葉や心の本質の探究が、ルネッサンス期以降人文や自然科学の学問の進展と連動して国際的に、飛躍的に発展した。エリオットは私たちの無意識の世界にも係る心の虚像と実像を見事な言葉で表しているのである。また東洋仏教異文化の縁起、ニルヴァーナ、唯識、無常観、無意識の探究が深まった時代であった。エリオットは、チョーサー同様、異文化言語の宗教、哲学書の翻訳で、心の本質に迫っている。特に、登場人物の話中でも、著者の語り手の言葉で、人間の心の本質について語っている。エリオットの傑作『ミドルマーチ』には赤子のあどけない顔に仏教文化の心の無意識世界についての行がある。彼女の最後の小説『ダニエル・デロンダ』には、主人

公による有名な仏教説話、「捨身飼虎」の"語り"がある。東洋異文化の
人の心にも関心が深いエリオットは、中世から続いている英国の誇るオッ
クスフォード大学の比較言語学者、異文化の国ドイツ出身のマックス・
ミュラー教授の影響を直接受けている。特に仏教のサンスクリット語にも
優れたミュラーは、エリオットの親友の思想家ハーバート・スペンサーと
共に英国人の明治維新日本における啓蒙者の一人になっている。ミュラー
は、科学主義、合理主義時代に即した考えで、キリスト教も仏教も宗教の
ひとつであることを述べ、また言語学の発展にも貢献しており、さらに英
国におけるドイツ観念論（東洋的自然観の影響もある）の普及にも努めて
いる大学者である。

　エリオットは、特にチョーサーのように、宗教、文化の"愛の語り"に
関心が深いし、異文化世界を紐解く鋭い言語学的視点も身に付けているこ
とは見逃せない。エリオットは、自然科学的な思考の「神即自然」で有名
なユダヤ系哲学者スピノザの『論理学』を翻訳している。またスピノザの
影響を受けたドイツ観念論の色濃いドイツロマン派作家のゲーテも、英国
ロマン派の詩人ワーズワースもエリオットの尊敬する文人である。また、
フランスのロマン派（瞑想詩も含む）の作品を読み異文化の文学の影響を
受けている。エリオットは、「愛は人間を神となし、そして神を人間とな
す」；「神とは、いわば人間の心情が発する声に同意を与える単なる言葉で
しかないのだ」と神と愛について述べるフォーヘンバッハの『キリスト教
の本質』も英訳している。[4] エリオットが"神、God" "永遠、Immortality"
よりも大切にしている言葉は、"義務、Duty"である。[5] "Duty" も "love"
も語源を辿ると仏教経典のサンスクリット語とも係っているのが分かる。
また "The little children are still the symbol of the eternal marriage between love
and duty." [6]（小さな子供たちは、依然として愛と義務が永遠に結び付いて
いるシンボルです）の『サイラス・マーナー』では、時に、子供はエン
ジェルのような大切な存在として描かれているが、私たちの愛する現実の
子供は人の子供で、神の使いのエンジェルではない、というエリオット
の"虚"と"実"の"語り"[7] があるであろう。

　エリオットは、チョーサーの中世英語による異文化交流風口承文学から

高　野　秀　夫

英文学の“語り”の本質を受容し、言語学的視点の“語り”をも取り込んで、独自の文学を目指しているのである。

　チョーサーの文学は、口承文学なので、落語家のように絶えず話し相手の胸の内を意識して語っている。それ故、まさにユーモアとペイソスに満ちた、時に時空を超えた“哲学的語り”の言葉で、言葉そのものの、心そのものの、人生そのものの本質に迫って、時にわたしたちの精神文化や、物質文化の本質をも語っている。また中世における異文化の言語も受容して、ロンドンの標準語を話し、中世騎士道的宮廷風恋愛の心の豊かな語り手で、「愛の詩人」ともなっている。口承文学は、“語り”が命であり、まず聞き手の心を満足させることが大切なのである。いかに瞬時に相手の心の動きを捉えるかが勝負である。話し相手が神様なのである。チョーサーは話し相手の言葉を、心を、人生を豊かにする見事な表現を駆使して「英詩の父」ともなっているのである。

　エリオットは、チョーサーの“面白くて、ためになる”“語り”[8]に心掛けている。エリオットの名言に "It's never too late to be what you might have been."[9] “なりたい人に成るのに決して遅すぎることはない”がある。過去、未来よりも、特に今現在を大切にする東洋仏教文化の精神に通じるものである。心理小説作家と言われているエリオットに相応しい仮定法過去完了使用の見事な“語り”文である。私たちの心の働きはいかようにも変わるのは面白い。もし今私たちが愛する人を亡くしたとしたら、私たちはとても悲しい気持ちになる。“もし…ならば”という実際の会話の“語り”におけるイメージは、今、話をしている私たちが共有している今の世界が一瞬にして、素晴らしい天国にも、悲しい地獄にも変ってしまう。それは同情する方も、される方も、共に時空を越えて心と心が悲しみで一杯になり、我を忘れてしまうチョーサーのユーモアとペイソスのファブリオ世界である。心がひとつになる愛と悲しみの同情の世界は、心の持ちようでいかようにも変わるものである。そして私たちは本来の自己に目覚めることも可能であろう。この仮定法による美しい言葉の“語り”は、私たちの心の本当の姿を映し出してくれる。愛と悲しみの会話の言葉も、単語（one poor word）だけでは、曖昧で、融通無碍である。言葉は、単なる単語の羅列に

- 225 -

しか過ぎないが、並び方次第で宇宙が見える。言葉の"語り"は、本来崇高で美しい心の働きそのもので、すべてが自由である。他者と、心と心が連動し一体化する。神の"永遠の現在"と言うボエティウス[10]による心の表現の境地にもなる。チョーサーは、そのイタリアの哲学者ボエティウス作『哲学の慰め』の翻訳者である。また 13 世紀フランスの寓意的で異教的な内容で、女性観、人間観、自然観、風刺、教訓の詰まった百科全書的な騎士道的宮廷風恋愛物語りの『薔薇物語』の本も英訳している。その『薔薇物語』は、異文化的な内容で、シンボル、寓意、擬人化も見られ、詩人が夢のなかでバラに恋をするフランス古典文学の傑作である。エリオットの文学も、いろいろな異文化の言語による国際的視野で、時に、神、知性、自然、真、善、美、さらに東洋仏教文化の無常観、無意識の唯識等の問題にも通じる世界である。そしてエリオットは、その愛と悲しみの深層心理と、その絶妙な言葉の"語り"をチョーサー文学世界の"経験"と"権威"の"experience"、"authority"から受容して、自分本来の文学を築き上げていると言えるであろう。[11]エリオット文学にとってもその経験と権威の"experience"、"authority"の言葉は、特に主人公の変心にとって欠かせないキーワードである。

　エリオット文学の理解には、急進主義のジャーナリストでもあるエリオットが、特にチョーサーの宗教的精神文化の"語り"にも関心が深いことは、見逃せない。外交官の経験もあるチョーサーは、14 世紀の英国がまだヨーロッパの後進国であるので、未熟な中世英語の言葉によって自国の宗教精神文化を世界に発信しなければならないのである。言葉の危うさを痛いほど知っているチョーサーもエリオットの"soul's language""心の言語"、つまり国際的視野で異文化の人たちにも通用する心の言葉の大切さを常々感じていたことであろう。

2.　東洋仏教異文化の自然観：美しい心の愛の"語り"：ゴッホと漱石

　"ひまわり"の絵で有名な、日本人好みのゴッホ（1853-1890）は次のようにエリオットを評している。エリオットは"魂によって仕事をしている

ような芸術家たち、"現代文明の先頭に立っていると考えられるであろう
男女たち"に属し、そして"天才的な特質"の"一貫して誠実で善意にみ
ちた"作家で作品は"驚くほど「造形的」"であると把えている、という
ものである。[12]エリオット作『サイラス・マーナー』の主人公のサイラス
は、機織り人であり、その作品の影響もあると思われているゴッホの"機
織り人"の作品が30点もある。ゴッホはなぜそんなにエリオットの文学
に興味を持ったのか？『サイラス・マーナー』（1861年）の物語りは次の
ようなものである。

　サイラスは、若い頃親友にも仲間にもさらに恋人にも裏切られ、神をも
信じられなくなり、絶望の淵を彷徨い、住み慣れた故郷の町からラヴィロ
ウ村に移り、金だけが頼りの守銭奴になる。その金も盗まれる。その時、
たまたま家に迷い込んできた孤児エピーを、独身の身で英国の豊かな自然
の片田舎の大地で一生懸命育てる。村人たちの温かな心にも触れて、生き
ることの素晴らしさを知る。エピーとの深い心の愛の絆が生まれる。

　この物語りにおいてエリオットは、エピーとサイラスの時空を超えた
"完全な愛"[13]について"心の言語"で述べている。その人生の"語り"に、
ゴッホは感動したのであろう。ゴッホも、サイラスと同じく、癲癇の経験
もあり、ロンドンでは、言葉では言い尽くせないほどの人生の辛い苦しい
失恋の憂き目に合っている。エリオットの作品の美しい愛の"語り"は、
ゴッホの心に、過去の人生の悲しい記憶を呼び覚まし、深い愛の傷を癒や
したことであろう。19世紀のジャポニズムの影響を受け、世界を驚かせ
ている画家ゴッホは、晩年に弟の赤ちゃんの出産祝いに、四季の自然の美
を愛する日本人の心の象徴でもある桜の絵を送っている。ゴッホは、こよ
なく東洋仏教異文化の日本の美しい自然に憧れて、時空を超えた彼独自の
新境地の世界を築き上げたのである。

　ゴッホのエリオット文学についてのコメントは的を得ている。"文は人、
人は文なり"という言葉の通り、エリオットの人柄が作品のいろいろな人
物にはっきりと投影されている描写がある。サイラスとエピーは「一貫し
て誠実で善意にみちた」時に「驚くほど造形的」な人物である。この作品
は"大人のおとぎ話"と称されるほど擬人化、象徴化された表現も見られ、

寓意的で分かり易い。エピーの実の父親に嫁ぐことになるナンシーも時に美しい心の"完全な愛"の考えが象徴化されたエリオットの愛の概念として表わされている―"Once love, love always"、"一度愛したら、いつまでも愛すること"（11章）。また美しいブロンズの髪のエピーと金貨が、温かい心を持った人間と心を持たない冷たい金貨に、さらに精神と物質の文化の象徴として描かれている。『ジェイコブ兄貴』の物語りの終りには、東洋仏教異文化の因果応報の自然観、人間観にも通じるギリシャの因果応報の女神ネメシスの記述があり、そのような寓意的終り方の話が『サイラス・マーナー』なのである。

　ゴッホのサイラスの完全な愛による人物像は、チョーサー作『カンタベリー物語』「騎士の話」の二人の主人公が王女を時空を、死線を超えて愛することにおいて似ている。二人のその騎士道精神は東洋仏教異文化の色濃い日本の武士道にも通じる感がある。騎士道も武士道も最後まで人を完全に愛する道でもあろう。

　ゴッホはエリオットのようにジャポニズムを受容し19世紀西洋の古い既成の価値観を超えて、新しい時代が求める画家になったのである。

　19世紀、ジョージ・エリオットにとって日本は東洋仏教異文化の国でもあろう。夏目漱石は、その明治維新の目新しい女性の話し言葉の"語り"をも見事に扱い、禅文化（即心即仏）にも、また春夏秋冬の季語を入れる俳句にも、さらに"語り"の美を追求する落語にも感心が深い。夏目漱石の『三四郎』には、"Pity's akin to love."　"可哀相ただ惚れたってことよ"という"面白くてためになる"愛と悲しみの行がある。"悲しみは愛に似ている"は直訳であるが、"akin"の"kin"「自然」も"love"もインドヨーロッパ語族で、特に仏教経典のサンスクリット語にも係わっていることが分かる言葉である。英語の"pity"の日本語訳「悲し」は、旺文社『古語辞典』には「かなし」という音に「愛」の文字を当て、「愛し」とも書き、相手をいとおしい、かわいい、などと述べられている。英国人の心の本質や日本人の大和魂の本質をよく知ろうとしている漱石は、日本の古語の当て字である表意文字漢字の"愛"と口語の発音の「かなし」では、昔と今の言葉、文化、時代により文字の標記が異なる面白い言葉の妙味に

ついては熟知していたのであろう。日本語の表意文字と英語の表音文字の異言語文字文化の相違も面白い。言語はまさに私たちの世界観をも表していることが分かる。夏目漱石はロンドン留学後、日本が誇る東大英文学教授として初めて使用した教科書が『サイラス・マーナー』である。英語の教科書も道徳教育に資するべきだ、と述べている漱石に、『サイラス・マーナー』は、ぴったりのエリオットの作品である。漱石が西洋キリスト教英国の作家であるエリオットの"完全な愛"による"語り"の行を『サイラス・マーナー』の作品で読んで、精査していたことは間違いないであろう。

　エリオットは"sorrow is then part of love"[14]と述べている。この言葉は同じ女流作家の日本の樋口一葉文学にも通じる感があるであろう。だが漱石は、エリオットの真意を知っていたと思われる。日本語の"心"の意味の英語"mind"もサンスクリット語にまで係る語である。漱石文学も、異文化の言葉で言葉そのものの本質にまでも迫り、またいろいろな"心"で"心"そのものの本質にまでも、さらにいろいろな"人生"で"人生"そのものの本質にまで迫ろうとしている。漱石は、東洋仏教異文化の日本人として初めて、エリオットの"完全な愛"も視野に、独自に、悲しみが込められた美しい完全な愛の心の絆を模索したのではないだろうか。また晩年には、エリオットの死線や時空を越えた"心の言語"の人生の"語り"も受容し、一時自殺にまで追い込んでしまい、ひどく苦しい目に合わせた、愛する妻や生涯の文学の友としての正岡子規との人生の別れの"真実"と"虚構"について、大作『こころ』の作品で、人の"こころ"の本質を究明しようとしているのではないだろうか。明治時代の文豪の漱石は、今や、日本における国民的作家なっているが、漱石もエリオットやチョーサーのように"面白くてためになる"新しい時代の思想文学的作家でもあると言えるであろう。

　チョーサーは、中世英語のロンドンの標準語も異国の言語をも使いこなし英国文学史上初めて、優れた中世英語の言語的才知を活かして、見事なレトリックで英詩の本質に迫っている。チョーサー文学における人生の"語り"の伝統を、間違いなく、エリオットは受け継いでいるのである。

（注）

1. Text: Larry D. Benson（gen. ed.）, *The Riverside Chaucer, 3rd edition*（Oxford, 1987）
   西脇順三郎訳『カンタベリー物語（上）』（筑摩書房、2000）
   西脇順三郎訳『カンタベリー物語（下）』（筑摩書房、1998）
2. George Eliot, *Adam Bede*（A Signet Classic, 1961）p. 465-466.
3. Ibid., p.460.
4. Cf. 内田能嗣『ジョージ・エリオットの前期の小説』（創元社、1989）pp. 23-24.
5. Cf. 冨士川和男『ジョージ・エリオット文学の倫理性』（大盛堂書店、1977）p. 140.
6. George Eliot, *Romola*（The Penguin Library, 1984）p. 50.
7. George Eliot, *Silas Marner*（Collins, 1970）p. 132.
8. 西脇順三郎訳『カンタベリー物語（上）』p. 34.
9. Cf. 高野秀夫『ジョージ・エリオットの異文化世界』（春風社、2014）p. 18.
   チョーサー研究会／狩野晃一編『チョーサーと中世を眺めて』（麻生出版, 2014）
10. Cf. 河崎征俊『チョーサー文学の世界』（南雲堂、1995）p. 114.
11. Cf. Ibid., p. 6.
12. Cf. 大島浩, *George Eliot Newsletter of Japan*（ジョージ・エリオット協会、2011）p. 2.
13. George Eliot, *Silas Marner,* p. 144.
14. George Eliot, *Adam Bede* , p. 315.

「ラブ・ソング」の系譜 II——都市の「ソング」と黒死病

小　倉　美　加

　中世からルネサンス期にかけてのイングランドは民衆のエネルギーが満ち溢れていたようだ。[1]過去の遺産がどす黒い渦巻きの中へ吸い込まれ幾重にも渦を巻きながら、新たな大海へと押し流されていくような激動の時代。2020 年の状況と似ていたかもしれない。ジェフリー・チョーサーが生まれた 1340 年以降は宗教界の腐敗、フランスとの百年戦争、国内戦争、感染症の蔓延が原因となり、時代が激変し、結果的に激流が近代へ。新型コロナ蔓延による現代生活の激変も政治の腐敗と戦争と感染症が原因である可能性が高く、中世ヨーロッパ末期と状況が似ているように思う。そんな中、14 世紀半ば以降は封建制度に縛られていた民衆が自分の意志で生活の糧を探し、特に都市部では居酒屋を中心に、民衆娯楽がますます発達したようだ。フランス発祥で民衆起源の音楽祭の開催がこの時期から見られないのはおそらく百年戦争だけでなく黒死病の蔓延も原因ではないかと思われるが、娯楽の中心は音楽であった。中でも中世末期に人気を博した音楽詩にあたる「ラブ・ソング」は宮廷だけでなく特に民衆に力を与えた新しいジャンルだった。[2]

　いつの時代も愛の歌は人の心を揺さぶってきた。力強く歌われるのは、悲しくも情熱的な愛。14 世紀に流行した「ラブ・ソング」は悲恋や片思いを歌った。悲しい思いをことばにして自分を慰め力づけたようだ。特に黒死病が蔓延した 14 世紀末期は人々は「ラヴ・ソング」を歌うことで生きる力をえていた可能性がある。この研究ノートでは「ラブ・ソング」が熱狂的に受け入れられた背景を探り、「ラブ・ソング」と黒死病の関連性について考察する。

　中世末期になるまで民衆の音楽は記録に残ることはほとんどなかった。祈ることは歌うこと。キリスト教では、歌は神への愛を歌うものであり、現代の異性へのラブ・ソングとは根本的に異なる。しかしその異性への

「ラブ・ソング」もまた修道院で生まれていた。修道院では 10 世紀前後から西欧音楽の源流といわれるグレゴリオ聖歌が初期は単声で歌われていたが、徐々に 2 声、3 声と主旋律に装飾を加えるメリスマやネウマという方法が取り入れられた。難解なラテン語の性質をうまく利用し、聖職者たちは神の教えや聖歌にこっそり恋愛の詩を織り交ぜて楽しむ方法を編み出したようだ。それは日々の退屈なルーティン・ワークに明け暮れる僧たちを喜ばせ、夢中にしたに違いない。このような傾向は（古）フランス語圏で発達し、後にイタリアが加わったそうだが、修道院では距離に関係なく驚くほど写本に残された旋律が似通っていたという。当時のポピュラー・ミュージックとしていかに人気を博したかが伺えるエピソードだ。

　恋愛自体は 12 世紀の中世ヨーロッパで発明されたという人もいるが、その真偽はさておき、フランス王国内の宮廷で恋愛が花咲いた。12 世紀から 13 世紀にかけて宮廷風恋愛をテーマにし、王侯貴族たちが「ラブ・ソング」を自ら作り舞踊にも長けることが宮廷でのたしなみでもあったようだ。宮廷詩人や職業音楽家たちも即興で歌詞付の「メロディ」を奏でていた。[3] 職業音楽家たちは教会でも活躍していたそうだ。

　13 世紀以降かつては城塞のあった地域や、農業・鉱業・商業の発達や大学設立に伴う人工の増加で、都市 "city" が発展した。その都市の居酒屋では放浪学生や学僧がラテン語の恋愛詩や風刺詩を楽器演奏を伴って歌い酒に酔う。夜な夜な居酒屋では、客が喜ぶ流行歌や替え歌を歌いつつ即興で楽器が奏でられていたようだ。

　中世の「ラブ・ソング」は世俗の愛の歌である点は現代と共通しているが、当時としては新しいジャンルだった。現代なら「ラブ・ソング」と聞くと民衆のためのポピュラー・ミュージックを思い浮かべるが、まずは「音楽」（Musike）という語彙自体が大学 7 科の 1 つである重要な学問分野を表わすものであり、「ラブ・ソング」はこの学問分野に含まれていなかった。[4] 中世の「音楽」とはボエティウス等によって古代ギリシャの音楽理論が再編集されたものであり、難解な数学のテキストのように音程などを表わす数字の計算式ばかりで、楽器演奏それ自体には関心が向けられていない。「ラブ・ソング」がいつ発生したかは定かではないが、14 世紀

にフランスで花咲いた、多くの場合、「メロディ」のある異性への愛の歌を示す新しいジャンルであった。

　「ラブ・ソング」の人気は先ほど述べた13世紀以降の都市の発達に密接に関係し、人が集まる場所で発達しているという共通点があるようだ。「ラブ・ソング」は聖歌発のソングと宮廷発のソングと居酒屋発のソングと主に3種類あるようだが、どれが最初だったかは今となってはわからないという。しかし詩のある「メロディ」で愛を歌う習慣が人気を博したことは確かだ。例えば、フランスのギヨーム・ド・マショーという聖職者が、挿絵と楽譜付き詩集の写本を残しているが、ほとんどがいわゆる世俗の「ラブ・ソング」であり聖歌の数が「ラブ・ソング」の6分の1ほどであるという。キリスト教関連の祝祭日と音楽は結びついていたが、13世紀から14世紀中頃にフランスの都市で民間主催の「ピュイ」という音楽祭も行われていた。音楽付の詩などを披露するコンテストで、ロンドンでも開催された記録があり、宮廷でも貴族たちが真似事をしていたという。封建時代に民衆が宮廷に発信した文化とも言える。

　このような説明だけを読めば、当時流行した「ラブ・ソング」を明朗でリズミカルな現代のポピュラー・ミュージックと連想するかもしれない。しかし、14世紀までの「ラブ・ソング」はミサのように厳粛な雰囲気があり、静かに悲しげに歌われ、ほとんどが明朗な「メロディ」ではなく、むしろ陰鬱ですらある。激しい情熱を独白のようなスタイルで謳い上げるパートと、聖歌に似た厳粛なメロディ・ラインを繰り返すギヨーム・ド・マショーの「ラブ・ソング」もあるが、多くは現代で言うといわゆる片思いを静かに悲しげに歌う「バラード」に近いかもしれない。15世紀になるとデュファイの「ロンドー」のような春を思わせるような明るい曲調に変わる傾向がある。

　筆者はこれまでこのような14世紀と15世紀の「ソング」のメロディがなぜ「暗」と「明」に極端に分かれているのかが疑問であった。今までは14世紀は特に片思いの「ラブ・ソング」が流行したからとしか結論できなかった。しかし、その理由の1つは黒死病の蔓延と密接に関係があるという可能性が高いと考えている。ジョン・ケリーによれば、黒死病は

1340 年代から 1400 年頃から人口が安定してくるまで断続的に続いたという。[5] これはほぼチョーサーの生涯と重なる。『カンタベリー物語』のトパス卿の物語の中に登場するチョーサーは下を向いて暗い顔をしていた、とあるがこれもこの黒死病と関連があったかもしれないと思える。[6]

　今年 2020 年 1 月頃に中国から世界へと拡散された新型コロナは、日本に上陸して 1 年未満であるがそれ以来私達は家での生活が中心になっていることにストレスを感じ、先が見えない状況に疲れを感じ始めている。ジョン・ケリーによれば、「パンデミックの特徴は、個人だけでなく人間社会まで破壊しうる点にあるが、それを知識として知るのと、目の当たりにするのとでは大違いである」とあるが、まさにこの言葉通りである。この黒死病こそ、14 世紀の「ラブ・ソング」に陰鬱な雰囲気が覆う原因であると言えるのではないか。

　特にフランスとイタリアの中間地点にあたるアヴィニオン教皇庁やフランス・オランダ周辺のブルゴーニュ公国の宮廷では聖職者たちは聖歌にはほとんど見向きもせず「ラブ・ソング」を作っていたようだ。イタリアの作曲家フランチェスコ・ランディーニという聖職者に至っては 1 曲も聖歌を作らなかった。音楽理論や教会の権威が忘れられてしまったかのようだ。いくら祈っても黒死病の威力が衰えない現実を目の当たりし、神が信じられなくなった聖職者たちが自らの震える心を鎮めるために「ラブ・ソング」制作に没頭し、現実逃避していたと考えることはできないだろうか。そのある種の狂気と悲哀が音楽に表現され、多くの人々の心を惹き付け、熱狂させたのではないか。そう考えれば、中世の「ラブ・ソング」がフランスから海を越えてイングランドへ、アルプス山脈を超えてイタリアへ伝えられたとしても驚くにあたらない。その時代の風を強烈に感じたかのように初期のジェフリー・チョーサーも夢物語詩にこのフランスの「ラブ・ソング」を英訳し作品に積極的に取り入れている。[7]

　ここまで読むと中世の音楽の話をしているようだが、ここでいう詩（ソング）とはいわゆる文学作品にあたることが多い。中世では音楽と文学作品は分けて語るのは難しい場合がある。楽譜が残っていないからと言って、それが「メロディ」を伴わない詩とは言えないのである。音楽と詩を分離

することが難しいのが中世時代の特徴である。中世末期の不安事項を抱え
た人々は、悲しくも情熱的な「ラブ・ソング」を楽器を伴い歌い踊ること
で見えない将来への不安をかき消し、明日を生きる力を得ていたと言える
のではないか。

注

1. チョーサー研究会のニューズ・レターの第1回連載エッセイを加筆した。
2. ここで用いた「ラブ・ソング」は中世音楽用語「ソング」(“songs”) をわ
   かりやすくするために現代的な表現とし、現代な意味で用いるときは括弧
   なしとした。詳しくは小倉美加「ジェフリー・チョーサーの夢物語詩にお
   ける「ソング」の文学的受容とその意味について」『明治大学情報コミュニ
   ケーション学研究』2018年、第18号、105-124を参照。
3. 中世の「メロディ」は古代ギリシャ起源で、単旋律、つまりメロディ・ラ
   インが1つという意味である。
4. 音楽は中世の大学7科の学問分野としての「音楽」を示す場合は括弧をつ
   けた。
5. ジョン・ケリー(野中邦子訳)『黒死病—ペストの中世史』、14-17頁を参照。
6. 『カンタベリー物語』「トパス卿の話」「あなたはウサギを探しているように
   見える、なぜならずっと地面を睨んでいるのを私はずっと見ていたから」
   (“.... Thou lookest thou woldest fynde an hare, /For evere upon the ground I se thee
   stare....” Sir Thopas, VII) 696-7.
7. チョーサーの作品では夢物語詩、『トロイラス』『ショート・ポエムズ』な
   どに歌唱された可能性のある「ラブ・ソング」の歌詞が見られるが、意見
   が分かれている。

参考文献

上尾信也『吟遊詩人』新紀元社、2006.

金澤正剛『中世音楽の精神史』河出文庫、2015.

J・ギース、F・ギース(青島淑子訳)『中世ヨーロッパの都市の生活』講談社学術文庫、
　　2006.

ピエール＝イヴ・バデル(原野昇訳)『フランス中世の文学生活』白水社、1993.

ジョン・ケリー(野中邦子訳)『黒死病－ペストの中世史』中公文庫、2020.

執筆者一覧（五十音順、敬称略、所属は 2021 年 6 月 1 日現在）

有坂夏菜子　　Arisaka, Kanako　　（小山工業高等専門学校准教授）

池上　惠子　　Ikegami, Keiko　　（成城大学短期大学部名誉教授）

池上　　昌　　Ikegami, Masa　　（慶應義塾大学名誉教授）

石黒　太郎　　Ishiguro, Taro　　（明治大学教授）

小倉　美加　　Ogura, Mika　　（日本大学兼任講師）

貝塚　泰幸　　Kaitsuka, Yasuyuki　　（千葉商科大学非常勤講師）

狩野　晃一　　Kano, Koichi　　（明治大学准教授）

笹本　長敬　　Sasamoto, Hisayuki　　（大阪商業大学元教授）

杉藤　久志　　Sugito, Hisashi　　（日本大学准教授）

高野　秀夫　　Takano, Hideo　　（駒澤大学元教授）

多ヶ谷有子　　Tagaya, Yuko　　（関東学院大学名誉教授）

谷　　明信　　Tani, Akinobu　　（関西学院大学教授）

地村　彰之　　Jimura, Akiyuki　　（広島大学名誉教授）

原田　英子　　Harada, Hideko　　（明治大学兼任講師）

春田　節子　　Haruta, Setsuko　　（白百合女子大学元教授）

中世英文学の日々に
― 池上忠弘先生追悼論文集 ―

2021年10月20日　印　刷　　　　2021年10月29日　発　行

編著者 © チョーサー研究会／狩野晃一

発行者　佐々木　元

制作・発行所　株式会社　英　宝　社
〒 101-0032 東京都千代田区岩本町 2-7-7
Tel [03] (5833) 5870　Fax [03] (5833) 5872

ISBN978-4-269-72156-2　C3098
［組版・印刷・製本：日本ハイコム株式会社］